Praise For John Keene's COUNTERNARRATIVES

"Keene exerts superb control over his stories, costuming them in the style of Jorge Luis Borges.... Yet he preserves the undercurrent of excitement and pathos that accompanies his characters' persecution and their groping toward freedom."   —Sam Sacks, *The Wall Street Journal*

"Only a few, John Keene among them, in our age, authentically test the physics of fiction as both provocation and mastery. Continuing what reads like the story collection as freedom project, in *Counternarratives*, Keene opens swaths of history for readers to more than imagine but to manifest and live in the passionate language of conjure and ritual."
   —Major Jackson

"A gifted writer who seeks to immerse himself in the body of language so that certain ruling assumptions may open themselves up to an inner dialectical scanning."   —Wilson Harris

"I am mesmerized by *Counternarratives*, as much for John Keene's dazzling prose as for the sense one gets of his ability to conjure the dead. These stories read like a secret history of the new world."
   —Stephen Sparks, Green Apple Books

"A book that spans from the 17th century to the present day, Keene's ambitious, confident storytelling is matched by his complex, evocative, and compelling voice."   —*Vanity Fair*

"In *Counternarratives*, John Keene undertakes a kind of literary counter-archaeology, a series of fictions that challenge our notion of what constitutes 'real' or 'accurate' history. His writing is at turns playful and erudite, lyric and coldly diagnostic, but always completely absorbing. *Counternarratives* could easily be compared to Borges or Bolaño, Calvino or Kiš, but at the same time it is a deeply American, resolutely contemporary book, that asks us to reconsider our own perspectives on the past—and the future."   —Jess Row

"Who knows what book of spells Keene used to conjure these hypnotic, quasi-historical tales involving mystical convergences?"
—Katrina Dodson, *The Millions*

"The year's most historically rich work of fiction; you could easily retitle it *Counterhistories*. And whether Keene is rewriting a slave rebellion, witchcraft, or the material afterlife of a dead infant, his preternaturally beautiful sentences never fail to sting and release."
—Jonathon Sturgeon, *Flavorwire*

"Encompassing hundreds of fictional and historical characters over several centuries, and utilizing a mesmerizing array of styles—including slave narrative, historical document, stream of consciousness, fever dream, diary, field manual, concrete poetry—the book amasses a vision of epic capacity."
—Blake Butler, *Vice*

"Queering the script, defying the imperative to be silent, however, does not require confidence or a vision of what progress means. It is, rather, in all its uncertainty and risk, the most basic stuff of—the very matter of—life. It is also the crowning achievement of one of the year's very best books."   —Brad Johnson, *The Quarterly Conversation*

"In *Counternarratives,* John Keene's language is a machete slashing through the underbrush of the history of Western Civilization, 'tearing the white out' by giving voice to the marginalized, all the way to a basement in a none-too distant future in 'Lions.' Along the way, the book whispers in the code of those in bondage. Coded language, coded names, coded text, coded bodies and secret spaces all play pivotal roles in the passages of Keene's fugitive journey."   —D. Scot Miller, *Mosaic*

"A literary creation of quiet, unsettling power: Practically every sentence in the book perforates, stretches out, or pries open literary modes designed to be airtight, restrictive, and racially exclusionary. An expert generator of suspense, Keene also turns out to be a skilled humorist, a mischievous ironist, a deft, seductive storyteller and a studied historian."
— Max Nelson, *Bookforum*

Counternarratives

Also by John Keene
FROM NEW DIRECTIONS

Annotations

COUNTERNARRATIVES
John Keene

A NEW DIRECTIONS PAPERBOOK

Grateful acknowledgment is made to the magazines and journals
where some of these stories and novellas have appeared:
Agni, Encyclopedia, Hambone, and *TriQuarterly.*

AUTHOR'S ACKNOWLEDGMENTS: Please see page 305.

The map on page 9 is courtesy of the Map House of London
(www.themaphouse.com).
The map on page 33 is courtesy of FCIT (etc.usf.edu/maps).

Manufactured in the United States of America
New Directions Books are printed on acid-free paper
Published clothbound by New Directions in 2015
and as New Directions Paperbook 1339 in 2016 (ISBN 978-0-8112-2552-6)
Design by Erik Rieselbach

Library of Congress Cataloging-in-Publication Data
Keene, John, 1965–
Counternarratives John Keene.
pages ; cm
ISBN 978-0-8112-2434-5 (alk. paper)
I. Title.
PS3561.E3717C68 2015
813'.54—dc23   2015001269

2 4 6 8 9 7 5 3 1

New Directions Books are published for James Laughlin
by New Directions Publishing Corporation
80 Eighth Avenue, New York 10011

For Rudolph P. Byrd
and Gerard Fergerson
and in tribute and thanks
to Samuel R. Delany

CONTENTS

I

COUNTERNARRATIVES

Perhaps, then, after all, we have no idea
of what history is: or are in flight
from the demon we have summoned.
James Baldwin

The social situation of philosophy is slavery.
Fred Moten

So it is better to speak
remembering
we were never meant to survive.
Audre Lorde

MANNAHATTA

The canoe scudded to a stop at the steep, rocky shore. There was no slip, so he tossed the rope, which he had knotted to a crossbar and weighted with a pierced plumb square just larger than his fist, forward into the foliage. Carefully he clambered toward the spray of greenery, the fingers of the thicket and its underbrush clasping the soles of his boots, his stockinged calves, his ample linen breeches. A thousand birds proclaimed his ascent up the incline; the bushes shuddered with the alarm of creatures stirred from their lees; insects rose in a screen before his eyes, vanishing. When he had secured the boat and settled onto a sloping meadow, he sat, to wet his throat with water from his winesack, and orient himself, and rest. Only then did he look back.

The ship, the *Jonge Tobias,* which had borne him and the others across more nautical miles than he had thought to tally, was no longer visible, its brown hulk hidden by the river's curve and the outcropping topped by fortresses of trees. The water, fluttering like a silk shroud, now white, now silver, now azure, ferried his eyes all the way over itself east—he knew from the captain's compass and his own canny sense of space, innate since he could first recall—to the banks of a vaster, still not fully charted island, its outlines an ocher shimmer in the morning light, etching themselves on his memory like auguries. Closer, at the base of the hill, fish and eels drew quick seams along the river's nervous surface. From hideouts in the rushes frogs serenaded. Once, in Santo Domingo where he had been born and spent half his youth before working on ships to purchase his freedom, he peered into a furnace where a man who could have been his brother was turning a bell of glass, and he had felt the blaze's gaping mouth, the sear of its tongue nearly devouring him as the blown bowl miraculously fulfilled its shape. Now the sun, as if the forebear of that transformative fire, burned its presence into the sky's blue banner, its hot rays falling everywhere, gilding the landscape around him. He was used to days and nights in the tropics, but nevertheless crawled beneath the shade of a sweet gum bower. He turned down the wide brim of his hat, shifted his sack to his left side, near the tree's gray base, opened his collar to cool himself, and waited.

The first time he had done this, at another, more southerly landing nearer the dock and the main trading post, one of the people who had long lived here had revealed himself, emerging from an invisible door in a row of bayberries, speaking—yes, repeating—a soft but welcoming melody. Jan, as Captain Mossel and the crew on the ship called him, or Juan, as he was known in Santo Domingo, or João as he had once been called by his Lusitanian sailor father and those like him among whom he worked, the kingdoms of the Iberians being the same in those days, and before that M——, the name his mother had summoned forth from her people and sworn him never to reveal to another soul, not so distant, it struck him, from the *Makadewa* as the envoy of the first people had begun to call him—had stilled his ear like a tuning fork until he captured it, and with the key of this language that most of the Dutch on the ship assured him they could not fully hear, he had himself unlocked a door. Pelts for hatchets, axes, knives, guns, more efficient than flints or polished clubs in felling a cougar, a sycamore, an enemy. He had wrung a peahen's neck and roasted an entire hog, but despite having heard several times the call to revolt, he had never revealed a single secret or shibboleth, nor had he killed or been party to killing another man. So long as the circumstances made it possible to avoid doing either, he would. Someday, perhaps soon, he knew, his fate might change, unless he overturned it.

The envoy had, through gestures, his stories, later meals and the voices that spoke through fire and smoke, opened a portal onto his world. Jan knew for his own sake, his survival, he must remember it, enter it. He had already begun to answer to the wind, the streams, the bluffs. As he now sat in the grass, observing the light playing through the canopies, the shadows sliding across themselves along the sedge in distinct shades, all still darker than his own dark hands, cheeks, a mantis trudging along the half-bridge of a gerardia stalk, he could see another window inside that earlier one, beckoning. He would study it as he had been studying each tree, each bush, each bank of flowers here and wherever on this island he had set foot. He would understand that window, climb through it.

He stood and unsheathed his knife. Then he removed a roll of twine from his bag. Using the tools, he marked several nearby spots, hatching the tree and tightly knotting several lengths of string about the branches, creating signs, in the shape of lozenges, squares, half-circles, that would be visible right up to sunset. In nearby branches he created several more. There was always the possibility that one of the first people, whom he expected to appear at any moment, though none did, or some nonhuman creature, or a spirit in any form, would untie the markers, erase the hatchings, thereby erasing this spot's specificity, for him, returning it to the anonymity that every step here, as on every ship he had sailed on, every word he had never before spoken, every face he had never seen until he did, once held. If that were to be the case, so be it. Yet he vowed not to forget this little patch where a new recognition had dawned in him. If he had to commit every scent, every sound, even the blades of grass to memory, he would. He walked around, bending down, looking at a squirrel that had been looking intently at him....

Despite having no timepiece, he knew it was time to return. A breeze, as if seconding this impulse, sighed *Rodrigues*. He began sifting through his store of images for a story to recount to them, shielding this place and its particularities from their imaginations. He broke off two branches big enough to serve as stakes and carried them with him down to the bank and the canoe. Using his knife and fingers, and, once he had created an opening, the thinner end of his paddle, he dug a hole, and pounded the first stake into it. Using the twine he created a cross with the other branch, then strung a series of knots around it, from the base to the top, wishing he had brought beads or pieces of colored cloth, or anything that would snare the gaze from a distance. He stepped back to inspect it. He was not sure he would be able to spy it from the water, though it commanded the eye from where he stood. But, he reminded himself, once he returned to the ship, it would be for the last time, and he would have months, years even, to find and reconstruct this cross again, to place a new one. The first people would guide him to it, too, if they happened upon it. He replaced his knife and the twine, collected his anchor, then hoisted himself back into the canoe, paddle in one hand, in the other his ballast. He pushed off from the shore, out into the river, and as he glanced at the cross, it appeared to flare, momentarily, before it disappeared like everything else around it into the island's dense verdant hide. It was, despite his observations of the area, the one thing that he recalled so clearly he could have described it down to the grain of the wood when he slid into his hammock that night, and, when he returned a week later, his canoe and a skiff laden with ampler sacks, of flints, candles, seeds, a musket, his sword, a small tarp to protect him from the rain, enough hatchets and knives to ensure his work as trader, and translator, never to return to the *Jonge Tobias,* or any other ship, nor to the narrow alleys of Amsterdam or his native Hispaniola, the very first thing he saw.

ON BRAZIL, OR DÉNOUEMENT:
THE LONDÔNIAS-FIGUEIRAS

On Brazil

Male Found Beheaded in Settlement Ranked Among Most Dangerous in Metro Area

STAFF REPORT

The nude, headless body of a male was discovered shortly after dawn in an alley off Rua dos Cães, at the edge of the new and unauthorized favela of N., on the periphery of the industrial suburb of Diadema, by an officer from the São Paulo Metropolitan Police department. The department and the São Paulo State Police have opened a joint investigation....

According to Chief Detective S.A. Brito Viana, authorities still have not confirmed widespread rumors that identification found on the body indicates the deceased is banking heir Sergio Inocêncio Maluuf Figueiras, 27, who has been listed as missing since the early summer....

On Brazil

From the 1610s, the Londônias were the proprietors of an expanding sugar *engenho* in the northeasternmost corner of the captaincy of Sergipe D'El-Rei. The plantation began some meters inland from the southern sandy banks of the Rio São Francisco and fanned out verdantly for many hectares.

The first Londônia in New Lisbon, José Simeão, had arrived in the Royal Captaincy of Bahia in the last quarter of the previous century after receiving a judgment of homicide in the continental courts. Before this personal calamity, he had spent several decades serving as a sutler to the King's army. Because his first wife had died during childbirth while he was posted in Galicia, once he arrived in the land of the *pau brasil*, he promptly remarried. His new wife, an adolescent named Maria Amada, came from the interior of Portugal's abundantly expanding territories, and was a product—according to Arturo Figueiras Pereira Goldensztajn's introduction to the *Crônicas da Família Figueiras-Londônia-Figueiras*—of one of the earliest New World experiments: the coupling of the European and the Indian. José Simeão and his wife settled in the administrative capital, São Salvador; he worked as a victualler and part-time tailor, drawing upon skills acquired in his youth, and she produced several children, only one of whom—Francisco, who was known as "Inocêncio" because of his marked simplicity of expression—lived to adulthood.

Francisco Inocêncio followed his father's path into the military. Instead of provisioning, he became an infantryman. By the time he was 25, he had taken part in several campaigns against Indians, infidels, foreigners, and seditionists in the western and southern regions of the King's territories. His outward placidity translated, in the midst of battle, into a steadfastness that even his opponents quickly came to admire. Facing arrows or shot, he neither faltered nor flinched; when his flatboat capsized, he calmly surfaced on the riverbank, pike in hand. A commission and promotions were soon won. But there is only so much gore that sanity can bear. He eventually resigned to settle in the remote northernmost region of São Cristovão, Sergipe D'El-Rei, near the Captaincy of Pernambuco, where he set up a small estate. Not long thereafter he married the widow of a local apothecary.

Though his wife was not beyond her childbearing years, Francisco Inocêncio adopted her son, José, who was thenceforth known as José Inocêncio, and her daughter, Clara. From his mother, they say, José Inocêncio inherited a will of lead and a satin tongue. These gifts led to his greatest achievement, which was to ally himself with and then marry into the prominent and clannish Figueiras family, which had acquired deeds of property not only in the capital city but throughout the sugar-growing interior. The Figueirases were also involved in trade, as agents of the crown, in sugar and indigo processing, and in the nascent banking system. As a result, they were rumored to be *conversos*. In  any case, the royal court benefited greatly from their ingenuity, as did the colonial ruling class, of which Londônia soon became a member. To the connected and ruthless flow the spoils.

Within a decade, José Inocêncio had quadrupled the acreage of his father's estate, acquiring in the process several defaulted or failed plantations, some, according to his rivals, by shrewd or otherwise extralegal maneuvers. He had plunged into this business with the same zeal with which his father had once defended the crown, which is to say, relentlessly.

José Inocêncio was entering the sugar trade as ships were disgorging wave upon wave of Africans onto the colony's shores, and he viewed this as a rising historical and economic trend, the product of the natural order. The mortality rate for slaves was extraordinarily high in 17th-century Brazil. It was higher still on Londônia's plantation. He could not abide indolence or anything less than an adamantine endurance, so he devised a work schedule to ensure his manpower was engaged productively at every moment of daylight. Nightfall barely served as a respite. Those who did not fall dead fled. He was thought of by his fellow planters as "innovative," "decisive," "driven," a man of action whose deeds matched his few words; in the face of such immediacy and success who needs a philosophy or faith?

On the estate itself, things were moving in the opposite direction. The final straw came when he ordered Kimunda, a frail cane cutter who had collapsed from hemorrhages while on his way to the most distant field, tied to an ass and dragged until he regained consciousness. As stated in the schedule, which each slave was supposed to have memorized, Kimunda was expected to work his section of the field from sun-up to midday, circumstances be damned. The result was that a cabal from the Zoogoo region mounted an insurrection, seizing swords and knives and attempting to lay their hands on gunpowder. José Inocêncio quelled it with singular severity. Sometimes the fact of the lesson is more important than what is actually learned. Half a dozen of the plotters, including Cesarão, a particularly defiant African who had become the *de facto* leader of the coup, after torching a field of cane and a dry dock, escaped across the river into the wilds of what is now the Brazilian state of Alagoas.

José Inocêncio swiftly rebuilt his operation. He viewed himself as a man of estimable greatness, of destiny. It is undeniable that he had possessed what might be classed as an exemplary case of proto-capitalist consciousness, for afterwards he sought out as diverse and well-seasoned a workforce as possible. Growing markets have no margin for mercy. Several years before his death, he received a litany of honors from the crown.

The Londônias-Figueiras

The Londônia family: Londônia's eldest son José Ezéquiel strongly resembles his mother in appearance, his father in canniness and business acumen. Short, heavy-set, with a broad jawline covered by a thick, black, immaculately groomed beard, like most of the Figueiras clan. He is described in some tendentious contemporary accounts, according to Figueiras Pereira Goldensztajn, as almost "rabbinical" in mien. Eventually he inherits his father's estates, and his branch of the family gradually expands them along with his mortgage empire until the collapse of the sugar economy, despite which these Londônias head a new feudal hierarchy in the region for generations.

Londônia's youngest son Gustavo—emerald eyes, skin white as moonstone, a swan's neck, impressive height: all recessive traits, all valued highly by the Court society in Lisbon. Fluent in gestures, languages, charms. A career in royal law is predicted for him. By the age of twenty-four, he has infected several women in his social set before dying of the same blood-borne illness himself.

Maria Piedade, the only Londônia daughter, finding no adequate suitors, married back into another branch of the Figueiras family. The other children, as was common even among the rich in those days, died before reaching adolescence, except for the middle son, Lázaro Inocêncio, who possessed his father's tendency towards resolute action, his high self-regard, his inflexibility.

Lázaro Inocêncio

After two years at the Jesuit college in Salvador, where his classmates alternately nicknamed him "the Colonel" because of his assurance and hair-trigger temper, and "Guiné" as a result of his thick, expressive features, swift tan, and woollen locks, he chose a career that placed him near a center of power. He was by birth a Figueiras, nothing less was expected. He gained a commission in the King's forces, serving as vice-commander of a regiment based in Itaparica. During the final Portuguese invasion to recapture the capital city of Salvador, in 1625, he held steadfast against repeated charges. After the commanding officer had taken shot to the chest, Lázaro led his men in a daring advance through the rump of the lower city that resulted in the capture of a small batallion.

Despite the fact that his captives were all found mortally wounded, as soon as the Dutch retreated he was duly commended and promoted. His sense of superiority and bellicosity, however, caused problems in the context of the general state of peace. Continued battles with his superiors led him to abruptly resign his commission. A star does not orbit its moons. He returned to Salvador, and in a moment of even greater rashness, married the sickly daughter of an immigrant physician. He found the situation of his marriage and his estrangement from the army intolerable, and headed south, his goal the distant coastal city of Paranaguá, essentially abandoning his ill wife, who was, unknown to him, with child.

Fortunately for heroes fate's hand is surest. In 1630 a fleet led by the Dutchman Corneliszoon Loncq seized Pernambuco. Londônia, who had gotten no further than the town of Vila Velha, north of Rio de Janeiro, was located and recalled. His commission involved his resuming leadership of the remnants of his former regiment—Souza, Antunes, de Mello, Madeira—which was now under the general command of Fonte da Ré. The Portuguese forces were intent on retaining their patrimony, so adequate plans were being drawn up. Lázaro Inocêncio, however, pressed to participate in the first battles in Olinda. A farsighted man, Fonte da Ré recognized the looming catastrophe and ignored Londônia's agitation to take the field.

But Londônia did have a reputation for bravery, so Fonte da Ré, after receiving word that an official fleet was already bound toward the seized northern capital, ordered his commander to head west, up the Rio São Francisco, moving in a pincer movement into the rear flank of Pernambuco. He was to press into the leaner, bottom portion of that colony, then head back southeastwards, tracking the southern rim of the unforgiving sertão, then moving north again towards Olinda, which was under Dutch control. Rivercraft awaited him on the Sergipe d'El Rei side, provisions at the post west of the thriving town of Penedo in Pernambuco. He was not to attack any Portuguese colonials unless they declared allegiance to Nassau. In order to preserve manpower, he was not to engage in any other combat unless absolutely necessary. This course of action would keep him out of the main campaign, Fonte da Ré hoped, until Londônia's enthusiasm could be put to direct use in a clean-up operation. Two other batallions were added to his command.

After a journey by horse along the coastline to the mouth of the São Francisco, Londônia and his men set off on pettiaugers up the deep and refractory river. On the northern shores, past the sandy banks and the falls, settlements and plantations periodically appeared. The aroma of cane and the sight, from his boat, of *engenhos* and mills, goaded him like a spur. There was no genius comparable to that of his people; the greedy Dutch must pay. Within a day he and his men had passed Penedo and reached a small Portuguese outpost from which they would proceed into the interior.

As they moved inland on foot, Londônia's men realized he was as unfamiliar as they with the difficult, nearly impassably dense forest terrain. Unlike them, however, he was indefatigable. He wanted to drive forward, forward. A few of his men, however, began to fall by the wayside, to fevers and periodic attacks by Indians, who had been living somewhat undisturbed in the vicinity. Londônia demanded that his soldiers not flag: here we see history repeating itself, though in a guise bearing professional validation. One mutineer he shot outright, another he threatened with similar summary judgment. On they proceeded, through forest to clearings of scrub-land and then to forest again: soon, hunger, thirst and questions about the validity of the mission enjoined the men. Though they marched, there were no Dutch to be found anywhere.

One night, at camp, as the Colonel paced a brook in the distance, several of his men whispered among themselves the unspeakable word: desertion. The plan became moot at dawn, however, when yet another band of Indians launched an assault. Arrows and stones swarmed their armor like locusts. The Colonel's men had no choice; how quickly we forget the repellent aspects of personality in moments of crisis, which permit the illusion of unity against more dangerous foes. The clergy had one method for dealing with the Indians, soldiers another. The Colonel, no Jesuit, urged his men to pursue the last of the savages until they were incapable of staging even the memory of a surprise.

There were therefore no natives who could be pressed into serving as guides. As far as anyone could tell, they were well beyond the region of Portuguese settlements. As a result, the Colonel was unsure about the land on which he now stood. Sheer, green walls of trees that smothered the sunlight rose before them. An interminable carnival of beasts and birds crisscrossed the canopies above, while insects spawned in the pens of Satan swarmed the ground beneath their feet. The regiment had lost the curves of the river, but an impromptu compass devised by one of the men seemed as if it might guide them toward their goal; even the Colonel knew they could and should avoid the *sertão*, the graveyard of mortals, and trek back southeast along the river's line to reach Penedo, which he was sure was a staging ground for other units. This would ensure their participation in the expulsion of the heathen Netherlanders.

After a day of marching, they appeared to have returned to their initial spot. They were obviously lost. The men sat in frustration, enraging the Colonel. He ordered his adjutant, Pereira, to devise a new compass as quickly as possible. Wasn't there a man among them with Tupi or Xororó or other indigenous blood or experience who knew this region? A mulatto scout, dos Santos, meanwhile set out with a dowser, marking trees with twigs and hacks to guide his return. After a while, he heard an unusual noise. An infinity of unusual noises surrounded them, but he recognized this one: a berimbau.

Having grown up on a sugar plantation, he knew instantly what he was dealing with. Africans. Were they allied with the Dutch? Were they escaped slaves living under Indian protection?

Dos Santos spotted a clearing, just on the other side of the creek at the bottom of the low hill on which he stood. Lying prone in the brush, he could see beyond a fringe of mahogany trees a tiny settlement. Further observation showed that though the community was no larger than a cane field, it hummed with considerable industry. Small buildings, in the thatched style, formed a circle; several handfuls of men, women and children moved back and forth among tethered animals at its center. It was, he realized soon enough, a *quilombo*. Perhaps the residents, whom he figured to be independent in their allegiance, might lead his regiment back towards the river, or even provide a few warriors for the coming battle. He tried to recall the phrases he had learned from his mother: she had secretly practiced the Mina rites.

Dos Santos followed his markers back to where the Colonel and the regiment had begun to bivouac. He reported to his commander what he had seen; immediately the men, though thirsty and exhausted, were ordered to decamp. When the scout inquired about the Colonel's plans, he was thrown to the soil. The regiment beat such a quick path using his guideposts that it took dos Santos several minutes to catch up.

As a child, the Colonel had witnessed the Africans' failed attempt to raze his father's plantation, and more than once he had been told that their plans had included slaughtering every Londônia or Figueiras they found. So he tended to regard all blacks not in bondage or under the protection of the cloth as renegades. In any case, a *mocambo* might provide an ideal haven for any enemies of the Crown. Did the Dutch, who were heathens anyways, even sanction slavery? Who could be sure? At the hill, the Colonel told his men to slow their advance and follow the direction of the lilting music. He paused, all the men paused. He ordered them to draw their weapons. Dos Santos noted, this time aloud, there was no sign or seal of Dutch influence. This was evidently a free colony, he was willing to bear a message of conciliation, if so ordered. The Colonel told the scout not to mock him again; not only canestalks should fear the scythe.

As they crouched in the bushes, a phalanx of a half-dozen males, ranging from adolescents to adults, emerged from the trees. Maroons, they wore simple shifts; except for the one at the very head of the line, carrying what appeared to be a sacramental spear, they were unarmed. At their rear strode a tall, gray-haired African, of influential bearing. He carried a large shield made of braided and colored palms, a cross within a circle woven into its face, and a carved mahogany pike. A bright ochre sash fell across his bare, scarred but still muscled chest, at the center of which hung a small, leather amulet.

The train of black men began to mount the hill. As they approached the summit, dos Santos, the regiment's assigned emissary, rose reflexively from his haunches to approach the group. But the Colonel also sprang from his lee into the clearing. The group of free men halted, the shield-bearing leader extending his hand palm upwards, fingers spread, in a gesture of friendship. One of the other maroons announced in broken Portuguese that they were not subjects of the crown, and that they sought no hostilities. Perhaps they assumed the mulatto scout and the commander with his nappy mane, though clad in military gear, certainly would not harm them.

What the Colonel saw, however, was Cesarão. The big man, though he did not recognize his enemy, did realize immediately the danger he was facing. The Colonel yelled out a forward charge, in successive lines, and his men began dropping their adversaries by sword and pike as rapidly as they could reach them. The man the Colonel sought fled back down the hill into the compound; his cries, in a language unintelligible even to dos Santos, sent women, children and animals scattering in all directions. The Portuguese company hurried down to the perimeter of the settlement, where the first wave met poisoned arrows, knives, a long, spear-lined pit, which opened suddenly, like a lamprey's mouth. A few men toppled over each other into death: Souza, Madeira. The others dropped whomever they could.

The Colonel, from a position in behind a tree, reloaded his gun, felling one of the rebels. As his men subdued most of their opponents, he hunted down that Cesarão. The big man, running to grab his sword, had stumbled into another pit, this one filled with waste, on the periphery of the settlement, and was clambering like a crab to get out of it. The Colonel had one goal: the chief rebel's head. With one swing of his sword, he got it.

When the regiment was done, flames shrieked up from what had been the settlement like a monstrous blue bird-of-paradise. The Colonel ordered all the enemy who had not escaped or been slain taken prisoner. There must be at least some among them who would serve as guides back to the São Francisco, and since they had operated under Cesarão's control, they ought, he was convinced, to be returned to his father's estate. Cesarão's head, along with the infernal fetish, hunkered in its bloody, fecal glaze in a burlap sack.

The number of captives was few. None was willing, without coercion, to lead the tormentors out of the jungle. Finally, an older woman, sufficiently broken by the Colonel himself, conducted them to the initial outpost from which they had started. It was, unaccountably, no more than a two-day journey.

The Colonel, Viana

Another small regiment, under the command of Viana, had stopped there, awaiting further orders; they had been sent as backup to the Colonel, since he and his men had not been heard from in months.

Viana inquired about the Africans. Who were they, were they agents of the Dutch, how had they come to be so badly maimed? The Colonel demanded to see his papers. Had Fonte da Ré sent him?

An argument ensued. When Viana refused to listen any longer to the "obviously feverish and belligerent *cafuzo*," the Colonel ordered his men to seize Viana's weapons, commandeer his boats, which were anchored at the dock, and place the few remaining rebels on them. He had Viana and his regiment bound and lashed to trees, though they were, ostensibly, the King's soldiers. Viana promised that the Colonel would never see beyond the gates of a military prison once he got free; the Colonel's first impulse was to raise his sword; the festering burlap sack could surely hold another head, but dos Santos implored him to think better of it. The Portuguese sentries manning the dock and post opportunely vanished.

The boats plied the river back to its mouth. Every hundred kilometers one of the captives endeavored to leap into freedom of the currents, such that by the time the Colonel reached his father's plantation, only one young male, whom he had tethered to dos Santos, and two young females remained. José Inocêncio, now walking with the aid of a cane, and his elegant wife, Dona Maria Francisca, received their son and his men in the sitting room of their house. The son presented the recaptured slaves; his bewildered father was unsure that he could take such easy title to any of them, who in any case were too young and wild to incorporate immediately into his docile stock. He would have to consult his lawyer. Still, he had all three taken out to the slave quarters. The young male black, the elder man noted, looked vaguely familiar. At this point, the son presented to him the burlap sack, which by now was swarming and putrid. After a brief and horrifying examination, Londônia ordered it removed and cast out into the voracious river; very likely, like a vial bearing a message of incalculable importance, it rapidly made its way to the open sea.

Once he was fed, outfitted and properly horsed, which devoured nearly a month, the Colonel brought his men back to Salvador. As soon as he reported to his garrison, he was seized; a warrant had been issued for his arrest, for violations of the military code. Viana, already back in the capital city, had reported him. The Colonel was remanded to the military prison, to await adjudication of his case. He asked to meet with Fonte da Ré, but this request was denied on the grounds of practicality. His commander had been killed in battle at Arraial do Cabo, near the port of Nazaré, only a few days earlier.

The Tribunal

There was no precedent in the records of the military courts of Brazil, a councilor with connections to the colonial administrator and hired by José Inocêncio argued, for such a state of affairs, about which officers and prominent townspeople were buzzing. In the case of Lázaro Inocêncio Londônia de Figueiras, there could be no charge of insubordination. Viana held no titular rank above him; the commander only took the steps he did in order to complete his mission without delay; he had remained faithful to the original orders, as best he interpreted them, of his commanding officer; he had suffered an insult to his face, his dignity—there were witnesses. On the first and final counts, the argument appeared to have standing. On the second and third, questions lingered. Fonte da Ré, now deceased, was unable to attest either way. The men in Londônia's regiment had suddenly grown silent, and might have to be ordered to testify by the tribunal. Still, tying up a fellow officer and his soldiers, when they posed no threat of sedition, desertion or sabotage, constituted an extraordinary scenario. The councilor would have to consult with more learned authorities, and write to Lisbon for more guidance. During this interim, Londônia would remain in military custody.

Not only Londônia, but his father and relatives in high places found his circumstances intolerable. He was a Figueiras, strings must be pulled. But there were, oddly enough, no Figueirases among the upper hierarchy of the army. But there were many Figueirases who had the ear of the Church, the Crown's representatives, among the sugar-growing and ranching aristocracy not only of Bahia, but also of Parahyba, and Rio de Janeiro. But making an exception on behalf of this Londônia without the appearance of even a *pro forma* hearing might possibly harm morale among the officer corps during this critical period, as the Crown was engaged in a difficult war against the Dutch. But who was this Viana anyways, the son of unknown bumpkins from the south? But those same Vianas were landowners as well, had contacts. But Figueiras Henriques, his brother-in-law, was already on a frigate bound for Iberia, and would request an audience in Philip's court in Madrid, if need be. But there were witnesses. But, a war hero? But honor, duty, *esprit de corps*?

While the councilor consulted with knowledgeable parties, Londônia remained impounded. His connections, being what they were, insured that he would not suffer undue privations. He had to keep busy, so he had prisoners write letters to his parents, his elder brother, his nieces and nephews, members of his regiment. He organized athletic contests, drills. He assisted in the disciplining of slaves. His sister was permitted to visit him regularly, former classmates and fellow trainees sent tributes. Figueiras Henriques, on his return, met with members of the military command. The Bishop of Bahia received another influential relative. Some time passed, and the brouhaha waned, while the sequestration, though inconvenient, grew almost pleasant.

A closed tribunal of officers was finally seated at the urging of several key parties. A military lawyer from a less-distinguished family opened with his argument on behalf of the army, which is to say, Viana. He seemed, it struck all present, to be whispering into his chest, as if trying to perform an act of ventriloquism. One member of the tribunal had to be awakened twice. Then Londônia's councilor, deputized to appear before a military panel, delivered his defense. Such an elegant wig, such golden perorations, such learned command of the royal law. There was much nodding and noting of the councilor's key points. So it went. Viana's lawyer presented his rebuttal. It was noted that his Portuguese evidently carried fewer Latin eloquences than was common in continental courts of law; where on earth had he received his training? The tribunal broke for the Sabbath. When it resumed, the councilor intended to call Viana as his witness.

Meanwhile, Fonte da Ré's replacement, Nogueira, had reassigned most of Londônia's men to Viana's regiment, now reconstituted as part of a larger military unit which was to take up a position north of Olinda, close to the Dutch fort at Itamaracá. Capturing the fort would, Nogueira's superiors thought, prove decisive. Though Viana hoped that the tribunal would rule swiftly on what was by now an oft-mentioned punch line of his infamous humiliation ("tied up by that crazy nigger Figueiras, no less!"), there was a war to wage. The men shipped out on a navy vessel from the deep harbor at Salvador on the day the trial began; the winds were in their favor and only a short while later they had anchored off the coast of Pernambuco, as the general in charge deliberated on their plans.

Viana's lawyer, seeking to have him testify, learned that he had been mustered. An order must be issued not to send him into battle; his case was underway. His commander, Nogueira, for his part, had not received word of the trial, though it was taking place on the other side of the garrison. The lawyer requested a stay, until he might present further testimony. The tribunal, however, wanted to conclude the trial as soon as possible, as it was, by any measure, a distraction—the officers were needed for the ongoing campaign, and there were pressures from other quarters, in any case. Several of Londônia's men— dos Santos, Pereira—testified: they were rough-hewn characters, not entirely reliable, the members of the tribune conceded, but their tales of their commander's determination and valor would have persuaded the devil. Viana's lawyer elicited no counter claims; he returned to studying his written commentary. Again, he requested an appeal to be delivered to Nogueira, then rested his case.

Londônia sat to testify. The panel found his narration of heroism during the earlier Bahian conflict, followed by his campaign in the wilderness, enthralling. There was so much to hear, those Figueirases have a way with the word. Despite the seriousness of the affair, a current of easy familiarity passed among the men. Several laughed at Londônia's account of the circular march through the jungle; his route, he suggested to them, would eventually make a fine cow path. There were those Indians, of course, and other hardships, which need not be elaborated upon. He was no Jesuit, mind you. All he had to show for his exertions, however, was the unmistakable burnt-cork tan from wandering in the sun and forest for so long, and an amulet, which his councilor requested be entered into the record. Londônia even mentioned that he would have brought them back his pet monkey to exonerate him, only he'd forgotten it in his parents' home in Sergipe. When the session concluded, several of them thought he ought to be promoted on the spot, until they were reminded of the full slate of charges against him.

Back in Pernambuco the order came: Viana and his men boarded and launched small craft to reach the shore. The Dutch, surprised at the gross lack of subtlety, began their fusillade. The cannons at the fort let loose, while sharpshooters took aim, supplemented by a team of archers. Whatever men were not drowned and made it to shore fell quickly to the sands—Viana, who had never set foot on Pernambucan soil, was at least able to register this new achievement momentarily before closing his eyes for the final time.

Back in Bahia, the military lawyer waited; still no Viana. Nor did any other witnesses come forward. The head of the tribunal was losing patience; was this Viana unaware that the Dutch held territory as far north as Rio Grande do Norte? Things proceeded, arguments.... The councilor gave his final plea on behalf of the hero, which stirred nearly all present. Then the military lawyer spoke, so rapidly one had to strain to hear him. Arguments ended, the panel ruled. Londônia had grounds, there was the necessity of following his orders and the insult, so he would keep his commission, but he would be assigned, at least for a while, in a training capacity to a garrison near the city of Rio de Janeiro. Until such time, he should relax and reacquaint himself with civilization. All shook hands, the Colonel was released. Several slaves carried his numerous effects to his sister and brother-in-law's home, in the upper city above the Church of the Bonfim, where he would lodge until he set sail for Rio. Friends of the family paid visits; in his honor Mrs. Figueiras Henriques threw a sought-after farewell dinner, which concluded in dawn revels.

The journey to Rio was an unpleasant one, though Londônia had his comforts. From the ship, he could see that this second city, on the Guanabara Bay, was, despite its mythical mountains and bristling flora, markedly more rustic than the capital. But he had grown up on a sugar estate, far from the poles of civilization, and could adapt. As Londônia walked through the port area to hire a horse to reach the garrison, he found himself in the midst of a public scene. There was shouting, shrieks; a shoeless mulatto, his face and shirt and breeches clad in blood, scampered past him, followed by a large slave woman sporting a bell of petticoats, screaming. What on earth was this? Then another man, short, emaciated, with the sun-burnt face of a recently arrived Portuguese, emerged from the wall of bodies, his right hand thrusting forward a long dagger. Londônia tried to slip out of the way and brandish his sword in defense, but his reflexes, dulled after the protracted incarceration, failed him.

As soon as word reached the military officials in Bahia, he received several raises in rank; his body was brought back to Sergipe d'El Rei for a proper funeral. An auxiliary bishop officiated at the burial. It was only several months later that his wife, who had given birth and returned to her parents' home, learned of her husband's misfortune. She was now a wealthy woman. Their son, whom she originally named Augusto, was henceforth known as Augusto Inocêncio. She soon remarried, producing several more sons and daughters, and re-settled with her new husband, a soldier who was related on his maternal side to the Figueiras family, near the distant and isolated village of São Paulo.

On Dénouement

In 1966, the model Francesca Josefina Schweisser Figueiras, daughter of army chief General Adolfo Schweisser and the socialite Mariana Augusta "Gugu" Figueiras Figueiras, married Albertino Maluuf, the playboy son of the industrialist Hakim Alberto Maluuf, in a lavish ceremony in the resort town of Campos do Jordão. The event, conducted by His Eminence, the cardinal, in the Igreja Matriz de Santa Terezinha, with a reception on the grounds of the newly inaugurated Tudor-style Palácio Boa Vista, was covered in society pages across the Americas and Europe. They were divorced shortly after  the country's return to democracy two decades later, in 1987.

Their youngest son, Sergio Albertino, was known as "Inocêncio," a family nickname given, for as far back as anyone could recall, to at least one of the Figueiras boys in each generation. Sergio Albertino's marked simplicity of expression and introverted manner confirmed the aptness of this name, by which he quickly and widely became known. Yet from childhood this same Inocêncio—"emerald eyes, skin white as moonstone, a swan's neck"—also periodically exhibited willful, sometimes reckless behavior, engaging in fights with other children, committing acts of vandalism, setting fire to a coach house on the family's estate that housed the cleaning staff. He met with numerous and repeated difficulties in his educational progress. No tutor his mother enlisted lasted longer than a few months. Bouncing between boarding schools in the United States, Switzerland, Argentina, and Brazil, he developed a serious addiction to heroin and other illicit substances. An encounter with angel dust at a party thrown by friends in Iguatemí led him to drive a brand-new Mercedes coupe off an overpass, but he was so intoxicated that he suffered only minor injuries. After a short involvement with a local neo-Nazi group and repeated stays in rehabilitation centers, he dropped out of Mackenzie Presbyterian University, in São Paulo, where he had enrolled to study business, a profession which his family had long dominated. An arrest for possession of ten grams of cocaine, a tin of marijuana and three Ecstasy tabs led to a suspended sentence. His community service included working with less fortunate fellow addicts in other parts of the city. Quickly befriending several of these individuals—friends of his parents remarked in the most restrained manner possible that from childhood the boy had possessed uncouth predilections and tastes—he increasingly spent time in city neighborhoods in which most people of his background, under no circumstance, would dare set foot. The bodyguards his parents hired gave up trying to keep track of him. One evening in midsummer, he left the flophouse—where he was staying with a woman he'd met on a binge—to score a hit. . . .

> "Oh, this terrible ancient pain
> we feel down to our bones
> that fills the contours of our dreams
> whenever we're alone—"

On Brazil

São Paulo, once a small settlement on the periphery of the Portuguese state, is now a vast labyrinth of neighborhoods upon neighborhoods, a congested super-metropolis of more than fourteen million people, the economic engine of Latin America. As Dr. Arturo Figueiras Wernitzky has noted in his magisterial study of the region, millions of poor Brazilians, many of them from the northeastern region of the country, including the states of Bahia, Sergipe and Pernambuco, have migrated over the last four decades to this great city, its districts and environs, suburbs and exurbs, primarily in search of work and economic opportunities.

Among these *nordestino* migrants, many of them of African ancestry, were members of the Londônia family from the towns of the same name in the states of Bahia, Sergipe, and Pernambuco, who constructed and established unauthorized settlements, or *favelas*, across the city of São Paulo, lacking sewage and electricity, and marked by the highest per capita crime rates outside of Rio de Janeiro—murders, assaults, drug-dealing, and larceny, as well as well-documented police violence.

Among the most notorious *favelas* is one of the newest, as yet unnamed, only marked on maps by municipal authorities by the letter—*N.*—perhaps for "(Favela) Novísima" (Newest Favela), or "(Mais) Notório" (Most Notorious), or "Nada Lugar" (No Place), though it is also known, according to journalists and university researchers like Figueiras Wernitzky, who are examining its residents as part of a larger study of demographic changes in the region, among those who live in it, as "Quilombo Cesarão."

AN OUTTAKE FROM THE
IDEOLOGICAL ORIGINS OF THE
AMERICAN REVOLUTION

Origins

In January 1754, Mary, a young Negro servant to Isaac Wantone, wealthy farmer and patriot of the town of Roxbury, Massachusetts, gave birth in her master's stables to a male child. An older Negro servant, named Lacy, also belonging to Wantone's retinue, attended Mary in her prolonged and exacting labor, during which the slave girl developed an intense fever. For a half hour after Mary delivered the child, a tempest raged within her as she lay screaming in a strange tongue, which was in part her native *Akan*. Then her eyes rolled back in her head and she expired. Lacy uttered a benediction in that same language, and thereafter presented the infant to her master, Mr. Wantone, as was the custom in those parts. When he saw the copper-skinned newborn, eyes blazing, upon whom the darkness of Africa had not completely left its indelible stamp, the master, adequately versed in the Scriptures, promptly named him Zion, which in Hebrew means "sun."

Knowing his servant not to have been married or even betrothed at the time of the child's birth, Wantone rightly feared the sanctions laid down by Puritan and colonial law, which in the case of illegitimate paternity included whippings, fines rendered against the mother of the child, its father, and quite probably the master, be he same or otherwise. Wantone also might have to put in an appearance before the General Court. Though not a gentleman by birth (he was of yeoman stock and self-read in the classics), Wantone had fought admirably among his fellows in King George's War and had by dint of many years' toil built up an excellent estate. Moreover, he subscribed unwaveringly to the Congregational Church. And, on all these accounts, he declined to have his reputation or standing in the slightest besmirched by such a scandal. He had therefore conspired to conceal Mary's condition for the full length of her term by keeping her indoors as much as possible and forbidding her to venture out near the local roads, where she might be spied by neighbors or passersby. He also forbade his servants and children to speak of the matter, lest their gossip betray him. Toward neither plan did he meet with rebellion; so it is said that one's sense of the law, like one's concept of morality, originates in the home. The child's father, whose name the taciturn girl had refused to speak, Wantone identified as Zephyr, a sly black-Abenaki horsebreaker in the service of his neighbor, Josiah Shapely. Among the members of his own household, however, he himself was not entirely above suspicion, especially given the child's complexion. In any case, Zion would, according to plan, officially be deemed a *foundling*.

Wantone's wife, *née* Comfort and descended from an unbroken line of Berkshire Puritans who had arrived in the Bay Colony not long after the Mayflower, had for several years been growing ever more austere in her faith, and to the achievement of a glacial purity of relations. As a result she abhorred all spiritual and fleshly transgressions, especially bastardy, in which the two were so visibly commingled. Upon learning of the infant's imminent entry into the sphere of her family's existence, she ordered that it be kept out of her sight altogether.

Music

When Lacy had first passed the infant Zion to her master for inspection, the child began to cry uncontrollably. Wantone order him to be placed in a small wooden crib on the second floor of the house above the buttery: thereby he might learn peace. This weeping, which soon became a kind of keening, persisted for several weeks without relent. Meanwhile Wantone ordered his slaves Jubal, a native-born Negro who tended his livestock, and Axum, a young mulatto of New Hampshire origin who served as his handyman, to bury the deceased slave girl Mary near the edge of his south grazing fields. At her interment, the master recited over the grave a few lines from the Old Testament, and wept.

Lacy was nearing middle age, yet this chain of events soon bound her into assuming the role of the child's mother. Otherwise she was engaged in innumerable chores about the house or attending to her mistress, Mrs. Wantone, who did not like ever to be kept waiting. Lacy had not seen her own child since shortly after his sixth birthday nearly fifteen years before, because her previous master, then ill with cancer and disposing of his Boston estate, had sold the boy north to a merchant in Newbury, and her south to Wantone. Taking frequent quick breaks, she nursed the infant Zion from a suckling bottle, on warm goat's milk sweetened with honey and dashes of rum, of which there was no shortage in the cellar. She also sang to him the lively songs she remembered from her childhood along the lower Volta, in the Gold Coast, as well as Christian hymns when any member of the family, especially her mistress, was in earshot. Eventually the child calmed down appreciably, and Wantone allowed him to be carried about the entire house and grounds when the mistress was away.

Though these were years of increasing privation for many in the Colony as the noose of the mother country tightened, Wantone prospered. Not long after this time he purchased a likely young Negro woman, named Mary, for £11 from the Boston trader Nicholas Marshall, to replace the deceased Mary, who had attended primarily to the four Wantone children, Nathanael, Sarah, Elizabeth, and Hepzibah. New Mary was also expected to afford Lacy more time for Mrs. Wantone by also watching Zion. This became the only task to which she took with even a passing enthusiasm. She had been born in the region of the Gambia, where all were free, and quickly chafed under the weight of her new status. She ignored orders; she talked back. Moreover she was given to spreading rumors and painting her face and fingers gaily with Roxbury clay and indigo on the Sabbath, while declining to recite the Lord's prayers, as well as to other acts of idleness, gossip, lewdness, and truculence. For these offenses, to which the boy was a constant witness, she was routinely whipped by her mistress, who took a firm and iron hand at all times. Naturally, New Mary ran away, to Brookline, where she was captured by the local constabulary, and returned bound to the Wantones. She received ten lashes for her impertinence, another ten for her flight, still a third ten for cursing her mistress before the other slaves, and an interdiction not to leave the grounds of the estate under any circumstances. One can only temporarily keep a wild horse penned. For several years, as the child Zion was nearing the age of his autonomy (seven), New Mary endured these constraints, peaceably rearing the child with Lacy and the several Negro male servants, Jubal, Axum and Quabina. And then she ran away again, this time getting as far south as Stoughton, on the Neponset River. Again she was returned, duly punished, ordered to comport herself with the dignity befitting the Wantone household. Repeated incidents of insolence and misbehavior followed, however, including acts of a lascivious nature with a local Indian, the destruction of several volumes of books, and an attempted fire. The Wantones sold New Mary to a Plymouth candlemaker for £4. Zion was, for nearly a year, inconsolable.

Even during New Mary's tenure Zion had often shown signs of melancholy or unprovoked anger. Frequently sullen, he would often sequester himself in the buttery, or at the edge of the manor house's Chinese porch, singing to himself lyrics improvised out of the air or songs he had learned from Lacy and the other slaves. Or he would declaim passages from the local gazette which Axum or the Wantone children had taught him. At other times he would devise elaborate counting games, to the amazement of the other slaves. When caught in such idle pursuits on numerous occasions by Mrs. Wantone, who spared no rod, he did not shed a tear. Her punishments instead appeared only to inure him to discipline altogether. He began singing more frequently, and would occasionally accompany his songs with taps and foot-stamps. His master took a different tack, and hedgingly encouraged the boy in his musical pursuits, so long as they did not disturb the household or occur on the Sabbath. As a result the idling musical sessions abated—temporarily. Even so, Mrs. Wantone relinquished Zion's correction to her husband and eldest son.

As soon as Zion was able he began performing small tasks about the house and estate, such as restuffing the mattress ticks, mucking out the stables, replacing the chamberpots, polishing the family's shoes, and feeding the hens. His intermittent disappearances and musical-lyrical spells soon reappeared. At the age of ten, he entered an apprenticeship to Jubal, and then at eleven to Ford, the Irishman who oversaw the extensive Wantone holdings, which included twenty acres of home lot, fifteen acres of mowing land, twelve and a half acres fifteen rods of pasture land, twenty acres ten rods undivided of salt marsh, ten acres of woodland and muddy pond woods to the south, and six acres of woodland to the west, all in Roxbury and Dorchester; as well as a plot of forty acres of woodland in Cambridge, recently bequeathed by his late brother-in-law, Nathanael Comfort, Esq., a graduate of Harvard College and a gentleman lawyer. From Ford, Zion learned a number of Irish melodies, which he performed to the delight of all on Negro Election Day and other holidays. During the late summer evenings, he would accompany a nearby slave fiddler, and soon developed a name throughout the neighborhood as a warbler.

One afternoon around the time of Zion's thirteenth year Jubal heard fiddling out near the cow barn. On investigation, he found the boy creditably playing his master's violin and singing a sorrowful tune in accompaniment. The horses stood in their stables, unbrushed. Because he liked the saturnine child, Jubal waited until Zion had finished his performance. After reproaching him, Jubal seized the violin and returned it to the music room. When he returned to the barn, the boy was missing. Several weeks later Jubal again found Zion playing the violin in the afternoon, when he should have been at the chicken-coop feeding the hens; this time he threatened to tell on the boy if he took the violin again, to which Zion only laughed and dared Jubal to say anything. Jubal returned the violin without incident. The third time Jubal encountered the boy fiddling in the barn, he rebuked him vehemently, but before he could snatch away the violin, Zion smashed it to smithereens on a trough. For this, he eventually received stripes from both his master and his master's son, and a ban on singing of any sort. The boy's wild mood swings and moroseness waxed from this point, to the extent that the other slaves, particularly Jubal, took care not to offend him. Wantone himself remained unconcerned, as he was the master of his manor, and an oak does not quiver before ivy.

Around the time of his fourteenth birthday, Zion, now so strapping in build and mature in mien that he could almost pass for a man, ran away for the first time. Absconding in the dead of night, he got as far as the town of Dedham, some nine miles away. There he remained in the surrounding woods undiscovered for a week, until his nightly ballads and lamentations betrayed him to a local Indian, who reported the melodiousness of the voice to the town sheriff. Returned to his master, Zion received the following punishment: he was placed in stocks for a night, and then confined to the grounds of the estate, with the threat that any further misdeeds could result in his being temporarily remanded to the custody of the local authorities. Within a fortnight the boy had run away again, this time with one of Wantone's personal effects, and a pillowbeer of food. A search of the surrounding towns turned up no clue of him. As a result, Wantone was forced to advertise in the local gazette for the return of his lawful property.

Flight

From the *New England Weekly News Letter*, June 18, 1768:

> Ran away from his master Isaac Wantone gentleman of the
> country town of Roxbury in Suffolk County, in Massachusetts
> Bay Colony, a likely Negro boy aged fourteene years, named
> ZION, who wore on him [an] old grey shirt homespun and
> pair of breeches of the same cotton cloth, with shoes only, and
> a kerchief about his head, carrying a silver watch, clever, who
> sings like a nightingall: WHO shall take up said likely ZION
> and convey him to his MASTER above said, or advise him so
> that he may have him again shall be PAID for the SAME at
> the rate of £4 1s.

To Pennyman

Three months had advanced when the sheriff's office of the town
of Monatomy, in Middlesex County, returned to the Wantones
the fugitive child, who had been arrested and detained on a series of
charges. These included but were not limited to breaking the Negro
curfew in Middlesex County; theft (of various small articles, including watches and food); disturbance of the peace; brawling, gambling
and trickery at games of chance; dissembling about his identity and

provenance; and masquerading as a free person. Most seriously the young slave had beaten up an Irish laborer outside a public house in Waltham, and threatened the man's life if he reported the beating to the authorities, local or the King's. For this series of offenses, which broke the patience of the Wantones, the General Court of Middlesex County arraigned, tried and convicted the slave, to the penalty of thirty-five stripes, and a fine of £10, payable to the victims. After the boy received his public lashes, his master settled the fine and issued an apology for his slave's behavior to the General Court, which was printed in all the local papers. He then promptly flogged Zion himself before restraining the boy in a stock behind the cow barn. During this time, the Wantones considered their options, and agreed it would be in their best interests to sell their intractable chattel, who, they supposed, still had arson and murder waiting in his kit. This they promptly did despite the rapidly deflating nature of the local currency, for the sum of £5, to a distant relative of Wantone's, the merchant Jabez Pennyman, then living on a small estate in the Dorchester Neck.

Pennyman, a widower and veteran, ran general provision shops in Dorchester and Milton, the latter purchased at a sharp discount from a Loyalist recently emigrated to Canada. A native of the Narragansett Plantations, he had earned a reputation for probity in all matters financial, and rectitude in all matters moral, and had acquired Zion both because of the low cost and because he required the services of a slave of considerable strength who could read English and reckon figures. The menagerie of Pennyman's home, the slave soon learned, was utterly different from that of the Wantones'. Instead of sleeping in his master's small but bearable attic, his quarters now consisted of a windowless, zinc-roofed shack, which might once have been a toolshed, furnished only with a pallet bed and a rusted chamberpot, several hundred yards away from the main edifice. His daily routine also diverged markedly from that of his earlier life in Roxbury: for Pennyman expected him to ride out with an assistant to one of his shops six days a week, and spend the entire workday lifting, lading, packing, unpacking, registering and moving stock, such as apparel of all sorts, furniture, books, kitchenware, provisions, yard and garden tools, and farm and estate implements. There were no other Blacks, or even Indians, in Pennyman's household; only his Irish maid, Nellie, a Welsh manservant, James, and his assistants in the shops, all boys of English or Yankee heritage, none of whom showed the least inclination towards socializing with a Negro. Unless the situation demanded it, in fact, none of them, including Pennyman, spoke to him at all.

Although Zion worked commendably at his new post for almost six months (without even the smallest infraction beyond purloining several bottles of Malden rum), the long rides, the isolation and lack of companionship, his continued bondage, and the lure of the nearby ocean had begun to affect him perniciously. He especially bridled at Pennyman's austerities: the provision of a minimum of food, and no spices at all, at meals; a moratorium on singing or celebrations of any kind, particularly during those hours that he set aside for his ledger books or to read the Gospel; and the requirement of clothes of a plain nature especially on holy days, for Pennyman had not been awakened by the preachings of Edwards or any other deliverer great or small. One morning, after unloading cases of sugar, flour, molasses, salt, suet, cranberry bread, sweet currants, and apples, and casks of rum, French brandy, Boston beer, and Madeira wine, Zion began singing aloud one of the songs he had learned from New Mary to pass the time, when he thought he overheard one of the shop assistants noting how perverse it was that "music should arise from a tarpit." Confronting the man, who peppered him with epithets, Zion could no longer restrain himself and flattened the man with one blow. A bullet, once fired, cannot be recalled: Fearing the repercussions of his action, he fled on horse northward to Boston, tinderbox of liberty. After abandoning his mount in the marshlands near Boston Neck, he ran until he had reached the famed Beacon Hill portion of the Trimountain. He concealed himself in a stand of box, waiting for the cover of darkness before proceeding to the home of a cousin of Lacy who lived in Green Street, near the Mill Pond. Here and at another safe house run by free blacks he remained for several weeks, before shipping out without a permit from Hatch's Wharf on a clipper bound for Nantucket.

The sea momentarily opened a new chapter in the book of Zion's life. He sailed on a Kittery-based sloop, the *Hazard*, which ventured as far south as the English Caribbean, and on which he experienced the freedoms and vicissitudes of the maritime life. Next came a whaling tour, during which he served in a variety of capacities for a year, enduring an ever-rising tide of depredations that culminated in his being chained belowdecks, without food or water for weeks, for theft, attempted mutiny and insulting the honor of the whaler's drunken captain. Only the intervention of a galley slave from the Barbados, who held the captain's affections, and most importantly, brought him fresh water and salt cod at twilight, saved his life.

Liberty

The 1770s: great changes were blowing through streets of the colonial capital. The Crown's troops had irrevocably stained Boston's cobblestones with the blood of Attucks and others; the promise of freedom sweetened the air like incense. When Zion was freed by his captain upon return to Sherburne, in Nantucket Island, instead of a duel to restore his honor, the young man stowed away on a brigantine returning to the port of Boston. Penniless, carrying on his person only a pocket pistol and several cartouches he had stolen from the whaler captain's wares, and finding that both Lacy's cousin and the safe woman had moved or been moved from their residences, leaving no place to stay, for the town appeared to his eyes to have evacuated its entire black population, Zion grew restless and proceeded to rob a tanner's store. He was captured within hours by the Crown's authorities and confined, pending his arraignment, to the city prison on Queen Street. After a short period of time, the under-magistrate discovered that he was a fugitive slave, and returned him, pending his trial, to Mr. Pennyman, now thriving handsomely with five shops throughout Suffolk and Bristol Counties. Pennyman determined to get rid of him. His personal scruples, however, did not permit him to entertain simply manumitting the slave. He must first earn back his investment.

After Zion's conviction and brief imprisonment, he was again returned to Pennyman, and the businessman ordered him to be flogged for his effrontery, which to his preoccupied and rigid mind had assumed the character of outright treachery. He then sent him south to work in a shop in Attleborough, far from the negative influence of the sea or Boston, where the atmosphere fairly crackled with sedition. Zion—who yearned either to take up residence in Halifax, which he had learned about during his time at sea as a free man, and from there to ship out on a frigate bound for parts unknown, or conversely to return to the only settled home he had known, that of the Wantones, where he would be again among those who knew him best—did not take kindly to this turn of events, and revolted. After only a week, he fled towards Boston, following the coastal route and getting as far as Duxbury, where he stole two cakes of gingerbread, a package of biscuits, and a pint of milk out of a horse-cart heading north. He secreted himself in a nearby marsh. He was discovered a week later, arrested and housed in a local jail. He swiftly broke out by eluding his guard, commandeered a piebald, and headed south by southwest along the lesser roads and trails. The local authorities again captured, tried and imprisoned him, not only for his crimes but for his defiance of the social order, yet his realization of his own personal power had galvanized him, making life insufferable under any circumstances but his own liberation.

During Zion's second incarceration, Pennyman had quick-deeded his ownership of the slave to a fellow reformed merchant, Simon

Warren, of Boston, who in return promised to pay full, rather than wholesale, price for several cases of contraband liquor Pennyman was trying to unload. Zion left jail in May of 1772, and for a brief spell worked agreeably under Warren. Within the year, however, during which the enslaved man resumed a life of debauchery, including but not limited to periodic flights to Middlesex and lower Suffolk Counties, allegedly fathering several children by white, Indian and Negro women, drunkenness and brawling in the streets of Boston, celebrating on the Sabbath day, breaking curfews, threatening shopkeepers, openly praising London, and selling wine stolen from his master, Warren found the situation so unbearable that he gave him to another merchant, his second cousin, Job Hollis, of Boston.

Hollis, who had once held positions of prominence in the shipbuilding trade in Marblehead, was now reduced to running a scrap metal-working and trading shop on Lynn Street near the Hunt and White Shipyards. Possessed of an increasingly liberal mindset, and realizing almost immediately that he could only loosely control Zion, he afforded his charge some berth by giving him traveling papers. With these the slave immediately took the widest latitude, for had not the Reverend Isaac Skillman preached in that very year that "the slave should rebel against his master"? One midday he took Hollis's horse and a fiddle he had bought with some of his earnings, and rode out to a cornhusking at Medford. Here his singing and strumming, striking appearance, and lively manner at the husking hall attracted the attentions of a number of the local women. The one on whom he set his sights, however, was a married white lady in her late 20s, Ruth Pine, of evident gentility. She coldly rejected his serenades all afternoon. By the early evening, armed with rum, he demanded that she accompany him back to a local inn, a suggestion that visibly offended her, leading her to denounce him in the strongest terms possible. He responded by slapping her so hard that she passed out. This led to a great commotion in the hall, wherein there were numerous calls for the Negro's death. He promptly fled. Pine's husband, a stout local farmer, was enraged that his wife might be so mistreated by any man, let alone a black one, and even more incredibly a slave. He pursued Zion on horseback all the way to Boston, where he finally overtook the offender and engaged him in a battle of fisticuffs in Orange Street, the city's main artery. An officer of the courts walking by glanced at the boxers, then continued on his way. Within minutes Zion had reduced Pine to a heap of bloodied flesh and linen. To celebrate, he mounted Pine's horse, his own having galloped off, and proceeded to Cambridge, committing a series of burglaries of homes and carriages along the way.

Bounty

Items stolen: a bottle of rum, several pieces of jerky, a tricorner felt hat, nine pounds sterling four shillings, suttler's markee, some chocolate, twenty pounds sterling, a flask of French brandy, a pair of moreen small clothes (which did not fit and were thus discarded in the Charles), a man's white linen shirt, a leg of mutton, two weight of salt pork, eleven pounds sterling six shillings, five pence, a carbine and two pocket pouches, a magnifying glass, a map of the easternmost British provinces in Canada.

Advertisement

A likely Negro Man aged about 18 or 19 years,
that speaks very good English
of great strength and brawn
sings and plays the violin
sold on reasonable terms by Mr.
Ebenezer Minott, trader over against
the Post Office in Cornhill, Boston.

(There were no takers.)

Spree

After settling this most recent plight with the Middlesex County magistrate, Job Hollis arranged to place Zion on board a vessel bound for Virginia where he would be sold at auction and his wildness might finally be whipped or worked out of him. Only under such conditions would this slave learn respect for the common and hardworking citizenry in whose colonies he had been fortunate enough to dwell, Hollis reasoned, and if Zion continued in his ways down there, the penalties would be swift, and ultimate. Hollis walked Zion, hands bound, the requisite papers pinned to the slave's tattered coat, all the way to Hancock's Wharf, where the South-going vessel was to dock. He wished the young bondman a safe passage to the southerly port, saying a prayer for his soul as they stood before the open water. To drown out his master's voice, Zion began singing. On this note of defiance, the exasperated Hollis departed. For an hour or so the slave stood there singing and whistling on the wharf as the bailor and a customs official sat lubricating in a nearby ale house. When the ship, a frigate, did not arrive at the stated time, Zion charmed a Dutch whore strolling by to untie his bindings, whereupon he set off to find the first loosely hitched horse. As he ran he proclaimed himself free. Under duress one's actions assume a dream-like clarity. An unattended nag stood outside a tavern, and off Zion rode.

After a spree which stretched from the city of Boston west to the edges of Middlesex County, the slave played his worst hand when he committed lascivious acts just across the county line on the person of a sleeping widow, Mary Shaftesbone, near Shrewsbury. Having broken into her home and reportedly taken violent liberties with her, unaccountably Zion did not flee the town, but entered a nearby tavern and began a round of popular songs, to the delight of a crowd of locals and the horror of the violated woman. The sheriff arrested him without delay. When he realized the notoriety of the criminal he had in his hands, he suggested to the local magistrate that, although this most recent felony had occurred in Worcester County, the criminal ought to be returned to the General Court in Boston, which had the apparatus to deal with such evil. The magistrate responded that given the current worsening political situation in the capital, it appeared unlikely that the slave's crimes would receive rapid adjudication. Mrs. Shaftesbone, demanding justice, or at least compensation, therefore had word sent to Job Hollis, who was negotiating the sale of his business in the anticipation of an assault against Boston's northern waterfront. The violated widow suggested a cash settlement, with the proviso that Hollis sell the criminal out of the colonies, preferably to the French West Indies. Hollis, who still held title to Zion, agreed to this arrangement, and collected him, now restrained in wrist irons, from the town jail. They rode westward, where Hollis's real plan was to sell the slave down at Albany to assure a good price and guarded transport down the Hudson. But on the way, in the town of Pittsfield, they encountered the Hampshire County sheriff, who claimed to possess warrants for the Negro from Worcester and Suffolk Counties. In the confusion arising over the validity, scope and authority of the documents, Zion, as if aware of the tenuous state of justice for blacks in New York State, seized his master's musket, knocked both men out, mounted the sheriff's horse, and rode back eastward.

Jurisdiction

The following day, the Crown's military authorities captured Zion in an alder wood outside Worcester and placed him in the town garrison under heavy local guard. But at nightfall he inexplicably slipped away. He then committed a series of robberies and violent acts throughout the entire span of the county until his capture on September 17, 1774, again by the military authorities, who pressed to try him under the statutory laws of Britain, though that country's influence was now nearly at ebb tide. The colonial judiciary objected, and instead rushed this particular case along, despite a growing criminal and civil case backlog. Problems of jurisdiction always mirror much greater crises of authority. At Worcester, Zion was tried and found guilty of rape by a judge who considered the slave's affinity for civil disobedience and social disruption to be intolerable in light of the present state of alarm throughout the region. He ordered a hanging. Mindful of his rights under the law, Zion implored the court for a "benefit of clergy." This the General Court of Worcester County, after half a year's consideration of his records, with documentation from the neighboring courts and his former owners, denied.

Confession

The night before he was to be led to the gallows, Zion sang a dirge that brought tears to the eyes of a townswoman standing nearby. He then gave a short testimony of his life and self-destruction, which ended with the following admonition, in a keening voice, to all bondsmen and women of the colony and of New England: "To all fellow Brothers and Sisters of Africk and other wise in Bondage in this common Wealth of Massachusetts take heart that ye avoid Drunkenness and Lewdness of the Flesh for the only true Liberty lies in holding Free—do keep the Faith—"

This confession was duly witnessed and indited by an Anglican minister from Leominster, who included it among his personal effects when he returned a year later to his home parish outside London. The account was subsequently lost, however; he was the only one of those present who later recalled it.

Theory (Outtake)

The prevalence of the doctrine of liberty may be accounted for, from another cause, viz., a false sensation or seeming experience which we have, or may have, of liberty or indifference, in many of our actions." *David Hume*

Eclipse

On the morning of April 1, 1775, the authorities did not find the Negro named Zion in his cell. Given the severity of the crimes and the necessity of preserving the ruling order, another Negro, whose particular crimes are not recorded, was hanged in the Worcester Town Square, surrounded by a sparse gallery of onlookers, among them the widow Shaftesbone; and the newly-married Sarah Wantone Fleet and her husband George, of Worcester, a Lockean and member of a local militia. Also present was Jubal, now calling himself Mr. John Cuffee, a free laborer and leader of a Negro brigade in Boston.

Of their response there is no record. The rest of the town, absent from the proceedings, was preparing, one must suppose, for the swiftly approaching conflagration.

A LETTER ON THE TRIALS
OF THE COUNTERREFORMATION
IN NEW LISBON

*"What is the nature of the recurring irrationality of culture which pre-
cludes a victory of modernizing rationality?"*
Aby Warburg

"If I could fly to you on the wings of eagles ..."
Yehuda HaLevi

"I want the essence. My soul is in a hurry."
Mário de Andrade

"The disquiet that lurks beneath the placid surface ..."
Manoel Aries D'Azevedo

June 1630

TO:
Dom Inácio Lisboa Branco
Sacred and Professed House
Second Order of the Discalced Brothers of the Holy Ghost
in care of the Bishopric of Bahia
São Salvador da Bahia dos Todos os Santos
New Lusitânia (Brazil)

DOM FRANCISCO,
I write you in the expectation that you will soon discover this missive,
concealed, as you regularly instructed the members of the professed

house in Olinda, during the period that you led it, within the binding of this book that has been sent to you and which you, having discovered the letter, have just set down. The book is the very *Lives of the Martyrs* you bequeathed to those remaining before your flight in the spring of last year. The Netherlandish authorities under Nassau-Siegen persist in demonstrating toleration, and reason, not only in matters of the Faith, and though they are masters at war, proceed without cunning concerning our vernacular handiwork; and so it is unlikely that they will have seized this innocuous volume as contraband or scuttled it on censorious shores before it moors upon your writing table.

Nor is it likely that they will have laid a finger on the few other and sundry effects of yours, which include a rosary of colored Italian glass, an embroidered muslin handkerchief, a chasuble of black silk, embroidered in resplendent hues of violet, and a tattered and faded red vest of common linen that I am told you once wore faithfully during your conversions along the upper Capabaribe River. These effects I have entrusted separately with Amaro (Gaspar) Leite, the messenger who sails to your city under a letter of safe passage, and who, upon seeing you, shall pass on the shibboleth that confirms the existence of the very communication your eyes now feast upon.

All these gifts he brings to the new house in which you and those who departed with you have now settled, in the name of the gentle and good Provost there, Dom Felix Silva Matos, whose name was passed on by those who knew him well during his years in the *aldeias*. As a man of the Faith he never once laid an injurious finger on native or African, nor on any who shared the bloodlines of the two. Moreover, in sending these treasures, including the book, to you, I am of the mind that no officials of the Crown, nor the Bishop of Bahia, nor least of all the Holy Office, if it should make a visitation, will impound them.

The most valuable of all, however, is this written missive, as you will certainly soon agree. As you also shall see, you will gain full access to it only by the application of another trick you conveyed to those in your care, underlining how well your lessons took root, like cuttings, even in distant fields. Thus the special care I have taken. If you should please see fit, do let the lit candlewick linger upon this document once you have read it, as that would be in the utmost order, though it is of no matter to me, for it should be declared that I am beyond the reach of those laws, earthly or divine, that would condemn you, on the very fact of possession of the written account I shall shortly begin.

Do know that the one to whom you had intrusted the preservation of the Faith is in no immediate harm. This letter sails to you, in its clever guise, out of an abiding desire to convey to you the truth of what occurred at ALAGOAS; rather than let the waters of rumor fertilize the vineyards of discussion in the capital, I have dowsed for you here the spring of truth. I gather that you already foresaw the calamity, at least from the perspective of the Lusitanians, that would descend upon this land, which is why you began to employ the vehicle of the Gospels to arouse a spirit of resistance not only among the members of the Order, but among the citizens of the Captaincy and the far and nether regions; for, as you often said, and I have heard many times repeated, while we do rightly fear the saber and the carbine, it could be a single man's tongue, and the written record of its issue, that mark the greatest danger.

Yet even knowing this, did you foresee what was to come at Alagoas? Did you not foresee the implications of sending Joaquim D'Azevedo as your spiritual agent? Evidently not, and so I shall now recount to you how that absence of portents, like your Scriptures, failed you. That is, I shall now tell of that series of events, unforeseeable at least to some of those who lived them, that inverted worlds, bringing those whom you knew, or thought you knew, intimately, northward in retreat to Olinda from the south, just as you bore only the clothes on your back and your Bible in your departure south for the capital city of the Savior. How do I know these facts, their recounting never having passed any man's lips? This, as with so many other things, I shall reveal in due time.

To return to the present narrative, I cannot be certain that you have heard even a single account from any of the other members of the Brotherhood who were there; no knowledge has revealed itself of where those creatures went who had long been in residence, or where they are today. Perhaps they too are at Bahia, or, like the numerous ghosts that haunt the coast of this infernal land, slipped onto a ship and are now promulgating their vileness in Cape-Verde or among the Luandans. May even Hell be rid of them. I ask only that you understand given all that has transpired since you last spoke face to face with any of those at that now accursed house, that some who have been condemned to the most foul contumely do reside, nevertheless, in Truth, and so this missive proceeds from that strange and splendid position.

It was, you will remember, during the period shortly preceding All Saints' Day, which is to say in late October of that year, 1629, that you sent a certain priest, Dom Joaquim D'Azevedo, from Olinda to assume the position of provost of the foundation at Alagoas, in the southern region of the Captaincy of Pernambuco, of the Professed House of the Second Order of the Discalced Brothers of the Holy Ghost. You made the appointment; the order came from your hand. The Alagoas monastery had been without a leader since the untimely drowning, under mysterious circumstances, of the prior Provost, Dom Affonso Travassos, also sent by you, in the waters just after the Feast of Saint John, in June 1629; and one year before that, the prior leader, Dom Luiz Duran Carneiro, had succumbed, allegedly, to the temptations of the Devil himself, and disappeared into the interior. These occurrences were hardly known by anyone in the order, beyond those remaining at Alagoas, but you were unsure whether the news had spread throughout the various precincts of the nearby town and region. Yet either way, without a firm spiritual base the monastery there, much like its pastorate, risked falling into moral and mortal decay.

What most knew was that Padre Duran Carneiro and Padre Pero had constructed the foundation of that House by hand only a decade before, while D'Azevedo, that obscure figure and youngest son of that family of tax-farmers who had settled in the distant north, in the city of São Luis, in that former French colony of Maranhão, that one whom you would soon send as a shepherd to gather the flock back into the pen, was still engaged in private tutorial at home, and had not even set sail for studies and ordination in Coimbra. That was all that was well known.

This, then, is where it begins. At some point between Padre Travassos's death and that fateful time in the spring of 1629, you, with the counsel of the Vice-Provost and several senior members of the Olinda House, decided that D'Azevedo would be the emissary of renewal in Alagoas. You selected him for what you took to be his scriptural acumen, his meticulousness with whatever task he undertook, his pecuniary skills, and literary gifts. There was also his youth, and his personal probity. You expected that he would right the Alagoas house like an overturned raft, and at every stage write you of how he did it and would next proceed.

Indeed this is what you would tell him once one of the novices— having beckoned him as he re-inspected for a third time the casks of wine in the house's cellar to insure a correct count, his gift for precision and detail having already gained note— led him to your office. There you also delivered a brief speech about the importance of the house to the Faith in Alagoas and the priests' role in establishing it, about which D'Azevedo was only dimly aware. You presented him with his letters of commission, written out and signed and sealed by you, as there was no time to gain the approval of the authorities in Bahia, let alone Lisbon. You told him that there were at Alagoas two priests, the said Pero and another, Padre Barbosa Pires, and one brother, Dom Gaspar Leite, sent from Olinda half a year before, whom D'Azevedo had just missed upon his return from Europe, as well as a peck of servants, all of them Africans and mulattos. Of the entire ménage he heard only the essentials. You did not speak even obliquely of the malevolence lurking in that small outpost on the Atlantic Coast.

Padre D'Azevedo, cognizant of his oath and the necessity of duty, accepted willingly. He returned to the wine cellar, finished his inventory and handed it to a slave to submit to the Brother Procurator, then went and packed his trunk. Maybe he prayed, read several passages from Ezekiel or another book of Scripture which he thought might cast a light before him. He had not a single map of the plans or full estate, no contacts in the town, no specific orders written in your hand or any others, nor any guide but what might have suddenly taken root in his head. The next morning he boarded the skiff to Recife, to catch the ship to Alagoas.

D'Azevedo arrived at the port of his chief destination as evening was falling. The voyage, not far, but over unusually turbulent seas, spent him. The heat, heightened by the approach of summer and the shoreline humidity, drained him more. He had vowed, however, to launch, like an arrow aiming for its target, into the heart of his new position as soon as he touched upon land. Though you had ostensibly sent word of his imminent arrival, it apparently had not reached Alagoas, so the house there had not dispatched an emissary to meet him. Rather than lodging at an inn, as was the custom for people arriving so late in the day, he hired a driver and cart and, after explaining his destination they headed there, climbing an undulant escarpment along the bend of the river, along whose southern banks spread a town of indeterminable size, bracketed by pockets of forests and, to the north and east, the immense lagoon, at this hour dark as mourning cloth, from which the city took its name, and then further west, inland and upland until the landscape bowled into pasture, amidst which stood the monastery's main gate as the wall of the nearby forest and the moonless night's utter blackness, from all sides, enfolded them.

The Brotherhood's House in Olinda, which D'Azevedo had just left, rose up in two windowed rows with bracketed latticed balconies, its walls white, its rooms commodious, its doors hewn of the finest Brazil wood, a vision of order, with a church of estimable beauty at one end, and a dining hall and kitchen at the other, with a library, a balneary, and comfortable lodgings for guests, all ringed by ample, well-tended fields, as well as a number of smaller, skillfully constructed structures. The structure that D'Azevedo now faced, presumably the monastery, lit by a single lantern suspended from a pole midway between the gate and the façade, down a curving, rutted, sandy path, leaned mean and squat, a single long storey. It was impossible at that hour to discern its color, though it hardly looked as if it could even under the brightest light be considered white. Its shutters, the ones he could make out, listed from their hinges; bushes and small trees bowed, trailed by monstrous shadows, away from its walls; its large battered wooden front door appeared to have been cut by someone little acquainted with doormaking. Almost invisible in the black cloak spreading from the lantern's penumbra, what he took to be buildings shimmered like foxfires in the landscape round it. He could not, however, spot the monastery gate's farther rims. Though he had not initially noticed it, when he looked around and up to take it all in, he spotted a crucifix, barely lit by the lantern's dim light, which tilted off one end of the main building's roof. A heavy sea breeze, it seemed to D'Azevedo, might easily topple it. Not a soul, priest or layperson, broke his line of sight.

He opened the gate, which promptly tumbled from its hinges. The driver, a withered type who had passed the entire trip in a barely controlled tremor, did not help him unload his coffer, nor accompany him to the door, but as soon as D'Azevedo had done so, the man sped off into the darkness at a clip far faster than during the entire journey from the port. D'Azevedo stumbled down the path, dragging his bindle and the heavy wooden box filled with other necessities behind him, and knocked gently on the main door, so as not to wake anyone but the person who might be keeping watch. When, after a great while had passed, there was no answer, he rapped harder. Still, no one responded. He began to wonder if he had been brought to the right building, for there were no addresses in this part of the world nor was there any proof, save the lantern, that a living soul still occupied or visited this building.

Out of the corner of his eye he detected movement—a human? an animal?—in the distance, the darkness wavering as if it were trying simultaneously to conceal and reveal the perceived entity to him, and he turned, only to see nothing but the shadows of shadows. Whether it was a person, a wild creature or a mere phantasm he could not be sure, though it was common knowledge that although the Portuguese had made great strides in civilizing the wilds of this vast terrain, creatures beyond the knowledge of the wisest men in all of Europe still circulated throughout it. He called out to the area where he had spotted, or thought he spotted, someone passing, but there was no response, save a light echo of his own voice. He considered walking around the building, but was unsure of its dimensions, fearing he might get lost or plunge into a ditch once he left the lighted façade, so he seated himself at the base of the main door, his luggage on either side of him, and prayed, until even his sight, against his wishes, surrendered to the dark.

He awoke on a cot in a room just larger than a cubicle, a shuttered, unpaned window just above his head admitting thin razors of sun. The barest minimum of stones paved the floor; the room's walls sat barren of any adornment except a table, a chair, a battered chamber pot, and a crude crucifix, carved from tulipwood, that hung above the door. Brownish-black mold engendered, he imagined, by the dampness that plagued the region, licked its tongues from the corners to the ceiling. He had been undressed—he had not undressed himself, he could not recall having done so—and placed on the cot, a thin knit blanket, fragrant with sweat and mildew draped over him. He sat up and looked around for his personal effects. The coffer, already pried open, sat in the corner, atop it his bindle, also untied. His doublet, cassock and cincture hung from a hook beside the table. Beneath them, his sandals. How had he not immediately noted them there? He felt heavy in the head, as if he had downed a potion, though he had not eaten or drunk anything, save two cups of coconut water to refresh himself, since arriving at the port. Yet he did not feel even the slightest pang of hunger.

On the desk he saw a small clay bowl, a pitcher of similar material (filled, his nose confirmed, with plain water), a second, smaller fired pitcher (filled with agua de coco), a tin cup, and a rag. He was sure when he had looked at the table just seconds ago these were not there, and this led him to pinch his hand to ensure he was not still wandering about in a dream. The flesh stung between his fingertips. He drank a bit of the coconut water, relieved and washed himself, dressed, reviewed his menagerie to make sure everything was where it was supposed to be, and it was. He gathered his papers then left his room to meet the men over whose lives he had been entrusted with spiritual and earthly command.

As he stepped into the hall, one of his brethren, Dom Gaspar, a short, skinny, sallow man, of the type that abound in the hinterlands, approached him, and embraced him, offering greetings and inviting him out into the cloister, open to the sky as was the tradition, where the other members of the House, having finished morning prayers, were already assembled and seated. Dom Gaspar said that he had hoped to bring the new provost to morning prayers, which took place at 4, and then provide a tour, but D'Azevedo had been so soundly asleep he did not dare wake him.

Following Dom Gaspar, D'Azevedo tried but could not get a sense of the geometry of the house; from outside, the night before, it had not appeared to be even half as large as the building in Olinda, yet they proceeded down a long hall, without hard angles or corners, and far longer than he would have imagined, until they finally reached a large wood door, which he saw faced what appeared to be the monastery's front hall and main door.

"This leads to the cloister?" D'Azevedo, trying to get his bearings, asked the brother who, he realized, was only a year or two older than him.

"Why of course, my Lord, Padre Joaquim," Dom Gaspar responded, in tones that sounded as if they were meant as much to reassure himself as D'Azevedo. He clasped D'Azevedo's ample sleeve, and led him outside.

It was summer, and morning, so the sunlight at first blinded D'Azevedo. Squinting, he saw standing side by side the two other members of the House. Dom Gaspar guided him to them, and made introductions. Here stood the chalky-faced Barbosa Pires, his beard a coal apron suspended from his lower lip, a richer black than his thinning tonsure. He had, D'Azevedo noted to himself, a humped back, and a severe stutter. Beside him towered Padre Pero, a robust man of middle age, deeply tanned, his mouth framed by full voluptuous lips that drew the eyes to them, a laborer in build, worldly in the manner of someone who had been reared near Portugal's European capital. Dom Gaspar, the hospitaller, expressed the gratitude of his fellow monks for D'Azevedo's presence, but said that they had not known when to expect him. Padre Pero, to whom you had written a letter announcing the decision, said he had never received it: Padre Barbosa Pires, in his torturous manner, seconded his elder.

Resuming his comments about the monastery, Dom Gaspar could see that D'Azevedo was growing unsteady on his feet, and with a gesture summoned a stool, which a tiny man, dark as the soil they stood on, his florid eyes fluttering, brought out with dispatch. They continued on in this manner, Dom Gaspar speaking—Padre Pero very rarely interjecting a thought, Padre Barbosa Pires mostly nodding or staring, with a gaze so intense it could polish marbles, at D'Azevedo—detailing a few of the House's particulars: its schedule, its routines, its finances, its properties and holdings, its relationship with the neighboring town and villages, and with the Indians. The servant was one of eight people owned by the monastery, several of whom had been rented or leased out to various people in the town. D'Azevedo's family still held bondspeople, though on the larger matter, particularly as it related to a professed house, he was agnostic.

When it was his turn to speak, D'Azevedo explained the threadbare plans as you had broached them with him, augmented by others he had conceived during his passage by sea: the proposed changes to the house, how he would take some time to identify his second in command, how there would be a renewed effort to bring the town and neighboring villages into doctrinal line, how eventually, with satisfactory growth, this house might ultimately gain its independence from Olinda, how a college might rise with it as well. He emphasized in particular nurturing whatever roots of faith already existed here, and in the nearby region, so its residents might assist in the House's work, ultimately, he said, repeating your exact words, "to propagate the Lord's Word far and wide."

The brethren listened, though Padre Pero seemed at times to be looking through him, while Padre Barbosa Pires was inspecting some point deep in his own interior. Dom Gaspar, however, hung on every word. At one point he paused to look at them and could not tell the three men apart; all had full black beards, all had a hump, all were deeply tanned. He closed his eyes until he felt a finger, Dom Gaspar's, tap his shoulder, and when he looked again, all three men were as different as they had been minutes before. After D'Azevedo finished, with obvious effort, Dom Gaspar helped him to his feet, and ushered him to his office, where he might review the various ledgers and other important documents, alternating with rest, until the midday Mass.

As they headed back into the building, Fr. D'Azevedo asked, "My dear brother, whom shall I thank, in addition to our Father, for bearing me to my room and putting me to bed? I should like to offer my especial thanks, given my state of exhaustion last night, and, apparently, this morning."

Dom Gaspar turned to D'Azevedo, who was bracing himself against a wall, again trying to orient himself in the white maze of corridors, and answered, "Then you shall have to thank yourself, for you did so yourself, your Grace." The provost halted in a spot where one hallway twisted into another and, clasping the loose fabric of D'Azevedo's sleeve firmly, lest the unsteady man fall away from him, Dom Gaspar continued, "I am not sure which of the Negroes bore your coffer; perhaps the one named João Baptista, whom they call amongst themselves Kibanda, who brought you your seat in the cloister.

Maybe another. None of us heard your Grace come in last night, though the slaves reported to us this morning that you were here." At this D'Azevedo paused, trying again to recall anything of the previous night, any assistance, especially by the black who had brought the stool, whose face he could not at all remember, but Dom Gaspar, like a horse drawing a plough across early spring soil, tugged him forward, onward, and before he knew it he was seated in his office, the Provost's.

D'Azevedo started to arrange the books on his desk, but promptly fell into a delirium. He was borne back to his monastic cell, and stayed there, tossing and turning for several days, attended periodically by Dom Gaspar, who was also the infirmarian, and, he thought, the Negro João Baptista, until he recovered. As soon as he felt fit enough to leave his room, and resume his duties, about a fortnight after he had arrived, Dom Gaspar took him on tour of the monastery's grounds, which were ampler in acreage than he had imagined. There was the main house, consisting of the main building with two wings, bracketing the cloister, which was enclosed on its back side by a stone wall. Several other buildings dotted the grounds to the north: the stable, the slave quarters, a coop, a work-shed, a privy. The monks kept several horses, a dairy cow, and chickens; grew maize and tobacco; maintained a garden, despite the poor soil, with European and American vegetables and herbs; and husbanded a small nursery of trees: avocados, papayas, acerolas, tangerines, limes, mangoes. Palms bearing coconuts formed a towering ridge beyond the gate. What they could not consume the house had contracted, under patent with the governor of the captaincy, to sell in the market near the port, as well as at one held monthly in town.

Tending to all of this, as well as all of the domestic tasks the monks did not undertake themselves, Dom Gaspar said, were the bondsmen, several of whom had arrived with the monk postulants themselves, one of whom was a gift of the leading local landowner, another a bequest, and two of whom were the result of natural increase by

women on neighboring plantations; these two boys had been returned to the monastery when they reached working age. The last
of the men had been won in a lottery. Three had been lent or rented
out to planters in the neighboring towns, but were now back until
the fall harvest arrived. None were women, as the presence of that
sex would, as other houses of the Lord had witnessed, have posed
an insurmountable threat to the monks' oaths. Dom Gaspar recited
the slaves' names, and D'Azevedo had them written down: Aparecido, Benedito (commonly known as Bem-Boi), Jorginho (who they
called Zuzi), Miguel (Muéné, who was frequently called Negão), and
Zé (José Africano), and the children Filhinho (either Fela or Falodun) and Zé Pequeninho (sometimes called Ayoola). It was only
after he finished that D'Azevedo told him his count was off, and
Dom Gaspar remembered he had forgotten João Baptista, whom, he
added, they sometimes called Jibada. D'Azevedo requested that Dom
Gaspar show him where all the records, of the slaves and every other
aspect of their property, were kept, so that he might have the clearest
sense possible of the monastery's holdings.

As with the house and estate themselves, so with his brethren:
with each day their personalities came ever clearer into scope. Most
senior among them, Padre Pero, having been present at the monastery since its founding, might have served as a fount of knowledge
about its history and development, as well as that of the region, but
was by his very nature, D'Azevedo learned, ill-tempered, and taciturn. After a career in the military, he had exchanged the sword for
the Word, preaching the Gospel in the countryside, evangelizing
among white and native alike, later serving as a liaison and spiritual
counsel to the municipal administration. He among the monks also
kept a close watch over the bondspeople, with much the same intensity as he oversaw the livestock. Next, Padre Barbosa Pires, with
that jet beard, who scuttled from task to task. He rang the bell in the
morning and evening, called everyone to prayer and dinner, prepared
vestments for Mass, oversaw the kitchen. He too was laconic, and

appeared always to be trying to decipher something in D'Azevedo that the new priest kept scrambled. Ever at Barbosa Pires's side was the honey-cheeked child Filhinho, whom he referred to playfully, but without humor in his eyes or voice, as his "punchbag." And then there was Dom Gaspar, sent but a year before, as D'Azevedo had been sailing back from Europe, diligent, eager to help, so gentle in manner, the person best equipped to welcome visitors and now watch the monastery's books.

With his sense of his brethren firm and the slaves fully at his command, D'Azevedo commenced his restorative work. He had the monastery's entire exterior washed and whitewashed. He had the gate, from one end to the other, repaired and restiled. He had lanterns placed at regular paces about the front and rear of the grounds, so that a night traveler would not find himself in darkness so utter, and took care to prevent that any of them should lead to a conflagration. He had signs carved and mounted throughout the corridors, so that anyone could, by reading them, reorient himself. He had markers placed in even rods amidst the fields to identify and segregate the differing crops. He had a visitors' book placed in the front hall. He had new rules written and distributed to his brethren, and had Brother Gaspar, as D'Azevedo looked on, recite them to the slaves. He requested a periodic audience with each of the three monks, and a regular gathering of them all, outside of daily prayers and Masses, once a month. From Padre Pero he asked for a short, written census of the town's residents, and an oral report of the status of the Faith in the town and surrounding villages. Also once every several months one of the fathers would have to offer the divine sacrament of Mass to the slaves, and although he did not want them to read the Holy Scripture, or anything else for that matter, as much of it as that they could understand would be told to them, and they must confess their sins too.

In all things, save work and prayer, he reminded his brethren, their order required modesty, chastity, renunciation, mortification, dedication to the interior life. Less food, less wine, no chatter. At the austere morning meal and at dinner, at which he would always pass on the stews and dried meats, they were to read aloud from the first five books of the Bible or a similarly pious text. At the gravesite of Padre Travassos, which Dom Gaspar had pointed out to him and which bore no stone, he himself placed a new one, topped by the last coins from his doublet pocket.

In this way the house settled into a new and heretofore unfelt rhythm. Padre D'Azevedo's abiding aim, it appeared, was the sustenance of the foundation, but he did exchange letters of greeting with its municipal officials, the judiciary, the militia leaders, and the representatives of the wealthiest families, many of whom were one and the same, and then rode out to meet with several of them, opening up correspondences which he faithfully maintained. Given the constant threat of the French, though co-religionists, and the Netherlanders, who were not, he felt he must act to ensure a front line of defense, secured through amity and a shared belief in the preservation of the Faith. D'Azevedo meanwhile submerged himself in the monastery's archives, initiating the process of expanding its subscriptions and soliciting books from the main house in Olinda, as well as from the capital at Bahia, and from Lisbon, Coimbra and Évora, in preparation for a library that would benefit the priests, and, perhaps down the road, the envisioned college. He read and reread the ledger books, so as to wring out every possible *real* that might be hidden or misentered there.

Each of his fellow monks saw him as though through a prism, each viewing a differing facet of a carefully cut, rare stone. They all would have concurred in calling attention to his knowledge on an array of matters; his scholarship, so evident in his individual and group remarks with them, in the letters he drafted to the mother house in Olinda and to a range of correspondents across the country, and in his impromptu Scriptual tuitions at Mass; and his faithful obeisance to the rules he himself had established and would not rewrite depending upon the circumstances. He wrote in a clear hand; he did not equivocate in his speech; he quoted the Old Testament in Latin from memory perfectly. None inquired about, though Dom Gaspar was intrigued by, his private theological-philosophical project, to which he devoted a portion of each day, and he spoke nothing of it. He did not lead by force, or intimidation, or legerdemain, or threat of recourse to the Olinda House, which is to say through *you*, but by example. In the main, though he knew he was dealing with several refractory personalities, he detected no disquiet. To Gaspar, to whom he assigned greater duties, including now serving as his secretary and novice master when new ones arrived, and in whom he placed great confidence, his presence appeared not just a ballast, but a blessing.

Long hours spent in the study of any text will reveal inner, unseen contours, an abstract architecture. This is as true of sacred books as of those poems written in the pursuit of courtly or earthly love, or even of language itself. The ancient Mosaic law had accommodated this insight to the disadvantage of the surface layer, of images, while the Roman Church, akin to the preliterate cultural forms from which it in part arose, allows for the existence of a mystical understanding and experience of these abstractions. The careful scholar cannot but help but become aware of the conflict: when one speaks of the word, or Word, what is one truly speaking of? Who is the architect, man, and—or—a—God? Attempts to apprehend this new reality, these tensions, went initially by the names of philosophy, theology, science. What is it to know, know deeply? Is knowledge not always a form of power that, taken too far, cannot be turned against itself? The texts continually opened these doors and subsequent ones for D'Azevedo, who conveyed them, using ciphers, to some of his distant correspondents.

Several months into the new provost's tenure, after a brief campaign that, he believed, had successfully changed perceptions of the monastery in the town's eyes, he began weekly tutorials for a small cohort of boys he selected from the upper ranks of the town's citizenry. Though each of these boys had their own personal tutors at home, D'Azevedo suggested to their parents that in the event they did not receive training at another college, and to ensure adequate preparation for further study in law, medicine, the classics, or the priesthood, especially should they seek to serve at the Royal Court or in the administrative center in Bahia, he might provide them with supplementary training. As a result, each Tuesday through Thursday, amidst his other duties, D'Azevedo guided the sons of the Espinozas, the Palmerias, the Cardozos, the Alonso Lopeses, the Figueirases, and the Pimentels, in the study of the Old Testament; Latin and Greek; the natural sciences, especially botany, and mathematics; in disputation and philosophy; and Hebrew.

The boys rode out to the monastery or arrived by coach, bunked in a room furnished only with cots, stools, a wash basin, and woven baskets for their personal effects, that D'Azevedo had set aside especially for that purpose, with one of the child slaves their only attendant. Early Friday morning they rode back to resume their own usual routines at home. In this way he was planting the seeds of a school, and, it seemed, doing the very work you had tasked him to. He alone taught the boys, and maintained an atmosphere of utmost rectitude. It has often been subsequently said that this small cohort, once spread across the Empire and beyond, never lost sight of the ethos he nurtured there.

One Wednesday evening, weeks into his courses, shortly after the turn of the new year and the feast of Our Lady, once he had concluded Vespers and tucked in for the night, D'Azevedo awoke to what he thought he perceived as the regular beating of a drumhead, though so low it was almost below the level of audibility. He rose, slipped his doublet over his nightshirt and stepped into his sandals, then made his way through the tunnel of dark, for the monastery was kept lightless until 4, the hour of morning prayers, to where he thought the sound emanated. Perhaps, he considered, the boys had snuck in a jug of any of the many types of liquors that were the fruits of the abundant sugar crops, and were continuing Christmas celebrations, frowned on though they were; but he would only chide them, gently, and remind them of the House's rules, for though they were guests and youths, they were expected to carry themselves in the manner expected of any who lived between these walls, let alone boys of their station. Tracing his way to them, he opened the door, as quietly as possible, and entered the room. All were soundly asleep. Soft snores rose from their slumbering forms. In the slender ribbon of light the moon cast through the half-closed shutters, the Figueiras boy, curled beneath his sheet, was murmuring the gibberish of dreams. D'Azevedo closed the door, waited for several minutes, then went back in. Not a body had shifted.

As he closed the door he could again hear the drumming, faint but now accompanied, he perceived, by a low wail, like an animal caught in the crevice of a deep shaft, or wire upon wire. He left the boys and tracked his way back, ever so carefully through the blackness, until he reached the main entry hall. The noise was coming, he thought, from the cloister. He passed through the large wooden door, now so familiar to him, out into the cool air, to find not a single soul or sound but those of the summer night, the light of the moon and the stars, the soil and grasses and flowers and stones. Everything lay in its usual place. He stood still and listened but the sound was gone. He strolled the open space, checking in corners, scanning the back wall, examining the wings, with bedrooms, including his own, that extended from the long, low main building. He saw and heard nothing. He sat on the ground and kept vigil for a while, until he grew sleepy and felt his head nodding. It was as he was opening the door to go back indoors that he again heard drumbeats and, out of the corner of his eye, he spied a shape, a shadow, moving along the rear wall, and he turned to spot something, someone, its hair fanning over its shoulders, gliding over the stone barrier. D'Azevedo ran to the wall and leapt up, seizing its top to wrench himself high enough to peer over it, but there was nothing, neither drum nor cry, only the nearby barns and stables, the slave cabins, the fields, the vast forest with its peculiar soundscape, and enveloping it all, the dense, impermeable silence of the night.

D'Azevedo crept back to bed, but could not sleep. Despite no sounds beyond the usual ones of the house, his entire body, like a sentinel, kept vigil. He went early to the chapel, before the bell, and as soon as he had mouthed the last syllable of the Latin imprecations, he turned to his fellow monks and told them that he would like to meet with them straightaway in his office. They walked there together in silence, and it was not until he closed the door that D'Azevedo noticed the slave João Baptista sweeping his office. He promptly ushered him out. The provost opened the gathering by noting its irregular nature, and apologized for calling his brethren from their appointed duties. He recounted the strange incidents of the prior night, and made clear that he had not merely dreamt them. He had heard drumming, and had observed someone vaulting over the wall. With barely suppressed shock he noted it might even have been a woman, given that none of the monks—and he surveyed them as he spoke—nor the slaves, had long hair.

Had any of them heard anything? Seen any odd characters traipsing about the monastery's buildings or grounds? All said no, they had heard nothing last night, seen no one. Padre Pero noted that sometimes the blacks consorted with women in the town, without permission, but that in any case, this would occur in their quarters and never within the cloister or main building. He promised to conduct an inquiry and severely punish anyone found to be violating the rules. Padre Barbosa Pires asked whether D'Azevedo was certain it was none of the students he had brought into the house; there were forces at work in the town that the Holy Office might well need to address. D'Azevedo dismissed this comment, noting that the students' behavior had been unimpeachable, and awaited Dom Gaspar's thoughts, but he expressed none. With that, D'Azevedo thanked them all and sent them on their way. He wrote out a letter asking you for guidance, and prepared it for posting, though, he noted to himself, he had not heard from you or anyone in or around Olinda for some time. Finished, he felt lightheaded. Before he could call for assistance, João Baptista knocked to enter his office, with an urn of fresh coconut water, and a bowl of cashews, which are said to be good for the nerves, and the remedy set him right for the rest of the day.

Things proceeded without account, until, several weeks later, after a private meeting and dinner at the monastery with several members of the powerful Pimentel family, local plantation owners and brewers who were considering becoming patrons of the future school they hoped their younger sons might someday attend, at which alcoholic spirits from a newly gifted cask had flowed, though the abstemious provost had not drunk more than a cup, D'Azevedo invited Dom Gaspar into his office to record the leader's thoughts on the event. Once Dom Gaspar had done so, and drafted a letter of thanks to the Pimentels, which D'Azevedo signed, the provost, calmed by the sweet and potent liquor, the fellowship, and the knowledge that they had roughly a half hour or so before evening prayers and bedtime, asked his charge to remained seated, and said, "My dear brother, I am so grateful for your assistance here. I do not know how I would have gotten this house into the shape it is in without you by my side."

The brother, his lips and mind also loosened by wine, unbuttoned the top of his doublet and replied, "And I am so thankful to you, my Lord, for the changes you have wrought here. How different it was before you arrived! In the absence of a firm tribune of the Father, Son and Holy Ghost this House was approaching the precipice. There was not just a laxity of practice but of the Faith, of spirit. That wickedness, either preached by the devil's handservant Luther or by Satan and his agents themselves, when they are not one and the same, was rising like a fever through these walls. I shall not call out any names, but I must testify to you, as I have not yet dared even in Holy Confession, that I did not always appear for prayers and on Sundays I did not always rise from my bed before midday. I hoarded food and ate eggs raw rather than let them be cooked. I raised my voice to the Negroes and even once took the Lord's name in vain. I—"

"My dear brother," D'Azevedo started, his face crimsoning at Dom Gaspar's torrent of words, but the charge continued:

"I tell you, my Lord, the slaves themselves often forgot their places; they refused to work, they talked back, some vanished for days on end and cavorted with the Indians, they even dared to order the monks around. The one called Damásio, who was sold off shortly after I was sent here, threatened to murder Padre Pero in his sleep, I heard him say it with these two ears. Padre Pero beat him, then had him bound and sold at the market at the port, and sold off another that same day who planned to murder us all as well and have the other slaves rise up in revolt."

"My dear brother Gaspar," D'Azevedo said again, "perhaps some queer things may have transpired here in the past—"

"And, I, I am sure I glimpsed—for if not, let my eyes be struck blind by the Lord God Himself ..." Here he broke off, momentarily gathering himself, his face flushing and his tongue in tremor. "My Lord, by the Blessed Father, the Son and the Holy Ghost, and by the force of the Holy Office of the Inquisition itself, for I only heard and now dare to repeat it, O Lord Christ strike my tongue dumb, but Padre Barbosa Pires told me that he saw a Negro woman, and one of the slaves, he could not make out which one it was, ordering Padre Travassos around, the elderly priest on his hands and knees in the center of the cloister at twilight not but a week, I believe it was, before he died, and he wore not a doublet, not a robe, not a single stitch, and the Negro man was riding him like an ass, and driving him with a crop, and around the white man's neck he held reins tight, for in his mouth was a bit, and the white man was not uttering a single sound, only making the sounds of a beast, that much he glimpsed—"

"Mercy, Brother Gaspar," D'Azevedo said.

"—and that is not all, my Lord, for not only did the slaves come and go but the house had received a steady stream of visitors, they were coming before I arrived and some came after, few of them fellow monks or anchoresses or even priests from near or distant dioceses, nor pilgrims in search of spiritual salve, nor lay mendicants, not faithful from the nearby towns, nor even the savages that populated the forests or runaway slaves, but men and women who brought vile thoughts and vicious deeds in their wake, including sometimes persons whose kind one could not discern, man or woman or some other creature, and they usually appeared just at the fall of night, and Padres Travassos and Pero did entertain them, Padre Barbosa Pires told me, and then I saw him enter the room and entertain them himself, and the Negroes took part in the revelries too, the three priests did entertain them, as was said did the former founder Padre Duran Carneiro, before his flight, for why do you think those two boys here are mulattos—"

"Mercy of the Lord—" D'Azevedo said.

"—inviting them in, your Grace, and transforming the solemn holidays into scenes of lasciviousness, with rituals so diabolical it would cause even the Lord Jesus Christ to turn his face away in horror, and there was said to be witchcraft and sorcery of a kind so powerful in this house and outside it, such that creatures worse than those that issue forth from Mephistopheles's bowels were roaming this estate, and I heard tell that a beast with multiple heads and another beast that could both swim and fly, and another beast that bred with every other animal including humans, including humans living here—"

"Brother, stop," D'Azevedo said, "I think the spirits—"

"—and so great was that evil and so present that sometimes even though we have all walked arm-in-arm with our Father since you, my Lord, crossed the threshold I can still sometimes feel it, if only you knew of the rituals, in which they defiled the chapel altar and the Host, and daily that Negro woman gave sooth, and one told me in confession that it was one of them, our blacks, parading around in women's garments, and that the priests sometimes did the same, sometimes even going out as women to meet their lovers in the town, just as there were men and boys from the town who came here during these monstrous frolics, and Padre Travassos took eager part in them, and Padre Duran Carneiro too, I have heard said, before he fled, driven out by that slavewoman, and Padre Pero—"

"Gaspar, please, no more of this, I command—"

"And it was only a year ago, around the time weeks from now when the Lord's Son will rise from the dead and redeem the World, that some of the townspeople, who are said to be of those accursed faiths, the Jews and the Muslims and the followers of that German monk, Padre Barbosa Pires having denounced some of them even in his childhood, and people believing in dangerous spirits and having no beliefs at all, including the Negroes, and aboriginals who were enticed from their forests, arrived here to participate in the most abominable revelries, and I had begun to barricade myself in my cell, but a female visitor appeared very late one night at the threshold of this very house, I could hear her knocking, and she was so heavily cloaked despite the heat that I could not see her face, and out of Christian duty and hospitality I let her in, and lo I quickly found myself thus at the threshold of the door of the room where she was lodging, as if at her beckoning, which had not required a single word nor even a gesture, as if by sorcery, and only at that moment I fell to my knees, my Lord, and implored our Father for the requisite strength to still these desires and mortify this flesh, and return me to the sanctity of my vows, though as I did so I could hear the drums and the moans and the most extreme and exquisite pleasures occurring only steps from me, just beyond every surrounding wall, and that creature opened the door, though I did not go in, and lifted her skirts, and made me promise not to utter a single word or I would be struck dumb and deaf and blind—"

With this Dom Gaspar fell silent, his whole body shaking like the string of a berimbau, and D'Azevedo shook too, unsure of what to say, until they both heard the ringing of the bell, and realized it was time to go pray.

"My dear Brother," D'Azevedo said, barely able to summon words, "we must hurry to prayers. But we shall not speak of this again, until I have had time to investigate it further, and seek counsel from Olinda. Do you understand? Do you?"

The brother assented, and as he began to say something there was a knock on the door, and with D'Azevedo's permission he opened it, and the slave João Baptista was there, lamp in hand, to guide them to the chapel. D'Azevedo looked at Dom Gaspar, who had calmed down, and then toward the slave, whom he could not see because of the lamp's glow, except for the flash of his large, expressive eyes.

Throughout the prayers, D'Azevedo could not shake Dom Gaspar's tale from his head, and kept getting lost in the words, the Latin sounding more like mere rhythms than sense. Only when they were nearly done did he calm down. What he told himself was that the cane liquor itself bore terrible spirits, so powerful he could still smell its aroma, and these had gotten to Dom Gaspar's already nervous mind and caused the terrible flight of fantasy, the nightmare that had overtaken his waking thoughts. He nevertheless intended to put this too in a letter to you, hoping that you or someone in Olinda might advise him. He wavered between the final words of the prayer, Dom Gaspar's account and thoughts of his tutorial with the boys tomorrow. Once the Vespers had finished he hurried to his bedroom without saying a further word to Dom Gaspar, who also went straight to his room, or to either of his fellow priests, who too duly vanished.

D'Azevedo slept fitfully; he rolled about on his pallet as if he were on the deck of a yawl in an Atlantic storm. During one stretch, he saw looming above him a creature, cloaked in a black caftan, its skin white as quicklime, with reddish horns, a beard so matted it appeared woven of copper, the napping becoming an orange flame, and coiling above its head, a tail armored with razors, and when he raised his hands to push it away it transformed into a creature as black the bottom of a pit, the face, a negro's, sublime in its geometry, its hair alive, a writhing mangrove swamp, which began turning into snakes before D'Azevedo's eyes, while the body, its black, black body covered with those same tentacular appendages, held D'Azevedo flat against the pallet, and as the creature neared D'Azevedo its bared pelvis sported a rod of such virility that D'Azevedo was sure it would tear his insides to pieces. He screamed out as loudly as he could, though he could not hear a single note issuing from his throat, but the apparition vanished, and he realized that he was sitting on the edge of his bed, sheathed in sweat and moonlight scattered like coins through his shutters. He opened them to admit more, which led him to spot a palm-sized folded slip of paper someone had pushed beneath his door.

Because it was still night and he did not want to wake anyone, as quietly as he could he fished a flint and firestone from his trunk, and lighted a candle, taking care to place it near but not in the window so that the tallow smell would carry into the open air without the light waking anyone. The paper was blank. He held it closer to the candle to make sure he was not missing print too tiny to view in the darkness, and like magic, the tiny, elaborate script, definitely Portuguese, umbered before his eyes as if being written right there on the paper: *"They are coming lest you fear watch and listen trust the seer."* The message startled him so he dropped the page into the flame, leaving only ashes on the sill. He returned to his pallet and tried, using the tools of reason, to understand what was going on, from the message, to the nightmare, to the tales Gaspar had told him, all the way back to the unusual circumstances by which he had ended up in this very room the very first night he arrived here. When he made no headway he knelt on the stone floor, his Bible before him, and prayed, remaining there, until exhaustion conquered his efforts, and he did not wake until the final ring of the next morning's bell.

D'Azevedo rose from the floor, where he had passed out after his mental exertions, washed himself, and threw on his cassock and doublet, then rushed to Matins. Padres Pero, Barbosa Pires, and Dom Gaspar were all already there; in their faces and gestures he did not detect even the slightest disquiet. They proceeded through the Breviary without halt; D'Azevedo found himself struggling to concentrate on the words, as his mind was again cycling. It was only when Dom Gaspar extended his hand to help him up from his knees that he grasped the prayers had ended. They exchanged greetings, though the other two priests left the chapel straightaway. D'Azevedo went directly to his office, where the materials for the day's lessons sat in neat piles on his desk. As he perfunctorily penned a plan to explain several refined points in Biblical interpretation, he would periodically feel a tingle in his cheeks or thighs when the images of the night before flashed in his head.

Not long before he was to head to the scriptorium, where he held the classes, D'Azevedo could hear voices rising like a choir tuning itself, and suddenly, hammering on his door. He went to open it and Dom Gaspar, as red-faced as he had been during his possessed reverie, ran in, crying out:

"They've sent a messenger, along with coaches from the town, calling all of your boys back. There's news that the Dutch have laid successful siege to Olinda, and the boys may be needed to participate in a local defense until the Crown's forces arrive from Bahia and elsewhere."

"Have they reached our port," D'Azevedo asked, pulling the stool out for Gaspar, who did not sit, "at Alagoas?"

"Not yet, my Lord, but they say it is only a matter of time before the heathens begin their drive to seize everything and raise the Orange standard above us all."

D'Azevedo, with Dom Gaspar behind him, went straight to the room where the boys lodged. All were collecting their personal items to prepare home.

"Lusitania has successfully defended her territories from worse threats than this," D'Azevedo said to the boys, who paused momentarily to turn to him, "and the Netherlanders, like the French, will not triumph. You can be certain we shall reconvene in a fortnight or less, no matter what the threat. In the interim, continue with your lessons on your own, when you can, and if it is possible, send me word of your progress and of what is happening in the town." When they had finished, he, Gaspar, Zé Pequeninho, who was assigned to serve them and carried as many sacks as he could, and João Baptista, always present, who carried the rest, accompanied them to the stables, where their horses and the coaches to fetch the rest of them awaited. D'Azevedo watched each depart, then returned with Dom Gaspar to his office to formulate a plan in the event that the Dutch did make headway inland.

D'Azevedo asked his charge to notify the other monks that he would like to meet that evening, just before Vespers, to discuss the crisis. Before then, he would examine the house's inventories to find out what weapons and munition they, lacking a cannon, possessed. From what he could tell there were but a few: several very old swords, a hatchet, perhaps a pike and mace (at least that was what someone had noted down before), and all the agricultural tools, like flails, hoes, and scythes, that could be put to use if necessary. Also listed was a firearm he had never seen, some shot, and a small amount of gunpowder. Nearly all save the pike and farm implements were kept under lock and chain in a vault that he had never entered but knew was accessible via the chapel's nave.

He followed this with inventories of all other aspects of the house: its finances, the food stocks, the state of the crops, the animals, the slaves. He had heard throughout his time in school on that the Dutch, unlike Lisbon's ancient allies the English, were especially brutal to adherents of the Roman faith, even though he had also heard the Dutch Church had survived the pox spreading outward from Saxony and that seductive false prophet of Eisleben. If the local forces retreated here in their march toward the interior, the monastery would be able to provide sustenance and shelter; if the Dutch managed to vanquish them, D'Azevedo reasoned it would be beneficial to have at hand every means to ensure their magnanimity. In the event of a siege he tried to figure how long he and the monks could hold out. On the back of a letter from the municipal authorities, concerning rules that had been implemented as of the turn of the year, he designated which bottles of cane liquor and wine, casks of English beer, horses, sacred implements, including the gold-plated chalice and the patin, gifts of the Albuquerque family, that were the pride of the Sacristy, as well as slaves, could be used to curry favor. He wrote two versions of this, one which he would entrust with Dom Gaspar, and one which he would keep on his person, to be presented personally to the Dutch commander if necessary.

Throughout the day messengers to the monastery brought notice of the approach of the Dutch fleet, the preparations in town, the lack of response from Olinda and Bahia, or Heaven forfend, distant Rio de Janeiro, the unlikelihood of reaching either Lisbon or Madrid, or, as some fancied, London. D'Azevedo wrote out an appeal to the mother house, but having heard nothing from them in over a month tore it up, and tried to busy himself with other preparations. He checked the food rations again, and requested that all the ovens be fired for extra loaves in preparation for the first waves of refugees and soldiers; explored the feasibility of fortifications, and ordered cordons of rope tied around the perimeter of the various fields to prevent them from being trampled; conducted a tally of candles, lamps and palm oil, and had new candles fashioned out of the latter so that the house would have sufficient light; and, just before the day plunged into the unquiet evening, climbed onto the roof himself to roll a white sheet to be unfurled, if needed, along the house's façade as a sign of neutrality. The visits from the outside world ceased completely. D'Azevedo returned to his office to await the brethren. Only Dom Gaspar appeared at his door.

"Where are Padres Pero and Barbosa Pires?" D'Azevedo asked. He peered around Dom Gaspar into the dark, open hallway.

"There has been an incident, my Lord—"

"Dom Gaspar, we are facing an imminent attack—"

"—at the slave quarters. Indeed I came to fetch you...." D'Azevedo noted how the light from the lantern Dom Gaspar brandished before him contorted the deputy's features into a mask of fright. The provost set down his quill and followed his charge outside.

During the time D'Azevedo had led the professed house, he had often ventured near the shacks where the slaves made their homes, usually during the early morning, usually to conduct a quick inspection to ensure that things were as they should be. Not once had he noticed anything amiss. Nevertheless, as he now trod the hard, hot soil trail behind Dom Gaspar, it was as if he were stepping into a completely different world. Behind one of the shacks, straight ahead, he saw Padre Pero, shirtless and wearing only a bandanna around his neck, soiled work britches, and shoeless, dressed in the manner of a slave himself, holding a black woman by her neck, her wrists bound behind her back. Her wild hair cascaded about her narrow shoulders, covering her face, down almost to the waist of the gossamer linen frock that stopped just above her ankles, which D'Azevedo could see were also bound tightly with rope. She was slender, slight almost, and appeared to be standing only because Pero held her up. Before her, up to her knees, rose a pile of wood, and beside it several urns, smelling of palm oil, and several long coils of rope. D'Azevedo tried to piece all these clues together but they made no sense. It was only then that he noticed that there were only two other adult male slaves present, also apparently bound by their wrists, behind Padre Pero. Three, he realized, instead of the eight that should have been there; though little Filhinho stood almost within the prodigious beard of Padre Barbosa Pires, who wore only his cassock and no doublet, he grasped that the other child, who had served his students and whom he had seen quite recently, also was missing.

"Padre Pero, for heaven's mercy," he called out to the older priest, who maintained his tight grip on the slavewoman's neck, "what is the source of this commotion?"

Pero released his grip on the slavewoman, and raised his other hand, in which he held a large hunting knife. "These creatures were going to burn us all to ashes in preparation for the heathens' arrival, led by this beast, isn't that right?" He cuffed the woman hard on the side of her head, knocking her to the ground. One of the black men stumbled forward to assist her, but Pero brandished the knife and the man froze. The fallen woman struggled to her knees, before Pero pushed her back down with his foot, holding her there. "I have a mind to take care of it myself right now."

"Padre Pero," D'Azevedo said again, "in the name of Our Father, and the Holy Bible, and the Holy Roman Catholic and Apostolic Church, and the Captaincy of this Province, and in my capacity as the Provost and head of this Professed House of the Second Order of the Discalced Brothers of the Holy Ghost, I command you to desist. If this person, these persons, have been engaged in any mischief, such as a plot to harm this house, especially at this fraught moment, we will address it according to the laws and rules already set down." D'Azevedo took two steps toward the woman, who continued to writhe about until she rose to kneel, and then was again standing.

As D'Azevedo asked, "Can someone tell me whence this African woman came?" Pero reached out and yanked the curtain of hair from her head, revealing the slave João Baptista, whom, D'Azevedo could see, was also gagged. Lacking words to express his astonishment, D'Azevedo staggered backward, until he felt Dom Gaspar's arms bracing him.

"This João Baptista, or Quimbanda as they call it," Pero said, "has long been a source of mischief, well before you arrived. It—she—he sent away a number of the slaves, as you can see, as part of his, its mischief, and was planning to dispatch the rest of us to that blackest place, well before the Dutch could."

"T-t-t-throw him on the w-w-woodpile," Barbosa Pires shrieked, startling D'Azevedo, who was just regaining his composure. "T-t-t-there may be more p-p-plots afoot in town given w-w-what this one is capable of."

"I concur with Padre Barbosa," Padre Pero continued, "that we hurl this pillar of evil on the very woodpile it was assembling"—and as he uttered these words he approached the bound slave and whispered something D'Azevedo could not hear, the knife in his hand grazing the back of João Baptista's neck—"then put all the rest of them on there, lest those filthy Dutch or anyone else get their hands on them."

"T-t-there is a plot afoot," Barbosa Pires screamed.

"Padre Pero," D'Azevedo said again, "Padre Barbosa Pires, we will not and cannot proceed in this manner. We have laws and rules and will deal with this person, these persons, as they compel us to, and we shall follow them." After saying this, D'Azevedo stood silently, neither he nor Dom Gaspar nor Padre Barbosa Pires nor Padre Pero nor any of the enslaved men, save João Baptista, stirring at all, until he finally said, "Dom Gaspar, I want you to bring this person to my office, immediately." He turned to Padre Pero, who was still holding the knife and glowering at João Baptista as he was led away, and Padre Barbosa Pires, who was holding tightly onto the boy in front of him, and, collecting his words before he spoke, D'Azevedo said, "My blessed brothers, I want you to untie these men and take them and the boy to the barn. Order them to stay there. Then I want you to get dressed, and prepare yourselves so that we might discuss not just this matter, but the far graver threats we face. We shall meet in the chapel in one hour."

D'Azevedo did not move until he had watched Padre Pero cut the manacles of rope off the two men, before guiding them, with Padre Barbosa Pires following him, Filhinho in tow, toward the barn. If it came down to the Dutch offering these men their freedom he would emancipate them all on the spot. He decided to draft a document to this effect as soon as he was done with his initial interrogation of João Baptista. When Dom Gaspar returned, he asked the brother to collect the wig, the rope and the oil; the first two he should bring to the chapel for the meeting and discussion, the second he should deposit in the kitchen. D'Azevedo went straight to his office.

The slave João Baptista stood waiting outside the door. D'Azevedo led him inside and, taking a rare step, locked the door behind him. At first sight, the slave looked wretched and forlorn. The thin linen shift was smeared with dirt and grass, and a large patch of soil, where Padre Pero had pushed him down, covered part of his neck and cheek. Down the white back of his shift rilled a thin band of blood. There was also blood on his lips, and on his slender arms. D'Azevedo removed the gag and untied the rope binding João Baptista's hands and feet, guiding him to the stool facing D'Azevedo's desk. Into one small glazed bowl he poured well water and into a second coconut water from the very urns that João Baptista brought to him several times a day, then handed both, with a rag that sat on his table, to the servant so that he could refresh and clean himself.

Now that he was looking João Baptista in the eyes, he considered that he had never really observed him, never seen him before. The face was crystalline in its familiarity, but not from regular viewing; it was if he had glimpsed this face somewhere else, on an inner mirror, and what he had seen for nearly his entire stay at the house had been merely an outline, a mask, a shadow. João Baptista's face was very dark, like ebony bark with numerous threads of navy woven through it, the ageless features full but at the same time delicate, the contours sharp but pleasing to the eye. As woman or man he was, D'Azevedo considered, striking. The eyes seemed to blossom from their pupils outward, fixing D'Azevedo's own. He had to look away, toward his books, to settle his thoughts.

What he thought was: he had never conducted an inquiry of this sort before, and although he had halted Padre Pero's savagery, supported as it now appeared by Padre Barbosa Pires, he had no idea of how he should proceed. He had immediately sought to question the slave to ascertain the depths of his mischief, which included but was not limited, given the cross-dressing, to the alleged plot. Were there time, D'Azevedo thought, he would seek the counsel and lead of the Olinda House, appealing directly to you. But he had not heard from you in a month, for he, like nearly everyone in that house, was unaware that the Dutch had already seized Olinda and were on the verge of doing the very thing of which the person sitting there was charged: burning most of it down.

D'Azevedo searched the shelves for any books that might provide guidance, but his eyes landed upon none. Instead, after a few minutes, he sat down at his desk, looking straight at João Baptista, whose return gaze induced a steady, intensifying calm, and said:

"You, João Baptista, have been accused by Padre Pero of very serious charges, do you understand?"

João Baptista, still in the process of self-cleansing, nodded.

"Can you speak?"

"Yes," the slave said, his voice as soft and distinct as crumpling vellum.

"Very well, please speak your answers, João Baptista," D'Azevedo said. "Padre Pero alleges that you were planning to burn down this monastery and all of us in it. He also alleges that you sent some of the slaves, the property of this monastery, like yourself, into flight. There is also the matter of your dressing in the manner and likeness of a woman, and there may be other evils and vilenesses that I shall learn about when I have further opportunity to speak with Padre Pero and Padre Barbosa Pires."

João Baptista set the rag on the edge of D'Azevedo's table, and smiled. "Before we proceed, I would ask that you call me Burunbana, as that is my name."

The impudence of the black man took him aback. Not only was it not a slave's station to challenge a white person, let alone a superior, but he had only ever heard João Baptista, like all the slaves, respond in the most basic fashion.

"João Baptista, I will not have you speak to me in that manner." He continued: "In this house we use Christian names. I have read the record by which you came here, by acquisition via a lottery after the death of your owner, a lay brother at a now shuttered Carmelite friary at Sirinhaém, north of here on the Pernambucan coast, and there you were baptized João Baptista."

"Your records do say such a thing occurred," came the reply. "They may baptize me a thousand times in that faith, with water or oil, no matter. The one who died was named João Baptista dos Anjos, by his own hand, and they imposed his name upon me as a penalty because he took his life, though that is another matter. I would nevertheless ask again that you call me Burunbana, as that is my name."

"Did you foment a plot to set fire to this monastery and kill all of us in it, and did you assist in the escape of any persons bonded to this house?"

First laughter, then: "Fire? We could have slashed your throats with daggers, we could have poisoned the stews or the wells; we have done none of these, and not just because of the threats and brutality here, which you have closed your eyes to, or because of the authorities in Alagoas or Lisbon who would hang us. Now I ask one final time that you call me Burunbana, as that is my name."

D'Azevedo slammed his palm on the tabletop. "I am the Provost of this house, and you will not speak with me this way. When you speak with me you will use your Christian name—"

"As you use yours, Manoel Aries ben Saúl?"

The priest shot up from his seat and retreated toward his wall of books. "What did you say?"

"As you use yours, Manoel Aries? Or should I call you Joaquim D'Azevedo? Which do you prefer?"

"How do you ... where did you hear ... that name?"

"I would ask that you take your seat, and call me as I have asked, Burunbana, as that is my name."

D'Azevedo returned slowly to his own stool, never removing his eyes from Burunbana. "Buranbana," he said.

"Thank you," Burunbana replied. "I know that you are Manoel Aries D'Azevedo, the son of Saúl, known as Paulo, and Miriam D'Azevedo Espinosa, known as Maria. I know that they fled Portugal and settled among the secret community in the city of São Luis, once belonging to the French and now under the aegis of the Portuguese—"

"But how ..." Aries D'Azevedo said.

"—and that at the urging of your parents you assumed the last name of your mother, D'Azevedo, when you left your home and entered this order, where you took the name Joaquim, which both faiths honor. I know that you have written to her in that tongue you speak among yourselves; that you have written to others in Olinda and in the town in that tongue; that your thoughts come to you first in that tongue sometimes before they transform into the language of the Lusitanians."

"Who are you?"

"I know that you do not peer into the water to see your reflection, though you have one; that you have never once willingly tasted the pork or shellfish served in the stews and soups the local women bring here; that your loins are cut as are all the men of the Book and as the followers of Mohammed. I know that you conceal limes for one of your holidays, and beneath a secret floor in your coffer harbor marbles for another, and special candles for a third. I know that you placed not just a stone, but coins and a ribbon at the grave of Padre Travassos, whom you had heard might be one of your own."

Aries D'Azevedo lowered his voice while glancing at the door, which he remembered he had locked. "What evil spirit do you have familiarity with, or who has revealed all of this to you?"

"I know all this and more, such as that you are giving those boys from the town special knowledge for they, as you do, wear the Roman faith like a mask, so that you can send them out to sustain the heritage of your ancestors, just as I do mine. I also know that you are in great danger if you remain here, because you are in the presence of real evil, but that evil is not mine, nor, in your case, will it come from the Dutch."

Aries D'Azevedo walked around his office. Although he was sure Burunbana did not turn a single degree, it was if those eyes were accompanying him from point to point.

"Why were you dressed as a woman, and what is this evil that you speak of?" He was now standing behind Burunbana, who, though physically quite small, seemed to be taking up an increasing amount of space.

"I am a Jinbada, or as one says in your language, Quibanda. I can read the past and the future. I can speak to the living, as now, and to the dead. I can feel the weather before it turns and the night before it falls. Every creature that walks this earth converses with me. I am such a one who is both. Sometimes the spirits fill and mount me as one and the other. Truly I was not familiar with your evil until I arrived on these shores. From the time I landed here the devils bade me serve them, forcing me to lie with them when I did not want to, and commanding all the women, men and children to do the same."

"Burunbana," Aries D'Azevedo began, but the illogic of what he was hearing, coupled with the revelations already uttered scattered his thoughts, like his secreted marbles, about the room.

"Those two have put all the Africans to wickedness and grief, from the sun's rise till it sets. When the brother Gaspar first arrived they took care to cloak their malevolence, as your Satan often wears a cape when he strolls in the sun. I read you when you first passed through that gate, and believed you could assist in our and your own liberation. Padre Pero slew Travassos, drowning him in the lagoon, because that one tried to prevent him from using me for nefarious purposes, and Barbosa Pires drove away Duran Carneiro by denouncing him, as one of your people, to the civil officials here and to the representatives of the Holy Office in Bahia."

"By any of the laws, of nature or state," Aries D'Azevedo started, but before he could complete his sentence, Burunbana whispered, "*They are coming lest you fear ...*" rendering the priest silent.

"Is it now the hour when you are to meet them? Go straightaway to collect Dom Gaspar, as he will be departing with us. Do not go anywhere but to the chapel, and do not inquire of those two, and bring the head of hair that he brought there, and come straight back."

Aries D'Azevedo stared at Burunbana, trying his best to decode the person before him, but could only register how empty his own mind was, more so than it had ever been. At first he could not move, but somehow did and, since it was already past nine and the house was darkening despite the summer sun's long tail, he took a lamp and went directly to the chapel. The hallway narrowed as he walked, and felt so cool that for a second he wondered if he had somehow entered a secret passage taking him underground; moreover he felt the impulse to visit his room and pack up a few of his things, at least a sack's worth, but every time he began to turn around he rebuked himself and kept forward. Soon he found himself in the chapel. Dom Gaspar was kneeling, saying a rosary, weeping.

Aries D'Azevedo lifted his fellow monk from his knees, and pulled him toward the door. He started to ask where Padres Pero and Barbosa Pires were, but remembered Burunbana's warning. He also thought to tell Dom Gaspar about the servant, then thought better of it. Instead, he had Gaspar hand over the wig and they left the chapel, arm-in-arm, bearing swiftly back to the office, relocking the door carefully behind them.

Burunbana was standing at the windowsill, peering into a bowl and muttering something barely audible. He had splashed the water from the urn in various places on the floor, a pattern Aries D'Azevedo could not discern, then annointed himself with a bit more. Another bowl sat to the side, and Burunbana drank from it, then traced symbols on his forehead and crown, and chest, and shoulders, and stomach, and loins. Aries D'Azevedo did not, dared not interrupt him.

"You must give him the list you wrote and the hair to me," Burunbana said without turning around. The priest complied. "Now we must make haste. Extinguish the lamp. We will depart through this portal."

"Where are we going?" Aries D'Azevedo asked.

Burunbana didn't answer, but cracked one of the shutters and peered out into the lightless cloister. From somewhere erupted three consecutive cannon booms. Aries D'Azevedo began to examine various papers on his desk, trying to figure out which he ought to grab, and scanned his shelves and walls to identify any books or documents he ought bring with him.

"Extinguish the lamp," Burunbana repeated, his voice a feather splitting stone. Aries D'Azevedo complied, and Gaspar filed behind him. Burunbana opened the shutters completely, and tossed the water out into the black cloister, hoisting himself up through the window and out into the warm air. The line the water left, a long diagonal across the stone walkway, into the yard's center, and towards the rear gate, glimmered as if studded with flecks of phosphorus, or miniature stars. Aries D'Azevedo could not believe his eyes, but he kept up, and soon he and Dom Gaspar were up over the back wall, then the gate at the rear of the estate and into the curtain of trees, moving along a path that glowed only when Burunbana trod on it.

They continued in this way, through dense brush, in a tunnel of blackness in which only the ground offered light, for what felt like hours, until finally, they reached a clearing, and there stood the two boys, Zé Pequenhinho holding a dim candle, and two of the three remaining Africans. Burunbana did not ask where the other one was, and none of them spoke. It was only as Burunbana blew out the candle and they resumed their trek that Aries D'Azevedo registered that both of the former adult workers wore priests' white doublets.

I shall conclude this letter by noting that the final destinations, much like their destinies, differed for the Africans and for your two men, Aries D'Azevedo and Gaspar Leite, for, as Burunbana assured them, under the Netherlanders each would be able to fulfill his liberty, which included practicing his faith and profession, whatever those might be, while no such freedom was guaranteed to the Africans unless they claimed it themselves. Aries D'Azevedo and Gaspar initially asked to remain with them, as brothers, in that place of refuge to which they initially went, and the provost assured the enslaved ones of their emancipation there on the spot, but Burunbana countered that they were already free and neither writ nor oath, from the Church, Dutch or Portuguese, could trump that. In any case, he provided the priests with a guide, who would connect them to a network of guides providing safe passage and the necessities for survival, leading them along the eastern base of the mountains north, all the way to Olinda, which you, and other members of the House, fearing persecution after Corneliszoon Loncq had raised the flag of Nassau, had already fled.

As for Aries D'Azevedo, who now once again goes by the name of Manoel, he has abandoned the cloth and practices the faith of his ancestors without worry, repeating the motto of that Greek philosopher: "When I saw all this, and other things as bad, I was disgusted and withdrew from the wickedness of the times." Yet in his writings and study he pursues a thread of thought that steadily brings him into conflict both with the training his schooling, in Coimbra and elsewhere, imposed on him, and also with that of his people, for whenever one looks too deeply beyond the surface of this world of *men*, one may find truths submerged that not even the most long-held beliefs and traditions can withstand. As for Dom Gaspar, he will alert you, in case you did not think to examine the martyrology's binding, to the presence of this history. He suffered a crisis of the soul upon his return to his native city, but clove ultimately to your faith and thus returns to you.

As for the Africans, they now live in such a place as does not exist on your map, though you will eventually find it, even if you can never lay claim to it. There is no *leader*, only a community, with elders who consult and concur amongst themselves about our habits and practices. Many from the town also come here, and from other towns, including your people too, the sugar plantations having bled so that they appear likely to die for lack of cultivation, though we can be sure that the Dutch will show as much industry as the Portuguese, and will install new gears to insure the smooth running of their machine. As for that Burunbana, who is a Jinbada and was known as João Baptista, that one continues spirit work among the people, who is their agent and their instrument, their conduit and gift, that one is *I who write you this letter*, for as my sister will write in the distant future, "it is better to speak / remembering / we were never meant to survive," I who know what I am meant to know and am where I am meant to be, writing in tribute to my dear brother Manoel Aries with whom I maintain a correspondence, it is thus that I close this letter with the proper date, Elul 5390, signed, as you will see when you have raised this page to the candlelight,

N'Golo BURUNBANA Zumbi

GLOSS ON A HISTORY
OF ROMAN CATHOLICS IN THE EARLY
AMERICAN REPUBLIC, 1790-1825;
OR THE STRANGE HISTORY
OF OUR LADY OF THE SORROWS

A History of Roman Catholics in the Early American Republic: 1790–1825, Jos. N. O. de L'Écart-Francis and Ambrose Carroll Meyer (Boston: Flaherty & Smith, 1895)

The status of the ancient Faith differed on the eastern shores of the Mississippi and its southerly tributaries. A convent and school, established at the turn of the nineteenth century, are referred to indirectly in the records of His Holiness Bishop John Carroll of the Diocese of Baltimore, whose curacy extended at that time to the far western frontiers of the virgin Republic's lands. A specific reference may be found, however, in the personal papers of Fr. Auguste-Marie Malesvaux, a native of Saint-Domingue, whose evangelistic labors encompassed the Spanish and later French territories from Louisiana as far north as the Great Lakes. Malesvaux offers brief notations on the convent and school, which he asserts were the first in this region. Flemish Nuns of the Order of the Most Precious Charity of Our Lady of the Sorrows established both near the village of New Hurttstown, in this frontier region of western Kentucky, in 1800. Because the convent and school suddenly vanished without a trace, and within several years the order itself disappeared as well, and as the nearby non-Catholic settlement suffered through a series of calamities before dwindling to near-extinction until its reestablishment in 1812, no other definitive records of this foundation remain.* It was not until the Reverend Father Charles Nerinckx, the native of Herfe-

---

* Carmel was the lone child among the handful of bondspeople remaining at Valdoré, the coffee plantation to which Olivier de L'Écart returned in late July 1803. The estate, over which his elder brother Nicolas had presided for more than two decades, clung like a forget-me-not to the cliffs high above the coastal city of Jérémie, west of the Rivière Grand'Anse, in the southern district of the colony of Saint-Domingue. Nearly all of Valdoré's able-bodied bondswomen and men, who at the height of the estate's prosperity numbered more than one hundred and twenty-five souls, had fled or been slain during the successive waves of liberation, revolt and retribution that had convulsed the colony since the first flash of rebellion in France. By edict of the Revolution, they had already been freed, first across the sea and on these shores again by Sonthonax's pen, against Nicolas de L'Écart's and the other plantation owners' wishes. Then under the threat of Napoleon's guns they had been captured or forced to return to Valdoré, and just as soon, many had swiftly escaped—parents, children, all—into the surrounding green maze of forests, hills and mountains, eventually joining or merging into the various rebel fronts, including those led by the leaders Plymouth and Macaya, that coursed throughout the long dagger of peninsula upwards into the Artibonite Valley. Others nevertheless had pledged their futures and future freedom to the Tricolor's military in its repeated campaigns to reclaim what had for years been France's Caribbean mint.

Carmel's father, Frédéric-Kabinda, a quiet, meditative man, had been stolen across the Atlantic in his ninth year. He had lived his entire life since then at Valdoré, first working in the groves until Nicolas de L'Écart happened upon a makeshift safebox he had cobbled together from scrap mahogany, after which he was apprenticed to a polymathic Mandinkean artisan on the neighboring estate of the Comte de Barcolet. Frédéric-Kabinda, known by other names to the enslaved from his region, eventually learned to craft metal grills and finials, carve and fashion furniture from any type of wood, blow small glassware, and above all paint; eventually he was commissioned to repaint the entire exterior and interior of the nearby de Barcolet estate's main dwellings. Over the period of a decade, he decorated the walls of the manor house's dining and visiting rooms, upper parlor, ballroom, and sunroom with a series of murals of the Burgundy countryside that merited praise as far away as the capital, Cap François, and the Spanish administrative center at Santo Domingo.

So refined did visitors to Valdoré find Kabinda's sense of composition and line that Nicolas de L'Écart eventually agreed to hire him out to the local gentry. In early 1801, while returning from working on a ceiling portrait of colonial nobles at a neighboring plantation, he was seized and pressed into service by one of Valdoré's former residents, a mixed-raced commander affiliated with the French; to this man it was inconceivable that someone of such aesthetic gifts could ally himself with the black hordes. Because of his metalworking skills, Kabinda was set to crafting knives, small armor and shot. He was also forced to sketch maps, battle scenes and caricatures for his fellow soldiers' amusement. His repeated attempts to escape to Valdoré were unsuccessful. During a counterattack against the rebels at Les Cayes, one of the Cuban attack dogs imported by the French turned on him, opening his throat, with the precision of a masterly brushstroke, in one bite.

Carmel's mother, Jeanne, was also known as la Guinée (Ginèn). From early girlhood she had been in the personal staff of de L'Écart's mother until the elder woman's death from poisoning a decade before, after which she joined the estate's general domestic staff. In her spare time she was said to practice divination, and later, as the systems of social control disintegrated, she increasingly served as a translator and courier for several groups of insurgents headquartered near the south coast. She had learned her divination skills from her mother, Gwan Ginèn, as she had from hers, and had performed it when necessary and without de L'Écart's knowledge, as a secondary mode of manor religion and justice. Most of her fellow slaves therefore gave her a wide berth, though it was widely recognized that she seldom put her gifts to malevolent uses. Just days after her husband's death, she too fell, in factional fighting near the Spanish border. Her final utterance, according to the account of a fellow rebel from Valdoré, was a curse on all who had even dreamt of betraying her.

When Olivier de L'Écart returned to Valdoré, Carmel was twelve years old. She stood just over five feet tall, and like her father, possessed milky brown eyes that always appeared to be half-shut, as if she were on the verge of falling asleep or weeping. A shy and reticent child, she wore the same raggedy calico shift over her gossamer frame every day, her waist like her head wrapped in faded crimson Indian cloth, her lone thin snakelike braid concealed beneath her turban's sweaty folds. None of the bondspeople still present—nor her master Nicolas de L'Écart, for that matter—could recall having ever heard her utter a single word. Many whispered that her mother had either cut out her tongue or cast a spell on her so that she would not reveal what she had witnessed either in the womb or at any second in her presence thereafter.

Since her seventh birthday Carmel had assisted in the cultivation of the coffee plants and the vegetable gardens during the growing months, and then during the harvest and market period in picking, drying and sorting the beans for the mill. Each day when she had completed her chief tasks, she joined the crew that gathered what remained of the withered coffee fruit for use in salves and tonics after the baggers collected the beans; the de L'Écarts had acquired a royal patent to sell some of these concoctions, properly packaged, to the poor whites and the free mulattoes across the island. Like many of younger females, Carmel had intermittently been reassigned to the housekeeping and serving staffs during the period running from Advent to Pentecost so that her master could entertain visitors, especially from the neighboring islands and the home country, in the grand style.

By the turn of the new century, however, L'Ouverture had sunk those once halcyon days far into the sea's black depths. The plantation again began bleeding workers, which soon left its fields fallow and the entire property susceptible to attack. Nicolas de L'Écart, who'd lived his entire life among Blacks and had little confidence that they could completely overthrow French rule, refused to emigrate. Instead, he pressed all his remaining able-bodied males into patrols, meanwhile dedicating the healthy adult females into what remained of coffee cultivation. Carmel and another female under 15, Albine, were assigned full-time domestic duty. They patched sheets, tablecloths and draperies, washed clothes and windows, walls and floors, husbanded tallows, candles, oils and spices, and kept strict count of the table services, silverware, china and crystal—there was little hope, except by shipping them to vaults in France itself, of securing jewels or precious metals, which vanished on a daily basis.

After even more slaves, including Albine, stole away or were killed by marauders, Nicolas de L'Écart, who was highly reputed for keeping his charges in line, sold off to American brokers a particularly troublesome quartet who'd hatched an assassination plot against him and neighboring planters. As a result, Carmel's responsibilities expanded to include maintaining full casks of rainwater in the event the insurrectionists or vandals set fires to or near the manor house, and verifying the other remaining slaves' reports on all departures and arrivals. She also had to feed the dwindling supply of chickens (their eggs were pilfered before she could reach the coops), and milk whatever cows and goats had not been carted off or carved up.

Up until this point de L'Écart had not really noted her presence, considering her no more extensively than one might remember an extra utensil in a large hand-me-down table service. He remembered having lashed her once—or thought he remembered he had—along with all of the other slaves under forty, upon finding ten gold pieces missing from his library safe, but the fact that she was female, along with her customary silence, ensured that she did not otherwise command his attention. After he survived his third attempted poisoning, however—and personally shot the chief conspirators, an elderly cook named Mé-Edaïse whom he had misbelieved to be too old to be caught up in the Negro frenzy, and her son, Prince (called by his fellow servants Bel-Aire, for the enchanting aura he left in his wake), his driver—he assigned the cooking responsibilities to Carmel and required her to taste his food before it touched his lips. Her skills were rudimentary at best, but at this point in the maelstrom of political and social disintegration, cuisine was the last thing on de L'Écart's mind.

THE ROLE OF DUTY

Under the circumstances, are there any benefits to dedication, devotion, honor—responsibility? What, in this context, is the responsible action? Is it even possible to invoke a rhetoric of ethics? Only repetition produces tangible benefits, which include the stability of a routine (however precarious) and the forestalling of longer term considerations that might provoke the following emotions: fear, indecision, paralyzing despair. In the absence of a stable context, the question of ethics intrudes. What kinds of responsibility? The maintenance of the established order, that is: labor. What is the non-material or spiritual component? In the private sphere: to the ancestors, their memory, to the elusive community of the self and its desires—constancy or consistency. What if these are in conflict?

During her rare moments of respite, when she was not identifying new hiding places in the event French troops or their black deputies or enemies commandeered the estate, or scavenging meals for herself from the waning crops and provisions, Carmel would spend her free moments drawing. She had access neither to blank paper nor ink, nor any of the other usual artistic implements. Instead, she would sketch elaborately detailed figures or images in the dusty banks of the Grand'Anse, etching them with sharp tipped branches or scraps of tin on tree boles, tracing chits of charcoal across swatches of old gazettes or in the end pages of the gilt-edged, uncut, and long unopened leatherbound books that lined the shelves of Nicolas de L'Écart's library. Her imagery ranged from the plantation itself to the seascapes and hill-ringed plains around Jérémie, to imaginary realms she conjured from book illustrations, dreams, nightmares, and her rare night visitations with her late mother. She often drew detailed pictures of her parents, the other plantation slaves, and the hierarchy of angels and saints, for she had been baptized into the Roman Church, and her father had sculpted half a dozen wooden sacred reliefs that encircled the sanctuary of de L'Écart's limestone chapel. She sometimes transposed these with figures, such as loas and spirits, from the folkloric accounts she had heard from her mother and other elders, often depicting them in colloquy in the images' foregrounds. Although she had never been taught to read or write, she would add to the bottoms of her pictures verbal fragments, names and words she came across or invented.

After her master began to spend long periods of time away from Valdoré coordinating the efforts of the local militias with the French troops to patrol the western end of the peninsula on which Jérémie sat, she took mahogany charcoal sticks to the mouldering wallpaper and paled, cracked walls of the manor house's numerous unvisited rooms. She was careful not to be caught drawing by any of the other remaining slaves, a risk that diminished as their numbers steadily fell.

Often in the middle of her creative process she would remind herself that she needed to break away to make tributes and create protective or curative powders and oils, as she had seen her mother do, in case the plantation was attacked or her master discovered her handiwork, but she would then fall back into her reveries, ending only at the point of exhaustion.

When at Valdoré, Nicolas de L'Écart was too preoccupied to notice the slavegirl's peculiar gifts. More urgent concerns beset him: in addition to holding onto his plantation, even in its advanced state of neglect, and serving as one of the leaders of the area's civil defense, he was engaged in a pitched battle with what remained of the municipal bureaucracy to clear several incorrect tax judgments and collect monies that were owed to him. He could usually be found in the main salle, where he met with the ever-waning cadre of his fellow planters or Army representatives, or in his library, poring through his financial records, or in the cool cellar chapel his father had built, his favorite manservant and groom, a tall, slender, muscular homme de couleur man named Alexis, praying beside him, sometimes under the tuition of one of the few priests still circulating in the district, the young, intrepid Fr. Malesvaux. Frequently the trio slept together there, loaded muskets at de L'Écart's and Alexis's sides.

De L'Écart, in short, was holding out for the restoration of the prevailing order. As soon as the governor—General Rochambeau—or another French leader suppressed the hordes and reclaimed the colony—whether or not France and Britain signed a peace—de L'Écart aimed to acquire a slew of new, well-broken slaves to rebuild his patrimony. Both Leclerc and Napoleon had promised not only the rounding up and return of all fugitives, but the complete resumption of bondage. There is order, and there is the order. For more than three decades Nicolas de L'Écart had been one of the prominent grand blancs in the South District, administering the estate that his grandfather, Lézard L'Écart, an indefatigable naval mechanic in the employ of the French crown, had established at the end of the long reign of Louis XIV, the Sun King. While de L'Écart found it inconceivable that Napoleon's forces would fall to unlettered gangs and maroons, in the event that the blacks did triumph, he had nevertheless drawn up plans to depart for Santiago de Cuba, where he had purchased a large plot of land for coffee cultivation. Were things to reach that nadir, he planned to take only Alexis and several of his able-bodied adult male slaves, and as many of his possessions as he could fit into several large carriages. He was determined not to leave the world under conditions substantially reduced from those in which he entered it.

One morning in mid-summer 1803, after the British bombardment had abated, Nicolas de L'Écart rode west with Alexis to attend the funeral and auction of his cousin, Ludovic Court-Bourgeois-L'Ecart, a fellow coffee planter, whose estate, Haut-les-Pins, perched high above the coastal town of Cap Dame-Marie. Court-Bourgeois-L'Écart had perished after a bout with the creeping fever, and the news of this turn of events, along with the murder of several neighboring planters— and in spite of the French Negro ally Dessalines' campaign to return escaped slaves to their plantations, which was succeeding on estates near Mirogoâne and Jacmel—had finally convinced de L'Écart that he should depart for Cuba. As he and Alexis headed east, cannonade shredded the hills in the far distance.

The night before, de L'Écart had abruptly ordered Carmel to prepare his emergency trunks. As per his orders, she filled them with freshly scrubbed and sun-bleached ticking; sheets and pillowcases; towels; several cotton nightshirts; a month's change of gentleman's wear, including scarves, cravats, city shoes with brass buckles, as the gold and silver ones had already been stolen; an oilcloth cape; an overcoat of boiled wool; two horsehair wigs with sanitary powder; several boxes of French lavender soap; a writing set (without embossed stationery); a cube of wax with the de L'Écart seal; several shell combs; two straight razors, a strop and a whetstone; fragrant honey soap;

a square of lye; a mother-of-pearl-edged mirror; a deck of playing cards; several bags of gunpowder; the engraved, amber-handled pistol and leather holster; a box of lead roundballs; a briar pipe with a tin of Santiago tobacco; a tinderbox and wrapped wicks; Alexis's favorite toy, a palm-sized Mexican rubber ball; another large carved and polished rosewood implement, like an arm-length squash, that smelled vaguely of the outhouse; and the Latin Bible de L'Écart had purchased during his year in the Roman seminary.

About her own fate, he said nothing.

While taking a break to begin supper for her master, Carmel felt a strange and powerful force, unlike anything she had experienced before, seize her. As if she were in a trance, she rose and staggered down to the cellar where she found a small stub of coal, and then as if pulled back up by an invisible cord, rushed to de L'Écart's second-floor bedroom. She had the sensation of wanting to cry out, as if someone were twisting the sounds out of her throat, though she knew no sound would issue. On the buttercream-and-buttercup covered wall facing his bed, whose chief additional adornment beyond a crucifix was waterstains, her hand took over.

WHAT CARMEL DRAWS

A road winding along the Grand'Anse through the hills above Jérémie, which she covers with such dense and darkened foliage that she gouges the surface of her father's mural. A white horse, astride which sits a tall, gaunt black man, wearing a field cap, a workshirt, and breeches. He carries a musketoon slung over his back. Alongside this rider and horse, another horse, black, its teeth bared and its reins swooping upwards but unheld, forming an arch. It bears no rider. Instead, high above it, a saint—no, a Frenchman, short and lean in the hips hangs upside down, a cocked hat still on his head and his hands extended as if he were diving. A pair of pince-nez hover before him. She adds clouds, a moon, and beneath the respective white and black steeds the block-lettered names LXI and MONS, before crossing out the second one: ~~MONS~~.

When she finally drops the black nub, Carmel is too drained to wash the wall or hide. She returns downstairs and falls dead asleep beneath the kitchen table.

Nicolas de L'Écart did not have an opportunity, however, to view her creation. As he and Alexis returned via a road that descended through a hilly pass above the Rivière Chaineau, a band of rebels shot up out of the ground before him. He reached for his flintlock, which he always kept loaded, and cocked it to fire, but before he could, his horse reared, hurling him into a deep and jagged crevasse. An insistent bachelor with no issue, his estate by will and law passed into the hands of his younger brother, Olivier.

‡ ‡

From 1780, Olivier de L'Écart had practiced law in the kingdom's colonial centers. In his private hours, he conducted studies on boundary and treaty disputes, producing a monograph entitled *On the Legal Matters Pertaining to the Royal Survey of the Antillean Islands* in 1785, as well as various pamphlets on related topics. In the autumn of 1789, as the revolutionary clouds massed in Paris, he went to New York to advise the French delegation on its negotiations with the new American republic. By the coup d'état of 1792, he was in Philadelphia, where he successfully sat for the bar. By the 11th Germinal, he was again assisting French diplomats, this time in Santo Domingo, with the civil ramifications of the Consulate's proclamations; when he learned of his brother's death, he had lived there for exactly two years. His American wife, Grace, came from an old Anglo-Catholic family that owned extensive tobacco plantations in the Maryland Tidewater. Their only child, a daughter, Eugénie, was nearly fourteen.

Olivier de L'Écart, like his brother, had been raised in the provincial milieu of southwestern Saint-Domingue, and educated in Paris. He had supported the King's laws and penal codes across the new world colonies through his advocacy, and now his late brother's slaves were his own. He nevertheless was a man of feeling; he had always maintained a strong inner revulsion towards absolutism and the dominance of the aristocratic estate over the others. In the tome-lined safety of his library in Philadelphia he had even cheered those who had forced the royal hand on the tennis courts of Versailles, and later seized the state outright. He aimed at some future stage in his life to resolve this contradiction, though he had grasped at an early age that law presented the best compromise. That the cause of equality, or liberty, seen in another way, had culminated in brutality and the militarism of Napoleon, however, just as Sainte-Domingue also had degenerated into its own terror, did not surprise him. The rhetoric of the Enlightenment was a more powerful stimulant than that which had enriched his family, because equality, he had more than once penned in his journal, was the proper guiding principle, though in practice it required severe restraint: "As distant as heaven is from the earth, so is the true spirit of equality from that of extreme equality..." (Montesquieu).

Upon learning of his brother's death, de L'Écart planned to dispose of the estate as quickly as possible. He was not unamenable to selling it to one of the local propertied mulattoes, since he had known several of them since childhood and foresaw that ultimately much of the island would end up as scraps in dark palms. His wife, however, pushed him to identify a buyer first from his own station, or at least from any Frenchman who could post a bond. It would, in any event, be sold. The capture just months before and the subsequent death of L'Ouverture, who had cooperated repeatedly with French aims only to see his loyalty betrayed convinced de L'Écart that quite soon, the blacks, now awakened to their fate, would hereafter consent to be betrayed only by blacks. As his parting act and as a gesture of his magnanimity, a virtue in which he took considerable pride, he also planned to emancipate whatever slaves were still at Valdoré.

Before departing for Jérémie, Olivier de L'Écart shipped most of his personal effects forward to the home he had purchased in George-town, as he intended to resume his law practice in the new capital of the United States. He had also thought of sending his daughter on to the United States, but his wife insisted, despite the perilous situation in major portions of the colony, that the family not be separated, as the sapling flourishes best in the forest. He did not bring the few ser-vants who also belonged to his ménage, despite his wife's request that he do so. From what he recalled during his last visit several years be-fore, there was still a small but loyal cohort on the plantation, which would suffice for the purposes of his scheme.

Grace de L'Écart was not so eager to dispose of Valdoré. She imagined the possibilities of society in Washington to be promising, especially given her familial connections, but she had also dreamt of becoming a plantation mistress, a role for which her upbringing had most thoroughly prepared her. As it was, she had had to endure the snobbishness of the créole planters and their spouses, and the vulgarity of the government functionaries and the rich traders, as a barrister's wife; though her husband possessed both wealth and pres-tige, and was of the landed colonial classes, even adopting the *de*, as became his father's right by the King's quill-strokes, he had spent his adult life among this sphere essentially landless and in the service of a government in Paris whose aims had long been held in mistrust.

Given this new change of fate, she was thus quite willing to endure Valdoré's oppressive tropical heat and the summers of fever-bearing mosquitoes, which, her husband had once joked to her, were the col-ony's true masters. She was also ready to take reins over her own retinue of slaves, even if the blacks of Saint-Domingue had tasted freedom and would only return to their prior condition at penalty of death. If it meant a life among French-speaking whites with airs and mulattoes grown so presumptuous as to declare themselves on equal footing with their former masters, she would weather it.

As soon as he had planted his trunks in the main salle and inspected the house and near grounds, de L'Écart deputized three of the male slaves that remained to serve as personal guards. A ricketed hunch-back of about 16, named Beauné or Boni, whom he found sleeping in the stables, was to guard his wife and daughter; the second, Alexis, his brother's former groom, who moved through the house as if it were his, was to accompany him at all times; and the third, the mid-dle-aged Ti-Louis, whose right hand had been lopped off at some point in the past, was charged with guarding the grounds. De L'Écart then rode off to the town hall in Jérémie.

In the meantime, Madame de L'Écart had Ti-Louis gather the re-maining female slaves. There were four—Amalie, who tended the few remaining animals and the garden—she was Alexis's sister, and, younger than him, in her late 20s; Joséphine, an elderly woman who was deaf and partially blind; Jacinthe, another elderly woman of regal bearing who could barely cross the room; and the long-legged, mute creature named Carmel. The Madame immediately set Amalie and Josephine to cleaning the ground floor, while directing Carmel to the upper storeys. The ungainly, very black woman-child who could not talk particularly unnerved her.

When the tasks were underway, Mme. de L'Écart scoured the pan-try. The shelves contained half a dozen pulpy mangoes and sabrikos, three furred malangas, a stalk of blackened bananas, covered bowls of horse chestnuts, wormy meal, jerky, numerous tins that had been emptied of their spices and nearly empty jars of English preserves, and a circle of hard, heavily molded cheese. Roaches wove a sepia tapestry on one shelf, ants another on the floor. Jacinthe, who had never labored in the de L'Écart kitchen, was told to prepare a proper supper for the family. Mme. de L'Écart did not trust that the slaves would not attempt to poison her, but she was certain, based on her quick review of them, that the elderly Jacinthe had the most to lose by destroying the source of her sustenance. Still, she stood watch in the kitchen until the meal was complete.

Carmel brought her tureen of lukewarm water, frothened by lye shavings, several large palms and a handmade broom, up to the front guest bedchamber. She had tied several washrags around her wrists. The room like many on the upper floors lay shrouded in old sheets, smelling of woodrot and disuse, so it must be cleaned in order for the daughter of the new Monsieur de L'Écart to sleep here. One of Carmel's charcoal tableaux, though not as fantastical as the one in the master bedroom, covered the largest wall. She looked right past it. She raised the window and opened the shutters, then hauled the Tunisian carpets onto the sash overlooking the balcony. As she began to pummel the ends of the rug with the broom handle, a nasally voice snapped from the closet: "Girl."

Carmel instantly stopped cleaning the carpets and turned around. Before her stood the white girl she had seen earlier, her shoulder-length, greasy, hay-colored hair falling in green grosgrain-ribboned braids behind her ears; her eyes, beads of cooled nickel, floated above her hawkish nose. She wore a pale green short-waisted dress of lawn, with a matching green girdle cinched by a darker green silk bow that set off her growing bosom. It had been years since Carmel had seen a young white woman on the grounds of Valdoré, let alone in such a brilliantly colored dress. She clenched her fist around the broom handle, and took a step to the side.

"What is your name?" the white girl asked, in melodic French.

Carmel mouthed her name, though no sound emerged. She

wanted to resume her work, but the white girl circled, observing her closely. She paused, leaning close enough to Carmel that her nose momentarily touched the enslaved girl's cheek. Carmel froze.

"I know your name. This is my father's plantation now. But he's going to sell it." She smiled conspiratorily. "We'll be leaving for Georgetown, where I was born. Father has a house there too. I'll have to have a handmaid, Mother says. Tu restes avec moi." She perched on edge of the high canopy bed, wheeling her legs about. "I had one in Santo Domingo named Carolina." Carmel nodded. "She would sass Mother all the time, the black witch, but Father doesn't believe in whipping Negroes. But that's not a problem, because you can't sass me." She then said several things in a language Carmel did not understand, and laughed.

"You don't seem lazy, though," she continued. Carmel returned to battering the carpets. The white girl grabbed her shoulder and wrenched Carmel towards her. "Can you keep secrets?"

Carmel, unsure how to respond, nodded a second time. The white girl looked her over once more, and said, "Of course you can, how could you tell? My name is Mademoiselle Eugénie. But that's not a secret. I'll have to figure out a way to teach you to understand English soon. Then I'll share a few with you." She bounded out of the room just as Boni poked his head in. Carmel splashed lye soap water onto the pine floorboards, and untied one of her wrist-rags to start scrubbing. Through the window wafted the faint scent of burning cane.

‡ ‡

Within several fortnights, Olivier de L'Écart had identified a potential buyer for the property, a creole speculator who lived in town. The price was a robbery. The rebellion had yet to fully turn to the blacks' favor, but they now controlled large stretches of the colony from the border with Santo Domingo all the way to Jacmel, and where they held sway their administration was as vengeful as that of the French.

In fact, reports of the slaughter of whites were as common as the fires from distant plantations painting each night's sky. De L'Écart set about settling his brother's chief debts, hired an agent to handle the remaining fiscal and land matters, sent trunks on to Washington, and purchased passage for his family. Although his original plan was to free the slaves—because he was finally ready to take a radical step not just in mind but in action—his wife suggested that because there were so few still at Valdoré, they be included as part of the estate to bolster the price. She also wanted him to retain several for their personal use. They would be keeping Carmel because Eugénie must not be left without an attendant of her own.

In fact, Eugénie so dominated Carmel's waking hours that she was unable, at least for the first few days, to do anything but serve the white girl. Eugénie followed her everywhere, continually demanding her assistance in everything, ordering her around and insisting that Carmel play games with her, often in the midst of the slave girl's required tasks. She taught Carmel to deal cards and comprehend the Spanish cursewords she had picked up in Santo Domingo. Or she practiced her amours with her servant, cuddling and caressing the younger woman, commanding her to brush and braid and unplait her pale hair, showering her with a level of attention Carmel had never experienced. In this way, to Eugénie's way of thinking, an understanding took root between them.

Within a few weeks, Carmel and Eugénie had developed a means of communication consisting of hand and facial gestures that only they could comprehend. When Carmel couldn't make herself clear in this rudimentary pantomime, she mouthed the words in her version of French. As she brushed Eugénie's hair, Carmel would intermittently pause to stand before her mistress to pantomime brief tales about Nicolas de L'Écart, her late parents, the other slaves and their escapes, the various battles in the mountains, the rebel outposts in the nearby hills and mountains, the British sailors who had seized the port, and the waterlogged, mutilated bodies she'd discovered up on the banks of the Grand'Anse—none of which interested Eugénie.

The white girl only wanted to know who had done the drawings that covered many of the walls. Their crudeness of execution, substandard media and haphazard placement all about the house were proof, as Fr. Malesvaux had stated in the library one evening as Eugénie played a pleasant minuet in a corner of the room, that, contrary to Monsieur de L'Écart's appraisal that the images had been created by one of the penniless graduates of the École des Beaux Arts circulating in the colony's formerly flush days, that the artist had received no formal training and was evidently a Negro mimic of the usual sort, but the exacting and strange details, marked by jarring juxtapositions of nefarious symbols, such as snakes, rainbows, hatchets, fish, coffins, swords, and unidentifiable abstractions, showed that their creator possessed an inestimable capacity for evil. Her father was less convinced of the drawings' maleficence, though the large, wildly sketched figure on the cellar wall depicting an image of a man he took to be his late brother did unnerve him, and so he followed his wife's counsel.

> "If the fox be unseen
> though his scent fills the air,
> the glen is dangerous
> for more than the hare."

Monsieur de L'Écart and his wife slept armed in the small guest bedroom across from Eugénie's, at whose door stood Ti-Louis, his machete at his side. Alexis was now the house sentry. It was only a matter of time, Eugénie had overheard them saying and told Carmel, before the ex-slaves, led by some houngan, fulfilled the end of some prophesy with the last of these de L'Écarts.

Carmel had often thought about flight and knew the hilly terrain near Jérémie, as well as the coastal route towards Cap Dame-Marie.

But what would her prospects be? What if she encountered French soldiers, or one of the fighters who had slain her mother, or insurrectionists who believed she ought to die solely because she already had not fled, or pledged to one faction or the other? She had no way to argue her position in the face of a bayonet or barrel, let alone some soldier's unbuttoned … Amalie, who had spoken with refugees from neighboring plantations, told of horrific murders: by Rochambeau's troops, by the rebels, by enraged petits blancs who now saw no place for themselves in the new system. Carmel did not distrust her fellow slaves, but she also perceived that because of her mother's particular history, they'd kept their distance from her such that there was almost no possibility of deeper ties.

Olivier de L'Écart scheduled the first Friday in August 1803 to ride down to Jérémie to notarize the contract of sale and transfer the deed. The next day the family, with Alexis, Jacinthe and Carmel in tow, would board la Pétite Bayadère, a frigate bound first for Cuba and then for the United States. Carmel thus spent all of Thursday draping what furniture still sat in the house and packing away all of Eugénie's personal effects. She had stowed her own possessions in a flax sow's ear.

The de L'Écarts sat down in the dining room to eat their supper. Olivier de L'Écart had never avoided discussing the grave state of affairs across Saint-Domingue in front of his daughter, so now he broached the topic of the uneven French campaign and the rumors of Dessalines' planned treachery against his former masters. Several plantations to the southwest had already been razed, their owners tossed into the Bourdon, while the French forces were again massacring rebels in the north. The goal of the masses was to tear the white out of the Tricolor. His wife chattered peevishly about the lack of correspondence from Santo Domingo. Reason, unlike the oleander, cannot take root where the soil is poor. Eugénie ignored both of them, slipping away from the table when neither was watching.

As soon as Carmel finished assisting Amalie in the dinner service, she descended to the cellar to wash down its floor and recount the casks of wine and rum, which she had swaddled in straw for their journey. Suddenly, she felt dizzy, and then a loud voice overwhelmed her ears, as if filling them with a command. She fished a lozenge of coal from the bin. Down the center of the limed wall in front of her she drew a series of wavy double lines. Atop them she etched a formless mass, into which she set what quickly materialized as Valdoré. Her hand was moving so quickly she could barely control it. All around the estate's grounds, she drew what she initially took to be mountains, though they looked more like arrowheads. After a few minutes she had covered both sides of the road with a hundred of the serrated peaks. At the base of the wall, she drew two horses, atop one of which sat Alexis, then another horse, with no mount. Beside him lay a thin, whiskered white man. Her hand traversed the wall so rapidly that her entire body was shaking. Over the horses' feet she drew a boat, a coach, two white female figures; around them still more triangles such that whole sections of the wall appeared to move outwards as if in three dimensions. At the very bottom she scrawled TOUT, then crossed out both Ts. OU. Her fingers cramped, loosing the nugget. She felt so spent she fell to her knees, but as soon as she recovered she doused her lantern and fled upstairs.

Eugénie found her lying by the side of her bed, and slapped her. Carmel instantly sat up. "What were you doing?" Eugénie demanded. She glanced at her unbound trunks. "Don't think because Uncle Nicolas is gone you can get away with anything."

Carmel rose and picked up a length of hemp. She saw that her palms were black and wiped them on her apron. She was trembling but began to wind the rope around a trunk. Eugénie reclined on her bed.

"Mother says the French are dying like horseflies," she said. "Did you know they also get the fever in Georgetown too?" Carmel finished one knot and began the next, without glancing up at Eugénie, who had crawled under the covers. "Father is going to write a book about this plantation. Are you listening? Here's a secret: in Santo Domingo I had an admirer. He was a creole boy in the seminary there." She lowered her voice to a whisper. "Actually I had two. The second was the uncle of my tutor, Madamoiselle Rossignol. That's why Mother dismissed her."

Carmel kept tying. Although she had considered telling Eugénie about the drawings, she thought better of it. She wound rope around a long, knee-high case that had once held hat presses for Monsieur Nicolas. She couldn't remember what she had packed in it just hours earlier.

"Oh, stop that," Eugénie said with annoyance. She climbed out of bed and snatched the rope from Carmel's hand. "Busy, busy. My last handmaid could sing, did you know that? Don't you have any talents?" Carmel remained frozen, quivering. Eugénie pushed her toward the door. "Draw my bathwater, girl," she groaned. "Can't you see I'm tired?"

THE ROLE OF DUTY

"It is true that it has been said of blacks through the ages that 'they don't work, they don't know what work is.' It is true that they were forced to work, and to work more than anyone else, in terms of abstract quantity." —Deleuze

Within the context shaped by a musket barrel, is there any ethical responsibility besides silence, resistance and cunning?

———

The next morning de L'Écart rode down to Jérémie with Alexis at his side. He wore his holstered pistol and carried one of his brother's rifles, while Alexis carried only a well-honed machete and a pike. Meanwhile at the dining table Mrs. de L'Écart wrote missives to her mother and dearest cousin, who was married to a planter living outside Savannah, and with whom she often commiserated by letter. Eugénie pretended to browse through an illustrated copy of Aesop's Fables while her mother was occupied, but eventually she invented solitary card games till she grew bored. She then tracked Carmel, who had continued to clean the house and pack up goods.

By late afternoon, neither Monsieur Olivier nor Alexis had returned, though Mme. de L'Écart affected not to show concern in front of her daughter. She ordered Carmel to find Boni or Ti-Louis and have either venture into town for news. Or Amalie, who had grown increasingly inattentive. This task provided Carmel with an opportunity to shake loose of Eugénie. But her search of the house, the near grounds, the gardens, the sorting house, the stables and barns produced neither man. Nor could she find Amalie, whom she had seen that morning preparing the day's supper, a spiced squash soup, nor Jacinthe. Their absences filled her with unease. She went out to the mostly deserted slave quarters, which sat on an undulating ridge to the west of the house, away from the river; she had not visited them since the de L'Écarts moved in. There she encountered Joséphine, sitting on an overturned milk bucket in front of her shack, gumming a charoot. Carmel mimed a query to Joséphine, asking if she had seen any of the other servants or knew where they where or what was going on. The old woman offered only a smirk in reply, a grayish-blue question mark of smoke unfurling above her head.

Carmel ran back to the house. She mimed to her Mistress that she could not find any of the other servants, except Joséphine. Mme. de L'Écart, who was disposed to ignore slaves' histrionics, ordered the girl to set places for herself and Eugénie, then complete her tasks. She planned to have a glass of rum with her bowl of soup, read, and wait for her husband to return.

Carmel returned to the cellar. She paused in front of her drawing. The mountains—or whatever they were—appeared to leap from the limestone wall towards her. The image as a whole churned her stomach, yet she could not pull away. Suddenly, she felt fingers clasping her wrist.

CONCERNING THE IMAGE

What does it mean, Eugénie calmly asks Carmel, I watched you cover this wall last night. She pulls Carmel close to the wall. Why did you do this? Carmel sluggishly shakes her head. Who told you to do this? Carmel shakes her head again. I don't believe you—

Eugénie approaches the image and studies it, touches it. She swipes her finger through one particularly dark, iridescent region, stopping on the male figure laid out just above the O U. She wrenches Carmel's wrist. Carmel is silent, she doesn't know.

Answer me! Carmel, though still unsure, considers her earlier experience of the drawing with M. Nicolas, and tries to mime what she lacks the gestures for: they are going to TEAR THE WHITE OUT.

Still holding Carmel's wrist, Eugénie ran upstairs to alert her mother that a terrible plan was afoot. Madame de L'Écart sat at the dining room table, her dinner bell, her untouched bowl of soup and several of her late brother-in-law's meticulously detailed catalogues of purchases stacked in front of her. She had regularly strived to break her daughter's tendency toward theatrics, so she ordered Eugénie to choose between her supper or her room. The daughter repeated herself, a murderous plan was underway. She had no appetite. Mme. Lézard de L'Écart dismissed both girls and, despite the indelicacy of reading during dinner, returned to her book.

As Eugénie, still tugging Carmel, made her way upstairs, she glimpsed through the kitchen window the surrounding hills, which were glowing like an amphitheater at a night carnival. Without a second thought, she ordered Carmel, who also saw the lights rising just to the east of the plantation, to get them safely to the quay.

A DIALOGUE

[…]

Where am I supposed to go?

[…]

According to Amalie they've seized control of both banks of the Chaineau and are advancing up the Grand'Anse.

[…]

But I've never been over the water—

[…]

Where am I supposed to go, and what I am to do when I get there?

[…]

What am I supposed to do when I get there?

[…]

———

With Eugénie holding the rifle that both girls knew first Nicolas and then Olivier de L'Écart always kept loaded, Carmel entered the library and stuffed the family's important papers in a leather satchel. In the dining room, they found Mme. de L'Écart lying on the carpet, retching. Carmel kneaded her stomach to speed the vomiting, then fetched a pitcher of vinegar water, which she poured down the agonizing woman's throat.

With Eugénie pressing the gun to her back, she raced upstairs and packed a large sheet with two changes of clothes and toiletries for both of her mistresses, to be loaded in the small, flatbed wagon that sat unused in the meadow near the stables. Carrying the knotted sack under one arm, she returned to the library and guided Madame, white as chalk and barely able to stand, to the wagon. There was only one horse in the stables, a swaybacked nag, which Carmel bridled and hitched as she often had witnessed Alexis do. With the mistresses hidden under a tarp that M. Nicolas had kept in the wagon for a similar purpose, she cocked the rifle, which Eugénie had only grudgingly handed to her, lifted the reins, and galloped off towards the byroad that tracked the Grand'Anse.

What Carmel remembers: nothing of the ride beyond the stench of burning coffee and bush. Not the dizzying descent down the path beside the treacherously churning Grand'Anse. Not the call of the lambi reverberating through the foliage. Not firing once into the darkness, nor the blunderbuss's powerful report. Not Eugénie's intermittent shrieks from beneath the rug under which she and her ill mother lay. Not the manor house erupting behind them like a immense gladiolus. Not even Monsieur Olivier de L'Écart staring up at them from the grave of the underbrush, his gaze as it met hers as impassable as a collapsed bridge, when the wagon swerved onto the main road into Jérémie.

Of the drawing, only what she now realized had covered the wall's expanse: flames.

‡ ‡

A year and a half after the establishment of the Haitian state, the orphan heiress Eugénie Mary Isabelle Margaret Francis de L'Écart had yet to settle in at the tobacco plantation of her maternal uncle, Colonel

Charles McDermott Francis, outside Washington. Neither Colonel Francis, who had readily taken in his late sister's child, nor his wife had so far proved capable of dealing with Eugénie, who, they both believed, had yet to recover from the depredations she had endured in the slave colony. Under a different scenario, they might have recognized that she was entering the full bloom of an innate rebelliousness not unlinked to the one she had just lived through. Like a weed, Eugénie's libertine attitude was beginning to take hold among the Francis' own two adolescent daughters. In addition to her repeated disappearances and her inappropriate behavior at social gatherings, there was a near-scandal involving an immigrant day laborer on the Francis estate. As it stood, there was no possibility of marrying her off, without adequate finishing, to a respectable young man among the local Catholic families. Colonel Francis therefore decided to send Eugénie to a convent school out west, where he and his wife hoped the nuns might instill in her not only discipline but also encourage her domestic talents and cultivate her reacquaintance with the basic social graces.

In the late summer of 1806 Eugénie de L'Écart entered the Academy of the Sisters of the Most Precious Charity of our Lady of the Sorrows, near the village of Hurttstown, Kentucky. The small and élite order had originated in southern Wallonia in the waning years of the Counter-Reformation. It was known for its industry and thrift, as well as for its effectiveness at spiritually molding young women of means. When the Directoire's gendarmes targeted the order in 1797, the nuns dissolved the convent, fleeing first to the Netherlands and then on to Spain, where they established a new foundation. A handful of members, however, envisioned great potential in the young American republic, with its guarantees of religious liberty against the ravages of reason, and after a brief sojourn in the city of New Orleans, established a convent and school in the far western corner of Kentucky in 1800.

The convent consisted of six nuns and novices, with eleven girls living as boarders at the school, and a trio of enslaved people, a young woman, Rochelle who attended to the nun's needs, and two older men, Hubert and Moor, who served as groundsmen, guards, grooms, and general factotums. The convent's estate comprised what had once been a large whitewashed mansion, in a rough version of the new Federal style, with a similarly designed carriage house and outlying buildings, as well as the extensive grounds—all partly constructed on the site of an Indian burial mound—of one of the region's first white settlers, the farmer, soldier and land speculator Joseph Hurtt, a native of Maryland who had fought against the Shawnees in the final battles of the Revolutionary War. When he succumbed to pleurisy at the turn of the century, his childless widow, whose mother had studied with the nuns on the continent, promptly donated what remained of the estate south of the creek to them before repairing to the federal capital.

The Tennessee River separated the convent's spur of one hundred and twenty-two acres from Chickasaw territory to the south and west; a steep hill and valley, interlaced with woodlands and traversed by a rocky road which abutted a wide, bridged creek, the grounds enclosed the entire length of their perimeter by a high, stiled fence, separated them from the miniscule, hardscrabble town of Gethsemane, which was also known as Hurttstown, to the north and east. There were no Roman Catholics among the townspeople. They consisted primarily of migrating Virginians from the Piedmont region who had intermarried with a small band of pioneers from the lower Ohio River and Big Sandy River valleys. Less than a handful held slaves; there were no free Negroes in the town. Most of the Gethsemane residents, touched by the religious revivals racing like wildfire from the Atlantic, were quite suspicious of the brown-habited, French-speaking nuns, who now not only occupied the largest share of what remained of the one great estate in the area—the rest having become Hurttstown itself—but also ran a school that did not admit the locals, though none of the elders of Hurttstown believed, in any case, in the education of girls. The Reverend Job White, pastor of the United Church in the town and variously mayor, vice mayor, councilor, and sheriff, was known to inveigh regularly against the advances of the Popish virus, which had given Indians airs and the false promise of equality. The nuns lived and functioned, then, in a low-grade state of siege.

The first Catholic evangelization attempts in the area near Gethsemane, to the indigenous people and the whites, around 1797, by a French-speaking missionary priest from St. Genevieve, Missouri, had been rebuffed with violence. An effort two years later by two Dominican friars from New York to raise a chapel along the creek had ended in their flight from the town at dawn. The nuns, aware of this history, proceeded with great care, taking every opportunity to maintain a provisional truce they had established with the townspeople, and refraining from any direct outreach to the Chickasaw. The sisters in fact did not themselves visit the town without the accompaniment of at least one local who periodically worked on the convent's grounds, and one of their black manservants.

The convent's Mother Superior, Sr. Louis Marie, a formidably tall woman whose habit always smelled of lye, was of the mind that the greater threat lay not in the gospels of finance, freemasonry and Protestantism, which were preponderant in America, but in that other dangerous product of the post-Reformation age, excessive liberty, poisoned by rationality: what, after all, had provoked the savagery that had clotted the streets of Paris with royal blood? What had brought nearly all of the great European kings and queens, divined by God, so low, and elevated the sons of merchants, with their abstract doctrines of progress, and the new, utterly alien secular order? All of the girls were required to develop the Christian aspects of their character by living austerely and working in rotation in the convent's workrooms, kitchens, and on its small farm and printing press, which produced pamphlets to spread the Word, and the world it might help to maintain, far and wide.

They were instructed in deportment: modesty, charity, gentility. The nuns usually accomplished this through positive reinforcement and penance, though they turned to more forceful methods when needed, for not only sunlight gilds the marigold. The curriculum consisted of the practical arts, as well as courses in basic theology, introductory mathematics, and French and Latin grammar. Only amongst themselves did the girls speak English. They were taught to sew, weave and darn; appraise the quality of materials and goods and be judicious; to bake, cook simple meals and supervise more elaborate ones; to conserve household resources for times of need; clean and oversee workers to ensure a proper home; preserve produce and meats; and propagate a sustaining and decorative garden. Like Eugénie, several of the girls were from border or Southern states and had brought a slave girl or woman. The nuns permitted these bondswomen to receive a minimal instruction, in French, in order to follow along in the recitation of the Bible and prayers, during the thirty minutes of repose after the Sunday Mass.

SELECTED RULES (printed and bound at the Convent of Our Lady of the Sorrows)

7. Girls shall not take the Lord's name in vain or utter any blasphemy, nor repeat any calumny against or concerning the Holy Roman Catholic and Apostolic Church.
8. Girls shall not dishonor or disrespect the Blessed Sisters or their fellow students.
9. Girls shall not gossip or engage in idle or slanderous discourse.
10. Girls shall not promenade around the Convent or its grounds as if on display, nor journey about the Convent or its grounds unsupervised except in groups of three (servants shall not count toward the total).

11. Girls shall not under any circumstances venture into the village of Hurttstown without the escort of a nun and a townsperson.
12. Girls shall not send notes or communicate with or enter into any written intercourse with residents of the town.
13. Girls shall avoid all license and provocation, in thought and deed.
14. Girls shall treat all of God's creatures, even those of the lowest station or caste, or of the smallest size, with love and respect, for whatsoever they do to the least of His brothers, that they render undo Him.

After only several weeks Eugénie found the routine intolerable. She bridled at the endless carousel of classes, courses in domestic arts and etiquette, prayers in the chapel, and labor. As in all convents, the greatest practical evil, after apostasy, was idleness. She had been neither pious nor obedient under more favorable circumstances, and she lacked any foundation for managing the conditions at the convent, which offered her no means for fostering personal happiness. She was inattentive in class, insolent to her superiors, indifferent in chapel, and at all times indolent, in the manner she'd witnessed since childhood among women of her class and which would have been suitable under the dictates of a different and vanished social order, which is to say, normal circumstances. Under her requisite mud-brown frock, which covered her wrists and boots, she sometimes secretly wore a lace shift pilfered from her late mother. Although the nuns forbade any forms of physical adornment, she would sometimes apply carmine blush, which she hid in a tin box below a loose paving stone in the dormitory floor, to her white cheeks after sundown.

Eugénie had always mistaken Carmel's dutifulness for devotion. Now she saw her slave as her primary means of emotional support, so she was initially kind and solicitous, assisting Carmel in making her bed and plaiting her hair, though she quickly tired of extending herself in this manner, and reimposed their longstanding hierarchy. She subjected Carmel to tirades about the food, the heat, the difficulty of the coursework, the chilliness and poor French and comparatively low stations of the other girls, and about her aunt's and uncle's unremitting cruelty in having sentenced her to this fate. Carmel stood at the side of Eugénie's bed, staring at her mistress and awaiting an order, thereby giving the impression of agreement.

Carmel's true enthusiasm lay in Eugénie's books, from which she devised her own curriculum. She enjoyed the ecclesiastical Latin, which she learned to read and write; she had already begun assimilating the rudiments of English, as well as French grammar, during her Maryland sojourn, and spent part of her free time perfecting them. During the convent meals on Saturdays, which the schoolgirls themselves were required to serve, and the periods before evening prayers and lights out, Carmel worked her way through the Bible, the Catechism and the Martyrology; she used her readings to wordlessly tutor Eugénie, who could not be bothered to open a book unless she was in class. She usually wrote out Eugénie's lessons, while the white girl lay on her bed under the flickering lantern light and whispered rambling monologues, half truth and half apostatic fantasy, on her exploits earlier in the day, in Maryland, in the capital. Eugénie claimed to have been courted by a banker; proposed to by a prosperous trader, as well as a sitting Senator; and to have slept overnight in a rooming house of dubious repute not far from the White House. She claimed to have slipped away and combed the streets of Hurttstown, which she pronounced nothing more than an overgrown sty, and to have explored the woods and valleys near the Indian encampments. Carmel accepted these tales without astonishment, committing them to memory, and when she could find pen and paper, sketched some of them out, concealing the papers in a gash in her mistress's straw mattress so that the nuns could not easily find them.

In general, Carmel found her routine bearable, since it gave her numerous breaks from Eugénie and opportunities to experience the world, even if that world was the severely restricted space of the convent and of her required duties. She enjoyed her own weekly, half-hour Catechism sessions with the nuns, which allowed her to expand her grasp of grammar and rhetoric, and the periods of common-work, during which the other slave girls and women, under the supervision of one of the sisters, sometimes convened to undertake joint projects.

Carmel had grown accustomed to isolation and solitude at Valdoré and valued every moment away from Eugénie as an opportunity to learn and cultivate herself. No matter; the other slave girls took offense at the fact that she did not sleep in the cramped and spartan quarters out back with them, not realizing that her mistress had demanded special dispensation on her behalf. They took offense at her height, which stamped her with an Amazonian air; at her self-possession, which they read as arrogance; they took offense at her bookishness, which struck them as pretentious; they took greatest offense at her unbreachable silence. Almost to a person, they read this as a white contempt; her unassimilable refusal to communicate in a sensible way defied their sense of shared suffering and solidarity. All of them maintained their distance, gossiping about her constantly, spreading stories, when possible, to the few slaves in town: she only spoke when casting spells; she was actually a zombie; she might not really be a female at all. She responded by focusing more intently on whatever task was at hand, to the point that some of the nuns thought her the very model of industry and dedication.

After the first month, Eugénie spent her free time developing affections for classmates. She was devoted to a skinny, raven-headed girl from Bardstown, Kentucky, but dropped her for the polished admiral's daughter from Delaware, before heedlessly pursuing another recently arrived young white woman from Vincennes. Eugénie had Carmel write out long, passionate notes to each, slapping her hands when she miswrote, before ordering her to burn them. After lights out, Eugénie would practice her affections upon Carmel, who usually concentrated as completely as possible upon a text she had memorized that morning or a drawing that she'd been working on, until her mistress tired and fell asleep, at which point she would get up and draw for an hour by candlelight on scraps of paper she had salvaged furtively from the printing shop earlier in the day.

CARMEL'S DRAWINGS

Her mother serving as a lookout in the banana trees along the road to Valdoré—Christ on the mountain top—Christ among a crowd of rebels, giving a sermon on the banks of the Grand'Anse—Ruth—her father at the Francis homestead on the Potomac—General Napoleon and president Jefferson chatting on a Washington street—M. Nicolas reclining between the thighs of Alexis on a divan in the library at Valdoré—Jacinthe standing above the Christ child's manger—an exterior of the convent after a heavy snowfall—St. Benedict the Moor—INRI in the outline of a fish (repeated until it covers the tiny square of vellum) —Africans genuflecting in the chapel at Valdoré—Saint Monica—Kiskeya—General Dessalines on his black-throated horse in the main street in Jérémie—the Mermaid-Divinity La Sirène—tous les loas—Mam'zabelle standing over a shallow pit behind the slave quarters as her mother solemnly drums on the maman—her father in the whale's throat—in the Cuban dog's—a circle of Chickasaws building a fire—micha ai illi aiokhlileka okfah kia ak ayah mak osh—her young mistress recumbent as an odalisque on a filthy pallet in an Alexandria rooming house—a map of the surrounding area—the county—a map of Kentucky and Illinois territory—a map of

Eugénie's second assigned rotation required her to assist one of the novices in arranging, labeling and packing up pamphlets, printed on the convent's press, as well as sundry dry goods in the storehouse. These included fruit and vegetable preserves, votives and other religious artifacts, such as rosaries, which Rochelle in her free time created, which were then sold through peddlers to Catholics living further south and west beyond the Northwest and Louisiana territories. The nuns also brewed their own spirits from harvested apples and berries, though they kept these for personal use, as they dared not provoke the temperate among the townspeople. A young carpenter from Gethsemane named Jacob Greaves, nephew of Reverend White, who had helped the nuns construct their still and oak casks, was again on the grounds to build a new annex to the storehouse. It did not take long, Carmel quickly noted, for something indistinct to begin spinning between Eugénie and Greaves, like a thread of freshly blown glass: brittle chatter, sly and expressive glances, a note catching in the throat for a second too long. No one else around them noticed a thing. Carmel detected periodic upswings in her mistress's mood, and Greaves's name surfacing more than once in Eugénie's monologues to her.

The late fall began its collapse into winter. Each night the hearthless bedchambers chilled like tombs, and the nuns, to maintain a proper atmosphere of asceticism, permitted only one heavy wool blanket and quilted eiderdown per girl. The conditions only magnified the hardship for Carmel, who half-slept on a low cot, bundled in her clothes and her mistress's cape. Eugénie had become increasingly distant, moving about as if in a dream, to the extent that she often appeared to forget that her slave girl was even in attendance. On certain nights after lights out, Carmel would hear her slip away, as she had done in Washington, though she always returned before dawn. Once she reappeared with the fragrance of apple wine on her breath; another with her woollen shift's back blackened with peat. One thing she rarely forgot was to have Carmel artfully pack her bed with a sack of rags and place her bonnet at its head, in case the nuns conducted a room check. She swore the slave girl to silence—she was not to reveal anything, not even in confession, though this was unlikely since Carmel bore on her conscience none of her actions on behalf of Eugénie's schemes; she was only carrying out her duties as commanded. In any event as far as she knew none of the priests who visited periodically accorded slaves that rite.

Carmel usually spent the immediate half-hour or so after her mistress's departures at her favorite pursuit. She had completely filled one of the spare handbound diaries that Mrs. Francis had sent her niece, and was now beginning another. The mattress could no longer hold all of her work including the books, so she began concealing them beneath the false floor in her mistress's trunk. She hid her tin thimble, which served as an inkwell, and the old quills she'd collected from the convent's scriptorium in the corner behind her pallet. None of the regular, official inspections of Eugénie's room had uncovered either.

On the last night of October, a severe chill settled in, then a light rain began falling. Eugénie vanished not long after evening prayers. Carmel, who for a week had been feeling alternately restless and easily peeved, had wanted to show her that earlier that day she had finally passed into womanhood. Since Eugenie was gone, however, she readied her mistress's bed, but noticed that the sack of rags, along with several pieces of Eugénie's clothing, were missing. She'd put the clean laundry away and balled up two petticoats to fashion a sleeping body. Once she'd tucked it in, she fished out her book, her quill and her drawing book, and returned to a drawing she had been working on, depicting the meadow, spread out like a sheet of lodencloth, behind the convent. Though she had only black ink, she found herself wanting to work in color and envisioning other methods for realizing her fertile imagination, such as embroidery and painting. The nuns would forbid either option unless she were depicting religious scenes. The white rain, rhythmically painting the windowpanes, began to lull her. The room assumed a strange and heavy dampness. As she started to crosshatch a poplar tree, her eyes rolled into the ceiling. On a blank page was drawn a rough map of the region, labeling the convent, the nearby town, the brown scythe of the Tennessee. Halfway through Gethsemane-Hurttstown, a line, but abruptly it broke off. Instead the quill punched in wavy lines, some of which gouged the paper; these stretched from the center of the river all the way across the town itself. Her fingers began moving more and more rapidly, drawing the waves automatically, until she bowed the quill completely back, nearly snapping it. Spent, her forehead veiled with sweat and her eyes still cycling, she trembled, unsure where she was, but out of habit tamped the wick so as not to arouse the nun conducting that night's inspections. She slid the book, under the bed, and—

Some time later, she felt something tugging at her hand and foot. Carmel momentarily fought back until she realized it was Eugénie, in the darkness, pulling her from under her bed's wooden slats. Carmel could feel that the white girl's hair and clothes, what few she wore, were completely soaked. Still partially asleep, she groped around the room for a spare blanket and patted her mistress dry. In utter darkness, she rolled her mistress's wet garments up, pressing them into a corner, and slid the white girl into her nightgown. She stuffed the cape against the door and lighted a tiny tallow candle, which took a few minutes, since she had to orient herself to find her mistress's trunk, in which they kept the tinderbox and a few votives. Once the flame spoke, Eugénie told Carmel of her adventure getting back to the convent: out of nowhere the heavens tore open and torrential rains fell. The sky thundered repeatedly, and then lightning struck as she was ascending the half-mile long road between the town and the convent. The path and the little bridge across the creek were swiftly and almost completely washed out behind her. Tree limbs, uprooted bushes and boles lay strewn like chicken bones down the surrounding hillsides. She had

had to run as fast as she could to avoid being swept backwards by the downrushing water, which was falling as if a celestial dam had split. After hurdling the gate and crawling through the basement window she always used, she had peeled off her muddy boots, stockings, cloak, and dress in an alcove next to the coal room, bundled and hid them in a secret compartment in order not to leave footprints on the stone floor. She'd made her way to her bedroom in only her petticoat and undergarments. Exhausted, Carmel wanted to pacify her mistress and put her to sleep, so she embraced her and rubbed her back.

At that moment, the ringing of the alarm bell in the front hall broke the girls' brief, silent spell. Outside the room, bare feet scurried along the stone floors. Then the two girls heard the Mother Superior's voice shuttling towards them: "Mesdamoiselles, emergency assembly in the front hall!"

Carmel took her book and, as Eugénie searched for her robe, quickly hid it in the trunk. Both girls opened the door just as the Mother Superior's hand pressed from the other side: "To the front hall, mesdamoiselles, immediately!" Eugénie and Carmel arrived to find all the other girls, the nuns and novices, a few of the workers, and the enslaved young women, in various states of night-dress, milling about.

The Mother Superior clapped her hands, and the girls formed their well-known rows. The head nun took a quick headcount, everyone was accounted for. She ordered the slave Hubert to check the cellar. Because the convent and its acres sat on high ground that drained into the creek and river, flooding in its buildings was unlikely, but she wanted to be sure. Before Hubert could report on the status of the cellar Moor was ordered to prepare cots in the upstairs library just in case. When they had gone, the Mother Superior described what Moor, who had served as sentry that night, had witnessed at the front gate: Clouds as huge as Hispaniola had anchored over the hill and town below, then burst forth with rains the likes of which he'd never seen in his entire life. As the river leapt its banks on the Gethsemane side, he'd rushed in to alert the nuns and the other slaves, so that they could bring the few field animals into the barn and secure the horses in their stables. Turning back in amazement at the ferocity of the unexpected tempest, he'd noticed a ghostly specter hurrying toward the gate, but by the time he'd been able to go back outside, it was gone. You must, the Mother Superior continued, now return to your rooms and stay there until morning prayers, but we shall each appeal to the Heavenly Father and Our Most Blessed Virgin to ensure that little harm is done to our neighbors. Ave Maria, gratiae plena, Dominus tecum....

Carmel and her mistress returned in silence to Eugénie's room. Carmel closed the door, and promptly dropped to her knees. She didn't have a rosary, but she knew the sequence of devotions well. Eyes closed tightly, her body trembling, she launched into the Lord's prayer in her head, in French. Behind her, she could hear her mistress pulling her blankets over her head as the rain unleashed its curses upon the glass.

At a morning assembly several days later, after the storm had dissipated, the Mother Superior delivered a short verbal report on the state of the convent and grounds. She pointed out that according to the male servants, nearly two dozen people in the town, whole portions of which still lay under an icy blanket, had drowned. In fact, while conducting a walking inspection Hubert had come upon the body of the convent's factotum Jacob Greaves, grounded like a barge in the creek's new banks at the base of the hill. A waterlogged sack of his clothes and a few personal effects moored at his side. Though the convent had received no notice, Carmel overheard one white girl telling another, it appeared as though he was quitting not only their employ at the convent but his hometown as well. The nuns, Carmel later learned, had wanted to attend his funeral in town, but they had been warned not to set foot on the other side of the river; nevertheless, when the next priest came through they would ask him to say a special Mass for Greaves and the other deceased, which included one of the old milk cows. The students and most of the nuns, who were quite fond of Greaves, erupted in tears. Eugénie bawled inconsolably. Carmel, standing at the rear of the room with the other bondswomen, many of whom were weeping too, stared at her mistress, who briefly turned around; her face had contorted into a wet, stone grimace. Turning away, the slave girl noticed that her fellow slaves, through their tears, were observing her, their expressions a mix of emotions shifting so rapidly she couldn't fully grasp them. She trained her eyes on her bare feet until the Mother Superior had finished her remarks. After a recitation of the rosary, the girls were dismissed to prepare for supper. Carmel waited until the nuns, the girls and the other slaves had departed, then she returned to the room.

She immediately thought of her work. Were anyone to find it, they would suspect the worst, and she might be punished and then sold off. She wasn't even sure how Eugénie might respond. As far as she could recall she hadn't experienced such an episode for the entire time that they'd been at the Academy of the Sisters of the Most Precious Charity of our Lady of the Sorrows. She entered the room cautiously. Eugénie did not acknowledge her. Silent, the white girl continued balling up her dirty clothes to be taken down to the washroom. Carmel perched on her cot and watched. When Eugénie was done with the clothes, she sat at her desk and began to brush her hair, which had come loose from its knot. Carmel did not move. When Eugénie had finished, she tied a brown ribbon around the ponytail, smoothed her frock, and sat back down. She still said nothing. Carmel crossed the room and started to re-sort the laundry when she felt something rap the back of her head. She looked up to see Eugénie stepping back, her forehead and cheeks dark as port, her eyes swollen.

"We never even got as far as the river," she spat out, preparing to strike Carmel again. From the folds in her skirt Carmel withdrew her rosary. Instead of administering a beating, however, Eugénie pushed closer to the door, whispering only: "Parce que le diable ne s'arrête jamais." Because, it is true, the devil, tireless, rests only for the devil. With that, Eugénie snatched the rosary and fled the room.

A DIALOGUE

Are you going to waste yet another opportunity to save yourself?

[...]

If you use your time wisely you'll be ready to take action.

[...]

You can take the wisdom you have at hand, scant as that is, or my counsel, which is to consider the consequences of repeatedly following the path you already know.

[...]

‡ ‡

the worst winter ever horrible cold mlle E still not speaking to me except orders fais ceci fais cela as always do this do that a pere ~~malevo~~ MALESVAUX here since after the flood say mass every morning in the chapel all of the S allowd to stand in the back i can say it by heart mlle E alw talkg to him she tell the other girls he ws a good frend of mon oncle she workg in the kichen i on garden detail we had to shovell snow off roof so v v cold then knitting stockings for the winter first for mlle E then nuns she made me ~~promesse~~ PROMISE no drawings no no none wrote out english sentences & sd 1 rosary befor slp

‡ ‡

so v v cold the creek a knife of ice sky same color today we shovelld off the roadway down to the fence and the town mlle E sd to me but not to me bc she is not speakg to me parts of the town of Gethsiminy is froze over the nuns send some breads & soup down but the revd mayor refusd I polishd mlle E new boots from her tante Mme ~~François~~ FRANCIS & sweaters sewd her collars & tear in her cape she

haves anothr handmade book fr her tante on my cot but when I sd
merci she ignore me after a while she gone out quo puella fugit rido
latin sentences & 1 rosary bef slp

‡ ‡

Frigidissima haec hiems est I overhrd one Sr say that the govnr wd
sending some help becouse the town sufferg so bad still they refuses
bread and soup today we scrubd the cellar floors & the attic of the
convent not to disturb the girls we clean the 1st and 2nd storeys on
Satrday the other S did not speak to me but sd to each othr pointing
to me why dont it save us the trouble and clean them with a spell they
laughd mlle E still not speakg to me say I shd keep my nose out of all
those books a ngr with a head full of figrs is as useful as a broom that
know arithmetic I rolld my eyes mind yrself girl english sentences &
1 rosary bef slp

‡ ‡

still so cold woke early almost dr but decide to read insted mlle E
punishd bc she did not finish her french assignment had to sit the
penance rm w SRS & pray ros which she nevr do save in chapel &
mass even then she only mouth the wds I can say it in my lang french
english latin & greek she did not speak when she return to rm but
pulld my hair when my back was turnd etiam hieme cor gelatur today
we washd down 2nd flr and 1st flr all the classrooms & workrooms &
the ballroom where the Srs and the girls eat later after evening prayers
fr MALESVAUX went down the hall & a little while later mlle E
gone too latin & english sentences & 1 ros bef slp

‡ ‡

V cold today Sunday mass I stood in the back w the other S I sd the
whole mass to myself they fell aslp or touch their dresses or gossip
aftwrds we had our theology class w the nuns of course Sr did not

call on me but all my writ answers was correct later she sd to hrself
but I heard her what a loss if only she were wht she might be worthy
of taking vows later in the room mlle E order me to clean up I dustd
everything swepd the floor refold all her clothes she did not speak
later after lights out she gone english sentences & 1 ros bef slp

‡ ‡

Finalement cold breakg at morng prayers Sr askd us to pray for
townsp who died fr the cold she sd ten but i hear one S sd many
more & they blame the convent if the Srs dont stop their wickedness
there will be under siege again there is something or someone terrib
evill up there sd the revd mayor then the S all look at me rolld my
eyes washd cloths all day then hung to dry in cellar later mlle E &
her friends JOSEPHINE & MARY MARGARET sitting on her
bd J sd do you think your S ever get lonely & MM sd of course they
seem human too but mlle E sd no bc they have us she refusd to nod
off finally then english & latin sentences & 1 ros bef slp

‡ ‡

Still cold mlle E lookd strange this morn sd i know it was you i combd
her hair straitened her bureau made her bed she just repeatd i know it
was in the garden det today a new S ~~FEDRA~~ ᴾᴴᴱᴰᴿᴬ the nuns call her
PHÈBE-MARIE aft the Bib belong to mlle JOSEPHINE O'G fr
savannah her old S was NISI who the nuns called NICOLE-MA-
RIE sent back to georgia she never speak i am hope PHEDRA/
PHÈBE more friendly her eyes a secret waiting to be solved mlle E
not speaking tired went to be early so & 1 ros

‡ ‡

Monday so cold mlle E not speakg to me for 4 days often w father
malesvaux he still do not appear to reconize me am teaching ~~PHE-
DRA~~ ᴾᴴ my signs swept washd down room floor washd out mlle E

clothes w other ones so v dirty alws hung to dry in cellar only saw
PHedra|PHèbe brief tday she used 1 sign while knitting stocks heard
1 S say to another S in Eng CARMEL-MARIE is putting poison in
the food im not i signed they ran away caelestia mihi vires read mlle
E Bib & wrote latin & englis sentences & ros

‡ ‡

cold cold wheres spring mlle E still not speaking disaprd last night
like past came in early morning cloaths v wet cold struck me several
times said if y scream or bang the walls I SHALL KILL YOU on
garden det ground hard as stone then patched tablecl serviettes curtains today all day fingers tired swept PH at first no speak then we sat
for few minutes she knows twenty signs now we talkd for as long as
we cld mlle E held my face down in the washbas you had better watch
out she sd then i cd breathe english sentences we declare these truths
to be self evident & 1 ros

‡ ‡

Monday still v cold tho PRINTEMPS – SPRING mlle E sick again
had to lie down did not want to go to infirm did not want to see pere
malesvaux he is still here she sd stop staring at me you witch her face
full and red after attend mlle J PH met me in the hall we sat for a few
minutes and spoke she knows almost 35 or 40 signs now I give her
a drawg do not let anyone see it she kissd me on my cheek english
sentences ~~& drawg~~ & ros

‡ ‡

Early wake mlle E sick again I will take you to the infirmary no she
said I cleaned up her mess all of a sudden very hot today like home
wkd in garden on det after through w mlle E who will spend summer
here say mme/mrs FRANCIS aunt of E she dont want her back
there fewer girls now PH beside me we digging put in seeds 2 S told

PH dont you know she disappears at night we seen her above the conv from the attic windows on her broom I signed they ran to the other end of the garden PH got very quiet I give her a drwg later mlle E could not keep her food down sd if you are poisoning me girl you will be sorry as if rido latin sents & 2 ros

⁂ ⁂

No entries for ? wks mlle E refused ink dei gratia she relented v hot they say there is a drouth in the town one of the male S HUBERT was in town spk with the 1 or 2 S there sd they tell them mayor towns people say: is those nuns wherever the POPISH cult take root there also grows evil had an entire baskt of woolens to darn PH had another detail until aft supper we ~~seen~~saw each other outside the dining hall missd you she sd in signs she tells me abt georgia mlle J family how she born on island down the coast her fathr sold off to louisiana I give her small 2 drwgs careful fold 1 of her later cleand the room swept washd down w soap back to the knittg finished six prs so far mlle E's ankles swollen I caressd them till she fell aslp was v tired & 1 ros

⁂ ⁂

Wk early not sure wh mlle E returnd sick as always cleand it up she will not go to infirm cannot fit one pinaf blamd me for shrinkd it she got ready to strike me and I lookd at her she laid down the drouth in the town continues made candles with Sr FRANÇOIS-AGNÈS kepd 2 fr myself Deo volente saw PH when I went to draw water fr the well she touchd my face I tell her about Ayiti mlle E family valdore how we escapd gave her 1 dr hid in hem of my frock mlle E followd me around till she fell aslp v late aft lights out & 1 rosary

⁂ ⁂

No entries for 2 wks mlle E hidden my book threatd to give it to MO-THR SUP she still sick face red cannot fit her bodice angry at me

~ 128 ~

today v hot at mass like in Ayiti sat in balc as always PH held my hand afterw group of S told her you will be just like the witch if you dont stay away do you know she can really talk but only speak the devils tongue PH laughed and then 1 S named MARILENE-MARIE slap her they nearly fight but I stoppd it they ran off we got a piece of chicken in tonights soup gave her 1 drwg of MY self mlle E went to bed early night visit did not work & 2 ros

‡ ‡

Woke early mlle E crying what have you done to me I didnt do anything I sd she tried to strike me with a brush stop it you sorciere you bruja diablesse but I didnt do anything I fight her back take off the spell SR CHARLES ISABELLE came in mlle E sd CARMEL is being insolent SR did not believe her but she orderd me to say penance and the ros, I saw PH brief she hugd bef she went back to her mistr mlle Josephine mlle E fell asleep bef lights out in the corner tryd night visit did not work no & 1 ros

‡ ‡

Woke v early my back sore fr cleaning the inner halls my det this wk the other S kepd turng over my bucket one took the rags sd make the water run back into the pail I will I threatd they grew quiet mlle E upset you wk for me she sd I sd I know but she did not listen PH askd me do you know any spells from Ayiti I sd no spells but my mother knew how to call upon the other worlds but I do not have those powers she sd oh I think you do we laughd she gave me a hand of violet PHlox as we heading indrs 1 S girl sd to her looks SHADOW like you finally found your BLACK they laughd PH did not answer mlle E v tired made me lie beside her stroke her hair deum misereatur as I fall slp she sd somethg is wrong are you doing somethg to me CARMEL I answered I havent done a thing God have mercy on me fin she slp english sent ~~r dr~~ & 1 ros

V hot by early morn like in Jérémie several nuns were sick the few wh girls left not feeling well mlle E cd not get out of bed pls CARMEL she sd use your powers I shake my head what powers we prepared pamflets to be sent to other Caths in the west several wh men arrivd w horses wagons mlle E wantd me to descrive them I sd I cdnt remember she was v angry but fell aslp then I saw pere malesvaux w them he to stay aft they leave PH & I stand behd wagon she kissd me we hrd something & stayd for a little while then we left I give 1 dr of us in eveng when I checkd on mlle E she still sick had a fevr I bathd her head tryd a night visit no luck & 1 ros

‡ ‡

V hot today men loadd up wagons we put in preservs sev trunks of cloaths also got much merchdse from east mlle E up and abt she doesnt eat look ill but face flush I combd her hair some fall out she big as a calabash v quiet stared at me but say noth when wagons & men leave PH and I hid und the stairs so we cd talk I gave her dr hid it in my hair & she sd your power is in here & touches my brow later mlle E sd where was you dont lie to me then she wd not talk again tryd a night visit no luck latin sentences & 2 rosaries

‡ ‡

Fri woke v early v hot day like mid sum mlle E awake alr made me take out her slip and pinafore do not let the Srs see I did not see PH all day mlle E said well you think anyone here cares about you but me even some other S she laughd I startd crying but she pulled my hair your only concern is me I fight her back she stopd I overhrd 2 S whisp pere malesvaux leaving heading west to St Louis after mass Sun like it was a secret where is PH did not see mlle J tryd night visit but did not work da meliora & 3 ros

Sat woke v early v hot day alr mlle E awake v quiet she was read the
BIBLE she never do that did not speak to me I went downst to beg
wkg on the new cloths w Sr FRANCOIS-AGNES no PH I sewd till
dinner 1 S sd to another now you see she made her shadow disappear
I lookd at them oh where is yr shadow PH now they laughed anothr S
sd I think her mistr sent her home she was turning into a witch hrself
or was it the witchs mistr who got her send her home they laughg I
turnd away cd not finish my din made sev errors w the stitchg later
mlle E silent not sayg anything when she aslp I did not cry tryd night
visit saw my mothers face but thats all & no ros

‡ ‡

Sun v hot wk early mlle E already awake staring at me at mass pere
malesvaux sd it v fast sat alone aft we assembled on the back lawn to
say goodbye to pere malesvaux he wldnt return until the late fall or
early winter MOTHR SUP sd the wagon to carry him off wd arrive
that aft sev nuns prayd I went downst to sew cloaths did not see mlle
E at dinner we got soup w sweet onions some jerky & sweet bisc I
sewed until nightf Sr FRANÇOIS-AGNÈS said go back to your rm
when I got there did not see mlle E her bed empty a circle of ashes
? on the floor near my cot I waitd until v late no mlle E quiet outsd
checkd my books and papers all there sd rosary tryd night visit but
no luck then on a swatch of paper no larger than my palm & began —

DRAWING

River—or creek—a hill—
          a clearing—two figures—no faces—
girl—male—older male

—convent—barns—fence—gate—
hedges—trees—woods—
—convent—grounds around the convent—
beeches—mulberries—black willows—dense
trees—so dense two bars of black—
rain—light rain—falling—river—
convent —barns—fence—stiles—
a figure—girl—lying —cylinder—
water—dark water—river—current—
flood—circle—blood—empty—
empty circle—shore—empty—
shawl—doll—blue—empty—
eyes—black—tongue—
torethewhiteout—~~I—N—F—A—N—T~~—

———

Krik krak, a week later at midday, as I sat in the cellar workroom in the rear of the nunnery, making new blouses out of old linens under the nominal supervision of Sr. François Agnès, who had slipped away to make a toilette, I heard a hubbub emanating from the first floor. The summer brazier that been pressed to the sky above the convent and town had yielded to several days of light, intermittent rain, but the basement remained humid as a cave, and I found myself intermittently reciting lines of Scripture, switching from English to French to Spanish to Kreyòl to Latin to Greek to myself in order not to fall asleep. Sr. François Agnès's Bible sat on the table beside me, open to the Gospel of John. As I brought the needle to the sleeve, the warm, dense air, which filled the air as if I had conjured it from my childhood, enfolded me like a lullaby. ...

When I awoke, having not missed a stitch, I could still hear a din above, though now it was feet scurrying rather than voices. Sr. François Agnès had not returned, nor had any other nuns or enslaved girls. I set aside my needle and fabric and hurried out of the room to find out the source of the commotion. Down the hallway, I saw Sr. François Agnès huddled with Sr. Ambrose Jeanne in the doorway to the storeroom, their whispers caroming off the walls. I wiped the sleep from my eyes and lips and slowly, step by step as if to render myself invisible, approached them.

Sr. Ambrose Jeanne was telling Sr. François Agnès that given the circumstances, the Mother Superior had no choice but to conduct an inspection, it was a disgrace that such events should come to pass in a house dedicated to the Lord, but under the circumstances there was no choice. Sr. Ambrose Jeanne shook her head violently; it was simply impossible that any of the nuns, let alone the girls, had been involved in such abominations. Sr. François Agnès agreed, pausing to look in my direction, her gaze arrowing past me towards the far wall, but added that the Mother Superior had no other option—the sheriff, Reverend White, had given her an ultimatum, and if she was unwilling to examine the girls, he would bring a party similar to the one that had just accompanied him, firearms in hand and deputized by the Commonwealth of Kentucky, to the convent's front steps, either do his work on the premises or take the nuns and girls by force to the town.

At these words both sisters embraced each other tightly, and Sr. François Agnès held Sr. Ambrose Jeanne as the latter sobbed her astonishment away. The examinations were to occur early that evening instead of supper, and as it was to be, so be it. Then they knelt on the warm stones and prayed, and after two rosaries, both nuns headed quickly down the catacomb-like hallway to the stairwell. After a pause of my own and still unsure of what was going on, I followed. When I was almost at the stairwell, I could hear other voices rounding the corner. It was two of the schoolgirls: Josephine O'Grady from Georgia, and another girl who was not Eugénie. I leaned back against the limed wall and crouched to listen.

The girls' voices trembled with shock as well. Josephine, her English thick as a magnolia petal, asked the other girl who on God's earth could have possibly done such a thing? She ticked off the list of nuns, not a single one had been with child, of that both were sure. They saw them daily at breakfast, at supper, at dinner, in class, in chapel, not one was with child. How could anyone have assumed such a thing? And then there were the schoolgirls themselves, only five now in summer residence, Josephine and Mary Margaret, both speaking to each other now, who were each sure that the other was as virginal as their other classmates, Catherine, Dorothy Angelica, and even the sickly, greedy Eugénie—none of them could possibly have been with child either, it was as clear as the reflection on the chapel patin. Sr. Germain Ruth, who ran the infirmary, would attest to that. And it had not come from any of the slaves, Josephine assured Mary Margaret, because, as they'd seen with their own eyes when the sheriff had thrust the tiny corpse into the Mother Superior's hands, Mary Margaret gasping at the very memory, its tiny fists seizing at the air, its mud-caked face petrified in a shriek, its icy blue eyes staring out fishlike as if glimpsing the netherworld for the first time, its azure placenta eeling out of its swaddling, and most horribly, the calligraphy of marks and hatches, as if a demonic stylus had been drawn across its forehead and chest, it had been as clear to everyone assembled, all the nuns, all the schoolgirls, all the slaves, and the sheriff and his party of a dozen, that although the withered infant body had been found bundled in what appeared to be a slave girl's shift, it was not a product, as he had clearly noted, Josephine's voice breaking, "of that infernal race."

The stench, Josephine continued, she could not ever forget, even less than that horrific image. And its unheard cry was still ringing in her ears. But, she told Mary Margaret, shortly after the sheriff and his party had descended the hill, aggrieved and barely satisfied, and everybody had been sent to their rooms or stations until another order was to be given about what would occur next, she had spied the Mother Superior and several of the other nuns, including Sr. Germain Ruth and the disciplinarian, Sr. Charles Thérèse, in the parlor looking at the small, bloated body, which they had placed on a table, and she had heard them saying that it did not appear to have been mutilated or used for some diabolic ritual, as the sheriff and most in his party had alleged, but rather as if it had simply been expelled from its birthing place too early, and been buried in that shallow grave just on the other side of the creek, at the rim of one of the many tiny sloughs the flood had created—a tiny blue waxen doll, not murdered by some mortal hand, despite its pose and cry and open eyes, because it was already deceased, though in the sheriff's conclusion, the two amounted to the same thing.

Given that there was no priest in residence, Josephine added, as Fr. Malesvaux had departed by coach for Saint Louis only a week before and no other priests were scheduled for several more weeks, she thought it only proper that the nuns bury the child themselves, praying for its soul and returning it back to the earth, on the convent's grounds. The entire incident was even more terrible, she added, than the flood and its aftermath, and the unspeakably bitter winter, and then the heat which now seemed to emanate from the gates of Hell itself, and the problems with her second slave girl, Phèdre—at whose name I moved away from the wall, nearer the speakers, neither of whom appeared to notice me—once so gentle and passive, who had gotten airs and become defiant and begun behaving as if she were in a bilious humor, even engaging in strange rituals, such as drawing crosses on the floor and talking in riddles and murmuring almost as though in a trance, so much so that she and the nuns had had, as Mary Margaret already knew, to remand the girl back to Savannah and request that her parents send her another in her stead. As Mary Margaret also knew, the new girl had not arrived and, this was news, as soon as Mlle. Josephine returned to her room she was going to write her parents a letter entreating them to remove her from the school as quickly as possible, she was not sure she could last another term.

Mary Margaret assented: she did not want to stay any longer either, though both would have to endure the inspection that evening, and then wait till as long as the post would take to travel to their respective homes before they could return, since the nuns would not send them on their way otherwise. I then heard both girls scramble up the stairs, and when there was nothing but the general sound of movement, I ascended the stairs myself on my way to the bedroom.

At the landing, I saw two of the bondswomen who, during my entire stay at the convent, had mostly kept their distances from me, though today, as in recent weeks, they did not bolt but unexpectedly lingered, as if they were gliding into my orbit. Though they still pretended not to want to sit beside me during our brief meals, today, as when we were in the same room undertaking our various tasks, they were drawing closer, closer still, until we sat or stood only fingers apart. We did not exchange a single word, but these two, who had been given the ridiculous names Daisy and Avondale, I had chosen to rename respectively Diejuste, because of her usual genial manner, and Ayidda, because twice while working in the gardens in her presence I had seen garter snakes. Each gave me the hint of a smile, as if I had shared with them some secret that offered a clue to the brouhaha now unfolding, and though I had not, I returned the slightest smile to each of them.

In the bedroom I found Eugénie slowly taking inventory of her personal effects, strewn across her blanket like a market stall. She moved as if performing a masque. I tried to get her attention and pinched her gently on the arm, but Eugénie pushed me away. She went to the door and, using a loose corner floorstone, wedged it shut. As soon as she'd done this, she crawled down under her bed and extracted a small bundle from the corner behind the portion of headboard nearest the wall. The stinking, reddish-brown mass of fabric made me retch, but

I knew what she wanted me to do, so as soon as she handed it to me, I slid it under my own cot.

The white girl, still not uttering a word, approached me and, seizing both of my hands, plunged them in one dead swoop between her thighs. I drew them back, but the white girl grabbed ahold of them and again buried them between her thighs, clamping down so they were vised in there, a rosary bundled between the flesh scraping my knuckles. As she did so she mumbled several prayers, though I could not make out what they were. For a while we struggled as an onrushing current surged through my fingertips, my fingers, my hands, my arms, until I was finally able to break free. I settled on the end of my cot farthest away from Eugénie, and looked away.

She appeared satisfied by my actions, and resumed cataloguing the clothes before her. When she had finished, she carefully folded each of them up and stacked them into neat little piles. Then she turned to me and pointed to them, which meant that I was to pack them away in her trunk. She stepped back to watch me work. I carefully placed each of the garments in the trunk, counting as I did so. I tallied combs, wool stockings, bodices, bonnets. There was one petticoat and one pair of small clothes missing: these, I guessed, were the dried carbuncle I had stored beneath my own cot. When I was done, Eugénie gestured for me to open my own sack of garments. I did so. She ordered me to pull everything out.

On my cot lay a long, threadbare linsy-woolsy shift, spangled with patches, that I alternated with the slightly newer one I now wore. There was my other linen head scarf, a faded rose castoff gift from her aunt, Mrs. Francis. There were my mismatched pair of repeatedly darned woolen socks, which I had not worn since the winter. Finally from the bottom of my sack I extracted my several tattered petticoats, which had belonged to Mme. de L'Écart, my own small clothes, and my woman's garments, all of which, though gray from reuse and repeated washing I kept meticulously clean. Where was my other shift, the gray wool one I, like all the other slave girls, wore during the winter? I was sure she had not removed it from the sack in months.

The white girl pointed to one of the petticoats and one of the pairs of undergarments, and indicated that they be placed in her trunk. When I hesitated, her blue eyes smacked me so hard it was as if I had been struck by an open palm. I folded a petticoat and the small clothes, and layered them atop her pile. I sat back down on my cot without permission and replaced my small menagerie in its store-place. Then we stared at each other, in silence, until Sr. Ambrose Jeanne appeared at the door to fetch Eugénie for her inspection.

As soon as the door closed I tidied up the room, then returned to my cot. I considering saying my rosary but did not.

EXCERPTS FROM A REPORT BY SR. GERMAIN RUTH ON THE INSPECTION OF THE PUPILS

On the 25th day of August, 1806, in the convent of the Holy Order of the Most Precious Charity of Our Lady of the Sorrows, in Geth-semane, Kentucky, under the supreme guidance and counsel of the Heavenly Father and our patron, Most Blessed Virgin Mother, Medi-atrix of Grace, and in the presence of our Reverend Mother Superior, Sister Louis Marie K., as well as our Associate Superior, Sr. Alphonse Isabelle D., I have, in accordance with the teachings of our faith, the wishes of our reverend leader, and the rules of our order, prepared the following report on the requested examination of the pupils en-rolled in the convent's school concerning the matter that is the case. This activity, extraordinary in light of the habitual occurrences of this house, was conducted to ascertain the possibility of a particular and unspeakable trangression by any of those entrusted to our care and formation. The particular case encompassing, in short, the tragic series of events that unfolded one week prior just across the estuary separating the convent's grounds from those of the town.

Each of the young gentlewomen was conducted individually into the calefactory. Verily, each was asked to be seated in a chair facing away from the window overlooking the west meadow, and was presented a series of questions concerning the evening under scrutiny. The inquiries also assessed any and all potential associations with any male person the pupils may have had, their behavior in the weeks leading up to the above-cited events, and the general and specific perceptions the reverend sisters may have had about each. With one exception, the alibis provided by the young ladies were in various states of conflict concerning their whereabouts between the evening inspection, conducted by my person, and the morning call. With one exception, that being Miss Eugénie de L'É., none was able to reply to any of the subsequent questions with persuasion. Several of the girls appeared to be in advanced states of agitation, which could have been the result of sin, ill or uncertain humor, or some other cause. Only the aforesaid Miss de L'É. was able to reply with a demonstrable measure of calm. It should be noted that the inquiries were conducted by all three of the sisters present, though the author of this report served as the primary inquisitor.

To go further, though in each case the child under inquiry was able to cite a fellow room occupant, usually a fellow pupil, who could vouch for her presence in her room throughout the entire period when the said events are alleged to have occurred on the said evening, each mentioned a detail or details that contrasted with the testimony of her schoolmates. In several instances there arose conflict over the very question of whether the girls were asleep for the entire period or even in their rooms. In the sole case of Miss de L'É. there was, the inquisitors noted, a solid story, to which another figure in the house, in this instance her bondswoman, might attest. One pupil, Miss Mary Margaret S., developed considerable disquiet during the inquiry, specifically on the question of her actions on that evening. Despite the general concurrence of her answers by her roommate Miss Josephine O'G., she became so discomfited at this particular question that she expelled the contents of her stomach. The sisters present were not completely inclined to believe them.

‡ ‡

After this initial period of inquiry concluded, the pupils were then individually asked to lie supine on the large serving table, which had previously been cleared of its usual artifacts in preparation for this portion of the inspection, against the east-facing wall. A white sheet was draped so that it concealed both the upper and lower portion of their torsos. Each girl was then told what this portion of the inspection would entail, which provoked several exclamations. In the case of said Miss Mary Margaret S., Sr. Alphonse Isabelle had to spend several minutes attempting to pacify her, and when this did not succeed, she was held down, by force, until such time as she was sufficiently becalmed, in order that the inspection could be properly undertaken.

The small clothes of each of the inspected were removed. In several instances this was only achieved with great difficulty. In the case of Miss Mary Margaret S., further force had to be applied to ensure that she would comply with this action. The author of this report, having served as the director of the convent's infirmary since its establishment, and thus possessed of deep familiarity with the human anatomy and physiological principles, proceeded to examine each of the inspected. In half the cases the results were inconclusive. Although it did not appear as though any of the inspected had recently given birth, this inspector, having viewed in manuscript illustration the essential parts at the conclusion of such an event, was unready to make a decisive declaration. On this point the other nuns concurred initially, although the Reverend Mother Superior, on continued examination, adjudged decisively that the inspected were still in an unmolested state. Only in the case of Miss de L'É. did it appear that the observed anatomy appeared incontrovertibly unchanged, as it ought.

Given that none of the sisters was in the least suspected in the matter, this second part of the inspection left all of the inquisitors present with great disquiet, though each duly was subjected to a similar examination, in the author's case the determinant being the Reverend Mother Superior. In none of the reverend sisters, by the Grace of the Holy Mother, did the observed anatomy appear incontrovertibly transformed.

‡ ‡

In every instance in the inspection concerning the matter that is the case, the effort was made to preserve the inspected's dignity....

Sr. Germain Ruth M. deP deK.

The nuns' official report, I heard Sr. Ambrose Jeanne telling Sr. François Agnès early one morning several weeks later as I sat undertaking piecework on the other side of the sewing room, having been delivered to Gethsemane's mayor by the white driver and mechanic who had returned from Missouri with Fr. Malesvaux, who was sojourning at the convent before returning east to Maryland, appeared, at least temporarily, to have soothed the passions of the sheriff and the townspeople, if not Reverend White. The summer heat, which had returned full blast, turning the air inside and outside the convent to glass, was, however, stoking the exact opposite effect.

Among their own population, Sr. François Agnès explained, they had identified a possible suspect: a white woman, the daughter of recent settlers in the town, was thought to have been secretly with child. Sr. François Agnès's expression, and the clipped, elliptical quality of her Latin, the language into which she and the other nuns sometimes slipped when they hoped to avoid being overheard, suggested she thought the penalty ought be severe.

After the hubbub waned Eugénie had for several weeks remained in bed. The summer air cottoning everything had wrapped her in fevers and induced fainting, from which she now appeared fully recovered. The ranks of her classmates had, however, thinned only to three white girls, two of them Josephine and Mary Margaret, neither of whom had been fetched home as she had requested, though Josephine's replacement servant, an often surly young woman named Marvel, who quickly took up with Diejuste and Ayidda, and whom I renamed Marinette because of her temper, had shown up, a sack in hand, on a coach from the east. The only other white girl was Annie Lawrie Geddes, who may or may not have been from New Jersey. These three white girls moved about as if in a state of shock, or suspended animation; their regular classes having ended, they had only to attend a daily course, after breakfast, that involved close reading and study of the Scriptures, in English, and because of the heat to participate in the various light indoor domestic tasks in the convent, such as replacing candles in the chapel, or helping to dry herbs and blooms and the first summer fruits for preservation, or copying out passages from English-language religious books to be sent to Catholics elsewhere in the countryside and country. At all other times they were allowed to read, or knit, or embroider, or sketch. None showed enthusiasm in anything she did, Eugénie even less so than the rest.

Sr. François Agnès concluded her conversation and called me over, telling me that I should wrap up my sewing and attend to Miss Eugénie, who would be finishing her breakfast and heading to class. I ascended the stairs slowly, as I had of late ceased to move with dispatch, unless it was absolutely necessary. Since the incidents of several weeks ago, Eugénie, recognizing the changes in my behavior, had responded accordingly. She no longer expected me to wash with her waste water; she took good care not to hand her comb to me in expectation that I would run it through her hair, or point to her chamberpot unless I was ready to touch it. In the hallway I saw Marinette; she was sweeping, but paused as I passed, and greeted me with her eyes. I replied in kind. The main floor was otherwise quiet; I imagined the sisters were either in the refectory or the chapel or downstairs, or otherwise occupied. At the stairwell to the next story, I saw Ayidda polishing the banister; we exchanged fulsome waves. The stairs themselves seemed to melt as if wax under my feet; it took me a while to reach the bedroom.

Eugénie was not there. I had already made my bed so I fiddled a bit with hers. I bundled her dirty clothes up and, exerting no real effort, lined her books up on her desk. She had forgotten to cork her ink bottle, to put her nibs away, to grab her writing book for class. I thought of taking it to her but decided not to. I set the main lamp outside our door so that it could be refilled for the evening, lazily brushed her shoes and beat out her pinafore, then closed up the room. This floor also was mostly quiet, though in the large room at the end, I knew, the class was unfolding. Behind me someone was padding quickly, and I turned to see Diejuste gathering up my lamp; we parried smiles. I proceeded down the hall until I reached the door of the class, which stood slightly ajar. All four of the white girls sat in a row at the first table, Eugénie on the end nearest me. I could hear Sr. Alphonse Isabelle's voice rising and falling like a rattle. I stared at Eugénie until she was compelled to look in my direction, though by the time she, and the girls beside her, would have done so, I was already on my way back to the sewing room.

ON DUTY

What is duty?

His maister had not half his duetee. (Chaucer)

Wherefore duty?

We have done that which was oure duetye to do. (Luke xvii.x Tyndale's Bible)

What duty is due us?

To do one's duty thoroughly is not easy in the most peaceable times. (Pattinson)

Whither duty?

No conciliation is possible, for of the two terms, one is superfluous. (Fanon)

———————

The summer heat grew ever more tropical, provoking fainting spells and transforming the upper floors of the convent to a kiln. By late June, the nuns canceled all activities for the white girls and themselves, save prayer, from midday to the early evening, that could not be undertaken in the basement. We thus rose just before dawn, before the sun broke, to fetch water, empty chamberpots, clean, cook, cultivate the garden, move all unused tools and implements, including a store of gunpowder, indoors, prepare whatever else was required for the white girls, and assist the sisters as they saw fit. The religious class moved into the sewing room, which had been my refuge, and I and Sr. François Agnès moved to a smaller room down the hall, a large closet really, which had been used for storage. It was far more cramped, but cool and peaceful, and as she assembled or disassembled garments, knit, embroidered, and darned, I worked on what I had at hand and tried to let my mind float free of everything around it.

Though I still read just before going to sleep and maintained my journal, my entries now tending towards a brevity so extreme that sometimes only a word or two, at most a sentence, resonant for my memory and me alone, would suffice, and I filled whatever space remained with minute line drawings of my fellow bondswomen, of the animals, of the grounds; and with caricatures of the nuns, the white girls, and the glimpses I had gotten of the townspeople and of the convent's visitors, including the Reverend White's son Job Jr., whom the nuns had contracted to repair damage caused by the rainstorm, to the front portico and to re-wash, in white, limed paint, the entire façade, I seldom undertook the more elaborate drawings that had been my regular practice since arriving with Eugénie, though from time to time I would extract the journals in which I'd drafted them, documents I kept carefully hidden in a storage space underneath the head of my cot, which I had dug out over a period of months and re-covered with a large paving stone, to review them, usually with a bit of bemusement at the queer constellation of imagery and signification that I had developed—what on earth or in the heavens had I been thinking?—and with admiration that, despite all the constraints I had faced, from lack of materials to disapproval to potential punishment, I had produced so much and, I was not unashamed to say, of such a high quality. Of course no one else beyond Eugénie knew, and even she was unaware of the full extent of my efforts, not that she would have been able to appreciate them anyway. Sometimes I had the thought that I should share this work, at least with the bondswomen, but I decided that I would wait until I was surest the right time had come, and undoubtedly, it had not.

My other mode of drawing had not made an appearance for some time before nor once since the last and most egregious set of incidents, and it struck me that perhaps I was outgrowing my youthful lack of control, that I might be shedding whatever tether held me to realms which, despite the otherwise deepening clarity of my perception of the worlds around me, stayed still so concealed. In terms of my own will and gifts, I had begun to figure out ever more about how to initiate the night visits with my mother, summoning the door before my eyes, though I had not yet found the right key, among the many arrayed before me, that would open it; and as for whatever lay on the other side of those drawings, with their arsenals of augury and admonition, I had not yet developed a theory of knowledge by which to understand them. Or rather perhaps I had, but lacked a language to characterize and describe them. It struck me that the spells and the drawings themselves might be a language, but this seemed so exploratory and fantastic, that I set aside further consideration of it, and instead reflected, when the thought struck me, on the process of my experience and practice of those episodes.

The air, though cool, was heavy; the room, lacking any windows, hunkered near to darkness. Sr. François Agnès, having begun to tell me how "Hell had come to St. Francis," the "embrace of the tropics had forced the relaxation of the convent's routines" and that "this was, pains seize St. Agatha, the sort of liberalization one would never see in the Low Countries," had promptly tumbled off to sleep, her snoring gradually filling the room like water finding its level. I stood and decided to make a round, to see what was going on, and responding, if I were questioned, that I was on my way to one of my tasks, which, to be truthful, was the truth. As I often now did when I wanted to pass unnoticed from one part of the convent to another, I imagined myself the shadow I had been at Valdoré, where no white person, save Eugénie, had ever seemed capable of seeing me. Had M. Nicolas de L'Écart ever noticed my presence? Had M. Olivier? Had his wife? For that matter even the bondspeople had rarely seemed to register when I stood among them. I wondered where most of them now were, the ones who had successfully escaped Valdoré's vise, France's visible and invisible chains.

I glided along the wooden floors without a single creak. As usual I wore no shoes; my hem floated off the ground; my pace was slow enough that I might even have gotten behind time itself. The heat seemed to form a curtain through which I had to press myself, though I did so with a minimum of effort. In the sewing room all the white girls save Eugénie had stretched out on cots, and were sound asleep, as was Sr. Charles Thérese, who slumped over the table, the books arrayed about her like an archipelago. Quiet preceded me down the hall; near the kitchen, I could hear the gentle snoring of Rochelle, who had, I imagined, fallen asleep with the soup on boil, its aromas of barley and sage wafting through the door's slit. I roused her, by means of a thought, and the snoring ceased. Presently I heard wood against metal, and the beginning of a soulful melody she routinely sang.

Upstairs, on the main floor, the heat was stronger still, though I could smell the outdoors blowing in through windows open on the building's backside. My girls were seated in the refectory, on the floor against the back wall, their heads nodding in near-silent slumber. I did not want them to encounter any problems, so I woke them without entering the room, and could hear them stirring, as if to return to their duties, or at least to the semblance thereof. Across the hall I peeked in the chapel, where the Mother Superior, Sr. Alphonse Isabelle, and Sr. Charles Thérèse were curled into their chairs, the Holy Virgin Mother beaming down upon them, their books in their laps, their ivory guimpes and dun scapulars undulating rhythmically, their veils tousled over their shoulders like loose hair. For a second I drew the statue's gaze to my own, then proceeded on toward the back porch, which led directly onto the gardens and the fields. There was a low buzz, as if people were talking but wishing hard not to be heard. Through the open door and through a large pane I could see Hubert, a kerchief on his head, toiling away with a hoe.

As I approached the doors the voices became more distinct, but I saw no one in the room. Crossing the threshold, I approached the window in which Hubert's dark shirtless back and kerchiefed crown bobbed, like a millpiece, and I paused only when I reached the glass, which gave off heat as if it were molten. The voices were now clear, and clearly in French, behind me. I turned around to see the brown, hooded cassock of Fr. Malesvaux hunching over something fast against the wall. I hid myself beneath the table beside me, though given his lack of reaction, he evidently had not seen me. He shifted the angle of his cassock and from behind it emerged Eugénie, her face flushed, her hair plastered to her head. Both her pinafore and Fr. Malesvaux's gown, I could now see, were soaked through. The two struggled, in silence, he holding her wrists tightly and saying without saying *in two weeks in two weeks* while trying to extricate himself, she responding *you don't understand you don't,* until finally he caressed her face, her hair and hurried out the door.

Eugénie stood alone, against the wall, looking as if she wanted to scream or cry, but knowing better. I thought of calling attention to myself, but I decided instead to observe her. For a while she remained in the same spot, alternately despondent and elated, occasionally looking toward the window and the outdoor scene above me, intermittently at the skirt of her pinafore, which she ruffled and smoothed. Her thoughts were cycling so swiftly and dully through her head she would not have been able to articulate them had she tried. She bent down and raised a discarded shingle, fanning herself for a while, until I grew tired of the episode, whose overall meaning had grown clear to me, and drew her eyes in my direction. She froze. She could not see me, of course, and peered all around her, as if I had placed my gaze throughout the room. She glanced at the table behind which I knelt, and after taking one step in my direction, she wheeled on her heel and fled down the hallway.

I resumed watching Hubert for a while, until he broke to head to the well, where I spotted Job White Jr. refreshing himself from the bucket. At this point I also left the closed portico and headed back to the basement.

A DIALOGUE

[…]

I refuse to think of them as wasted opportunities to save myself, but rather as stages in my careful process of preparation.

[...]

I am more than ready and willing to take action.

[...]

I think I have finally come to understand your logic.

———

Have I ever had a vision of Hell, that place to which this faith—in whose intimate and suffocating grasp I have passed the last few years of my life—and to which Eugénie, from our very first days together in Saint-Domingue, had constantly threatened the Heavenly Father would consign me? I have not. Or rather I have, but yet never have I devoted more than the bare minimum of my interest to it. I know the Hell of the Gospels and le catéchisme, the sermons of Fr. Malesvaux and other priests, the tuition and exams of Srs. Charles Thérèse and Ambrose Jeanne. I have pictured it, perhaps I have even drawn versions of it, though it has never meant anything more than the illustration of an exercise, a foreign mote of knowledge, to me. Have I however lived a form of Hell, lived in one, or perhaps several? Most certainly, and perhaps am in one now.

Of course there are Hells and there are hells, which is really a statement of banalities, for there are degrees of horror, of horrors, which we all witness and live through, sometimes directly, often indirectly, and it is the immediacy of horror, its sublimity and our incapacity even to reflect upon it, though we may indelibly remember it, that shapes our sense of what a particular hell, or Hell itself, may be.

The word itself had begun to foam, like spittle, on Eugénie's lips every time she eyed me, though she did not dare utter it, or cast a single aspersion in my direction. Instead, as the weeks crept forward through the infernal heat, she crept with utmost care around me, taking care not to offend me even in the slightest, as if she could tell, though I would not have deigned to tell her, that the departure of Diejuste and Ayidda, whose superintendents had finally been fetched home by their parents, opened a hole in my affections. We had not grown as close as I liked, but we nevertheless passed increasing amounts of time in each others' company, Diejuste's bright humor and wit clarifying as we sat and packed crates of pamphlets, Ayidda's skill at producing seemingly insignificant signs that needed only the right person to decode them providing me with an intellectual and spiritual workout of the kind I had not encountered before. I woke one morning, after a troubled sleep, with a severe headache, a novelty for me, and when I reached the refectory, I saw that there were two fewer white girls at the table and knew instantly that early that morning, Josephine and Mary Margaret, with Diejuste and Ayidda in tow, had gone. That left only Marinette, whose temper was still occassionally a challenge, as a companion, though we seldom found ourselves together for long.

As we passed in the hallways we would share thoughts, ideas, dreams: she longed first of being manumitted and going to live in Washington, where she had relatives and where she had been born, though she'd been sold off when the first estate to which she had belonged had been divided, at the death of its owner. Phedra, it turned out, was not her sister by blood, though they had been raised together as if they were. She had never heard of Ayiti. She also did not know much French beyond what she had picked up during her short stay, and no Kreyòl or Latin at all. I tried my best, in the slots of time alotted to us, to rectify that. Her temper, she realized, was like the wick of a lamp too often turned to its brightest setting, and though she had cause, as we all did, she was learning, striving, to lower it. We tried to arrange a time in which I might show her my drawings, but Annie Lawrie, who like Eugénie had been left in the nun's care, was now demanding as much of her time, if not more so, as Eugénie had previously required of me.

One night following a day so hot that it appeared to have scorched much of the foliage to a brown fur, I woke to hear Eugénie creeping past my bed. The room was black as the moment before a nightmare. She no longer bothered to force me to pack her sheets in her absence; everyone in the convent was usually so drained by the heat that they slept as if drugged. I turned over on my side, away from her, and tried to go back to my dream, in which Phedra and I were slowly walking across the river, but I could hear the white girl fumbling through my papers, so I sat up, as quietly as possible. What was she looking for? She tossed several things into a cloth sack, replaced the floor stone and bustled out of the room. When I was sure she was halfway down the hall, I trailed her.

She advanced through the darkness more quickly than I would have imagined, but I could still make her out. She was, I knew, going to meet with Fr. Malesvaux, perhaps to show him my handiwork, though to what purpose I could not foretell. Perhaps she now bore his child, and she was planning yet again to run away, this time with him. Let her go with him, I would not try to stop her, I had plans of my own. I was curious, however, about why she had taken my art. She made her way not to the first floor's rear portico, where I had seen them before, but continued upstairs, to the attic, moving almost soundlessly and without a single stumble, which made me realize that she probably had practiced and traced this route multiple times. At end of the hall, however, I could hear a din, almost imperceptible but enough to gain my attention, coming from the direction of the town. I pulled back one of the velvet curtains to see what was going on. There were tiny pinpricks of light flaring from Gethsemane, but intermittently. Nothing, at least from this distance, was clear.

Pulling myself from the window I went to the attic staircase and moved as swiftly as I could, catlike, my ears pricked, my eyes cutting through the murk. Voices, or at least one, issued from the main room there. The door was cracked and I slid through. To my left Eugénie was telling her lover that she had all her garments, some coins, sturdy boots, her cape, and the maps, mine, the ones I had drawn, which she had studied assiduously and was sure would serve them as well as any others. Her lover did not speak, but I wondered, given how frequently Fr. Malesvaux had come and gone from west to east and back why he would need to depend on one of my maps, drawn, in any case, from my inner vision and not cartographic accuracy. He persisted in not speaking and it struck me that he might be communicating with her in another way. Papers rustled in the darkness, until I could tell he was stilling her, calming her. She asked if the horses were ready, and he conveyed to her that they were. I stepped out of the way to let them head downstairs; I was not going to betray her to the nuns, since I was sure she and her popish paramour would not get far, at least based on the maps I had drawn, and they would find that out soon enough.

Right near the door, she turned, her shoulder-slung sack swinging and nearly hitting me in the face, and asked, "How long do you think it'll be before they discover you took all the money?" I was not surprised at this bald statement of duplicity and sin, and yet I was. Fr. Malesvaux, whatever he was or was not, had never seemed to me to be an evil man, let alone a thief. Even the Haitians at and around Valdoré had recognized this, French and ever liberal with Christian casuistry though he was.

The voice that responded to her, in a hard, somewhat stammering twang, in English, was not Fr. Malesvaux's, however, but another's. "Just like you told me to I put enough of it in their food they ought not figure I'm gone till midday." It was Job White Jr. who spoke. I must admit that his presence jarred me, at least momentarily, and I was determined to find out what was going on. I commanded the lamps to come on, and they beamed with an unearthly light. Eugénie and White, ready with sacks at their sides for flight, both suppressed their urge to cry out, but did back away from me immediately.

"What are you doing up here, you black witch?" she said to me, her voice breaking just above a whisper. I was going to answer, but I could hear the hubbub from outside growing louder and closer; with a clarity I have never felt before or since I could see the crowns of the torches gathering in the town square, before they made their way up the hill. I could see them, as I looked at Eugénie and White, who both were so pale as to appear ill. Despite this Eugénie repeated her question, and then said, "We are leaving, and you cannot stop us. I've placed all your demonic writings, your hellish illustrations, that diary full of gibberish and nonsense, in a flour sack just inside Sr. Louis Marie's door. We also left a letter for Job's father, Rev. White, and for others in the town to let him know that the nuns were harboring you, and you won't be able to say a word in your defense. Rather than wondering where I've gotten off to, where we are, they'll—" I silenced her, and exited the room. The door I made sure I sealed shut. Almost as soon as she began pulling on the knob, as he began heaving his shoulder into the wood, their screams started. Downstairs there was a shuffling of feet, and startled wailing. I got to work.

The wall outside the room leading down a storey was an expanse of paint the hue of buttermilk, but, I now knew, I no longer needed it, nor the charcoal I kept in my pocket. Instead as I walked down the stairs I urged Marinette, Rochelle, Hubert, and Moor, all asleep in their quarters out back, to go immediately to the stables and ready horses and carts, which they did, each dressing as quickly as possible, each baffled for a minute that they had had the same aim until they realized its source. I thought about letting the nuns counter the Reverend and the townspeople on their own, but it was not, it seemed to me, the charitable thing to do, and although they had assisted in the maintenance of my bondage, that would endure as a cross for their consciences to bear. I roused each of them from their prayers, their default response in the face of an approaching threat, as if they had lost all command of reason, and set them to motion.

The only white girl other than Eugénie—whose screams, now echoing throughout the upstairs and building, had turned into something almost animal—remaining, Annie Lawrie, had also never been a source of torment, so I hoisted her as if she were a marionette from the corner of her bedroom into which she had barricade herself, and spurred her to aid Marinette, in the process muting her so that she could not give a single order. Not one of the nuns, not the Mother Superior, not even Sr. François Agnès, in whom I had had some semblance of confidence, had thought to ring a warning bell, so I had her do so.

At another window that looked out onto the town below I could see the flames, at the base of the hill, ascending, like a wave of gold, towards the convent. Lamp and candlelight from the room seared through the dark. It was as if I were painting and in the painting at the same time, as if the inside and outside were fusing into one rich, polysensory perspective, and I almost had to stop for a second to steady myself. The nuns, amongst whom I passed though not a single one spotted me, were grabbing crucifixes from the walls, stuffing books and papers into bags, and reciting snatches of Scripture, in French. Their rosaries they did not think to look for, thankfully, since they would not have found them; I had already collected and disassembled them over the last week, so as to have the necessary tools at my disposal. I continued forward, forcing Annie Lawrie, weeping uncontrollably, down the main stairwell, where she had stalled, and outside to the stables, where Hubert and Marinette had hitched several carts, into which Rochelle had packed enough bread, water and dried food to keep everyone fed for at least a day or two.

When I reached the Mother Superior's room, the sack containing all my handiwork was not where Eugénie had claimed, but sitting beneath a desk. Whether she had put it there or the Mother Superior had moved it was unclear, but no matter. It was heavier than I thought it would be, but once I rifled through it I was sure that save for the maps everything I had accomplished since arriving here filled it. I hefted it over my shoulder and started to leave the room, when, glancing back, I saw Fr. Malesvaux, sitting on the edge of the bed, immobile as if stricken. I thought to leave him there, especially as in the blue of his irises and the sunburnt contours of his face I could read the pilasters and eaves of Valdoré, the crop of Nicolas de L'Écart, the fusillade of Napoleon, and L'Ouverture rotting in a forgotten cell, but I thought better of it, and stirred him such that he barreled past me, wearing only his dressing gown.

There was nothing in my own room that I needed to take with me beyond the pitcher of water and the washing bowl that sat beside Eugénie's bed. I made my way back to the attic, stopping briefly to peer first into the back grounds, where I could see everyone seated on horses or piled into the carts, which began to take off toward the river's oxbow, Moor's knowledge of the area enough to save them, and then out front, where a contingent of the townspeople, their faces lit white with torchlights, were belling around in a semicircle on the front drive, chanting for the nuns to open the door and show their faces, and to bring Job White Jr., Eugénie, and me out. I thought to turn them all into a giant, writhing pyre, but that time, I knew, would come.

The door opened with little effort, and I closed it tight behind me. Eugénie and White had folded themselves into a tiny ball beside a mountain of crates. Both had hollered and wept themselves dry, and neither moved as I entered the room. I paid them no mind and, taking a silver flask, engraved with the initials "NDL," which I knew she had filled with liquor from the cellar, I initiated my procedures, pouring a generous libation accompanied by prayers, drawing a circle around me with the wine, filling the washbasin with enough water that I could see my reflection. I sat beside it, formed a filigreed vane with the beads and closed my eyes. Before I could get too far into my imprecations, I heard a voice so tiny it almost sounded as if it were coming from another world. I opened my eyes. Eugénie had risen and planted herself right outside the circle.

"You spook," her voice boomed, "I command you to get up and let us out of here. And you're going to hitch up one of the horses right after you open that door. Did you forget you still belong to me? Now be a good heifer and do what I tell you!" I closed my eyes and continued my prayers, opening them only to peer into the water, onto which a variety of images, first two dimensional as in my drawings and then, as if looking into a magical screen in which life itself could be projected, took shape, color and form.

Nisi audiam no te exaudiam. The fragrance of fire taking wing through the bowers of trees fused with voices thundering just beyond the nearby pane to generate an effect not unlike a nervous system subjected to an intense and continuous shock. I trembled but pressed onward with my chant.

"Ma négresse," the girl said firmly, though no longer screaming, and still outside the circle, "ouvre la porte maintenant." White was yanking on the doorknob, but it would not budge. "Have you forgotten how close we once were? How you were ma pétite poupée? Ma chère, open that door." On the screen before me I could see those days, she in her pastel lawn following me from room to room, interrupting my tasks with questions, demands, how she kept me up late and woke me before dawn, how she would extend her thin pink ankle just before I took a step, her chamberpot in tow, sending it and me spilling down the stairs, how she placed the knife to the small of my back and ordered me to prepare the wagon and stallion to carry her and her barely breathing mother to the port.

Build a castle on sand, even with lime, and it will eventually be a gift to the sea. I did not even have to raise my hand to drive the pictures from the water's surface. Battering on the main door below began to resound all the way up to the ceiling above us.

"Carmel," the child said, almost softly, though I could feel the blade in every word, "let us go. You can join us if you want to. Once we get to the Northwest Territory I might even set you free. Don't you want to save yourself, don't you want to be free?"

I thought about her offer for a second—seeing the three of us, they on the one aged gelding still on the grounds, and I on foot chasing behind them as they galloped off into the dark, then me helping her across the Tennessee as White and the sack of coins he had emptied from his father's safes sank to its brown depths, and then me foraging on her behalf for something to sustain us as we proceeded through the land the Chickasaws still tenaciously had held onto, where she nevertheless would encounter her own people as well, as they had seeped like an underground leak from one end of this region to the other—but no longer. Instead, I rose and answered her, "Fòk mwen te manke w pou m te kap apresye w." The door swung open, sweeping her and White out. I resumed my position and continued searching in the watery mirror, until I finally found my mother's face.

A DIALOGUE

Are you going to waste yet another opportunity to save yourself?

Didn't I already tell you I refused to think of them as wasted opportunities to save myself, but rather as stages in my careful process of preparation.

So you are ready to take action?

Have you been so busy you weren't paying attention?

Don't forget who you are speaking to.

Don't forget who you are speaking to.

I think I have finally come to appreciate your logic.

Perhaps, I find myself recounting to Phedra, Marinette and others, it will be left to the patience of someone more devoted to the genre of literature than I to record the noises that filled that hot and moonless night in Kentucky, or the taste that lingered on the tongues of the few survivors after the gunpowder stored beneath the printing press caught fire, or the particular stench of burning brick and plaster and ink fused with flesh and hair, or the feeling of being thrown far, far into the black air with nothing to halt your eventual fall back to the parched, grassless soil ... I personally shall never forget how that scene—so distant from where I was then that it required all my powers to concentrate—reminded me of nothing less than a forget-me-not, white with bright scars of crimson and azure, holding fast like a last memory or reliquary of sorrows against the bluffs above a small, almost forgotten provincial island or inland colonial town.

II

ENCOUNTERNARRATIVES

Knowledge is submarine.

Edward Kamau Brathwaite

*I believe that if we have any notion at all of what has generally
been called human nature, it is because History, like a mirror,
holds up for our contemplation, an image of ourselves.*

Edgardo Rodríguez Juliá

*He never tires of the journey, he who is the darkest one,
the darkest one of them all.*

Adrienne Kennedy

THE AERONAUTS

S*cream* I holler to Horatio's, Nimrod's and Rosaline's laughter, then they're asking me to tell it to them again, though I plead how at this age I can't hardly even remember my name. Horatio says, "Red, come on, just one more time cause you ain't fooling us," and I start with how it began six months before all that happened, round the middle of May, 1861, when I showed up for my job as a steward at the final Saturday of the spring lecture series at the Academy of Natural Sciences of Philadelphia. I had spent that morning toiling under my regular boss, Dameron, helping prepare for a grand dinner party he was catering for a Mr. Albert Linde, president of the Philadelphia Equitable Mutual Insurance Company, and was glancing up at the wall clock so often I nearly cut my thumbs off dicing rhubarbs. Dameron couldn't afford an accident so he switched me over to kneading the bread and pie doughs, then had me stir the turtle soup stock. Finally he released me a little early with the promise that I'd be back promptly, at four o'clock. Dameron didn't gainsay me earning a little extra from my side job, but he also had warned me more than once about my tardiness. Although I was no great cook, hated being in kitchens and hated even more ordering anyone around, catering was going be my profession, cause as my daddy used to say, "Anybody can cook a bad meal for theyself but rich folks always welcome help to eat well."

I ran the eight blocks from Dameron's to Orators Hall on Broad, where the Academy held its Saturday talks, and almost as soon as I slipped in the back door, I heard Kerney, the head of stewards, ringing his bell, calling us to order because the lecture was about to begin. I was completely out of breath but I immediately shucked off my dingy gingham trousers and brown cooking smock, and crammed myself into my uniform, which had belonged to Old Gabriel Tinsley till he came down stricken on Christmas the year before. The Prussian blue kersey waistcoat and trousers, still carrying his regular scent of wet cinders, were almost too tight on my thighs and backside. I mopped the sweat off my brow, knotted my gray cravat from memory, cause there wasn't a mirror in the stewards' dressing room, and hurried out to the main hall.

All of the other stewards, including my older brother Jonathan, were already finishing up their tasks, gliding between the reception room and the main hall. They had emptied and polished the brass bowls of the standing ashtrays, transferred the Amontillado sherry from the glass decanters into the miniature crystal glasses, and brushed the last specks of lint from the main serving table's emerald baize cover. Jonathan nodded to me as several of the stewards began ushering the guests from the alcove to their seats, but I didn't see Kerney though I had certainly heard that bell. Several gentlemen, members of the Academy and their guests, entered the hall and as I attempted to head over to guide each to one of the other stewards who would be seating them, I felt fingers winching round my forearm, like the claws of an ancient bird the Academy would probably exhibit, and sour breath warming my ear: "Boy, if you had walked through that door there even a second later I would thrown you out in the street myself! Late one more time and there won't be no damn next time."

I turned to see Kerney fixing me with his red-eyed stare. I could smell he had been tasting, or how he liked to say testing, the sherry, and probably had been tallying every second on the main hall clock's little hand past the time I was supposed to walk through that door. I eased myself out his grip, his crisped apple face tracking me across the room, and took care not to look in his direction. Soon as I reached my assigned spot Dr. Cassin, the president of the Academy, Dr. Cresson, who ran the Franklin Institute, and the afternoon's speaker, another professor I recalled from a prior lecture, took their seats, the customary hush settled over the room, and the five other stewards and I assumed our places. Shoulder to shoulder we lined up, erect as a row of tin soldiers, facing the lecture hall's high, windowless, crimson wall. Stock still, thighs against the table edge, chins up, our white cotton-gloved right hands palm-down over the lowest button of our waistcoats, we were so quiet you could forget we were there.

In the front row next to Dr. Cassin, Dr. Cresson, the speaker, and the other Academy dignitaries sat as always almost completely out of my sight. The most recently hired of the crew, I had started only at the beginning of this year's spring series, in February, through Jonathan's intercession on my behalf with Kerney, and so I stood last in the row and farthest from the front of the room, though I could spot the dais and lectern. This month's crowd was noticeably larger than in April. Thirty-six white gentlemen in the room I calculated, from the furthestmost chair in the front row to the nearest one in the last, whereas at the meeting the month before, which had unfortunately fallen on the same weekend as the attack on the South Carolina fort, starting the war, only twenty members and their guests showed up to hear the speaker, Professor Benjamin Peirce of Harvard. He had delivered a talk on his discovery that the rings of Saturn were not solid and how he had proved the other researchers wrong, and even if I had not learned enough mathematics or natural science at the Institute to follow him, I enjoyed his lecture, despite his talking so fast that he lullabied most of the audience to sleep.

Afterward as I brought my sherry tray around I passed by Professor Peirce talking to City Councilor Mr. Trego and Dr. Leidy, both members of the Academy; a guest I didn't know; and Mr. Peter Robins, the son, not his father who ran the bank. As soon as he saw me young Mr. Robins started up the same "game" he had initiated every month since I had worked there, saying to his party, "I think Theodore here pays as much attention as we do," as if he was expecting me to say something in reply, but I smiled and instead lifted the tray of sherry glasses higher. Mr. Councilor Trego looked around the room, Dr. Leidy whispered something to his guest, while the Harvard professor was looking at me all quizzically, then Mr. Peter Robins again said, "Theodore always pays close attention, don't you, he's a *very* sharp boy," and I responded with another smile since I noted Kerney's glares. Professor Peirce turned to the three white men and said very rapidly as he combed his fingers through his gray beard, "Certainly my lectures can be a bit dense even for those who have had the benefit of reading them in advance, and my astronomical work and other proofs provoke particular challenges," to which Mr. Robins said, "Theodore, tell our distinguished guest one of the things you heard him speak about today." At that moment Kerney I could see was turning red as tenderloin and looking like he was about to come slap me if I opened my mouth.

Before Mr. Robins, also reddening in the cheeks, could repeat his request I said, "Well, Sir, the professor was talking about the universality of physical laws and the uniformity with spiritual law too, and said at one point that every part of the universe have—has— the same laws of mechanical action as you find in the human mind." Mr. Robins grinned and patted me on the head, and Mr. Councilor Trego and Dr. Leidy nodded approvingly, though Professor Peirce continued to stare at me like I was a puzzle. To break the silence I said, "May I take you gentlemen's glasses?" After they turned to walk away young Mr. Robins pulled out some coins and placed them in my hand, saying, "A special tip for your *far more amusing* contribution to our series." When he caught up to Professor Peirce, who had joined another nearby group, the Professor once again spoke, his words gushing forth, "Isn't that an articulate and clever little...."

Not that I can truly recall *everything* unless I am paying attention, and my mother was always warning me about allowing my memory or the past to overmaster me, let things go she would say, just like she would admonish me not to let my mind fly too far, too fast into such things, lest I couldn't bring it back down to earth, because, as she was fond of saying and my father was too, "Outside the most exalted leaders of our race what sort of life you think there is for us if our heads stay too far up in them clouds?" and if anything has to do with the clouds it's mathematics and astronomy and so forth, which unlike history or literature I had never disliked, and I wasn't too bad at figures, plus if you think about it, even I could see from all the preaching I had to sit through that the cloud talk also had to do with religion, which is what I also think Professor Peirce was saying but I couldn't tell nobody there that, all they all were trying to do at those lectures was figure out how things of this world and the next one worked but also to see if, outside of a church, they could reason Him out, and thinking about that reminded me of how when I was little I used to like to spend my Saturday afternoons reading about science and strange places and looking at the maps at the Free Library, which we too were allowed to visit, and I will never forget seeing a book on display there by Mr. Audubon, about whom Dr. Cassin, who was also a famous ornithologist, gave the lecture the month before Professor Pierce's.

At this month's talk Jonathan as usual was standing three places closer to the dais, and I spied him once again trying not to fall asleep, since every one of the lectures, no matter how interesting, he found boring. He clearly was also tired, because he also worked most Saturday mornings, like this one, as he did all week as a stockboy at Kahnweiler's dry goods store. Since our father had been taken out by that gang on the West Side, all of us had shouldered extra jobs to add to what my mother brought in from her sewing. Zenobia, who had just married, like Zephira, worked in the houses, while Lucius, the oldest, was a janitor at the Customs House, and he and Zephira already had their own households to support. Before he died my father on his deathbed said to me, "Theodore, promise me that you will have Christ in your heart, and take up a trade, and not turn idle or fall into the arms of iniquity, and not truckle or bow down to no white man, and whatever you do, do not be a burden to your mother, your brothers or your sisters, and always help out another colored person if you can do so, and keep your head, like your feet, on the ground." Of course I assured him I would do all that, and had already taken up a trade, and wouldn't bow down to white people, though his failure to step to the side and not argue back with that pack of Irish ruffians had consigned him to that very bed, and I especially stressed I would not be a burden to nobody, though my mother, when she grew upset at one thing or another, like my lateness or impetuousness or day-dreaming or failure to join her for church, predicted I was sinking into downfall's deep waters.

As I observed my brother I thought about how like our father Jonathan and Lucius were, tall, slender, almost military in bearing, charming but with God's fury if you crossed them, and how while we three had gotten our mother's open face and light brown eyes, I was the one, along with my sisters, who ended up with her slight, diminutive stature, cloud of auburn hair, and freckles that turned the shade of pumpkins soon as the summer sun rolled in. From the time I was ten or so I had hoped and even beseeched Jesus I would gain a few more inches, because at 16 1/2, despite my mustache and chin and chest hairs coming in, I always had to stand on my tiptoes at public events, or people were mistaking me for a child. Worse, after my best friend and former classmate Horatio, tall as Jonathan and twice as muscular, now standing beside me and also almost slumbering, had left the Institute for Colored Children six months before the end of the previous school year to start working, I had had to fight my way past taunts and punches nearly every morning and afternoon for weeks.

In the midst of my musings I heard Dr. Cassin clattering up to the lectern, but I knew not to look at him because Kerney was on the other side of the room watching me closely, and after the last lecture, by Professor Peirce, he had warned me about acting like I was one of the guests. Instead I stared at a random spot on the high red wall, well above the heads of Academy members and their guests, moving my eye between it and the gentlemen I could identify, including Mr.

Robins and his friend, Mr. Linde, a scientist who also always attended the talks. When I tired of that I mulled over my evening obligations. I had already washed and hung-dry the white shirt and hose Dameron lent me, and scrubbed away the dirt and stains from the black swallow coat and trousers—

Dr. Cassin's voice rung out: "Gentlemen, scholars and fellow members of the Academy, and to our distinguished guests and visitors to our beloved city and lecture series, I say good afternoon and welcome. Although I am a man of science, I am also, as they say, *un amateur du monde natural et scientifique,* and in that capacity I beg your indulgence. I should begin by invoking the esteemed philosopher Aristotle, as this Academy and the aims to which it and we are honorably dedicated, are to that greatest of the effects of the mind at work dedicated, that is to say, to the pursuit of the betterment of mankind through those means we yet have and are still developing, by which I mean: science, in her many faces, including the fields to which our most esteemed speaker today is devoted…." In this same way Dr. Cassin opened each introduction, his voice a rake dragging across winter earth, which made me think about how my sometime, Rosaline, little sister of Angelica, the girl who had candied Jonathan, had sent back my most recent note unopened. Far as I knew nothing bad had transpired between us, but something had caused her to cool.

A round of polite applause, and then another white gentleman, this one much younger, the one I recognized earlier talking with Dr. Cassin and Dr. Cresson, was standing on the dais. From his grey longcoat he extracted a thick square, his talk it turned out, folded several times over. He fumbled with it, smoothing it down, and though most of the gentlemen seated stayed silent, amongst some of them ran a current of whispers provoking frowns from Mr. Robins and Mr. Linde. Yet the gentleman at the lectern, who would certainly have heard the murmured censure, didn't appear in the least perturbed. Instead, he continue to assemble his papers, smoothing and arranging, not looking up, until he finally did and said, "My distinguished guests, I appreciate your indulgence and your presence this May afternoon. As the Academy's eminent leader Dr. Cassin noted, I am Thaddeus Lowe, and I appear before you to speak about the advances, with which many of you are already quite familiar, in the science of flight, human flight."

Horatio's weight was pressing in on me, and I saw he was about to topple over, so I hooked my foot around the back of his and kicked till I stirred him to attention. The very idea of human flight fascinated me so that I concentrated on everything Professor Lowe had to say. "For the entire history of mankind, he has carried not just in heart but in mind the dream of riding the air. Perhaps this is a vestigial phantasy born of our lifelong witness of the clouds, our long familiarity with birds and God's other flying creatures, with our thirst for knowledge of the heavens and of the angelic orders. . . ." I was training my gaze on that single spot across the room, while Professor Lowe spoke about the myths and history of human flight. He touched upon the Greek myths, Icarus and Dedalus, some Frenchman, a range of other pioneers including Americans like John Wise, and John Steiner, who was, he noted, a resident of this city just as he was. The professor recounted his own experiments and demonstrations, with ample details about different types of gases used and the materials the balloons required, his calculations and conversations with other members of the Academy, such as Dr. Henry, at the College of New Jersey, and the beneficence of Dr. Cresson and the city's Gas Works.

I found myself even more involved when he reached the technical elements of the flights. Professor Lowe launched into a story about how just weeks before today he had attempted to demonstrate to the people of Cincinnati something about the practicality of balloon flight by traveling in an aerostat to the federal capital, but ended up off course and drifted all the way south to South Carolina, *after* Fort Sumter! When he said this most of the audience sat up, and someone on the far side of the room emitted a noise somewhere between a cough and a harrumph. The simple country people who took him prisoner, Professor Lowe said, thought he might be an evil spirit, or at least a spy, so to prove he was who he said he was he announced that he had brought Cincinnati newspapers, which sat in the basket and which he handed out, but as he was a Northerner they were still quite suspicious, so he still had to wait until several brethren men of science, all Southerners, could fully vouch for him and guarantee his safe passage home.

Course I wasn't allowed to say anything, not even "Good afternoon, Sir," unless he spoke to me first, and even then not a thing more than "Yes, Sir" or "No, Sir," but when he finished and the question portion commenced, if I could have I would have asked him specifically about what it felt like when he was high up enough to see past the tops of the mountains, whether he could touch the clouds, was the sun brighter than on the ground. How, I wondered, did it look with all of Ohio behind him and Kentucky out front below? How was he sure he would be able to land and not just keep soaring higher and higher until he headed toward the moon? Then I estimated these would have been the most foolish questions ever asked at any Academy lecture I had ever heard, and was glad I had to stay silent and listen, though a number of the questions that started coming were not that much better than mine. One gentleman asked him if he wore special clothes to prevent from freezing when so high in the air, another asked him how did he keep the gas from blowing up, yet another pressed to know if he had ever crashed and broken any limbs. The scientists, all of them, asked better questions, it seemed to me, about flight patterns, machinery, and aeronautical science, though Professor Lowe responded politely to everyone.

Soon as he ended and before the audience applauded Kerney gestured that it was sherry serving time, unless we were on the coat detail which I wasn't. I fetched my tray, arranged the glasses on it soon as they were filled, and slipped into the smaller reception hall where the guests were milling about. I stayed in my assigned post till my tray emptied then went and loaded up again while Jonathan and one of the other stewards collected the empties, our routine until Kerney's signal to clean up. As I stood there, my mind alternating between the account of the balloon flight and thoughts about souping turtles, which I hated to do, all that shell and tendon and soft flesh, up came young Mr. Robins, with Mr. Linde. I extended them the tray of sherry and Mr. Robins acknowledged it with a half smile, as he said to his friend, "But they have always been unreasonable. It does not take the most careful student in the history of this country, Neddy, to grasp that every foot we have given them has been turned not just into an ell but a tyrant's mile, especially under Buchanan, and it was on the pretext of last fall's campaign, let alone victory, that they began the process for cleaving us in two. I view this mess as the opportunity to discipline them once and for all."

Mr. Linde did not say anything at first, but sipped his sherry and stroked his chestnut mustache, nearly as sparse as mine though he was, I knew, in his early twenties like Mr. Robins. Another man round the same age approached them, Rev. Hodge, whom I overheard tell someone's guest at my first shift back in February that he had only a few years ago graduated from the theological seminary in New Jersey. He said, "Peter, don't you think that if we pursue things as Lincoln appears likely to do this will all turn out very badly? Speaking not as a clergyman but as an American. There'll certainly be consequences."

Mr. Robins finished off his sherry in a gulp. I accepted his empty glass and passed him another. I glanced to my right and Horatio, perched like me with his tray almost empty, was watching me closely, as if he was trying to tell me something I should be able to figure out, while to my left I saw Jonathan collecting more empty glasses. I looked back at my tray and tried to imagine how many people would be manning and attending the party I was working tonight, if there'd be a band or not or two, like the event I had jobbed two weeks ago out at the estate in Merion. They had carried on so well past dawn that we all had to sleep on the cellar or attic floors till morning, then we helped the man's staff clean up and each of us got a little $2 more, because those people, Dameron said, had so much money it was flowing like the Bushkill Falls, and that man even provided us with special coaches to get back to the city so we didn't have to walk or hop the railway—

—"Neddy," Mr. Robins was saying, "is playing the taciturn but he has stronger convictions on the matter than me, Hodge, I assure you. He's still taken with Lowe's lecture, clearer to his mind than mine, but then he is the one who studied such things at the old college." At this Mr. Linde nodded. "Remember he's the one who made a pilgrimage up to Cambridge to spend a year studying at Lawrence. The whole time Lowe was lecturing he was probably transforming the words into equations."

Mr. Linde continued sipping for a bit before pulling a small bound notebook and pencil from his inner coat pocket. He said, tapping his temple with the book, "This is just between us," and, leaning in, Mr. Robins and Rev. Hodge bowing in close too, continued, "but if Lowe does get an aeronautic corps going, I'll be first on his list. I was planning to sign up in any case, but I especially fancy flying in one of those contraptions, even if we end up sailing off to Florida or some other preposterous place." He and Mr. Robins started laughing but Rev. Hodge shook his head. None saw the older Mr. Robins, Dr. Cresson, and Professor Lowe approach until they stood right behind the younger trio.

Mr. Robins senior offered his round of introductions, and young Mr. Robins, Rev. Hodge and Mr. Linde all praised Professor Lowe's lecture, thanking Dr. Cresson and Dr. Leidy, who I could see was circulating on the other side of the room, for inviting him. They launched into some small crosstalk until young Mr. Robins abruptly said, pointing to me with his near-empty sherry glass, "This boy here pays as much attention as we do, don't you, Theodore?" and I immediately grew nervous because I had never ever said a single thing in front of Dr. Cresson beyond "Yes, Sir," or "Thank you, Sir," and usually only played young Mr. Robins's "game" with his friends and the given month's guest. I smiled, raised the tray, and smiled again, but young Mr. Robins persisted, saying, "Come on, Theodore, why don't you tell our guest, Professor Lowe, at least one thing you heard him talk about?" Mr. Robins senior was looking at me, Dr. Cresson was frowning, and Rev. Hodge's cheeks were deepening to wine, but Professor Lowe and Mr. Linde looked like they expected to hear me speak, to respond to young Mr. Robins's request. I wanted to call Jonathan over, snare Horatio's attention, even have Kerney bail me out by snatching me away, because the whole room appeared to be pausing until I uttered my reply.

I said, "Professor Lowe say—said—that when he flew the Pioneer balloon last year, watched even by the Japanese ambassadors and their retinue, it rose to two and one half miles above this city, Philadelphia, and he experienced a 'mirror effect' in the clouds, then he travel—traveled—all the way to New Jersey's ocean-side before the lower currents brung it back about 18 miles to here."

Professor Lowe's eyes scoured my face, they all did, then he turned to young Mr. Robins and said, "This boy apparently took exceptional mental notes, I barely remember having said that, correct though it is, at all." He clapped, then they all clapped, save Rev. Hodge, who appeared somewhat annoyed. After Professor Lowe patted me on the shoulder, nearly causing me to drop my tray, they dispersed toward another group, except young Mr. Robins, who told me, "That was splendid, Theodore. Before you leave today you will get quite a treat." Mr. Edward Linde walked back over, and looking me straight in the eyes, said, "Like a little machine. I especially appreciated the details because my memory is like pumice stone—" to which young Mr. Robins said, "Though you can work anything out from first principles, Neddy, which is more than I or anyone else in this room can do." Mr. Linde handed me a carte de visite, which I tucked in my pocket, continuing, "so if you find yourself seeking work, write me or call upon me care of that address and you can join me at the Aeronautic Corps, wherever we are." Young Mr. Robins patted me on the head, as he usually did, and said to his friend, "You know, I'll even put Theodore in a balloon and have him fly himself down there to you, or perhaps in a BOX to do the same," at which he burst out laughing so hard he had to take out his handkerchief to wipe his eyes. He kept repeating "Box" to Mr. Linde, who did not appear to find it humorous, as they joined a nearby circle.

All the while I was wondering if Mr. Edward Linde was the son of or somehow related to Mr. Albert Linde, the host of the evening's event, and I thought given how he had addressed me that maybe I should say something, yet we were forbidden to talk to the members or guests unless they spoke to us first. Later, when we were done, young Mr. Robins before he left gave me several crisp bills about which he said, Mr. Edward Linde standing right there, "Don't tell a soul" although I knew Kerney, Jonathan and the others had seen him give me something extra after we played his "game," and I thanked him profusely and replied that I wouldn't. As he filed out Mr. Edward Linde, looking straight at me, once again tapped his temple with his notebook and stated in a clear voice, "Remember."

Once all the attendees had left and I was in back changing, Kerney for a change didn't pay me any attention, in part because he was busy counting out the money. Horatio, shirtless, looped his long knotty arm dark as roofing felt around me and said, "You going to meet me to hit the streets 'night, s'right?"

"I got a shift tonight, Ray-Ray," I told him, adding, "Party for Dameron, where I'm heading once I get change again, then I head out to it before sundown."

Horatio removed his arm from my shoulders and laid his immense hand on my knee. "Edray, I think you don't love ya boy no more." He directed this not just to me but announced it as if he was trying to make sure some of the other stewards sitting near us heard him. They chuckled but paid him no special mind, and continued dressing and cleaning up. Then he grabbed my goatee and pulled on it, hauling me forward until I slapped his hand.

"Watch it, now, ignay," I told him, as I often did since he wanted to keep on roughhousing around like we had as children, "don't be fooling like that."

"See what I mean." He rose and tucked in his shirt. "Y'ain't got no love for ya boy no more. I'ma still come by ya place and drag you out there, even if you sound asleep. Can't let these coins burn a hole in my pocket." He flashed the beacon of his large white teeth and I couldn't stay mad at him, but when he reached for my chin hairs again I put up fists, mock fighting, though I knew he could flatten me with a single punch if it ever came to that.

"Get your pay and you got to clear out of here!" Kerney had stacked the money in piles for each of us on a table, so we lined up and collected what was ours. When I reached mine he said, baring the yellow kernels in his mouth as if trying to appear friendly, "Better not end up in the bottom of them rivers, boy, cause I spect to see you come September, y'understand?" and I answered him, "Yes Sir, Mr. Kerney, and you have a good summer too." I grabbed my pay and raced outside, where Horatio and Jonathan were waiting.

"Where, you off to, Dameron?" Jonathan was rolling a moundlet of tobacco from a pouch he kept in his waistcoat in a piece of newspaper look like he took from the back room.

"Sure nough, what about you?"

"Bout to go relax these dogs for a little bit fore I go get Angie. She get off today round 4." He was licking the end of his cigarette but didn't have a light. "We sposed to be meeting up with Johnny and his lady, and Tut-Tut and Queenie, we probably go try to find a dance or something to get into."

Horatio was quiet, looking like he wanted to leave but I could tell he was waiting till Jonathan did so first so that we could walk together and talk.

"Well if'n I don't see you fore you head out I'll catch you when I get in," Jonathan said, "I don't need to tell you but I'm going to, Red. Stay out of trouble." We all slapped palms then he scooted off to light his cigarette at a pushcart down the street and cool wherever he cooled when he wasn't at home or Angelica's.

"You walking to Dameron right now?" Horatio asked, towering over me.

"Sure nough, I need them coins, what you doing?"

"Ain't on for no upholstering this evening, prolly just going to go home, you know it be like the circus up in there, can't hardly even breathe with all of them. Edray, I almost didn't have no shoes this morning cause Franklin walking out the door with mines." We laughed in unison at the thought of his brother, with even bigger feet than his, stumbling in Horatio's boots out the door. As we did so he winched his long arm around my shoulders. I could smell his underarms cutting through the rosewater he had splashed on himself in the backroom, and the combination was not at all bad. "Why don't we take some ladies out tomorrow after service for a stroll, that'll get you to hang out with ya boy, no?"

I paused there on the walkway. "Rosaline sent my last note back, she ain't want to talk to me at all when I seen her two days ago. Who I supposed to take out if I ain't got no lady?" Horatio stood in front of me.

"I'll talk to Rosaline, you remember how her sister Janie was sweet on me." And he was right, Janie, a year older than us, had been utterly infatuated with my best friend for several years, beginning when we were thirteen or so, until she gave her heart completely to Christ and chilled on everyone who wasn't always in church except her immediately family, and strangely, Horatio. "Say yes and I'll head over there right now." I looked up at him and he cupped my chin, drawing his face closer and closer to mine until I pushed his hand away, though for a second I felt I wanted him to put it back. Horatio slid back alongside me and was now looking off into the Saturday crowds, all the human hustle and bustle up Broad, the horses and coaches and wagons, people alighting on or off the street cars. I seized both his big hands, which immediately grabbed his attention, and said, "You talk to her for me and we definitely roll tomorrow," though I knew it probably would just be me and him in the park playing Takeaway or improvised cribbage.

"Bet, Edray," he said and I answered, "Bet and better be, Ray-Ray," we slapped palms, then I darted through the maze of traffic to Dameron's.

When I had finished all my preparatory tasks for the soup and the desserts, which the main cooks would take charge of, I beat a path straight home and lay down, feeling the day's work had wrung me out. My mother wasn't there, Jonathan neither, so I spread out on the bed I shared with him and just let my mind float free thinking about Rosaline and what I might have done to cool her so, and about Horatio, who did know how to talk to or least get the attention of girls, though he didn't ever really seem to want to. Jonathan also had that charm, girls and people in general had always flocked to him. I consoled myself by recalling that too much nectar, my mother would warn, would draw more than the butterfly. Always fumbling and stumbling and saying the wrong thing, I didn't have whatever it was anyhow. I forgot to look girls in the eye, bring them something sweet, special, cajole and inveigle them to reach that sweeter spot. Rosaline nevertheless had used to like to spend time with me especially during our last year at the Institute. As I traced circles on my stomach and thighs I reminded myself that truth be told I didn't want to be courting so hard yet anyway, although I knew having a sweetheart was best when the summer came and you could sit up on the riverbank and watch the steamboats streaming by, or walk the promenade late on a Sunday afternoon after services, and I liked when Horatio and me had gone courting together, I would be studying what he said and deploying my own version, and now I could feel my eyes leadening but I knew not to fall into a deep sleep, because I might miss tonight's job—

—And I heard Mama calling out, "Theodore, if you sleeping wake up, sugar, and get dressed," and I rose, washed up, scrubbed my teeth with baking soda even, donned my serving clothes. Before I left I gave Mama, who as soon as she set her sacks down had begun readying dinner, a big kiss on the cheek and some money then I headed off to Mr. Linde's.

I hopped on the streetcar that ran up Broad, since that one we could ride and the conductor was one I saw all the time, he never spoke but didn't curse me either. I let the white folks climb inside then I held out my coin and he snatched it, I grabbed on, wondering as we rode whether I might not be too early. I glanced around for a clock in a pane, and seeing none, asked the conductor what time it was. He consulted his pocket watch and said, "Seven past six." I had almost an hour and a half, so I rode up a few blocks to Prune. With the party two blocks east of Rittenhouse Square, I decided to kill time by walking a roundabout route down to the Schuylkill before circling back. Right outside the New Opera House I ran into Reverend Johnson, the pastor of our old church, who asked about my mother, and then once on Pine I saw the Holland twins, and Miss Catto, who wanted to chat for a good minute. On Aspen, I paused to talk briefly with my former classmate Simpson, shoveling up manure, who people called both Simple *and* Samson since he fell first off a horse, then off a roof, and had survived both. At S. 23rd I ran into another acquaintance and former classmate, Amos, sweeping the sidewalk outside a row of stores. He asked me why I was all dressed up, then said if Dameron had any openings to let him know. He also warned to watch myself near the river, but I assured him I already knew to be careful, and reminded him that steps from the Water Works near here they had slain my father one evening three months ago. I said goodbye to Amos, picking up my pace and counting down the blocks until I could see the wharves and boats, and be ready, if need be, to run.

A couple blocks from the river, near Cope, from behind the corner of a warehouse my first cousin on my daddy's side, Daniel Lyons, emerged, smoking a cheroot as thick as a tree limb, and soon as he saw me he tipped his brim and called me over. He had been a few years ahead of Horatio and me in school, though after Jonathan, but he had always seemed as if he were much older. People in the streets called him "Dandylion," though to me he was just "Dandy." The blue serge suit he sported was as fine as anything the white gentleman at the Academy this afternoon had worn, and even in the evening light the rings glinted from every other one of his stubby copper fingers. I hadn't seen him in a while but wherever he happened to be, my mother warned me constantly, so was trouble. Nevertheless I didn't know anybody walking the streets of Philadelphia who could stay so close to danger yet outside the lasso of the law or always have as good a time doing so.

"Uzcay, where you rolling?" He extended his cigar. I declined. When he pulled a flask out of his inner pocket and offer me some after he took a sip, I declined again.

"Work, Uzcay," I said. "An event. Near Rittenhouse Square."

"Ahh." He smoothed his full mustache, which looked like he had been trimming and waxing it for decades. He added, "Rittenhouse. That's some fancy pish, Red. What you doing over here? Little play before you toil the night away?"

"Just got some time, taking a walk to burn it off before I got to sweat."

"Sweet," he said. "What time they expecting you? I want to show you something if you got just a few minutes." His voice lowered, like he didn't want anybody, not even me, to hear what he was about to say. A man on a horse trotted past and he grew silent. "Something real good. Only for my blood."

"Oh no, Dandy," I said, registering at that moment that I ought to slap palms and run straight to the event, even if I had to expend a half hour to spare just milling about outside the back gate or in the square itself. "I can't be late for this, I swear."

"Why you think I'ma make you late? Edray, my little man, come on now. All I axing you for is a few minutes. Just got something to show you. Know you'll like it." He took off his hat and stroked his perfectly parted and pomaded head of hair, the shine on the black bales setting off his beringed fingers.

"What is it? Where is it?" I looked around and wondered at that moment what Dandylion was even doing over in this neighborhood with all the toughs and bandits and everything else, especially since these west-side white folks were known for jumping out of alleys ready to fight. I told him, "Look, Dandy, I wish I could roll with you right now but I got to get to work. Plus, this area over here—"

"See, Uzcay," he said, "you always wanna be like that. Hincky. Last time we cooled it ain't you have a good time?" and he was right, we had gone to a house south of here, ten blocks perhaps past the Naval Asylum, where some people he knew had set up a gambling parlor, with enough free liquor for a shipload of sailors, several fiddlers, and hours of dancing. There were even white folks there too. Before that, right after I turned fifteen I had ridden the ferry with him to Camden to attend a cockfight, and had had my first taste of beer there. "Rittenhouse Square is it?"

"Just east of there. I swear I can't miss work, Dandy, you know how hard things is these days."

"Red, cool your heels. You ain't going to miss no work, we only going a few blocks away, in the direction of Rittenhouse. By the time we done you could crawl there and still wouldn't be late." So he started walking but I stayed where I was, until I spied these two white boys, men really, across the street, they were watching me, not frowning but not looking neutral either, and at the very moment they started to advance in my direction I thought it best to follow Dandy.

At a three-story building that on the outside looked like any other on the block but also like one in which no one had lived for a while, he knocked six times on the weathered front door. I started to turn around as soon as we entered because it was very dark, except for a single lamp, not even gas, in the foyer, but Dandy took my arm, guiding me up the stairs, past a brother I didn't even see at first with a face so hard it could cut metal, though when our eyes met they contained the glimmers of assent, slightly reassuring me. We reached the second floor, which appeared empty though I could hear things going on in several of the rooms, cackling, flesh clapping against flesh, dice or marbles hitting a wall. Dandy proceeded up the stairs to the third storey, still holding my arm, and I knew then that I should turn around but I also wanted badly to see what he had in store.

We walked down a near-black hallway, and he again knocked six times on a door. To our left I noticed another door open but a crack. I walked over toward it and peeking in it saw a stairwell look like it led to the roof. The door Dandy had rapped on opened, baring a brother, face backlit by lamplight. Dandy pushed in, towing me with him. Before us sat a bed, face down in it, I saw squinting, lay a white lady, least I thought she was white, and a female, but sheets covered her legs, pillows concealed her head. Since she wasn't moving I didn't know if she was alive. The room stank of sweat and piss, no one had ever cleaned up in here, and I could also smell urine rising from the floorboards and the dark sheet shrouding the window. I turned toward the door and Dandy grabbed my elbow and said, "See, I told you I had something I know you'd like. Who don't want a pretty girl like that?"

The brother, double our age, probably 30, skinny as a knifeblade and just as ugly, whose presence I had almost completely forgotten, piped up from the shadows, "Who this little red bastard, you only sposed to be up here by yourself."

"This my cousin, slave," Dandy replied, placing his hand inside his jacket like he had a shank or revolver in there, and I really wished I had left him on Cope and just headed straight to the event. "What mine is my blood, plus you owe me triple anyway." While he was talking the white lady began moaning and lifted her behind in the air and spread her legs wide open. "Just think of this as partial repayment."

The man looked from me to Dandy, then said, "Y'all got an hour with her, and no mad shit neither," and Dandy said, "Slave, who the fuck you think you dealing with?" He reached into his jacket again, then said, "Where that special cigar you sposed to have ready?" The man pulled a cylinder, wrapped in what looked like butcher paper, from a cloth pouch slung over his shoulder. "Light it, so we know it okay." The man lit the cigar from a candle near the door, and drew hard on it three or four times, then he passed it to Dandy, and Dandy drew on it some before passing it to me. "You can get out now," he said to the brother, who stood staring at us, "we knows how to tell time." Soon as the door closed, Dandy pointed to the cigar, which reeked of burning trash, and I took a hit, I had smoked tobacco before but I still choked some because it was so strong. When I handed it back to him he took another hit, then rubbed it out on the wall.

"Now Red," he said, "you been with a woman, right?" I nodded, even though I never gotten any further than kisses with Rosaline. Dandy studied my face in the darkness. "That hinky midnight girl I seen you with before, she probably ain't really give you any, though. Nothing like this." Then: "You go first, my treat." I shook my head, which felt so light it might separate from my neck, and again started toward the door, but Dandy said, "You gonna get you some of this grade A first." I was trying to decide what to do when I saw the lady putting her hand between her thighs, saying something I couldn't understand, it was in a foreign language and I was already dizzy but getting excited too, I knew being in this room with this white woman was forbidden and if they caught us they would hang us, but Dandy was stroking the outside of his pants and saying "She and I is both waiting, Red," so I looked for a place to put my clothes. I untied my cravat and removed my shirt and waistcoat, then started to remove my boots when Dandy said, "Naw, leave everything on but tie and shirt, put them on this chair right here, we gotta hurry and I sure 'on't wanna see ya little red ass." He pulled a long knife from somewhere in his suit coat, which he draped over the edge of the chair. Following his lead I left my shirt, tie and waistcoat there, unbuttoned my pants, and shuffled to the bed, where the woman kept saying "Leave, leave." I told Dandy that she was telling us to go away and he said, "Fool, she saying she want you in German, hurry up." I climbed onto the bed, I could smell her woman smell, and from somewhere shit and vinegar, the sheets were damp but not soaked, I couldn't really see her face because she still was concealing it under a pillow, maybe I didn't want to see it, I could see her back curving up white as soapstone in front of me, her behind as fair arching, the thick fair hair on her sex, I leaned closer, kneeling, my knees sinking into the soft mattress, and—

—Dandy was next to me saying, "Put it in, Red," as she hiked her buttocks up to me and threw her head around to see me, I glimpsed her face and saw she was probably the same age as the brother at the door, her long brown hair falling all over her back as she took me in her, Dandy putting me hard in her, pressing us together and I thought of Rosaline and how this felt. I started to push into the softness, the woman sliding back and forth, I reached down to grab her hips and at that moment I thought about Horatio and how he had described this all once, I could see him and kept pushing harder, my hands on her sweaty hips, she pulling my insides out of myself and I shot out everything like I had never done before and cried out as Dandy pulled me away, handed me the knife and a handkerchief and said, "Use that bowl of water there to clean yourself up good," and I stepped off the bed as he clambered onto it, telling me, "Soon as you done cleaning up good guard that door," and she barked out something and he grunted and started pumping and I almost forgot to wash myself, his pants fell around his knees and he gripped down between her thighs and still hard and aroused again I couldn't stop watching them, his dark mounds hammering back and forth, her legs clamping onto his. "Red," he said glancing at me and I checked the door, it was still closed and he howled real loud and shook and she screamed out "Leave, leave" till he jumped up and said, panting, "You cleaned up completely?" and "That was good, right?" and "Way we did it she won't get knocked up by neither of us bulls," and he grabbed the handkerchief from me and scrubbed himself several times, as the woman sat up in the bed, now calling out to us. Dandy said, "See, you done made her forget her real man," then "Red, tie your tie, " he straightened it for me, took the knife, donned his suit jacket, when all of a sudden we heard a street whistle and banging—

—Dandy threw open the door, his eyes darting, "I seen stairs," I said, he seized my hand and I led him to them, there was a white cop's voice, maybe two, below us, no sign of the brother outside our door, we could hear chairs being overturned below us and somebody screaming as something tumbled down the stairwell, we were half-way up to the roof when Dandy said, "My hat, Cuz, you go on!" and I told him, "I'll wait, I can't leave you," and he say, "No, you got to get to your job," and I realized I forgotten all about it, I was probably already late, but I told him, "I can't leave you," the white voices were ascending, nearing us, we could hear the batons or maybe tire irons hitting the walls, bannisters, flesh, I stayed there on the stairs as he ran back and I heard a cop voice holler, "It's a god-awful hive of 'em," and Dandy yelled from the room, "You got to go, I don't want you to get sent up, they'd break our necks for that white girl," but I did not move till he came barreling up behind me pushing me through the hatch onto the roof, it was evening now, the roofs of Philadelphia like silver-black waves, strewn with pearls and gold.

Dandy replaced the hatch, but we could still hear voices just below us and he said, "Red, we gonna to have to jump," and I said, "Where, off the roof?" not even thinking about how we would reach the street, and he pointed, "Over there," from the stretch of roof we stood on to one lower, then there was another with a parapet, and the hatch started to open and he stomped it back closed and said, "Let's go," so we rared back and sprinted and soared—

—Onto the next roof half a story below, I hit the surface first and skidded to a halt, Dandy did the same thing, we stood and ran and jumped again, onto the parapet roof, rolling as we landed, "One more," he said and we leapt, over a gap my whole body length, closing my eyes upon as we crossed it, I spotted a chimney and a water tank and we hid ourselves behind them, Dandy clutching his hat and laughing, "Red, even in the dark it's clear you black as a chimney sweep," and I looked at myself and him, he appeared to be all smeared in tar, his face and palms and shirt, like my cravat and tie and waistcoat, my pants and palms all black and sticky, even my hair, a thick layer of pitch from one of the roofs all over both of us, and we could hear the cops yelling from the building but they couldn't see us, and they were not about to jump. I knew once we somehow came down there was no way I could show up like this at Mr. Linde's, and I tried to think of an excuse to tell Dameron, but began formulating plans to talk to his rival, Mr. Thomas Dorsey, first thing Monday about joining his catering company since I already foresaw what was going to happen. Dandy was still laughing and saying in a low voice that rode the blackness, "You hear them cops still up there trying to figure where we disappeared to?" and "You know I want to do that with you again," and "Red, Cuz, you really flew!"

Dameron fired me and must have sent word to Mr. Dorsey, who refused to bring me on, so I got only a few jobs here and there with the smaller caterers. Sometimes when I was julienning carrots or making a roux I formulated the extreme idea of working down on the docks, though I also thought it was a good idea to avoid being anywhere near the Schuylkill, because if the cops didn't spot me one of them from that house might, while the Delaware side, brimming with far more wharves, was not only locked down by immigrants, but Dandy's usual territory. Jonathan wanted to know what had really happened, though I would not tell him, but I considered asking if he could get me on with his boss, Mr. Kahnweiler, though in truth I didn't want another job in his shadow nor be a stockboy. I recounted the story to Horatio, only I said the woman was one of us, I was ashamed to tell him the truth, just like I didn't tell Dandy I'd thought of Horatio when I was with her. Nevertheless Horatio asked me to describe it over and over, to paint a spoken picture of me and then Dandy inside her. I tried not to think about what happened though whenever I patted my empty pockets I cursed and then grinned at the memory of that evening with my cousin.

Wherever I went now during my searches for work, everybody, black and white, seemed to be talking about the war, how the Southern states just kept leaving and the Confederates were eventually going to invade Pennsylvania, how there would soon be no more slavery and how, they said at the barber, they'd put us all in bond if Richmond was not defeated. There were appreciably more white men in uniforms in the streets. Sometimes the white people even seemed to treat us a little better than usual, sometimes, as I found in Independence Park or on the streetcars, worse. Once I was shoved off after paying, another time a rider, decrying the fact that there was a war going on at all, spat a brown stream of tobacco juice in my direction. The summer came and then was nearly gone, I all the while doing my occasional cook prep jobs, because there weren't that many special events or parties, hoarding every penny, just waiting for the Academy lectures to start again. Mostly I walked the avenues looking, for jobs, for something, anything, from one end of the city to the other, checking in at the Gas Works and the Arsenal, the railway stations and the hospitals, but nobody wanted to sign me on because they already had workers or weren't hiring us or because I was still too young.

One hot August Sunday evening I met up with Horatio near Washington Square. We were just ambling and sharing a cigar and, as if an invisible fuze exploded in my head, I said, "I'm going to go work with Mr. Robins's friend," and he said, "Who?" and I said, "'Member, at the last Academy talk, about the air balloons?" and he said, "How you even recollect that?" and he laced his arm around my shoulders and took the cigar from my lips and rolled it in his and said, "Colored can't fight in this war, specially not no 16-year-old," and I said, "I heard them talking at the barber about it, they asking the president to allow colored volunteers and troops," and he traced something on the back of my neck and said, "Well, you ain't even grown enough to muck out stables yet," and I pushed him away and said, "I'm telling you, I'm going to go work for Mr. Robins's friend, I still got his carte de visite," and I thought about showing it to Horatio, since I had been walking around with it in my pocket for weeks, but instead I said, "I'm even going to go to Washington if I have to," and he yanked me back to him, pushing the cigar in my mouth and said, "You can be a admay li'l ignay, Edray, know that?" then "What that white man name again?" and I say, "Mr. Edward Linde," and he asked, "Ain't he related to that man reason you got fired?" and I said, "Maybe"—though from the card I knew they shared the same address—"but the old man was throwing that party and he ain't know who was supposed to be there, Dameron got rid of me cause I never showed up *and* ruined them clothes, plus my latenesses, even though I only ever missed one other party and was late just a handful of times." Horatio paused, observing me, then said, "He give you your job back come September, can't nobody stay angry at you long," and I said, "Nobody cept Rosaline, though I don't care," and Horatio winked at me and said, "We both know why." But I didn't. Instead of asking what he meant I said, "Well, I'm going to go work with Mr. *Edward* Linde, and that Professor Lowe," and Horatio laughed and hugged me so tight I couldn't breathe and I wrestled him off me and punched him in his chest, he chasing me, still laughing, all the way up Locust.

The next morning I woke early, scrubbed myself completely, and put on my nicest shirt and trousers. As soon as Mama and Jonathan had left the house I headed up Broad to Mr. Linde's near Rittenhouse. I tried not to get all sweaty but it was hot as a griddle outside, and I was nearly soaked through when I reached the front door, so I patted myself down with the handkerchief Dandy had given me, my souvenir of our last adventure. The house sat back from the street behind a stone wall, broken by a black wrought iron gate with the letters AVL, in a circle, in its center. I let myself in since it was not locked, and walked down a brick path through a garden full of flowers and statues. Using the gold-plated knocker I rapped gently. A man with gray hair in a blue livery suit opened the door, looked at me then behind me, curiously, and said, "You got a delivery for Mr. and Mrs. Linde?" and I answered, "I am here to speak to Mr. Edward Linde." At this the man scrunched up his face, shook his head and said, "Boy, come again?" and I repeated, "I am here to speak to Mr. Edward Linde, Sir, the scientist." The man stared at me, then said, "Wait here," and I remained there, half-watching coaches passing, small groups of elegantly dressed people heading toward the square, wagons making deliveries. The man returned to the door and hissed, "Go out the front and come around the alley, I'll meet you at the gate near the stable." He was still looking like he couldn't believe I was there, but I obeyed his instructions, walked all the way around the wall till I found the alley, where he was waiting for me at another black gate, this one locked. I could see through it that the rear garden was even bigger than the one in front and the house, which was three stories, was immense too.

"What you want with Mr. Edward Linde, 'the scientist'?"

"I work at the Academy—" and before I finished he cut me off.

"If you got a message for him from them tell it or hand me the paper. I'll pass it on to him."

"No, Sir," I say, "I ain't—didn't—finish. I work at the Academy and I met Mr. Linde there, and he told me he going to work with Professor Lowe, who also a scientist working with balloons, and—" Shaking his large head, the silvery tufts rising like wings from the bluish-brown crown, he waved for me to stop.

"I'll go get Miss Katherine, this all too queer. Stay *right there.*" I stood for a while, stepping out of the way when two white men dragged a dray, loaded with several crates, alongside me, and like magic the man returned to unlock the gate and let them carry the crates in, though he repeated to me, "Right there." When the deliverymen left, paying me no attention, the older man returned with a tall young white woman. He said to me slowly and formally, "This Miss Katharine Linde, Mr. Edward sister. You can tell her what you want through the gate. Shall I wait here, Miss?" She shook him off and he went back into the house, though I figured he and probably everybody else in there was watching us closely. The young woman looked mostly like Mr. Edward, but in female form, with long, chestnut hair that she wore up in a comb.

"What is your name … how can I help you … ?"

"Theodore King, Ma'am," I said. "I work at the Academy on Saturdays at they lectures and I met Mr. Edward at the last one, by Professor Thaddeus Lowe, the balloon specialist, and Mr. Edward, who Mr. Robins say—"

"Excuse me, did you say Peter Robins?" She almost blushed as she asked this, so I momentarily looked away. She opened a fan and sat on a small stone bench near the gate.

"Yes, Ma'am," I said. "The very same. Mr. Robins was saying that Mr. Edward was studying science, and Mr. Edward say—said—that he was going to work with Professor Lowe."

"Theodore," she said, making me think she was about to tell me something, but she was just pronouncing my name. She looked me up and down, before staring at some of the white flowers, hovering like stars, beside her. "Mmm. This is so very odd. Do you have a message from the Academy for my brother? Anatole said something about a message."

"Well, Ma'am," I said, "Mr. Edward Linde give me his carte de visite and told me if I want to work for him when he was working for Professor Lowe, I should contact him. I ain't—didn't—know how to do that except come here so here I am." I passed the card through the gate to her, dropping it onto the opened fan. She stared at the face on it, scrutinizing it as if to make sure that it was her brother's visage peering back at her, and then at me, then passed it back. "Mmm. Truly irregular. But then these days the whole world is upside down, and then there is my brother. So Neddy gave you that card?"

"Yes, Ma'am," I say. "At the Academy, most exactly." I felt sweat rilling down my brow and neck again so I patted myself down. I realized I could use some water.

The white woman stood, cooling herself with the fan, saying, "It's scorching today, isn't it?" then "We can't blame the rebels for that." She turned away and I wondered if she was going to head back into the house without saying anything else, but she stopped and told me over her shoulder, "Well, Theodore, I will give my brother and *Mr. Peter Robins* your message that you came to the house and are 'eager to work.' Where do you stay, should they conceivably supply a response?"

"Thanks, Ma'am." I started smiling but restrained myself. "I live on Lombard Street, Ma'am, Number 723, second floor. 723 Lombard Street, in this city, with my mother Mrs. Emma Riley King and my brother Jonathan, who is employed at Kahnweiler's General Store and the Academy. I sincerely would like to work for Mr. Edward Linde if he need me."

The white woman continued looking back toward me just enough that I could read her brief half-smile as she proceeded toward the house. At the stairs the man I took to be Anatole materialized in front of her. He said quite loudly, "Everything all right, Miss Katharine?"

"Yes," she answered, and with her fan gestured toward me. "I'll pass on his message to Neddy and should he have a response, someone will have to relay the message to him." She disappeared past Anatole into the house. Soon as she was inside Anatole scampered toward me, still behind the gate, and, nearly spitting, said, "Listen here, boy, don't you never come rolling up at the front door of this house, never again, y'unnerstand? Never. And get your little black ass away from this back gate too, before I count to ten? If the police don't knock all the teeth out that smiling mouth I sure in the hell will."

I didn't answer him but left, almost whistling, and thought about calling out, "Anatole," but instead I headed back east to Washington Square to find a place to sit and, despite the heat, read the handbills and any discarded newspapers, and listen to speeches about the war.

A week passed, then two, no word from Mr. Edward Linde or anyone else. Then came the first days of September, though still no substantial cooking or catering positions. I put in at the House of Refuge, where I heard there was an open slot, and because they were always taking in orphans and bad children the work would be steady, but when I went back to inquire they apologized that they didn't yet have anything available. An honest job is an honest job, my Mama kept saying, so you best just keep hitting those streets, and I once again thought of seeking something at Kahnweiler's, or, come to worst, even casting my lot with Dandy.

That first Saturday of the month it was so late when I got home it was already dark out and I couldn't believe I had walked what felt like half of Philadelphia, all the way down Passyunk to the County Prison then over to the Schuylkill then all the way up to Girard College, where I practically begged to join their kitchens, then hobbled all the way back down Broad, not a single street car stopping for me, my legs and feet hurting so badly I was ready to cut them off. I came upon Mama, framed by the lamplight's glow, sitting in front room with the Misses Allen from upstairs. Soon as I greeted them all she said, "Theodore, somebody brung a letter for you," and I immediately worried it might be a summons from the police for what happened with Dandy, or maybe for Dameron's clothes that I completely ruined and still had yet to pay for. I said, "Yes, Ma'am, where is it?" and she said, "Right there on your bed," and there it was, a long tan envelope, addressed to "THEODORE KING." I ripped it open and read:

Friday, August 23, 1861

To Theodore,

This missive is even by the usual standards of my Correspondence a most eccentric Exchange, but I just received a note from my dear sister, Katharine, stating that she had forgotten to tell that you had come to my Father's house enquiring of me. I initially was unaware of whom she was speaking, until she made mention of the Academy, Professor T. S. C. Lowe's lecture, and my near-brother Peter Robins, and thus I recalled your peculiar yet delightful display of *Memory*, and my comments to you that Saturday afternoon.

As things stand in our continuing contributions to Science in the Defense of our UNION this corps fortunately does need *Hands*, though I cannot but certify my Good-Will and a miniscule Purse as guarantee. Peter kindly enquired of your arts and talents, and wrote that in addition to your memorial Skill you are also a Cook, which any corps must need, though we also have need of Elbows to undertake related tasks, of which I know you will not suffer undue abuse.

You will have to make your Journey to military headquarters in the Capital, and there interrogate *where to find me*. Peter has said that you may use his name alongside mine, should this matter still bear your interest. Please carry this Letter, and the Warrant it represents, along with my *Carte de Visite*, on your person in any case, and as I have gone on too long, *Sapientiae Scientiaeque,*

> *Edward Harrison Bartram (von) Linde, A.M., A.M.*
> *Technical Assistant to Professor T. S. C. Lowe*
> *United States Army Balloon Corps*

I had to read the letter several times to understand it fully, but once I did I decided that I was headed down there. I waited till after service on Sunday to mention the offer to Mama, who told me I was ten times more of a fool than she ever thought she could raise, because what sane colored person would ever risk his life to go down into the bosom of the slavers? She wept as she admonished me think before acting so rashly, then wept again when I said I would not change my mind. Jonathan, who had witnessed the exchange, responded that he didn't think I was a fool but instead probably trying to fool him and everyone with my claim. The next day in the park after he got off I shared it with Horatio, who began bawling like I had never seen him do before and assured me he was going to pray I never ended up in the traitor's arms, before narrating to me how when they captured me they would bind me and whip me before having their way with me as punishment. I replied that I was planning to leave for the capital soon as I could figure out a way there. I had saved up some money but I doubted I could afford the railroad or was even allowed to ride on it, and also did not think I could afford a horse or coach ride.

That evening and for several afterwards I read the Bible, which I seldom did, to find a divine answer to my quandary, feeling reassured when I came across passages such as when John says in 14:31, "Arise, let us go hence," and the 91st Psalm, verse 11, with its clear affirmation: "For he shall give his angels charge over thee, to keep thee in all thy ways." I tried respectfully to ignore Mama complaining about my foolishness to Misses Janie and Lucie Allen, or to my aunt, her younger sister Dorothea, who dropped by at the beginning of every week to relate what sounded to me like the same stories about the rich people she worked for and the poor people she worked with. Instead my mind kept turning on the axles of Mr. Linde's letter and Professor Lowe's lecture and the aerostats and Washington, the *war*, and how more than once over the years I had seen people drive the abolitionists out of Independence Square but now they often stood and listened, sometimes politely, a few even cheering, as the men and women, black and white, assured listeners that we would all soon be free.

A few days later I left Horatio at the Arcade where, when we met up after he got off from the upholstery shop, he wouldn't stop shouting that I was behaving with pure lunacy, though he also confessed that he had been dreaming of heading south with me too. As I departed Washington Square I heard a voice utter just above a murmur, "Red," and looked over to see my cousin Dandy, in a doorway, hat tilted low on his head, his charcoal jacket and trousers rendering him a shadow: "Where you heading?" I walked over to him and answered just as softly, "I'm trying to figure out how to get to Washington." He said,

"Running from somebody?" and I shook my head, said, "Naw, Cuz, I wanna go work with the Army," and he said, "Colored can't sign up for this war." I answered, "I'm gonna work mess," and he beckoned me closer and whispered in my ear, "I need to get out this town, been thinking about Buffalo or Boston, but seeing as all the commotion happening down there Washington'll do." I stepped away from him, a bit incredulous, and asked him, "How?" Dandy looked around us, and said as if each word would vanish soon as he uttered it: "Can you meet me here in three days as close to 6 pm as you can manage?" "For sure," I replied and he added, "Bring whatever money you got but don't tell nobody, just leave your Mama a note and a couple bits for rent, make sure you put something in your stomach," then he asked me my birthday and concluded, "We'll be in Washington faster than you can say Abe Lincoln."

Though I doubted Dandy's scheme would come to anything I did exactly as he said. I packed a few things each day while Mama and Jonathan were at work and counted out my money. When I left I had to go upstairs to borrow a scrap of paper, a quill and some ink from Miss Lucie Allen to write my letter, and grew so nervy I wanted to take a stroll but instead I heated up a potato and ate it, drank water, checked twice that I had put out the stove. Soon as I heard the church bells ring 5 I split to meet my cousin. Since I arrived early near where I saw him the day before, I milled about, finally asking a white man the time. He told me quarter to six, so I walked up to the square then raced back, counting the minutes, and right on the hour I saw Dandy there in the doorway, dressed as if he worked for the railroads, with a leather saddle bag and a second cloth bag slung over his shoulder. Dandy said, "We heading to the depot down on Washington," which I knew meant the Philadelphia Wilmington and Baltimore one, so I started up the street and Dandy said firmly, "No, no, Cuz, they coming for us," and he slipped back into the shadows till a cab came, the horse rearing when it stopped abruptly. Dandy ordered me, "Get in, fast," and we did and sped down Seventh to Christian, before I knew it we were at the depot. Dandy said, "Stay close, and whatever you do, from now on anybody talk to you keep your mouth shut." We went around the rear of the station, where we met a brother Dandy talked to for a few minutes, until he hailed me over, saying, "Okay, give him some change." I did, then Dandy gave him some more money from a roll he had concealed somewhere, and something else wrapped in burlap and twine, though I knew not to ask what it was. The man ushered us to a luggage car on a train bound for Washington, and whispered something in Dandy's ear, said we would know when we get to the capital because that was the last stop, these days no trains ran on to Virginia. We settled in behind some crates, curling up as tiny as we could. Another brother came in and spotted us but didn't say a thing. Eventually we heard the whistle, the train began to move. Once we were pulling out Dandy handed me a little pocket watch, all filigreed silverplate around the edges, a small cream envelope, then a swig of liquor from his flask. I sat up, listening to the music of the wheels along the track—

—And Dandy woke me saying, "Red, Cuz, gather your stuff up, let's go." Soon as the door gaped, he said, "Make it," and the two or three men stepping to unload the crates and luggage glared at us as if they were seeing ghosts, but Dandy said something so fast I didn't catch it, he winked and gestured to them with his fingers, and they let us pass. As we scurried out I saw white men dressed in different kinds of uniforms, probably all military, as well a lot of our people too. I counted what appeared to be twice as many as at home. I asked Dandy, "Are they slaves? " and he said, "Probably free as we is in Philly," then he added that we had to get to Q and 9th Street before sundown. He asked one of the men for some water and where we could relieve ourselves, then we exited the station. The city was no-where as built up as Philadelphia and unlike the initial perception the station offered appeared to have considerably fewer people. Neither of us was sure what direction we were facing so Dandy said, "Take out that watch." He stood so close I could feel his hot, sweet breath on my cheeks. He wrapped his arm around me as if cloaking us in invisibility and said, "See, on the back you got a little compass, so whatever you do don't lose your papers and don't lose this." I swore to him I wouldn't. I also saw that we were facing South and there, looming right in front of us, atop a hill ringed by buildings, was a gigantic white building with an unfinished dome. Astonished, I asked him, pointing to it, "Do you think that's the President's House or the Capitol?" Dandy shrugged. "Cuz," he said, "you got to act like you from here," so I dropped my arm, though it took me a minute or two to stop staring.

I glanced at the compass again. "Which way we sposed to go?" Dandy said, "They say due north up New-Jersey." We searched, as inconspicuously as we could, until we found that street. We started walking, not really talking because I could tell Dandy was striving hard to appear as ice as possible while also paying close attention to everything around us. He was not listening to anything I was saying, not about how much emptier and dirtier the capital was than Philadelphia, how there were twice as many soldiers everywhere, how every other person appeared to be like us. Most of them nodded in our direction and I made sure to nod back, but Dandy only tipped his hat and pressed forward, though every so often he would ask how I was feeling, if I needed any water or anything else.

All the while I was counting the street letters as we headed north, the grid not unlike Philadelphia's, thirteen blocks we crossed, the buildings thinning out eventually to meadows and pastures, dense thickets of alders and hawthorns, stands of oaks and ailanthus broken intermittently by shacks and lean-tos, almost like the far northeast or southwest parts of our own city. A strange thought struck me and I asked Dandy, "How you know there ain't no Confederates hiding in these bushes or trees," and he answered, "Cuz, you know I like me a joke but not one like that." I consulted my watch-compass and told him we needed to walk in the direction of the cluster of buildings to our west. Before I knew it we were there. As soon as I saw the condition of the structures, crude edifices of wood and tin, and towards the backs tarpaulin tented to extend some of the dwellings, I wondered were we really going to stay *here*? though I trusted Dandy. He approached and spoke with a couple of rough-looking men and a woman outside one of the buildings, a shack that could only generously be labeled a house, but I remained where I was until he called for me. "Here where we staying, Red," Dandy said, and introduced me to a short, dark walleyed man with a pointed beard named Cyrus, and a pretty woman in a yellow headwrap and dress named Eliza, who invited us inside. They seated us on stools around a stove and fed us, all the while questions about how we were feeling, but nothing about Philadelphia or the trip down. I remembered what Dandy had told me and let him talk, smiling but politely maintaining my silence.

Since we didn't have a map we had no idea where Army headquarters or the Balloon Corps might be, so I began creating a chart in my head of the streets we walked that first week. Where we were staying was in the colored section, Uptown, near the city's northern boundaries, but I walked down to Mt. Vernon Square, to the President's House at Lafayette Square, to the Capitol Building near where we first entered the city, to the Naval Observatory which perched on the edge of the Potomac. I took care to avoid attracting the notice of the soldiers, on guard nearly everywhere I wandered, same as I did the police, whose attention I crossed the street to evade. I spoke at length with no one except our people unless I had to, and none of them paid me any special mind. I remembered not to go beyond U Street north of where we were staying, nor anywhere near the Navy Yard, which was, Dandy warned, swimming and shooting distance from Virginia. He would come and go and somehow also knew his way around, which at first I didn't understand since as far as I knew he hadn't ever been beyond New-Jersey, but my father did used to say that like his father Dandy's mind ran like the finest phaeton but he wasted it on crisscrossing the sewers. I knew never to ask what he was up to, especially when he returned one evening with papers saying he was "Anthony Smith," and made me vow from now on when we were around other people I should make sure to call him that.

End of our first week I was walking back from the mall that stood in front of the Smithsonian castle—and not even Philadelphia had a building that could match—and an local officer ordered me to stop and when I tried to slip away seized my arm and demanded my documents. After he read through them the tiny blue eyes pricking his pink face scanned me up and down, then he reviewed the documents again, asking with a twang, "How do I know these papers are your'n?"

"Well, Sir," I answered, "them is mine sure as Mr. Lincoln is the president and Washington is the capital of the United States of America."

"Where were you born?" As he asked he hid the papers behind his back.

"Well, Sir, I was born free at my parents' lodgings at 701 Spruce Street in Philadelphia, Pennsylvania."

He brought them back before him and read them carefully then concealed them again. "What date and year?"

"Well, Sir, I was born on December 18, 1842." The officer again brought the certificate Dandy gave me from behind his back to study it, and I was glad I had studied it before the train left the Philly depot, since I actually was born in 1844, though in case I needed to be 18 to work Dandy had gotten somebody to add two years.

"So why are you down here in the capital? Philadelphia ain't just walking distance. Between the ones of you fleeing across that river over there and the ones of you maybe sent up to spy, why in the Lord's name should I think you're telling the truth?"

"Well, Sir, I came down because as that other letter say I am to be employed down here by the scientist specified in it."

He opened the other piece of paper and browsed it, and for a second I thought about handing him Mr. Linde's carte de visite, but I decided to withhold that until absolutely necessary. "How do I know you didn't memorize all this? Y'all can be so crafty sometimes.

If you're really free and from Pennsylvania and are working for this 'scientist,' read this paragraph aloud for me right now."

"Yes, Sir," I said, peering into the page, whose writing was swirling before me. "As things stand in our con-con-tinuing contri-tri-butions to Science in the De-fense of our UNION—this corps fortu-for-tu-nately does need *Hands*, though I can-not but cert-cert-ify my Good-Will and a mini-scule Purse as guaran-tee...."

"I'll be the devil," he said, snatching the letter from me, and read it again himself. "So why aren't you working with this scientist Linde and the Corps now?"

"Well Sir," I replied, seeing he was softening, "I been trying to fig-ure out where the Federal Army headquarters at so that I can find him. I had to pay my way down here to Washington, and now I got to find where the Balloon Corps is at."

The officer turned on his heel and pointed in the direction of Lafayette Square telling me, "The War Department is just east of the President's House, at Pennsylvania and G. You should go there straightaway."

"Yes Sir," I said. "I'm going there right now."

"You had better, and I don't want to see you wandering around here again. These days nobody needs any added mischief." I bolted up 13th, feeling his eyes train a target on my back and turning every so often, real subtly, to check if he was still watching me. I nearly stumbled into the street as a carriage was approaching but righted myself and paused against a hitching post, looking back to find him gone. Only a short while after that I reached War Department. All kinds of people thronged out front, mostly guards and, to judge by the navy uniforms, military men. I spoke to a white guard stationed near the base of the main portico, then to another at the main door, spilling my story to each, mentioning Dr. Linde, Professor Lowe, the Balloon Corp. After skimming my letter the second one called over a young man my exact size and build who was a good three years older, whom I at first thought was white until I got a good look at his nose, lips and hair. The white guard said to him, "You heading to the Potomac office?" and the young man said with a lilt, "Yessir," and the guard said, "Take this boy up there with you, and see that he speaks to someone about that letter." The young man didn't speak at first, he just reviewed me up and down as he was leading me to wherever we were going, but finally he paused and asked my name and where I was from. I told him and when I asked him the same question, he answered, "My name Nicholas, but they call me Nimrod." I added, "Well they call me Red. You from here?" He told me he was originally from Annapolis, worked as a messenger, among other things, for the staff of the Army of the Potomac and General McClelland, adding that he had never heard of any Balloon Corps and wasn't at all sure I was searching in the right place.

On the top floor after a guard examined Nimrod's papers and I displayed mine and the carte de visite, he guided me at an office where I eventually spoke to several different people. No one had ever heard of Dr. Linde but when I mentioned Professor Lowe and the balloons finally one official knew exactly who and what I was talking about. He said the Corps was *not* part of the military, but then, another official entering the office overheard him and told me it was, under the aegis of the Topographical Engineers, or perhaps the Quartermaster Department, no the Signal Corps, no the Engineers, then he interrogated me and perused my papers, taking the letter and disappearing for a while, which made me start to fidget in fear that he would not return with it. Finally he did and told me I would have to wait two days to head down to where the Balloon Corps was stationed. I would accompany Nimrod when he carried messages down that way. I thanked the officer profusely, but he ordered me to get out of his office.

Nimrod was waiting for me out in the hallway. I relayed everything to him and he told me I had to be here in two days, at 7 o'clock in morning sharp, that's when he was heading down to the camp to bring the messages and other information. I assured him I would be there. I beat the fastest path I could back up to the shack where Dandy and I were staying, dallying only at the market at Mt. Vernon Square to get some water, and buy a few provisions like bread ends, potatoes, and a cabbage to give to the people we were lodging with. That night as Dandy and me were lying on the cot we shared, trying to stay warm as the cool September air enfolded us, I told him my news and he told me *Anthony Smith* had a special opportunity in Baltimore. He urged me to be as careful as possible, first chance I get write Jonathan a letter he could read to the rest of the family, always guard my watch and money, don't spend a penny I didn't have to, and above all don't tell these people here the date I was fixing to leave. Finished with his litany he reminded me about all the fun we had had together, including the train ride down. Before I fell off to sleep I hugged him tight as if I might never see him again. When I woke up, Dandy and all his belongings were gone.

I spent the day just walking around 7th Street, peering in the shop windows, my head down and my ears perked, listening to every conversation I could hear. Half the time in Philadelphia it hadn't felt at all like there was a war, but here talk of it was constantly passing people's lips. Outside the market I even overheard one man saying to another brother that a federal general had set all the slaves free in Missouri. I make sure to stay circumspect as I eavesdropped, not walk too fast since things were slower down here, not waste a single penny except to get a drink of water, and avoid all trouble with white people. Finally as evening was falling I left the Northern Liberty Market and returned to the shack. I told them I wasn't feeling so good and went into the little area where me and Dandy were staying and quietly gathered all my things. My pocket watch handy, I took little naps till I glanced down and saw it read 5:35. I rose, silent as a shadow, everybody else was still slumbering, washed up best I could and used what passed for an outhouse, and grabbed everything of mine, including a new, well-fitting coat that someone had folded up and placed in my bag. I left some coins on the table for them, then rushed off to meet Nimrod.

At the western end of the War Department Building portico, a white patrolman asked me what I was doing there. I answered that I was waiting for Nimrod, an official Army messenger, but we went halfway through a document check before Nimrod appeared beside him with a white orderly who cleared us to go. The patrolman eyed me all the way off the War Department's property and was still watching me even when we reached the covered wagons waiting to take us down to where the Corps was headquartered. I asked Nimrod where we were going but he told he wasn't allowed to say. Once we had helped several enlisted men load all the supplies and gear, I climbed in the rear of the wagon beside several of them and other men and Nimrod, and we took off. It was a slow, bumpy ride. I held on tight to the back of the wagon, my other hand on Nimrod's knee, trying to make sure when we crossed a rut or uneven pavement I didn't go flying out the back. Between the journey's unpleasantness and my rising nerves I could hardly pay attention to what the men were talking about. The rocking of the wagon began to stir me so I forgot what was going on until someone broached how there were snipers everywhere, how someone else had almost gotten killed by an errant shell. I thought about asking Nimrod how close the Confederates were or we were going to be to them, but I just held onto the backboard and him, and listened, and peered out at the city streets as the day closed in.

Every so often the wagon would stop, and the driver would speak to patrolmen. At one such checkpoint I heard we were heading west into Georgetown. When we neared the water Nimrod said, "Red, you seen the Monument yet?" I looked to my right and there it was, the lean gray blade of obelisk slicing the blue morning sky. I wasn't sure, however, how it was supposed to represent President Washington, the capital or the Union. As we crossed the Aqueduct, as one of the men called it, across the Potomac into Virginia, I could again feel my nerves ginning, but Nimrod knew at that moment to calm me, patting my shoulder and assuring me the federal troops had full control of *all* of Alexandria.

Before I knew it we were climbing the road up through the green bluffs of Arlington Heights to our stop at Fort Corcoran. We stopped just outside the main gates and began unloading most of the baskets and crates, soldiers streaming past the high palisades and the piles of trees, which Nimrod called abatises, to collect them. I asked him before he ran off to deliver his messages where the Balloon Corps headquarters were, a query he answered by glancing first at the fort itself then at the cleared terrain ringing its walls, finally telling me when he found out he'd escort me there. As I waited I moved back from the main road, the wagon traffic, and pressed myself as close possible to the fort's walls. I observed the waves of blue-clad figures, most from the 13th New York Infantry Regiment, I would learn, all the other white men galloping up or off on horseback, the fusillade of commands and conversation. For whatever reason at that second I wondered what my mother had said about my letter, what Jonathan thought about it, what Horatio was thinking about and doing right now—

—"Let's go," Nimrod called and I followed him, my sack slung over my back, we two heading towards the rear of the fort, between the walls, buttressed by a revetment of riprap and soil, fascines and planks, and a long row of tents, toward a group of white men standing in a circle. Behind them I could see a balloon bag, uninflated and spread out like a flattened lampshade, its vast silk head trellised with linen cord, its large wicker basket double the size of a standard well, festooned on its sides with sandbags. The men didn't notice us at first and continued their discussion, one of them I immediately recognized by face as Professor Lowe, standing at the center of their circle and pointing towards the clouds. None wore the Federal's uniforms I'd seen for weeks, but instead dressed like regular working gentlemen I might see on the streets of Philadelphia. Nimrod engaged one of the men in conversation while I hung back, watching him and them, their exchange inaudible though the man looked over at me. He led Nimrod to the balloon, where I could now see on its far side more men kneeling and fiddling with strings and cables. Nimrod yelled, "Red, come on over here." I readied my papers in case there was any further confusion. On the ground, tinkering with a mechanical contraption and wires, a pencil, ruler, and notebook splayed opened before him and several other men, was Mr. Edward Linde.

"Professor Linde," the white man with Nimrod said, "this boy has showed up saying he's in your employ," yet Mr. Linde continued his work on the metal device, twisting and arranging the wires. The white man did not repeat himself but walked away, while Nimrod and I hovered there, until Mr. Linde finally raised his eyes, squinting first at Nimrod then at me, his face initially a portrait of bafflement, and I opened the letter to hand to him and prepared once again to recount everything when he stood, gathering up a ruler, notebook and pencil, which he passed to me, his expression suggesting that I had just accidentally dropped them there to undertake some other minor task, and said, "Ah, Theodore, there you are."

From that minute forward I was working alongside Mr. Edward, who insisted I call him "Neddy," although all the others, around whom I always said, "Mr. Edward," had to be correctly addressed: Mr. John La Mountain, Mr. John Wise, the Misters Ezra and James Allen, Misters Paullin, Steiner, Starkweather, the different assistants to each, as well as Professor Lowe and his father, Mr. Clovis, and his wife, Mrs. Leontine, who would periodically visit us. Soon as I set my bag down I was sharpening Mr. Edward's pencils, tracking the placement of his spectacles to ensure he didn't lose or sit on them, replenishing his stash of tobacco and filling his pipe, ferrying messages to the various other members of the corps, and posting his letters to his parents, his siblings, Mr. Peter Robins and other friends who had not volunteered. More than anything else I repeated verbatim what I heard him say whenever he was musing scientifically or assisting Professor Lowe, especially when they were devising a device, so that he wouldn't fail to record it.

Like most of the others Professor Lowe at first didn't really notice me at all. Then early one morning about a week after I had been there he said, "So you are Neddy's little computer key, the boy from Philadelphia," but I didn't grasp what he meant. Later that afternoon Mr. Edward told me, "That kindly *savant* Professor Lowe is convinced you are helping with my calculations, so please keep quiet and both of us in his best graces," before he added, lowering his voice, "though the rest of these characters are, as my father would say, a *Schlangennest*." I asked, "Mr. Edward, Sir, excuse me but come again?" and he replied, "Nidum serpentium," and I said I didn't understand, worried I was supposed to get what he was talking about, but he chuckled, "*Neddy*—and perhaps it's best you don't."

Usually I was referred to as an "aide to Mr. Edward Linde," or "Professor Linde" as Misters Paullin and Starkweather called him, and often when that particular combination—"aide" and "Professor Linde"—was uttered, shortly thereafter I found myself at far more tedious, difficult work. I slogged sandbags to the baskets, unfurled the telegraph wires that rode up with the balloons, arranged the necessary tools for the various aeronauts or others on the team, helping unpack or break down the campsites as we moved along the Potomac, either on the Maryland side when we weren't based at Fort Corcoran or temporarily stationed in one of the other ones along the Virginia banks. The periodic gunfire and talk of snipers made me always want to stay behind the cordon of federal troops and forts that guarded the north shore of the Potomac and Washington. I also always offered to lend a hand with the meals, though the white man in charge of mess, Paul Danahy, didn't want me anywhere nearby. Point of fact whenever Mr. Edward wasn't right beside me and I wasn't busy with one of their tasks nearly all of them ordered me to stay out of their way.

There was only one other colored man working for the Corps; his name was Ulysses Harris. Twenty-five and a good foot-and-a-half taller than me, he at first didn't say much of anything or even look in my direction. After he realized, however, that he and I had to eat together and do everything else personal together, sleep and crap in the same place, away from everybody else, he started to grow a little and then considerably more friendly. I learned he was born in Winchester, Virginia, up in the Shenandoah Valley not all that far from where we were or from Harper's Ferry, where the great martyr John Brown had launched his raid, and that he and his family escaped north to Maryland and then into Pennsylvania, where he had spent a few years near Greencastle. He said he had a wife there, Lizzie, a former escapee like himself, though she was from Martinsville, as well as a baby son, Lysander, and after the war wanted to be a minister rather than digging ditches, pitching tents and securing pulleys. I told him I lacked the introspection to be a preacher, the gift of insight to be a teacher, no contacts to undertake an apprenticeship, the strength to be a stevedore, the patience to be a waiter or porter, and no money to pursue any of the higher professions open to us in Philadelphia, so like my father before me I was going to be a cook and, I hoped, eventually a caterer, though I didn't say I was choosing this path mainly because I couldn't think of anything else. Sometimes in the evenings when Nimrod was free he joined us, and we sat and chatted, both of them asking a hundred questions about Philadelphia, which they really hoped to see someday, and me asking about Annapolis and Washington and Greencastle. I wanted to tell to them about my train trip down with Dandy and ask about slavery, though from Philadelphia etiquette I knew better and didn't dare. We'd gab until the sky grew black and our lids heavy, forcing Nimrod to hurry back or lose his post. When it started to get real cold at night Ulysses didn't even have a blanket, but Mr. Edward had given me one of his extras, a quilt with all of Pennsylvania's counties sewn on it, so I invited him under it with me and soon we were sleeping arm in arm.

One Saturday toward the end of September, General McClellan ordered Professor Lowe to ascend in the *Eagle* above Fort Corcoran and report on the rebel positions south of us, near Falls Church, in preparation, everybody was saying, for a battle. We were all commanded to stay inside the fort's walls, to the rear of it, well behind the line of fire. Though Mr. Edward said the Confederates were at least three or four miles away and we had nothing to worry about, my heart hammered whenever I imagined they might be closer. "Worse comes to worst you can play a bondsman," he said to me, drily, "but they will surely slit my throat with a bayonet since our dear President can't see fit to sign off on our commissions, and where, pray tell, would that get us?" I wanted to tell him I knew nothing about commissions but was not about to play, let alone be anybody's slave, but instead I kept quiet and calmed myself down by helping him and the other assistants ready the telegraph cable and the relay machine, the gauges, which he said he had ensured were perfectly calibrated, and several flags that Professor Lowe was going to take up in the balloon with him.

Soon as the balloon was filled, all the white folks, save Mr. Edward and the receiver operator, and Ulysses took hold of the cables, easing them through the pulleys. Up Professor Lowe rose into the air, slowly, then more rapidly, finally hovering about 1000 or so feet above. Mr. Edward and I reeled out the telegraph wire until Professor Lowe was so far up we could see only the basket's square brown wicker bottom and the immense tan curves and slope of the balloon's globe. Professor Lowe gave a signal for the cables to be tied and staked, though several assistants still held on. Where I sat, along the slope of the real wall's revetment near the telegraph operator I could see and hear Mr. La Mountain grumbling about something to Mr. Paullin, and Mr. Edward, approaching me and observing them as well whispered, "That one is the most notorious of vipers." I didn't dare reply but I had seen Mr. La Mountain and Professor Lowe, and Mr. Wise and the others arguing several times since I arrived. I continued watching them, Mr. La Mountain flailing his arms about then walking away towards a group of soldiers. As he left our area Mr. Ezra Allen came over and asked Mr. Edward how the transmission was going. The telegraph operator working at the receiver was writing down the messages as quickly as possible, which led Mr. Edward to say, "Just dandy," provoking a double-take from me. Finally Nimrod appeared with an older soldier who asked both Mr. Edward and the telegraph operator, "Do you have the coordinates?" and the receiver handed them over. This continued for a while, Nimrod and that white man coming and going, taking the pages with them—

—Till suddenly two orderlies rode up and all around us curtains of gunfire and the periodic boom of cannonade. Professor Lowe is making signals with the flags, though I can't tell what he's conveying but Mr. Edward says he is helping to calibrate the position of the guns. But I don't understand, and Mr. Edward repeats, "The guns, the position of the guns," when something batters the outer walls of the fort and we all slide lower down the revetment's slope, while others even lie flat on their stomachs on the ground. The fusillade continues without relent, more balls blasts the front palisades, while Professor Lowe continues high above making signs with the flags and Mr. Edward is raising his voice yet I can barely hear him above the gunfire, "We are taking the traitors out," and I say, "But Mr. Edward, Sir, what is Professor Lowe doing with the flags?" and Mr. Edward hollers, "*Neddy*, Theodore, *Neddy*—and why don't you just be quiet for a damned minute!" I shut my mouth as the orderlies ride in again, they and we all watching Professor Lowe, and this pattern persists, with fewer and fewer bullets or miniés falling our way though we can hear the cannons and field guns firing from our fort and the stench of the gunpowder lingers, Mr. Ezra Allen whistles, everyone, including me, stands and hauls Professor Lowe down, hauling on the cables as he releases the gas, descending, until the basket gently yet firmly hits the ground. All of us, save Mr. La Mountain, who has disappeared to who knows where, applaud him, as another military orderly arrives with a report from the generals.

After that there weren't any more close scrapes and we spent most of our time at the Navy Yard in Washington, where Professor Lowe and the rest were assembling a series of balloons as well as a balloon boat, as Mr. Edward called it, to carry and tether several of them at once up and down the Potomac. One afternoon I went to run errands for Mr. Edward, dropping off his post and, though I didn't tell him, mine: a letter to Jonathan and my mother, one to Horatio, and, on an impulse, one to Rosaline, recounting the vague outlines of my experiences thus far. I also was buying his favorite tobacco, Lilienthal's, coffee and tea, some lead-tin solder, and a few other things from the general store, taking good care to avoid any trouble. I checked my watch after I left the main post office and saw I had some free time, so I decided to head up to where Dandy and me had stayed when we first came to town, to see if anybody had seen or heard from him.

I retraced my steps back there, straight up 7th St. through Mt. Vernon Square, past the market and the shops, every street, every tree, every building both strange to me and yet so familiar, to 9th and Q, where I saw the shack, so tiny and filthy it was hard to imagine that seven or more of us had slept and eaten in there at the same time! As I approached it I saw a woman I recognized, though her back was turned to me. Her name was Mary Agnes and she had arrived just before I left. She was standing outside the front door. "How do, Miss?" I called out to her, asking if she had seen or heard from Anthony Smith. That name made her whip her head around towards me, and snap, "Who the hell asking?" I answered, "His cousin, I even stayed here with you, Mary Agnes, don't you remember, when we first came to the city—" and before I could finish the sentence she was shrieking, "Y'all, y'all, come out here right now, it's one of them northerners that run a game on us," and I said, "No, no, I didn't run no game," and she yelled even more loudly, "You gonna pay for what you did," and I said, "No, you got the wrong person, ask Cyrus," because I had even brought them food and left them money, but two men, both twice my size, came scrambling from the shack and across the street I saw another, wielding a carving knife, and I took off running, coiling my bag around my hand so I didn't drop it, and cut a left on what I guessed was P and just zigzagged across the street, even hearing a gun go off behind me, three times, but didn't stop running all the way to Mt.

Vernon Square, where I darted behind one of the stalls and dropped to my knees to catch my breath and examined myself quickly to make sure I hadn't gotten shot. Only then did I consult my pocket watch. When I peered out at the street I didn't spot anybody chasing me, but I thought I should be careful so I turned my coat inside out and tied a kerchief around my head, figuring as I did so that I ought to take the roundabout way back, while also realizing that Mr. Edward was going to be cross if I returned too late. I started running again, but nevertheless the evening was already filling the sky by the time I reached the Navy Yard grounds.

Soon as I entered our encampment, I first heard then witnessed Mr. La Mountain once again yelling at Professor Lowe, this time letting everyone nearby know that down at Fort Monroe he was able to fly unsecured above the Confederate territory without a problem and was convinced that if they could just get the go-ahead from General McClellan, which Professor Lowe alone could guarantee, given that he had "the President and Congress in his pocket," he, Mr. La Mountain would eagerly do so. He added, even more loudly, that he had never suffered the kinds of mishaps Professor Lowe and Mr. Wise had, downing balloons, crashing into enemy territory, that he could fly a balloon from "here to New York or New Orleans, if need be," with his eyes closed and hands tied behind back. For his part Professor Lowe as usual was ignoring him and speaking determinedly with other members of the staff about their projects. Mr. Edward, an observer to the quarrel like everybody else, sidled up to me and said, "You would think that man is on the other side half the time." While he spoke he extended his hand for the things I bought him, registering nothing about my lateness. When we were through I inquired of Ulysses if he needed any help, since I knew he had spent the entire afternoon assisting various members of the Corps' assembly team attaching and reknotting the web of ropes from one balloon to its basket. He said he didn't, he was done. But he asked me to fetch them, and by implication him, some water. At the pump, as I was filling the pitcher, Mr. La Mountain stormed over and shoved me out of the way to fill his cup. My first thought was to say something, though I wasn't sure what I could say to someone of his rank and stature and not get punished for. Instead I brought Ulysses the pitcher and headed off to help Patrick, if he needed me, with mess.

That night, before Mr. Edward sent me on my way, he asked me to stroll with him out toward the river. "Sir, is it safe," I asked, and he said, "Theodore, why are you always so yellow with fear? There are federals all the way south to Alexandria Town, and more troops all along the Maryland coastline"—indicating these phantasms with a sweep of his hand—"so there is simply no need to worry." Yet even after being down here for nearly a month, I didn't ever feel secure, so I aimed as slyly as possible to keep him between the water and me. "I had to tell someone," he was still going on, "since Johann—John Steiner—confirmed what Professor Lowe had promised, which is that I will get an opportunity to go up in the balloon first thing tomorrow!" I thought and then said, "Sir, that's your wish come true, Mr. Edward, just wonderful," and he said, "*Neddy*—and it is, Theodore, I almost can't believe it. You'll have to be up earlier than usual, because I need to be ready, and whatever trick you use to stay so punctual use it so that you are by my side as soon as the sun's up." Sure as the sun rose, I was.

The morning sky looked like it would split in two. For a while a heavy wind boxed the small balloon around, but it didn't rain and things calmed enough that once it had filled with gas Mr. Edward could ascend to test it. I stood beside Professor Lowe, who this time, rather than me, was holding the telegraph wire, Misters Steiner and Starkweather, and several assistants, who were manning the cables. We all watched Mr. Edward as he opened the valve to regulate the height, and backed up when he urged us to as he snipped open sandbags to ascend. All the while he was calling out various things I committed to memory, knowing that although he had taken his notebook with him he wasn't yet writing anything down. There was enough wind and slack that after he initially floated above the dock he hovered westward over the inlet, then rose higher and balanced not far from the buildings on M Street. The wind was strong and he coasted upward and eastward, until he was hovering above the neighboring market, then he floated over the open water, holding there for a while as most of the others, except the men on the cables, dispersed. Professor Lowe handed me the telegraph wire, and left with Mr. Steiner for a short while, both still talking animatedly about various aeronautical issues when they returned.

I trained my attention on Mr. Edward, who had gone so far up and grown so quiet I imagined he either was thinking or calculating. After a stretch of silence I grew nervous, and considered calling out, "Sir, everything well, Mr. Edward?" especially when out of the corner of my eye I could see Mr. La Mountain and Mr. Wise watching me, and when Professor Lowe and Mr. Steiner returned, they began glaring at them. The professor broke off his conversation with Mr. Steiner and said to no one in particular, as he stroked his thick mustache and studied his own notebook, "Linde should be brimming with observations." He called out, "Everything well, Linde?" to which Mr. Edward cried back, "Optimal, Professor, *summum visum*," then "I am beginning my descent!" Professor Lowe turned to find me still by his side, which startled him, and ordered me to not let go of the telegraph cable and retreat a little, while my boss slowly and carefully returned to the earth.

During a lull that afternoon, as most of the men played an impromptu game of baseball or listened to one of the naval bands, I went to fetch the mail, tobacco, stationery, and a newspaper. Along with the letters from Mr. Edward's family there was one I could see from Jonathan, care of Mr. Edward, for me. As I trod along the edge of the canal I passed the letter from palm to palm, eager to tear it open but afraid to, almost so excited to read it I nearly dropped it into the murky water. It wasn't until I reached the open expanse of one of the squares near Virginia Avenue that I grasped I had walked right past the Capitol, nestled serenely on its promontory, without even noticing. At the South Market, just blocks from the Navy Yard, I paused and squatted under a linden tree at the stalls' edge, making sure I stashed Mr. Edward's correspondence away so I didn't lose it. With the greatest care I opened my letter, which I read, first aloud, then with my eyes several times, lingering on the large, slanted script:

Phil. Penna. SEPT 1861

to Theodore,

I write for Mama myself Lucius Zenobia+Zephira and all the Family when I says we MISS YOU something terrible and hopes you taken care given what we hear about the War. Follow His Word in everything BROTHER. I speak to Mr. Dameron and he say he'll take you back so please think abt it. Red do a good Job for Mr. Linde son and we hold you in our HEART AND MIND always.

God bless+protect you big bro. Jonathan

At the very bottom of the letter I noticed something scrawled around a cross but at first I couldn't decipher it. The longer I looked, the clearer it became, and I grinned when I figured it out: *ra†io*.

I sat there for some time thinking about the letter, about Mama and Jonathan, about my siblings and in-laws, my nieces and nephews, about my boy HoRA†IO, *Ray-Ray*, about my city and my home and how even though I hated scaling fish or shucking oysters, even if I liked it less than all of this, a lot less than all this, wringing a chicken's neck was nowhere near terrifying as huddling at the rear of a fort or riding in a wagon while gunfire raged nearby, and for a second I began musing about the possibility of returning back north and how and when I might do so, what exactly I would tell Mr. Edward, maybe I could head back with him when he quit the Corps because he had shared with me one evening a week ago, out of frustration, when he thought he would never get to take to the air, that he was planning on further training in order to become a professor himself, especially if President Lincoln didn't get around to awarding him and the rest of them official military commissions, and, he added out of nowhere, he was going to marry Mr. Peter Robins's sister Alexandra. Soon as I recalled that I checked the time: I had been far too long in my reverie, so I ran the few blocks back to camp.

Mr. Edward was standing all by himself near the tents, waiting for me, his hands behind his back, spectacles on the tip of nose. He said, peeve coloring his timbre, "Boy, where in stars' name have you been?" I told him that there were military officers holding up everything all along Pennsylvania, checking papers and such, and he replied, with obvious vexation, "Well, there are Confederates and their sympathizers all around us so you should take care not to dally in the city." He looked in the direction of the water, which lay beyond the rows of buildings and boats. "They were looking for you to join Ulysses in a buck dance to entertain them but I told them you wouldn't be doing so." I could hear a banjo and clapping in the distance, so I said, "Yes, Sir, thank you, here is your mail, can I get you anything?" He raised his right hand, which was wrapped in a gauze, forming a tan mitt, and returning to his usual tone with me he said that he had burnt himself with the soldering iron. "Oh, Mr. Edward, Sir, I'm sorry." I asked him if he had hurt himself badly but he assured me that it wasn't as bad as it looked, but he would especially need my help now.

He had me sit down beside him, open and read his passel of letters. While his mother wrote about the family, her friends and garden and parties, the return of the fall social season, his father wrote to let him know his account was full, and to be careful and brave, and use "the sabre" of his great mind. His eldest brother Albert penned long paragraphs about his wife and children, his clubs and the insurance business. The middle brother, Frederick, spoke about his position at the brokerage in New York. His sister Katharine included clippings from the regular and society newspapers, and mentioned running into Mr. Bache, who urged that "Neddy" pay him a visit at the Coast Survey offices which sat just blocks from here. Most of his friends, after perfunctory comments about the "War" and the Corps, nattered on about the same things, themselves, clubs, businesses, marriages, trips, purchases, though Mr. Peter Robins punctuated his letter, nested in a copy of a new novel by Charles Dickens, with the question of whether Mr. Edward was ready to end his "experiment," and "liberate your Liberian." I studied Mr. Edward's face as I read the line, but it appeared not to provoke any response at all.

When we had concluded the letters I asked to be dismissed, but he had me read the headlines of the *Washington Daily Intelligencer*—a paper he claimed to detest but read only because timely copies of the *Philadelphia Enquirer* were hard to find—which I did as swiftly as I could. I raced through auctions, politics at the local and national level, the war in western Virginia, which he made me pause on; the demoralization of the poorer classes in Norfolk and Richmond, debates on the war in Europe, articles on Utah and California, announcements for theater dramas and farces. I did not utter but winced when I came across the request, with a $50 reward, for the return of "Hansom," a "small-statured Negro boy of sixteen years, light copper colored," to his owner living southeast of some town called "Bladensburg." After that I opened his tin of sardines and he let me have half the can, so I made sure to save some for Ulysses, then I packed his pipe with tobacco and lit it so he could smoke it, while he talked about the balloon and how he had been re-calibrating the altimeter, how he intended to go up at the end of the week with Professor Lowe, how someone had broken up a fight with … but I was halfway to Lombard Street in my head, paying attention only when I heard him say, "Thank you, Theodore, you're dismissed."

The next few days I undertook my usual tasks, including trips to purchase twine and paint brushes. I also assisted Ulysses and the others in rigging the bigger balloons Professor Lowe was putting on his boat, or "aircraft carrier" as Mr. Edward called it, which would soon venture down the Potomac. Every chance I could I reread the letter from Jonathan, struggling not to drift off into a daydream and end up injuring myself with a snapped cable or dropped tool. Mr. Edward continued his preparations, but a hour before mess, he asked me to take dictation for a brief letter, with the quill and ink, to his former professor at the Lawrence Scientific School, Dr. Joseph Lovering, about possible study in Berlin. To stop thinking about Philadelphia and the letter and my family, I engaged in my count-ups and downs, and even convinced Mr. Edward to play several rounds of Takeaway using twigs, he winning three games and I two. It was a relief that night that Nimrod joined Ulysses and me for supper, even staying over almost till next morning's bugle call. A few nights later, on the eve of the next early morning observation, I could barely fall asleep at first and tossed fitfully, hearing what sounded like thunder though I reckoned it was in my dream, but it wasn't exactly a dream, nor a nightmare, I couldn't see anything and attempted to speak it, describe it, to myself, but I couldn't, my mouth wouldn't open, there was a hand or hands over it, on me, holding me, heavy as an ironclad, down, I was sinking down into the earth and I fought whoever it was holding me hard as I could, I fought them off and leapt up, yawning, no one was there, Ulysses was still curled under the blanket, snoring. I kept yawning as I scrubbed myself in the cold October morning air before I headed to where Mr. Edward slept. I fished out my letter, reread it, at the same time wondering where Dandy was, somewhere here in Washington, in Baltimore, had he gone there? back in Philadelphia, had he ended up in Buffalo or Boston, wondering how I could see him again, send him a note.

I collected Mr. Edward and his bag, heavy with various items, and walked with him to the balloon. No one else was there. The sky was as gray as gneiss and the balloon, inflated the night before, was twisting about at the neck in the chilly wind whipping around us. I considered asking whether he would be ascending today, but he preempted me with, "Ah well, Professor Lowe hasn't arrived yet," and then "the wind is blowing north-east, north-north east, or maybe it's southeasterly," and then "I need to check the altimeter, which should be perfectly calibrated, and also just ensure the telegraph wires are still connected." He handed me his notebook but did not move. He remained where he was, staring at his bandaged right hand, patting his pockets, lifting his left hand to his face, and said: "Theodore, do you have my pipe and glasses?" I shook my head then felt around in the full bag I had brought from his room. He and I both had packed a great deal, but neither the pipe nor glasses were in there. "Mr. Edward, Sir, I can go back and look for them," I said, and proceeded to head to his tent, but he stopped me with his good hand and said, "You've never been in the balloon before, when you drop my bag in there, why don't you make sure the altimeter is lashed, the main valve is tight, and the telegraph wires are connected." I stood there looking at him, since what he said made no sense, I wasn't supposed to go anywhere near the baskets, but he continued, "You know exactly how they are supposed to look." Of course I had wanted many times to climb in the balloon basket, had even thought of hiding in there the first time Mr. Edward was to go up, but on the other hand, I knew my doing so was forbidden. Most of the white men could not set foot in that basket, and certainly neither Ulysses nor I had permission.

I had never defied him, but I said, "Mr. Edward, Sir, I don't think I'm supposed to get near that basket, Professor Lowe especially might get very cross. I'll gladly go get your pipe and glasses." He assured me, "*Neddy*—and Professor Lowe won't mind your being in there for a second or two. Really, Theodore, I'll be right back, I think I know where I left them." I nodded, but nevertheless hesitated and began to say, "Mr. Edward, we can wait till you come back," but instead, watching him walk back to his tent I took slow but steady steps toward the basket, and climbed in. I set his bag down, reviewed the altimeter, which was securely knotted, and the valve, tight as a balled fist, but when I bent to inspect the telegraph wire I tripped and fell against the edge of the basket—

—While out of the corner of my eye I see someone, a white man, darting from behind a shed toward where the rest of the balloons are lying in assembly, and I experience this strange sensation like the ground is moving, like time is slowing and I see Mr. Edward, bespectacled, pipe in his mouth, advancing toward me, running but not running, yet simultaneously moving farther away as he's crying out, "Oh my heavens, no, Theodore," and my first impulse, after realizing I don't understand what is happening, is to scream as the basket hooks upward to my left, then my right, my jaws snapping open, my eyes beading on the pale pattern and elaborate housing of the vast silk globe above me, I want to scream back at him, at anyone who's nearby that I'm up the air, I'm flying, I want to holler even if just to myself about how it's not at all like I had imagined, how my weight is dwindling to nothing, how gravity is flipping upside down, time stalling to a standstill, how my stomach is twisting itself into tiny knots catapulting themselves into my throat, and Mr. Edward, I can hear him clearly now, is screaming, "Who cut the cables? Oh stars, somebody cut the cables, Theodore—"

—And I feel something jerking on one of the cables, and peer over the edge to see him trying to hold on with his bad hand, and here come Professor Lowe and Ulysses and Mr. Steiner and Mr. Starkweather and Patrick, almost all the others, they are jumping and reaching for the ropes and Ulysses is hollering, "Jump, Red, I'll catch you, little brother, jump," and Mr. Edward is crying out, "No, Theodore, tie yourself to the inside of the basket, and don't stand too close to the edge." I'm thinking to myself this really is flying, I'm flying, the wind humming against the balloon's surface and the basket, and I notice for the first time beside me a metal flask, which may or may not be empty, two white flags, attached to metal poles the length of my forearm, bound by knotted waxed cording, as well as the rope descending from the valve over the balloon's closed hole, and I hold onto one of the coils of additional rope and wire ringing the rest of the basket walls and remember to tie myself to the hook in the floor, and I also remember to check the altimeter and telegraph transmitter, and from the bag grab Mr. Edward's notebook, though I remember pretty much everything he has been saying about aeronautics and balloons and flying since we got here—

—While all around me the sky is churning between silver and mother-of-pearl, and below the rigid grid of the federal capital, circling it on all sides verdant countryside, the hills and meadows, the farms and homesteads, the bends of the ochre river, some of it Virginia and some of it Maryland, one direction straight to Pennsylvania and the other to the Carolinas, one to the Atlantic Ocean and the other to the Bull Run and Blue Ridge Mountains, I can barely hear Mr. Edward, Ulysses, and the others calling out to me, their voices growing ever more distant, "Theodore, Theodore," and I sit in the center of the basket as it grows colder, knowing now that I am tethered to nothing at all, the basket and me now in a free float, a drift, a soar—

—And I stand and remember, can see out there all the forts and encampments and troops massed like tumors along the river banks, the ramparts and howitzers armoring the hills, the works teething at the edge of the foliage, the terrible danger snaking through the vast green and brown rolling land, and I feel something not quite fear and not quite elation, I can't put a name to it, I try to utter it but cannot, I place my hand on the valve string, then reach over and check that the sandbags are in place, pat my winter coat, feeling not only the weight of my papers and my pocketwatch but my heart, when my throat finally relaxes as if something, sound, will issue from it, to say *Mama,* and *Jonathan,* and *Horatio,* and *Neddy,* and *Ulysses,* and *Nimrod,* and *Daddy Zenobia Zephira Lucius Professor Lowe President Lincoln, Hansome,* somebody *HELP ME,* but only the gas hisses in assent as I pull on the string, as I open my mouth even wider and remember to—

RIVERS

What I'd like to hear about, the reporter starts in, is the time you and that little boy ... and I silence him again with a turn of my head, thinking to myself that this is supposed to be an interview about the war and my service in it, from the day I enlisted despite being almost a score years too old, having several mouths to feed, and running a tavern under my own name a grasshopper's jump from the riverfront, to the day we were sent by wagon and train down to Brazos de Santiago, where we launched the fight that ended on that spring day, ten years ago, along the Rio Grande on the meadows of Palmito Ranch, which, we learned later from a scout we captured from the other side was the final battle in the first great war for *our* freedom, or between the states as they like to call it these days, so I ain't about to devote a minute to those sense-defying events of forty years before.

Yet the mere mention of that boy's name, one I seldom think about, not even in dreams or nightmares, retrieves the sole two times since those years that I saw his face. That first time the name and face had become molded to the measure of a man, still young and with a decade before him but rendered gaunt and taut by struggles unknown to me and perhaps to that writer, also from Hannibal, who had made him, both of us, briefly famous. That face with its narrow angles and sharp agate eyes, with the sandy tufts of hair now framing it at the cheeks and chin, that glanced past me on Chouteau near the Pacific railroad tracks as I passed it and that other one I knew so well, on my way back to the public house where I worked, near the waterfront, ten years after that voyage down the Mississippi—my folly, when I could have crossed with my wife of those years, and my children, then still little, right there at Alton, and made my way east and we all would have been truly free—ten years before the conflagration that would cleave the country in two.

The other face, the Sawyer boy's, froze as it glimpsed mine, and when it had passed several steps beyond me said loudly to its companion, "Whoa, Huck, I think that was your old boy from Hannibal!" and then, "Old buck, hold up, now," and "Ain't you Jim Watson, you, that keeps on walking without stepping to the side when you see two gentlemen approaching, like you ain't heard one of 'em call out your name?" So I paused and turned around, and faced them. There they were, Huckleberry, now in his early 20s, and Sawyer, same in years, both taller than me now, still lean in their youthful frames, each one looking from their clothing alone fairly prosperous as so many were during those charging years, though in Huck's mien I could see that all the gold they had gotten from that mess in the caves had not alleviated whatever inner torments afflicted him. "Well, now," Sawyer said, brushing the sleeves of his worsted suit coat as he approached me, Huck behind him, "I should have figured we would come across you one day down here."

"Howdy now, Jim," Huck said, and extended his adult hand.

"Howdy, Huckleberry, howdy, Tom," I answered, tipping my hat ever so slightly and taking his palm only momentarily in mine.

Sawyer leaned against a stile and proceeded to tell me all about himself, how he was working during the day in the law offices of Judge Thatcher's brother and after spending a year at Centre College in Kentucky and another at the University of Virginia, President Jefferson's school he proudly pointed out, he was studying law at night at Reverend Eliot's new seminary not far from here, though he reminded me neither he and Huck had to work and that I certainly should not have forgotten why. He told me he had traveled down the Mississippi on a steamboat several times, including by himself, all the way to New Orleans, which is where he thought he might eventually settle if he didn't stay in St. Louis, since the culture and people down there appealed to him, and that he would probably write about it all when he was past the bar and in an equitable position. He kept talking for a good while longer but I confess that though my eyes never left his mouth I rapidly quit listening.

After Sawyer had finished his personal resume he spoke about Huck, who he said had gotten himself some schooling too up in Cambridge, Illinois, near Rock Island, where he had gone to stay with some distant relatives of his late father's, and between stints in the cooler for "minor infractions," which he did not detail and about which I wasn't going to ask, he said that Huck liked to sample a little of every kind of job. Tom chuckled as he spoke, Huck for his part peering off into the roadway, as though he was searching for a way out of the story Tom was telling and a new path into himself. Such a "river rat," Tom continued, his words bubbling with laughter, Huck was that he now served as an assistant foreman in the river salvage company run by Captain Eads. Just before this new position, Huck, Tom concluded, his laughter evaporating like mid-morning dew, had just returned from Kansas. "He went out there to see what the troublemakers were up to, the ones from New England and the East and Iowa and here as well, who want to overthrow centuries of civilization and take away our way of life and liberty and tell us what we can and cannot do and own."

I said nothing, looking intently at him and then at Huck, who finally said, "This winter I gone out to Lawrence, which is a good ways past the state border. I got up to a few scrapes but nothing serious," and then, "I don't think old Jim wants to be bothered with hearing about any of that."

"Hearing about it and us ain't no bother to Jim," Tom said, and trained his gaze on me.

"All the same, he don't want to hear some scuffle with a troublemaker. He sure looks like he been minding his business and it's good to see him."

"Thank you, Huck," I said, and nodded at Tom, who frowned.

"He ain't got no business that's more important than what we're doing, does he?" Tom said. "Can't be likely, can it?"

"Not certainly," Huck said, and when Tom turned away from him, he shrugged his shoulders for me. "Then again I don't know nothing about his business these days."

"When did you get yourself down this way?" Sawyer said, his razor lips cutting me a smile. "Cause I reckon soon as you knew you had got your freedom we all woke up to find you gone."

I thought to tell the boy that although once Huck and I got back and I learned Miss Watson's will had freed me, a man in town, La-Fleur, and his brothers, all later to take up arms for the Confederate cause, would come into the stables where I worked and keep on making jokes about selling me back into bondage since Washington had cut off the trade and our bodies were a premium further south down the Mississippi, so I planned out resolving the matter once and for all by crossing to the other side, practicing a number of times when I knew the tide was low, since I knew how to swim and even a blind man in a blindfold behind a high blind wall could see Illinois from Hannibal. One night when I was waist-deep in the water I had to remind a white patrolman strolling the levee I was emancipated and showed him my papers which I kept in a waterproof metal locket that hung around my neck, though they were also on file down in the main courthouse of Marion County, Missouri, and he said he ought to lock me up just for talking so freely, like I was equal to a white person, but since I had belonged to the late Miss Watson, God Rest Her Soul, he would let me go, which I knew well enough to nod to, before I crept carefully back to my little room in the black section of town, and resolved even more to flee.

I thought to say that I had sworn to my then-wife Sadie, who had taken up with another man when she thought I had murdered that white boy, Huck, that I would buy the children's freedom and hers, which I intended to hold fast to, but when I told her I was leaving she convinced me to take her and our children with me, though I was not about to bring her new man along, she could send for him later, and as for my children, at that time there was only two of them, Elizabeth, who was deaf and mute, though sharp as a whipsaw, and Johnny, who looked like a little me, and I was going to fetch them to their freedom soon as I had gotten settled in. When all the signs confirmed the time had come I brought us to the farthest end of the levee, where I had identified a raft I would commandeer, and we stuffed all our necessities in one small sack and a canvas traveling bag I borrowed from the stables where I worked, I say borrowed since I eventually mailed it back, postage paid, and I could see Sadie was looking around as if that man of hers was going to steal away with us so I told her she could go with me and the little ones or continue in her bliss with him. I was prepared to carry those children on my back like St. Christopher all the way to the other side, and her too if it came to that, but not her lover, yet we reached Illinois easily on that cool spring night, landing far north of where the main docks in Alton were since I knew there were patrolmen to ensure none of us made it, and I had been warned to watch out for a notorious Negro who would run straightaway and alert the white constable, but that Rastus wasn't anywhere to be found.

I thought to say I did spot the person who knew where to take us and put us on a wagon bound straight north along the river for Quincy, where Dr. Eells lived. We spoke in what they call our *gibberish* but to us it was a language full of secret keys, and that person guided us to another person, in these days despite the daily terror against us we are still free and I can tell the truth because nobody can prosecute them or punish them now, so I can say they were both colored women, the first one carrying herself in disguise like she had no home in the world and the second was clothed like a male night watchman's assistant. The second woman guided us to the wagon that brought us to Dr. Eells. Have you ever tried to keep a small child from laughing or crying because your life depended upon it? Have you ever hid with a spouse and two children, which was actually two too many for Dr. Eells, and I had to cajole him not to turn us away, recounting at least twenty times for him how I was already manumitted but explaining the danger my wife, since that she still was, and my poor children, faced, so for a week I implored him in his attic, which is where we stayed, mostly lying down in silence until he would come to question me periodically, because the slavecatchers particularly trolled that city, which was notorious for harboring fugitives, and I was sure the people who had laid claim to Sadie and the children, along with her spurned male friend, had sounded an alarm.

I thought to recount that finally after dawn on a Sunday a white woman came to Dr. Eells's house seeking the cargo to Elgin and points east, and Dr. Eells stowed us all under a false floor which my wife was convinced would be our coffin until I reassured her that was the only way we would be able to travel while eluding the catchers' grasp. We traveled in that shallow grave on metal wheels for what felt like days, riding the worst roads I imagine exist in the state of Illinois, though it was not even a whole twenty-four hours, and we stopped in a roadside grove along the way for water and to relieve ourselves and eat some cold porridge with walnuts and hardtack biscuits, then returned to our hiding place and when we climbed out we were in the city of Chicago, which was an impressive sight, to say the least, far more impressive than Hannibal, though Chicago wasn't even as pretty or built up as old St. Louis back then, and so not as impressive as it is today.

I thought to narrate that there is where we settled, and as soon as we could I made sure Sadie and the little ones each got their Certificates of Freedom from the State of Illinois, Cook County, as I got mine, making sure mine read James Alton Rivers, since I kept the name I had always been known by but added the town where I first breathed in real liberty, and since we had finally reached the other side of the big snaking muddy river which had been the dividing line our whole lives up until then, our long bondage on the one side in Missouri and that goal we sought on the other, then we crossed the Illinois River which we had reached at Peoria, and finally the forking river in Chicago which takes you out to the sea-like lake, and I didn't feel a single shred of remorse for having dropped the name of Miss Watson, since she wasn't no great mistress or lady anyhow. I had to learn to say Mr. James Alton Rivers instead of just Jim as white folks always called me, or Jim Watson, which everyone had taken to saying, like this Sawyer boy now, just as Sadie had to learn to say Sadie May Rivers, May the middle name she took to acknowledge the month that we arrived, though she was not so fond of the last name Rivers, and kept calling herself simply Sadie May, and Elizabeth went by Bessie Amelia Rivers, to honor her late baby sister, Amelia, who died in infancy on that farm off Bear Creek where she was born, and Johnny, whose middle name became Obi after my grandfather I never met named Obi, who was a pure African they used to say, as well as the old faith I had kept alive, even in Hannibal, was quickly saying Johnny O. Rivers without missing a beat.

I think to conclude to the Sawyer boy and Huckleberry, all adulted now, that I keep that certificate at all times and in all places against my chest in a leather pouch I bought for myself and it reads JAMES ALTON RIVERS, FREE PERSON OF COLOR, a resident or citizen of the State of Illinois, at all times in all places, and entitled to be respected accordingly, in Person and Property, at all times in all places, in the due prosecution of his—my—concerns, at all times in all places, signed with the Seal of said Court, at Chicago, on the 23rd of November in the year of our Lord one thousand eight hundred and fifty-two, and I have carried it all the way up to and through the time I returned to Missouri, settling here in St. Louis since I was not ever going to set feet again in Hannibal if I could help it, and even when some of the Hannibal people including those LaFleurs have happened upon me down here there is not a thing they could say or do because I had the states of Missouri, Illinois and the federal government on my side, though I've always made sure to have an escape route and a safehouse on the other side of the river ready to flee to given the trials the courts are putting Mr. Dred and Mrs. Lizzie Scott through.

Instead I said, "I was living in Chicago for a few years then I decided to come back home. I posted my bond to stay here, have been working steadily and decided to settle down."

"Chicago," Sawyer said, looking at Huckleberry, "sounds like our old friend has gone and got pretty fancy on us. What do you think about that, Huck?"

"I been as far south as Mississippi and over to Louisville, Kentucky but I never been to Chicago myself," Huck replied.

"All kinds of things going on up in Chicago," Tom said.

"Jim ain't said nothing about all that, just that he been there and come back here," Huck said.

"Some go to Chicago and get ideas," Tom said.

The angles of that face, like broken porcelain, pulled apart and recombined until I almost did not recognize him. "Well, sounds to me like Jim is keeping himself out of trouble, and the worst thing for anybody these days is getting caught up in all that trouble, getting involved with people like Lovejoy or Torrey or that new agitator writer Mrs. Stowe what likes to stir up a whole heap of trouble too."

I remained silent, thinking I should tell these two that two years ago, I consulted the omens and auguries, which told me that I should head down to St. Louis, perhaps continuing on to Kansas or Oklahoma territory, so I said goodbye to my children, promising I would write them every other week and send money for food and books and clothes, and goodbye to Sadie May, who could move to Timbuctoo with her new lovers for all I cared so long as she did not take my children there. I left Chicago first thing in the morning to walk back and hitch my way to my native state, though this time with my papers on me, saying James Alton Rivers, free in all places and at all times, determined nobody, LaFleur or anyone else, was going to put me under bond. Eventually I reached the city after crossing around the Indian mounds in Cahokia and lodged with my half-brother Ezekiel, who had been manumitted and left Hannibal first second he could, running around with the last name Carillon after the family that had held him, though I eventually convinced him to change it Rivers too. Through him I secured a job cleaning up and doing repairs on a tavern building owned by an older gentleman named Mr. Wallace

Wallace, who had gained his freedom in the 1830s and was said, because of his silver eyes, to be the unacknowledged son of one of the oldest families in the county. Soon I was running that tavern since Mr. Wallace Wallace had so much other business, involving numbers and cards and palliatives, and sometimes ladies and studs, to attend to. There was a good number of those white men in the city who liked the delights that Mr. Wallace Wallace provided, but you always have to be careful when you get too deep in the cut with those kinds of folks, because you can turn up like Mr. Wallace Wallace, with his silk ties and ruby studded pocketwatch and silver eyes and pearl-handed pistol, which he did not hesitate to brandish if needed, floating face down in the Des Peres River, with no cut at all.

You could say Mr. Wallace Wallace left a welter, I want to tell these two, if you are trying to be both cruel and truthful, but he had fathered a number of children by different wives and girlfriends, some free and some still in bondage, some on the Missouri side and some over in Brooklin, right next to East St. Louis, and I heard tell that he had left another brood all along the river far north as Minnesota from the time he gained his papers up till now. As it was, I spoke to several people of the kind who could resolve the question of the building's title while I took to running the tavern, though I had to finagle to get it into my name. As soon as I did I sold it to a white man who planned to tear it and every other building on the block down so he could throw up a warehouse, since in those days white people from every corner of their world, some from all across the free states and some from the Southern states, some from Ireland and some from Germany, were showing up as if the wind brought them, and they like to make money and take care of each other and that tiny tavern was in their way. I took the money, which was more than a servant's wages, and bought another tavern cheap from a man leaving for Kansas, even closer to the river near the railroad tracks on Sycamore, from the roof you could even see Duncan's Island where they carried out executions and lynchings. Ezekiel painted the sign with my name on it, Rivers Tavern, and I got down to business, always making sure that I watered down the liquor and allowed few tabs or overnighters, borrowing only when absolutely necessary, and I eventually found myself and Ezekiel a pistol each, mine nesting in the back of my trousers, to ensure nobody rolled us, though I regularly paid off the police and a representative of my ward's alderman every other Thursday, always in the morning and a few cents more than they asked for, which meant I never had any trouble, no trouble at all.

For all my success in business, I have never had any luck with women, which I would never dare share with these two, and the first one I took up with in St. Louis, just to have a woman more so than I really liked her, had something going with another woman at the same time. I broke it off but she sent the second woman to come talk to me, saying they could make accommodations if I could. The way it happens in the Bible the man would take several wives and not the other way around, but this woman, Augustine, had a way about her that could bend you to her will. The woman who came calling, with her tight curls and skin as black as mine and her limp, was named Louisa, and I ended up moving in with the two of them and Augustine's two girls who were halfway to adult age and not so amenable to their mother's guidance, especially since she was too caught up with her own business, a sure disaster when dealing with young people. Louisa was interested in learning about healing and reading the signs, and after a while I found myself growing quite fond of Louisa herself, and she confessed she had told Augustine she'd better keep me on as soon as she laid eyes on me, so she could get to know me, with my shoulders of coal and hairy legs and skillful way around a bar and a ledger book, and I found myself taken with this short skinny woman with skin the color of midnight and lips always parted as if posing a rhetorical question and her love of books, midnight eyes, and that leg broken during her bondage and never properly set, and that was how all that began. Still I warned her we ought to be careful, not just because of Augustine, who it turns out had other things happening on the side herself and was fine to let us have our own, but with her girls, and because of the law which saw fit to jail or send people down the Mississippi who didn't follow the rules and conventions. Louisa, in her fashion, said several weeks later, having joined me in running the tavern, don't worry about all that, we live in a frontier area, nobody cares about what we're doing, and if the law comes we can always flee west and request to live among the Indians, and there's nothing the law could do to us then.

Instead I said, "My business, Huckleberry, is just working hard and living my life, and I don't know nothing about no Lovejoy or Torrey"—though I knew good and well who they both were, what free man didn't know the names of the abolitionist heroes—"or the Mrs. Stowe lady"—and who in the last year hadn't ever heard of her or her book?—"and I haven't ever even considered going west."

Huckleberry nodded, but Sawyer was watching me closely. He said nothing for a while, until I moved to take my leave and walk away. As soon as I stirred he laughed, more a cackle than an expression of humor, leaned close to me and said loudly, as passersby looked on, "You'd better watch yourself, Jim, you hear me? Good thing we know you but you walking these streets like they belong to you, and they don't to no nigger, no matter what some of you might think these days, so you watch it, cause the time'll come when even the good people like me and Huck here have had enough." He clapped me hard on the shoulder as he said this, and I thought to cock him cold in his wire-lipped mouth, but I did not want to do anything to lose my tavern or my freedom, so I said, "I hear that, Tom," and he said, losing his laugh, though Huckleberry was almost smiling now, "You call me Mr. Tom Sawyer, Sir, old man," and I said, "YesMissTomSawyerSoilMan," so fast it wasn't clear whether I'd left out the "Mr." or the "Sir" or added the "Old Man," and he looked hard at me, almost smiling, reminding me in a firm, cold voice, "Boy, I'm warning you, you had better watch yourself."

Huckleberry seized my hand, clasping it so tight he brought back in a quick flood of feelings those years with the Widow Watson, and whispered as if he wanted only me and not his friend to hear, "You take care of yourself, Jim, and keep out of all that trouble, please, cause this world is about ready to break wide open, and I sure don't want to see you get swallowed up."

I told him I would not get involved in any such things, though I was going to do whatever I wanted within reason especially if it was going to ensure that no other person would ever be enslaved, and not a single thing except maybe death was going to swallow me up or see that happen to me, certainly nothing involving him or that other one. I offered the two my good wishes and farewells, not moving yet watching as they walked away, Sawyer's head and arms gyring like a nickelodeon picture, Huck nodding but never glancing back, until they vanished into the horizon near Mill Creek.

I never came across either one of them over the next few years, not even once, then the war began so perhaps both had moved away to some other place, Sawyer to Nevada or Oregon, where some of the local people were heading, Huckleberry to Kansas, or perhaps they had already headed off to fight on the Confederate side. There was a pressing question about which way Missouri would go since Governor Claiborne had sided with the insurrectionists, then General Lyon came and the Germans faced down and fired on the insurrectionists, all those scrubby Dutch with their rifles from the federal arsenal, though nobody I knew could believe white people would fire on other white people en masse like that. But they did and that was only the opening of the war here, as well as the sum of the fighting, at least for the people who stayed in St. Louis. By this time Johnny O. had come to live with me, and at first didn't take so well to Louisa, though he stayed with us for about a year, finding work down on the levee with all the steamboats bringing goods to provision the troops, and in his off-time studied the healing arts with me when I wasn't working the bar. He fell in love with a girl who was still bound to a family out in Bellefontaine, so I gave him money to go back to Chicago, so she could become free and they could marry. He left late one night and I was wrecked to see him go, but he wrote to tell me that after being stopped by the river patrols they got through, and he wrote me letters every other week, like I used to do with his sister and him, promising he was going to come back and fight.

Right around the middle of the summer of 1863 the army announced that we could sign up, at the Schofield Barracks, and though I was over 40 now, 46 to be exact, I felt it was my duty to contribute directly to the struggle, though I was sure they would say, Mr. Rivers, you are far too old, but rumor was an old black man had been the first casualty when the battles began in Washington, so if he was willing and able to serve why couldn't I, and I walked over there anyhow. Louisa protested my decision but, without conceding that what I was doing was right, agreed to stay in town and run the tavern while I was gone. It tore me apart to say goodbye to her, us never having left the other's side since we had taken up house together, but I knew both from all the signs at my disposal and deep in my core that at war's end I would walk through that tavern door and see her standing there.

They took me and we, the First Missouri Colored Troops, men mostly young but some old from in state and some from points north, west and south, mustered not long thereafter, and I will tell the reporter about all of this, about each battle from the time we crossed the Meramec, then headed to Helena, and the entire journey, with every battle and firefight all the way down to Texas, but only once I have finished telling him about the second time I saw that face, which was after we had already reached Los Brazos de Santiago, near Brownsville. Have you ever noticed how on the decisive day the light comes through the trees a certain way, how the patterns of the future reveal themselves as a ghost language and you got to do more than just pay attention but use all the knowledge and wisdom you have ever gained to interpret it? Because I had been studying on just that when Sydnor, from my company, ran right up to me hollering, all out of breath, "Colonel talking about how despite the cease-fire we might scrap it up one more time with the rebels," repeating himself until Bergamire and the rest of them closed his trap with their glares. I listened to him since the light that morning was not shining like on the morning that I chose to cross the Mississippi with Sadie May and the children all those years before, the sun's beams not drawing a path to the shore, not touching and catching and caressing the bluewood branches there in Texas just so, though in Hannibal it had been crab apples and cherries, the gleaming dressing the leaves with its omens and auguries, printing clues in shadowed patterns in the grass and soil you just needed to discern if you could, because the real test is always to go beyond mere guessing to following the map the world around you sets forth.

Soon enough here came Anderson, stomping over from the area of the officers' tents, grinning broadly like the lottery man had called his name, but unlike Sydnor he knew not to mess with me when I was studying on something, so he stood beside me as my eyes followed the light's shafts down into the greenery, tracing it with my fingers, smelling it, listening to the aftersounds and the silence enfolding it and only then did he utter anything, only when he was pretty sure I was done, Sydnor watching me too until he couldn't sit no more and hurried over to hear what Anderson had to say. Excuse me but what news you got for us, Pop James? is what this young man, once in bondage yet who knew how to write out notes like a schoolmaster and recite chapter and verse from the Bible and Longfellow without mixing up a single word, and who behaved like a gentleman when he spoke to an elder like me, asked me.

I answered, "I got to think about it for a little while more, but if you look at this sign here"—and I pointed to the cross of light with the faint shape of a heart hovering just above its center, a forewarning and lament—"and here, to the way the blades is bending outward on either side like an invisible arrow"—urging us to stay right where we were—"and to here," a patch so dusty it was as if the desert of solitary death had already laid claim to it, "this is not the time to attack, I can almost assure you on my parents' and my grandparents' graves of that." DeVeaux, who had also walked over, countered without even acknowledging me that my mumbo jumbo and hoodoo claptrap couldn't be right, that what we needed to do is fight our way to the next line, lay those Confederates and their French and Mexican infantrymen low like the reaper, and they all commenced to smiling and clapping, Johnson, Scott, Shepard, Morris who had his sisters kidnapped into Arkansas well before the first shot down at Sumter, Wilson, Patterson, Renard, Kelley, even Bergamire, nearly every last one of them. DeVeaux was on a roll now, his voice a common preacher's, which is what his father was, Anderson told me the first time I witnessed him going on like this, soon as he got free the daddy took up the Good Book and the son intended to follow that profession, these folks from the far northwestern corner of the state, near Nebraska, though he had shifted into testifying about how we all needed to go beyond shooting them down, we needed to kill at least ten apiece, have a slaughter to send a message to Price and Bedford and all the rest. When he had finally quieted down, Anderson reminded everyone we had orders to take them prisoner rather than go on a spree.

When he said this last word a few of them guffawed because they hadn't ever heard that word before, but Anderson was wont to speak real proper at times, like a dictionary would if a dictionary could talk, which made me think of my old lady back home. He and Bergamire and a few of the others would take turns teaching classes early in the morning and by the campfire, on spelling and speaking and math, not the kind of learning people learned in the fields or in the store rooms in country towns, but the right way so that you can pen your name when the time came, and understand what your documents were saying, and count your pay before and after it hit your pocket, instead of having to rely on them other folks to do so for you. I found myself growing close to Anderson, and would tell him what I was picking up so that he could convey it to the rest as if he had somehow assessed it himself, since they were more likely to listen to him.

But that day was not propitious, and yet Colonel Barrett ordered us to ready ourselves and proceed against the gray traitors, which meant eight companies of our United States Colored Troops, which is what we became when the Army federalized our Missouri brigade, would head with the white 2nd Texas Cavalry Battalion under the command of Lt. Colonel Branson through Boca Chica Pass to engage the enemy, driving them back to Brownsville and capturing any we could along the way. All day we prepared for the evening march, though it was already clear that four dozen of the white men would have to proceed horseless, but both Anderson and Bergamire circulated among all the companies to say that as soon as we overtook the insurrectionists we were to requisition as many of their mounts as we could. Between readying and packing equipment I sat and composed brief letters, which Anderson wrote out in his steady hand, to Johnny O., who was with a regiment still stationed in Tennessee, and to Bessie Amelia, who was raising money for the troops all across Minnesota and Wisconsin, and to Louisa, who loved hearing about nothing more than the tedium of my daily military life. A fine rain began falling in the late morning, and I pointed this out to Anderson, who thought it might let up, but by the time we had reached the pass, the downpour had thickened into batteries of water, and the sky cracked open with thunder and foreboding light. Our progress was glacial through the high, wet grass, which now hid all its secrets, giving off strange waterlogged sounds and odors, the cattails fizzling like flares, the figworts emitting their noxsome fragrance, the nightshade extending its mortal embrace, but we followed the curves of the river throughout the night and caught a brigade of the Confederates unawares. The Texans took three of the traitors prisoner, and sent some of our men to husband the supplies from their bivouac, though Anderson had me help set up camp for the night and read the surroundings for any clues about the following day.

I woke that morning and studied the omens, which were ill but not fully open to interpretation, so I kept them to myself. By midday we were creeping on our hands and knees like turtles across green expanse at the base of Palmito Hill when a fusillade, followed by a brigade of Confederates, engaged us. I usually kept to the rear as I was ordered to, but Anderson urged several of us to crawl out to the far edge of the field, near the river, where there was a stand of Montezuma cypresses, which I did and when I rounded them flat on my stomach, creeping forward like a panther I saw it, that face I could have identified if blind in both eyes, him, in profile, the agate eyes in a squint, that sandy ring of beard collaring the gaunt cheeks, the soiled gray jacket half open and hanging around the sun-reddened throat, him crouching reloading his gun, quickly glancing up and around him so as not to miss anything. I glanced behind to see if Anderson was nearby, but he and most of the rest were proceeding to the north of me, along the open field of battle, a blue line undulating forward in the high grass, their mismatched uniforms behind the white men in their blue streaming like waves on the one side and the gray of the insurrectionists on the other, the gunfire crackling like the announcement of the end of something terrible, and I looked up and he still had not seen me, this face he could have drawn in his sleep, these eyes that had watched his and watched over his, this elder who had been like a brother, a keeper, a second father as he wondered why this child was taking him deeper and deeper into the heart of the terror, why south instead of straight east to liberation, credit his and my youth or ignorance or inexperience, for which I forgive him and myself but I came so close to ending up in a far worse place than I ever was, and I heard Anderson or someone call out in the distance, and raised my gun, bringing it to my eye, the target his hands which were moving quickly with his own gun propped against his shoulder, over his heart, and I steadied the barrel, my finger on the trigger, which is when our gazes finally met, I am going to tell the reporter, and then we can discuss that whole story of the trip down the river with that boy, his gun aimed at me now, other faces behind his now, all of them assuming the contours, the lean, determined hardness of his face, that face, there were a hundred of that face, those faces, burnt, determined, hard and thinking only of their own disappearing universe, not ours, which was when the cry broke across the rippling grass, and the gun, the guns, went off.

PERSONS AND PLACES

Cambridge Journal: October ___, 1890

Fleeting Impressions on an Autumn Afternoon (Harvard)

Of what did this chilly afternoon consist? After lunch with Morgan in Mem. Hall, work and a swift visit to 20 Flagg, I took a round-about way from the Gymnasium for my breather. Past the Square terminus, dodging the chattering crowds and dust and clattering hooves that transform Cambridge at times into something of a mini-metropolis.

I was feeling rather out of sorts, for I once again had to put off Mrs. T[aylor] with a promise to pay in a fortnight and a smile. Throughout the meal I sat and ate, only moderately aware of my companion, Morgan. His jovial self as always, was he recounting to me last Saturday's Hill festivities and his impressions of some new young Ladies on visit from

After lecturing on thought and the color-sense, during which I pressed the students to investigate how the context of one's perception shapes mental impressions, I took lunch with one of Royce's students. A robust, poetically-minded young Platonist from New Hampshire, we navigated for an hour around the shoals of idealism and the literal embodiment of the Absolute in the lyric moment, to which he has rather romantically subscribed. Is that not a danger of the current state of the literary arts? He then inquired, *sub rosa*, whether the body, though withering on the vine of a man's life, might somehow be restored to its most dangerous state of beauty by thought alone. The perils, I thought but dared not

Philadelphia, or did I only imagine hearing him say this? In truth I was concentrating on my questions for the coming meeting of the Philosophical Club, where Santayana, that new graduate student and my likely tutor, is set to speak on "Spinoza and the Ethical Sensibility."

Indeed, as I was passing down Mount Auburn Street, I spotted his black-clad figure floating by. Ghostly, yet swarthy, an Iberian by birth, though perhaps not in temperament, something dangerous and daring in those black eyes. Our gazes met, glancingly. As he has been wont to do whenever we have seen each other, he abruptly turned away, striding faster than before he had caught sight of me. I continued on toward the river, where I thought I might walk for a while and observe the currents slowly pulling whatever traffic still lingered toward the Institute.

Why does he glower so? Is it fear, for certainly he has seen a Negro before, or can it be an acknowledgement of how deeply we are linked? Or does he, like nearly all the rest of them, *not really see me* at all? Of course say, of a little Wilde or Swinburne, a dose of Pater or, forgive me, William Shakespeare. . . .

Later, as I strolled along Mount Auburn Street, quietly composing, concepts racing in my head like the regattas these New Englanders love to hold, I noticed him again. The intense young colored man, a Negro most certainly, brow high, stern mien, walking briskly toward the river, his eyes fixed upon an invisible target, an imaginary star. This *Du Bois*, who, I am told by that collector of personalities, William James, fashions himself a philosopher, though gifted with scientific and other facilities. It is true that I have noted him haunting the precincts of the Yard, books peeking from his tattered leather satchel, his cheeks the color of tea into which several tablespoons of sweet cream have been poured, that gaze pressing intently toward some hidden point. Several times we have glimpsed each other, in wary appraisal, and I have, I shall not dissemble, hurried on. Perhaps he recognizes me as one of those who professes, an admirer of mental industry whatever the outward appearance of the there will be scant possibility of a friendship. Be he a Latin or the Statue of Liberty; for even Professor [Wm.] James, in all his eccentric allegiance, admits, when we are at the same table, of those unshakable walls that separate us. Still I know that at some point soon I shall have opportunity to probe his mind, share my inquiries—*he and I alone, in an upper room*—and he will come to appreciate our common humanity.

For fifteen minutes thus I stood, gathering impressions in the chill, until true cold settled in. Then I hurried back, darting between carriages and odd fellows, almost missing the news stand. I could only glimpse the evening headlines—a human bullet runs the 100 yard dash in under 10 seconds; the Abyssinian War continues; another lynching—making swift mental notes on all issues pertaining to my people, even though the various other national and international events of the past few weeks have not yet had a moment to sediment....

bearer; or perhaps through some profounder spiritual auscultation, divined the passion and ritual in my gait.

This *jeune philosophe*, like the other Negro students, the handful of unassimilable Easterners, Chinese, Mexican boys, must by necessity subsist on an island even more remote than that on which I sojourned during my College days, within this larger crimson archipelago. At one level, I imagine it would provide a place of refuge and some element of happiness for their small and scorned society.

He observes me as if he has already examined the catalogue of ideas and impressions which I shall tell him when we eventually speak, of the gulf between the true-self and the world outside and how the mind, through its exercises, bridges it; of the forests rising around the language of the physicist's thought; of the importance of doubt in the philosophical method; *of those fugitive joys and sincere ecstasies— that heaven that lies in the heart of the earth*; of my own long and unfolding exile.

ACROBATIQUE

H
i
g
h
e
r
,
I
h
e
a
r
f
r
o
m

somewhere far down there, below, from the sandy circle of the circus
floor or a seat in the lowest ring of tiered chairs, *plus haut!* the voice I
can easily discern, it's the ringmaster's, the crowd's, the words, now a
lone one in my head, *höher*, repeating, fleet and fluttering, soaring, past
me up into the rafters, scattering among the trusses, vaulted arches,
the cupola, clambering amid the bats and the blackbirds, across the
brickwork seen only by its masons and ghosts, though I see it, often
scale it with my eyes when I ascend, every night I am performing,
on the cables or trapeze, sometimes studying that map of bricks and
buttresses and plasterwork of this chocolate jewel box and nothing
else, this elaborate testament to human handiwork, rather than the
lights flickering blue-white against this hexadecagon's drafts, or the
violet Paris night flowing in through the high, narrow windows, or,

at least at first, the flaring faces of every evening's audience, until I dare myself to look at them too and do, all those brows and chins masked in chiaroscuro, all those muffs and fans and ruffles and opera spectacles, all those glowing pipe bowls, cigarillo embers flashing like starlight quilting the surface of the Oder on a mid-summer night, and I do but see no one, only a blur no more distinct than the ceiling's shadows, until I fix a face fixing me, lips agape, eyes firm as beads of beryl, amazement streaming out of them that I am hovering above, the mouthpiece in my teeth and no harness or net to rescue me, or more startling when I hang upside down with the cannon suspended from my teeth, its chain clenched like a whistle, which after the build-up of the horn and drumroll one of the assistants ignites, and when it fires everyone screams, but I have never, ever let it go, never dropped it, never come close to allowing it to slip, though the metal cuts my embouchure and my jaws and head and neck ache for hours after, and someone is crying out, *Bravissima, Madame La La, une miracle, magnifique,* followed by the barely audible But how does she do it? and another, My God, it is impossible, but she is an angel—or do I hear *an animal?—la mulâtresse-canon, la Venus noire, elle là la nôtre,* a marvel of nature, cheers, applause and catcalls fire, that mouth, that body, unnatural, such strength you'd see in a *monster,* as I prepare for the next series of maneuvers and rest my hips and torso on the bar while the clowns caper in reprise below, awaiting my sister butterfly, Theophila, Kaira la Blanche, her hands a doll's in mine,

       around my wrists, my ankles,

           our fearlessness locked together

               as we fly, and I think about that moment almost a year ago when a pallid, absinthe-cheeked frequenter of the local cafés ferreted his way in and asked her, as I sat beside her in the chamber where we ready ourselves and retire afterwards, about a new trick in which she spun like a corkscrew in the air before I snatched her from certain oblivion, What does it feel like to touch her, hold onto those muscles, do your fingers melt into that

skin, his gaze never grazing hers but grappling in its designs upon me,
Do you all live together here in the Montmartre district, can I come
visit you in your lodgings, and Kaira is shivering with embarrassment
as my own regard hardens to wrought iron, They say that you may
be closer than sisters, is that true? the drunkard winking, fingering
his lapel and drawing his chalky digits down to the open button at
the head of his fly, not once releasing his stare from me, even after I
dip my kerchief in the glass of peppermint water and bring it to my
tongue and arcade, letting the muscles in my throat relax as I turn
away; and I have heard everything, far worse, sometimes making me
laugh aloud as I lie on my cot for want of weeping, but much better
too, here and everywhere we have toured, greetings and grace notes
of gratitude and praise from people I could have never imagined as I
scrubbed the kitchen floorboards beside Mummi or walked from the
schoolhouse in silence watching the carriages clatter up the Grabow-
erstrasse in Stettin or sitting eating taffy with Lili and Ulli and Maria
in Töpffer's Park, I write them all whenever I can about everything,
they have heard every possible new technique I've acquired, every
wire I've walked, every new member of the company or employee of
the Cirque Fernando, though so as not to bore them I began to concentrate on the noteworthy things, such as how at the end of a performance last spring—May 18, 1878, I wrote out the letter before bed—I
received a peck on the cheek from elderly M. Dumas fils, received a
little melody, with camellias, from M. Saint-Saëns, how I have been
feted in Lisbon and Antwerp, bathed in a bath of gifted rosewater
and roses in London, how in Budapest a prince or count, I cannot remember, offered me his wizened gray palm and the castle and estates
he held in it, how in Naples, that ancient, southerly city, a gentleman
who I was told is richer than their king handed me a pouch of velvet
as light as breath and in it sat a band of gold crowned by a sapphire;
but I would never want to be entombed in a *palazzo*, however grand,
however many jewels in my tiara or necklaces, and I already am being
courted again by a former acrobat from England, my *Toffee*, with his

buttery voice and supple juggler's fingers, and I have not yet seen the busy streets of New York or the palaces of Saint Petersburg; and I also write about the daily miracles with the war now over and barely a memory, the Paris sky like a winter crocus, and the serpentine Seine under evening lamplight, and the thousand unforgettable treasures secreted—the restaurants, the cabarets, the music halls—along the byways radiating out from Boulevard Haussmann, and I write about the ugliness too, the throwaways sleep-standing in the nearby door-ways, the streetwalkers hurrying past with their frayed hems down the rue des Martyrs, all the people from the colonies looking and wandering as if perpetually lost, so like and yet so different from the Kaiser's capitals, and I detail the indignities also, the haggling over *sous* and Marks despite my contract, the pain that radiates throughout my collarbone, the battles to keep my costumes immaculate, acquire new ones, my inexhaustible appetite for new boots and perfumes, my hunt for the best *maquillage* for my complexion, pomade for my hair, the too-rich soups and meat dishes in sauces and the lure of sweets on every other corner, how last fall because of an extra-heavy flow and no time to get back to my rooms I had to stuff any gloves I could find into my tights and only Kaira knew, and we prayed like Catholic girls to the saints that there would be no accident—there wasn't, though their letters in return never mention those bits, nor do they repeat a single word about all the other things I relate to them, how I intend to spend every waking hour in the air, to soar with the brio of a sparhawk and glide with a sparrow's ease and float, as Kaira and I do, as the audience perches on the tips of their seats, with the lightness of two creatures who have fully emerged from the chrysalis, how I want to suspend the entire city of Paris or even France itself from my lips if I could achieve that, how I aim to exceed every limit placed on me unless I place it there, because that is what I think of when I think of *freedom*, that I have gathered around me people who understand how to translate fear into possibility, who have no wings but fly beyond the most fantastical vision of the clouds, who face death daily back out into the waiting room, and I am one of them, Olga, the *kleinste Bräunchen*, but no, Mummi—since Vati has only ever penned one letter I recall—never repeats any of this, instead writing *The night, especially in the city, is the Devil's playground* and *A groschen set aside keeps you out of the almshouse* and *Remember that not only an accordion makes a pretty song* and *Don't forget your family and your Prussian*, though how could I, whenever I hear that accent I pause to remind myself where I am, like the night a week ago when after our performance Jean-Michel said that several notable Parisians were waiting to meet us, meet me, one of them a poet I had never heard of and I prefer German novels anyway, I read the American and British ones in translation though I speak that language, my daddy's, fluently, and all he had to say to me was *Guten Abend* and instantly I knew, a Pomeranian, living in Berlin, a publisher's agent, he and one of the Frenchmen handed us each flowers and they all invited us to dinner the following night, then another group mentioning a salon exhibition that we absolutely must attend, and another with a journalist who asked me a few questions about my sense of balance, poise, not listening to a single one of my answers, and as I was heading back into our dressing room another man drew forward, bent down, gray threading his beard, his large, lidded eyes hard at me like lead shot, he introduced himself as M. *Edgar Degas*, a painter, he said, Kaira, I noticed, had moved to my side, I have not missed a single performance of yours these last few days, and I have been sketching you, here and at the Nouvelle Athènes, and I nodded, smiling and waiting to see his drawings, saying, *Merci, M'sieur, ça me plaît beaucoup*, but he did not show the sketches as he glanced from K to me and back, his eyes returning to my own, I would like to invite you to my studio on the rue Fontaine, bis no. 19, I will show you the drawings, I would even like to paint you but I know they will not allow me to set up an easel here which would be so helpful because of the complicated nature of the perspective and architecture, and I looked at K who looked at me, neither of us understanding what he was talking about, so I'll have to work from the drafts, I already have several, even in pastels, I nodded again, noting he barely blinked,

> his eyes pressing into me
> and tracing not only
> my outlines as if his gaze

were a pencil but my inner contours

as if they themselves were wet clay and I backed away, *Oui, M'sieur,* I would like that, and he extended his hand, which was trembling, in it a *carte de visite,* with his address, I will even make sure you have a chance to chat with my friend Gervex, also a painter, who is often here, and M. de Goncourt, do you know his work? he is writing a story on the circus, and I smiled and brought my palms and fingers together, and assured him I would call upon him as agreed, telling myself I would bring Kaira with me, and the strange, intense man bowed and seized my hand and kissed it hard, whispering *Fort enchanté,* African Princess, muttering something else beneath his breath then he spun on his heel, vanishing past a small new cluster of people waiting to speak with us, and it is early on a Thursday morning that I am now writing to Lili recounting the incident, though at first I sincerely could not remember his name, even though I will go to his studio the following day to meet him and his friend and see his drawings and exchange pleasantries, all I could recall was that he had claimed to have been drawing me, and how the next night after that encounter as I rose up on the tether, watching Kaira standing in anticipation below I remembered that after the painter left she said, Ooh La La they always come looking for you and I replied to her as I sipped my cup of tea, Yes, they do, they find me too, always, and as I rose, amid that collection of expectation and excitement, the gas lamps raking waves of shadows over them, there, in the ring's front row, to my right, I could have sworn I saw the board which held the paper, the hands moving furiously across it, the eyes darting from it to me, his eyes, large and tourmaline and climbing their own invisible ladder, trying to seize and hold onto my waist, my ankles, the perfect aerial cross of my body, this space, performance, the one whose name I could not remember, then I do, as I elude him and all of them, gliding higher, toward the freedom of the dome, high as the summit of Mont Blanc, the mouthpiece tightly in my bite, the name, severe and aristocratic in its brevity, reappears, him, the painter,

D
e
g
a
s,
l
e
b
l
a
n
c,

d
o
w
n

t
h
e
r
e
.

COLD

It's fastest, someone once warned you, when you let go. Here, in the sweltering dining room, you recognize no one, not a soul. Your mother took her supper at the usual hour and has already returned to her room. When you've come with her before or alone you've usually spotted at least one familiar face, from the City, or Philly, or Baltimore, since from June through the first turning of the leaves people arrive every weekend from all over. Like several other hotels in Catskill, Miss English's has welcomed you, your mother, almost all who'll pay, permitting stays without incident. There have, however, been a few: whenever one of them who has no clue about how the subtler rules

The dark-ies came in
full dress suits, with
low neck gowns and
pat - ent leather boots,
And all the stylish at
- tri - butes, The coun-

this side of the Mason-Dixon line function, how the law sometimes falls on the other side. There was that time in the hotel on Kauterskill when you were asked to vacate your room and move to the other wing because the Carolinian took grave offense that you shared the same linens and dishes, that you might brush against his wife in the hallway or stairwell, as if you could not walk a straight or even angled line away from her, as if you had no will, as if you ever cast a second glance at her or any white woman, and that hotel's owner, a round, pasty little man with a voice like a duck call had said that he wanted to avoid any trouble, please just go, he'd throw in a free whiskey as consolation. That afternoon in what felt like a stupor you had packed up and settled into your new chamber over here, from which you could see the creek and the mountains instead of your previous ampler river view, the one you'd reserved half a year in advance, and you fumed for a while until a bar, oh yes Lord, then the full song belled in your head and you spent the entire afternoon in bed scoring it. Even here you know better than to linger when the dancing begins or challenge one of them on the tennis court. The New Yorkers, city dwellers or upstaters, native or immigrant, do not so much as blink when they see you, staring mainly at the cut of your full dress suits and shoes, your mother's elegant's day ensembles and summer gowns, as if viewing an exhibit. Only one or two of them has ever known whom they were looking at, or, for that matter, uttered more than a simple slur.

The surface appears tranquil, beware the undertow. The tanned hand slides the bowl of soup beneath your chin. You return what feels like a smile but almost isn't. Vichysoisse. For the last month or two, or five, has it been year—why can you not remember?—these newest melodies you cannot flush from your head, like a player piano with an endless roll scrolling till infinity. Songs have always come, one by one or in pairs, dozens, you set them down, to paper, to poetry, like when you took the solemn melody of the spiritual Rosamond was whistling as you walked up Broadway and in your head and later on musical paper clothed it in brand new robes. Then somewhere along the way after the first terrible blues struck you tried to hum a new tune, conjure one, you thought it was just exhaustion, your mind too tired to refresh itself as it always had, that's why the old ones wouldn't go away. A few memory games, like rambling inside the rooms of your vast mental castle on the Nile, as you called it and the one song that resulted from it, filling each one with various quilts of harmonies from throughout your life, the sound of an engine starting, horses galloping up the road, boat horns from the direction of the Hudson: keys to release you from the musical bondage, from any of a thousand things you spot and listen to as you stroll up 136th Street, all the conversations, per-

All the hot dressed Coons -- of the black four hun - dred, -- the pub - lic won - derd, Why they were num - bered, -- Swell col - ored belles, -- would set you dream - ing, --

sonal or overheard, hymns, ditties, stomps, work songs, quadrilles, cakewalks, rags. None of those could dispel these new ones until they did, then more appear, stuck as if a band has struck up the opening notes to the *Black Four Hundred* in your skull and decided to keep playing it forever ... we have your trials here below, what's a poor brother to do? You fear you can sometimes hear the upper octaves combining toward a crescendo that, soon as you open your mouth, might explode.

Close your eyes and lay your head back. For a few seconds you recline in your seat, suppressing a cry, rise, eyes shut, after only a few spoonfuls. Your fingers trace canons around your temples. You should head up to your mother's room and tell her that it's getting worse, again, let her minister to you, she used to know how to calm you down with words, a touch, Mrs. Isabella, he's rattling on about something can't no one understand, settle what between your ears only once in a while back in the day became a racket. You should hurry to the phone in

A high-toned colored la
- dy whose com - plex
- ions kind of sha - dy
Has os - tra - cized
her - self from ev'ry
Ink - y Dink - in town

the alcove and have the operator connect you to Rosamond or his brother Jimmy, your big sister down in Atlanta, call Aida Walker or Bert Williams, whose traveling schedule you can't remember though you wrote down the dates in your notebook, even Erlanger or Klaw, at least leave word for them all, it wouldn't take that long for someone to drive up or hire a car or take the elevated to Grand Central and be here before the night is out. Fact is you should not have told the attendants at the Manhattan State Hospital for the Insane you were free of the interminable internal bellowing, you should not have assured them you'd be fully in Mrs. Isabella's care, that the tempest of those songs had died down, these ones like January storms that grind on all through the morning and evening, so persistent and fortissimo at times you can feel them chattering like piano hammers along your crown. As you stand at the table you recall that moment when you

couldn't stop caterwauling them, sometimes you're on the floorboards, how the neighbors banged on the walls, the front door, gathered on the stoop as they came and carried you downstairs, saying,
"Mr. Cole, you alright?"—"poor thing, you know he wrote the 'The
Girl With Dreamy Eyes'"—"I'ma pray for the man, er'rybody can see
how bad off he is"—"my sis saw his Sambo Girls Company in Hart-
ford and just keeping them in line's what broke him in two"—"Inky
Dink sold his soul to you know who to line them damn pockets" ...
all those comments tipped with interest, yes, and cheek, contempt
twinned with compassion, to the accompaniment of that sonorous,
infernal drone. Devil's arias, you penned them. Showfulls. In your
twenties it had all flowed so easily, you'd sealed the deal, the singing, the wisecracks, the dancing, all those godforsaken songs, that
cooning and crooning minstrelsy copping a mountain of green in
return, concreting a vision of you, of all of you in their heads, your
own, the nigger who could do no wrong with the Creole Show, the
All Star Show and later Black Patti's Troubadours, before you turned
it inside out again, alone and with Rosamond, his brother Jimmy,
these songs unlike the previous ones, these were yours, nothing to
feel the slightest pang of shame about, any colored person could
whistle them without a pause, did whistle them as you heard yourself
on the IRT. So easily, until these newest ones, undreamt, unsum-

Way down in Mis- si
- sip - pi Long before
the war, Lived Un–cle
Ras-tus and his wife,
-- he had twen - ty pick
- a - nin - nies playing
'round the cab - in door

moned, sonic suns blasting behind your
eyes, these terrible samplings of the old
and the unfamiliar. You should have told
the attendants how your agent and the
publishing firm's representative had said
in almost the exact same words about
your newest pieces, "Bob, what has gotten into you, these notes together don't
make any melodic or melodic sense," how the arranger had cack-
led with reproach, "Cole, you have *four or five different* polyrhythms
running concurrently, no man can play this," how Rosamund himself

whispered, this side of sorrow, as he clasped your hand, "Bob, this mess on the other side of sound." Everyone began to train the same look on you, the bank cashier, the postman, the barber, the Bajan shoeshine, the tiny boy black as a crow with the crowbar who cranks cars for a cent on Lenox, the humpbacked begger guarding the curb hollering, "Mister, you need my help?" as you sat there on the front steps trying to massage the rondos out of your brow, your sinuses, your freshly trimmed and pomaded locks, trying to express them out—"Mister, you need me to call somebody? Excuse me, officer, but I think that gentleman sitting over there humming and crying to himself need...."

Allow the foliage below an easy embrace. You mop your forehead free of the film of sweat the August heat has pasted there, wipe the dew from your chest's silver curls, crumpling the napkin beside the untouched knife and fork. Somehow the heat down in Mississippi, Georgia, Florida, like this interior clamor, has followed you north, everyone around you is fanning themselves, reclining on benches or couches, already displaying like the underarms of your violet linen suit the dark, wet badges of the season's relentlessness. Your mother, no stranger to heatwaves, has taken to afternoon naps in the still silent dark. Bad as it is up here, though, it's worse, you know, far worse down in Manhattan. You gulp down a glass of water warmer than the soup, polish off a second soon as it's poured. Sometimes the songs make you so dizzy you forget where you are, you've tried every manner of patent medicine, the one that tastes like licorice and the one that tastes like silver, the one that's made from coal ash and the one that's made from pine resin, neither whiskey nor gin nor cocaine nor hemp nor hashish does the trick, you can't easily get your hands on opium—only sleep, morphine and the unknown dulling potion the orderlies provide temporarily blot it out. Then soon as you stir you're back at this internal concert, on stage again inside your head as Willy Wayside, performing with Billy at the Standard in Kansas City, twirling that mahogany cane and jigging at the Pekin and Savoy in Chicago, only without the corked mask and zinced lips and red wig and patchwork coats and satin lapels and tails and popped top hat and tap shoes polished to the consistency of glass and the orchestra, without the after-parties and champagne breakfasts, without the evening ending and you being able to sleep a whole night through, without these notes pealing into bedlam nobody knows, why did you ever write them, who did you write them for, yourself *and* them, more them than you you did not

This strange a - malga-mation twixt these two fun-ny nations gwine to cause an awful jamble soon -- Twill cause a great sensation ov - er the whole creation

want to, do now dare to admit, these songs still reeling and unreeling, unreal, daily, hourly, by the minute, in you, your head, and you can't, simply cannot, can no longer bear it.

Open your mouth as if you intend to swallow. You set the glass down and head for the door. "Excuse me, Sir, but you finished?" the young man, so light only his features, hair texture reveal his story, murmurs politely, "Can I get you anything else, Sir, send something up to your room?" You pause, look him over, see the eyes catching yours, another time, you think, shake him off, force a half-smile when you catch his flash of recognition, or perhaps it's just that broader sense of a link mixed with abstract solidarity, so common wherever you see each other, our people, even if no one else fully sees you, until the stain of disdain seeps in, perhaps the young man stood at the doorway as you regaled everyone last night with a few of the songs your fingers played from memory since your mind would not cooperate, you could see your mother beaming from her seat as you completed "Under the Bamboo Tree," nodding, clapping, her eyes telling you that everything was all right although it wasn't, it isn't, perhaps years before he saw you staring back from a handbill, contentedly, unlike now, and he too secretly blames you, they all do, for how you all are viewed? You pass into the alcove, past the check-in desk. The doorman, dark as a pneumatic tire, in elaborate livery despite the heat, swings the door open. You flinch, seeing your own face staring back, your mug never so cool or placid anymore except in photographs, engravings, the same wide forehead, broad slender lips, lantern eyes bearing something outward while beaming back in, making you glad no mirror's nearby, that you never saw yourself on stage, made up and masked, always masked, that awful jamble thankfully never captured for the Nickelodeon or a gramophone, you recover and extract the sole bill—$10—you have and some coins from amid the goldweight and the paperweight you stuffed this morning in each of your trouser pockets and place the money in that other palm, sheathed in white cotton beneath which you know lies a square of pink ridged with brown like your own, as your grip tenses, relaxes. The hurdy gurdy in your head churns on. "Thank you so much, Sir. Shall I call you a driver,

All I wants is ma chick - ens My Shanghai chick - ens, Ma feathered pick - ens! I shan't leave here wid - out my chick - ens! I'll bet six bits I'll kill a coon if I don't get ma chickens back!

Sir?" the doorman asks, assuming correctly that you will not want to walk in this heat through the streets toward downtown, or perhaps you might be heading to Athens or across the river to Hudson. No thank you, you mean to say, if you there, staves and quarter notes stalling your tongue, spilling out, you think you assure the doorman you're fine with a wave and head in the opposite direction, away from the town and river, northwest instead, over the meadow toward Main.

The first response is to struggle but you should stifle it. On the lawn as you pass a seated trio is laughing. Beneath them spreads a lake of gingham. You know the couple, initially because of your stays here, later after time spent with them in the City and at their home, Luther and Anna, they travel down from Buffalo where he has a general practice and also runs the local colored paper and she teaches school. You chatted with them briefly yesterday when you got in. The other woman, pretty enough to be a movie star if colored women starred in movies, looks familiar but you cannot place her. Gwendolyn, they introduce her, from Boston, she was here last year with her parents, the father a bishop of some sort, now you remember, I'll bet six bits she was one of Anna's former students you'd said to yourself before you met her then, they are trying to make *that kind* of introduction again, she straightens the ribbons in her loose black locks before you take her hand and drop it. She is saying something to you about your songs, your shows as you think you hear Luther ask, Why don't you join us, Bob? he and Anna nodding, she adds, We'd like that, we haven't hardly seen you since you arrived. You cannot hear what Gwendolyn is saying, it's as if someone has a trombone against your lobes, playing an ostinato, the same long, low phrase, then the original song comes back and you feel light, almost giddy, whisper you are going to walk over to the creek, if you see yourself going along so, Luther looks at Anna, they lift themselves up to join you. You touch your hairline where the music threatens to erupt, as they gather up the knives and forks, the bread and honey, the corked bottle of lemonade, place it in

> *Mis - ter coon you're*
> *al - right in your place*
> *____ To as - so - ciate*
> *with you would be dis -*
> *grace ____ Don't come*
> *a - round my house*
> *a - gain, Cause I be -*
> *long to the up - per ten*

the basket, fold up the cloth, Luther's and Anna's manners each as precise as they always have been, as anyone would expect of folks of their station. Gwendolyn hangs back, fanning herself, her eyes trained on you. You mean to say something about the weather, but no words emerge, nothing about the food, the staff, your mother, Luther's suit, Anna's dress the shade of crème anglaise, Boston, Harlem, Rosamond or Jimmy, the Sambo Girls Company or your other efforts, touring, business in general, Gwendolyn in whom you'd never be interested, your other *friends* in New York you would never discuss let alone hint at, the train ride up, the last few months, years, the long winters of blue periods that have plagued you even before the music could not be turned off. Only a sound that sounds like the inside of a sound, a not-whistle, a not-warble, not-words, a code, a cloud of could and cannot, and Luther laces his arm in yours, Anna close by on his other side, the basket on her free arm, Gwendolyn somewhere behind them, humming, why is she humming? two live as one, she's humming one of your tunes, or is that you and the sound is escaping you, as it sometimes does, if you like a me and I like a you, as you proceed across the grass to the road.

There is no way to counter the initial pain, a burning sensation, but eventually it will subside. Luther's arm slows you, stops you here at the roadside, you pause to pat your cheeks dry, your chest, the late afternoon heat is intensifying, you all pause as cars and carriages barrel by. Anna is talking again, something about her people who came up from Richmond to visit, some other folks they met during a trip to Ottawa, the ones appearing every day in Buffalo from Kentucky to Kingston, their planned cruise to Venezuela, what do you think about all the lynchings so far this year, what do you think about the new National Association for the Advancement of Colored People in New York, those white liberals and our folk who belong to the upper ten, Rosamond and Jimmy know people involved with it, you do too, what do you think, Luther's agreeing with everything she says, his voice like hers softening as if to distract you, and though you cannot hear anything they're saying clearly anymore, hear anything beyond this interior echo, though you perceive somewhere in their tone something else in the rhythms of their words, the blade of rebuke, not even friendship can hide it, you know what you did, they want to say, what you wrote, how you helped to sow this sickness even in the minds of your own, you know you did and tighten your fingers on the weights, so solid the gold, so smooth the glass, sometimes you're up, sometimes you're down but they are anchoring you right here, what do you think, as you squeeze on the weights what do you think and you do not. Gwendolyn, whose voice tinkles like a triangle slightly out of tune, has taken your elbow in her hand, fanning you as she inspects your eyes, your trembling lips. She asks if you would like a drink of water. Luther pats you on the back and suggests you all continue to the creek, sit on its banks briefly and rest, then return to the hotel. You want to

I must a been a dream - in' ___ while all dis was seem - in' ___ Case I woke up wid a scream - in' ___ And my eyes dey was gleam - in' ___ Oh! my forehead was a steam - in' ___ Perspiration was a stream - in' ___ I must a been a dream - in' dream - in' all the time.

say you were heading there anyways, the shade of the paper birches and slippery elms letting you cool off before you continue on your intended journey. You wag your head, something issuing from your insides, something that is and is not the noise buzzing in your brain, your throat, all down the column of your spine, into your toes, you can almost arrest snippets, you know these songs by heart, how many times did you perform them by heart, stand before that wall of stares and pull everything from your heart, by heart, record them by heart, you could put on a show right now by heart, as you did last night by heart, here on this greensward by heart, anywhere you wanted to by heart, like you used to, like you did in the park by heart that night and the man, that midnight man standing above you just turned on his heels and ran, you squatting there and could not stop yourself and the entire routine of *A Trip to Coontown* came out, every single note, not one missed, and it wasn't until a small crowd out seeking just like you had surrounded you, their shapes stirring the black, that you realized where you were. Luther guides you to a spot they've picked, Gwendolyn dresses it with the gingham cloth.

As your mind goes black, begin counting backwards. The years? Where have they gone? 1911, 1910, 1909, nobody knows the trouble … finally words erupt from you: "I'm going to go for a swim." They look puzzled, Anna is whispering, reminding her husband she did not bring her swimsuit and you all can try tomorrow at the river, but you hurtle forward down the slope into the water. "Bob," Luther is saying, "Bob," and you're pantomiming, because no more words will flow, only the music, forehead steaming, you are miming swimming, waving to them and grinning, that wit and playacting that always got everyone, this time without the kohl or charcoal corking and the floppy hat, "Bob," and you do the crawl and the sidestroke and the breaststroke, your arms windmilling the air, can feel the creekwater in your shoes, halfway to your knees, your drawers, if you like a me, eyes gleaming, cold, and I like a you, you can hear it now too, the creek, streaming, the water, no wig or whiskers now, no polish, must a been dreaming, never again, "Bob, come on out," Luther is walking toward you, never again to croon a coon song, Uncle Rastus, you wave him off, the water at your chest, dreaming all the time you tried, Bob come on out, how you tried but it kept leaking in, moon don't make me wait in vain tonight, no whistling coon no more, no cane or jig now, oh soul you cut it out soon as you could, so loud, the music and those voices, Bob, all this was a seeming, you ducking beneath the surface, the hot hate floating, away, swimming away, No, Bob, maybe Anna now, someone crying out and crying, Gwendolyn please go get someone from the hotel and Mrs. Isabella, sinking, go soul, under the bamboo tree, Zulu from Matahooloo they never knew you, blues, the true you dreaming the true you nobody's looking nobody knows no coon no more two live as one they will never harm you at all fly soul no coon a man bending down into the mud it's quickest someone once advised you when you completely let go, because the surface appears tranquil but beneath there's the undertow, and you shut your eyes and lay your head back, knowing the current and weights in your pockets will do most of the work, allow the foliage below you its ready embrace, but just in case you open your mouth because you intend to swallow, battling then defeating the impulse to struggle, you feel the first stabs of pain, a burning in your chest no worse than the pain of that music you knew best, eventually it too will subside, that bonfire, the nightmare track as your mind turns back into the blackness you count backwards joining in your song no coon no more nobody knows the trouble I've seen nobody but Jesus if you get there before I do tell all 'a my friends I'm coming until the music breaks into a screaming silence that if you could describe it in a word would be no word or note or sound at all but fleetingly, freeingly *cold*. . . .

BLUES

He wanted to say something... but the English words at first eluded him ... when they met earlier that year ... at a secret party ... after the dinner given by Rafael Lozano ... at the German director Agustín's... the noted poet had been staying briefly in Mexico... even before then a few of them had shared his poems like talismans... reading them as if their lives depended upon it ... he had translated three and published them in a local journal ... the older poets had already dismissed this so-called literature, condemned it ... much like their peers in Harlem... all this pansy dust from the gutter passing for good writing ... this only spurred them to read more ... and talk about it more, write more ... unforgettable as his verse, each thought ... to himself when the American entered the living room ... a compact beauty, tea brown ... high brow capped by wavy black hair ... after receiving his drink he stood at the center of their circle... smile flashing... each was vying to get his attention... to their surprise he spoke decent, vigorous Spanish... in his soft melodic voice... all strained to hear him... maybe he was a *veracruzano*... who had grown up among gringos... a Mexican as the new star of American Negro literature... someone whispered this in laughter ... he mentioned his friend, José Fernández de Castro, the Cuban writer ... Carlos corrected that he was from Missouri, wherever that was ... his father, he told them, had managed an electric plant... run a ranch in Toluca... he had spent part of his adolescent years here... he had come to wrap up the estate... he was staying with family friends on the Calle de Ildefonso ... though grieving he still appeared gay ... something nevertheless held in reserve by that insistent grin ... so as not to keep him standing Agustín invited him to sit ... the American recited lines by López Velarde and Jiménez as he walked to the couch ... they scrambled to places beside him ... Agustín as usual slung his leg up over the easy chair's arm to show off his ample package ... Roberto, who already had a boyfriend, nevertheless daintily perched on the edge of his seat ... Antonieta, the lone woman among them, took it all in stride ... he winked at her several times as he spoke and she leaned forward too ... his English name was not so easy to pronounce ... Long Stone is how they all kept saying it ... he had no problem with any of theirs, forgetting not a single one ... complimenting the German on the furniture, his modern taste ... he, Xavier, sipped his punch and observed those lips polishing each syllable ... the nasturtium, rose incarnate ... of that mouth ... he hated comparing things to flowers ... but in that moment there was no other metaphor ... the houseboy brought in canapés and nuts and the American's eye trailed his low broad shoulders ... ah ha, some of them thought, campesinos are what he goes for ... the German could unrefine his touch as needed ... he unbuttoned his shirt collar, his fingers combing his chest ... the poet offered his observations of the city's literary scene ... who, he asked, were the politically radical, the experimental writers ... he spoke of the visual arts, his love of bull-fighting y los novilleros ... he beamed a smile which made them all smile more ... that's what he likes, the fighting daredevils ... they were going to take him to a party at a painter's house ... he agreed and after several more rounds of drinks they headed out ... the German's hand on the American's waist, Elías's clasping his left elbow ... he, Xavier, followed a few steps behind, chatting with Antonieta ... studying the visitor's solid back ... ample buttocks ... they piled into two cars, sped through the night to the painter's house ... after five knocks the man with the scar from his right eye to his chin ushered them in ... friends were already there, everyone wanted to meet the American ... a cross-dresser emerged from a stairwell, her conversation in mid-sentence ... he, Xavier, had another drink and then another ... a man named Rodolfo he had never met before whispering something in his ear ... the American disappeared into the darkness ... then suddenly Long Stone is at Xavier's side, smiling ... saying I will be staying in the city for a little while longer ... Xavier mentioning his fellowship to study drama at Yale ... if you get to New York send word, we'll meet up in Harlem ... he gives him several contacts in order to reach him ... before Xavier can answer a bullfighter's expert hands spear the visitor's arm from behind ... his eyes saying this one is mine tonight ... the two of them gliding away ... into the writhing hive ...

He sent a telegram from New Haven ... to the address on St. Nicholas Avenue, where Langston was staying ... he had heard through the grapevine about the Guggenheim ... the journey out to Los Angeles to write scripts ... he jots in his notebook that he enjoyed the train ride down along the coast ... he sat on the south side as his classmate had recommended ... observing the scenery of autumnal New York Sound ... the water indifferent in its blue undulations ... vanishing intermittently behind screens of greening trees and warehouses ... he slipped down for the holiday the Americans celebrate to honor the Genoese Columbus ... he would miss a single lecture ... but will be able to catch at least a weekend matinee ... he has told no one though he may send Salvador and Elías each a letter ... he paused to photograph the great vault of Grand Central Terminal ... from the taxi to the New Yorker Hotel he stared up into the midday sky ... the height of the towers astonished him ... he imagined the shadows sleeping in the caverns between them. ... the pace, still more fervid than Mexico City at lunchtime ... all the colors of these people, their vivid, hungry faces ... some made him forget that there was a Depression ... others' eyes scored their suffering right into him ... he saw through to their inner solitude ... you should not stay up in Harlem, a friend had written ... they rioted in March, another warned, attacking every white person ... another said it was fine, spend a night at the Theresa ... No problems for Mexicans but Negros are forbidden there ... he wanted to explore that and other neighborhoods ... perhaps he would venture up there even before meeting with Langston ... after a nap that first evening he wandered the streets ... then took the subway down to the West Village ... ambling slowly around Washington Square, avoiding the beggars, cars and buses ... he happened upon the Italian district ... a meal of pasta with red wine ... in a little tavern he downed a few drinks ... his eyes lingering on the men but he said nothing ... no one to help relieve his loneliness ... he knew there were places nearby ... a bottle of whisky and a pack of cigarettes ... he retraced his steps back to Times Square. ... the doorman's gaze tracking him inside ... he sat at his desk and worked on several drafts of poems ... smoking a cigarette he penned a new one ... then the meal and trainride hit him and he lay down ... stretched across his bed atop the covers ... studying the sliver of midnight sky, scarred with stars ... he wondered how well or if the poet even remembered him ... no messages at the front desk, he will call the number he has tomorrow ... friends had sent him the names ... of several countrymen and other Latin Americans to meet ... new Yale friends provided him with others ... there are other writers he would love to encounter ... his intention during his return after the new year ... he thinks of Salvador, of his Agustín, Lazo, not the German ... and falls fast asleep. ...

He peers at the telegram and tries to recall ... the poet's face remains an empty screen ... he met so many people in Mexico City ... he should consult his notebooks, carbons ... so much he will never put into print ... he ponders, which one could this one be ... the party after Rafael's, at that apartment ... not the movie director, not Salvador, but Xavier ... quickly they loom into view, the immense eyes, hawkish nose ... wide mouth, glass vase complexion ... a tiny beautiful thing, almost passarine ... he is trying to figure out if he will even have a minute to respond ... should he call anyone else, or meet this man alone ... the premiere of the play is just over a week away ... everything that could go wrong already has ... because of the rich ofay producer-director ... whose changes have warped his vision ... into something monstrous, a mess on stage ... who keeps demanding more of his royalties ... silence from his drama agent, Rumsey ... despite his constant appeals ... maybe he should let Max handle this too ... he sips his coffee and smiles at Toy ... his second mother, Em his father ... his own mother sent a brief letter from Cleveland wishing him well ... her sincerity and false confidence as evident as her shaky hand ... the tumor cannibalizing her insides ... how can he be there and here ... always the need for more cash ... how can he even think to write that novel ... poems keep grinding themselves out of him ... the trip to Minnesota days ago feels like it took place last century ... all those students cheering at his words ... how to bring that world more frequently into view ... maybe he has mixed this poet up with someone else ... so many there, such beauty ... if only he had a Beauty now to listen to him ... lean on, lie beside as he barely slept ... black, Mexican, it wouldn't matter ... the sunlight crept in though he had only just halted a nightmare ... the cast on stage performing and the theater empty ... Jones refusing altogether to pay him ... critics writing reviews condemning the language and structure ... he could use the air and light of Central Avenue now ... the beach and orange groves, those California Negroes ... even the tenements and singsong patter of his Cleveland and Chicago neighbors ... he hugs Toy goodbye and heads out ... more battles at the theater await him ... he knots his scarf against the October chill ... feels the telegram folded into fourths atop cards in his jacket pocket ... the subway platform not so busy at midday ... the train whining its swift approach ... he finds a seat in the middle of the car ... exchanges glances with a silver haired man who winks, slyly ... shall I make a record of your beauty ... he extracts a poem tucked inside the script from his portfolio ... uncaps his pen, begins to mark it up ... he realizes only as the train slumbers into 34th Street ... that he has missed his stop. ...

He spent all of yesterday touring Manhattan ... first thing after breakfast the ultramodern Chrysler Building and the Empire State fortress ... both a brisk stroll from the hotel ... the Independent subway line to Bookstore Row in the Village, Wall Street, Bowling Green ... the Aquarium at the little fort at the island's southern tip ... he walked to the foot of Brooklyn Bridge, imagining Crane's steps, Whitman's ferry crossing ... rang his hotel from a nearby booth to find out if anyone had rung him ... a cab then train to the Public Library's main branch on Fifth Avenue ... trekked up to St. Patrick's Cathedral, Rockefeller Center ... snapped photos, ate a late lunch at an automat ... sipping a cola and polishing off a bowl of soda crackers and chicken noodle soup ... watching the patricians and penniless stream past the window ... on the street he struck up a conversation with a Puerto Rican ... who gave the names of restaurants to visit in East Harlem ... a walk east to Madison's haberdasher shops, where he bought hand-kerchiefs and a scarf ... and the Interborough up to the Metropoli-tan Museum of Art ... he could only manage the exhibit of Hogarth's prints ... so exhausted he stumbled out into the violet street ... no time left to visit Harlem ... no messages waiting at his return ... in the hotel lobby he called a painter friend of Carlos's ... to meet for a meal tomorrow ... he had dinner in his room, began reading ... through his gathering poems ... he penned a letter to Salvador but crumpled it ... thought he might see what lurked out in the darkness ... signs, stars, blue tattooed letters ... but slumber gripped him and he was out ... he returned to his hotel after leaving the chatty Guadalajaran ... and a Broadway matinee of *Porgy and Bess* ... he was searching for the right words to describe it ... the songs kept pealing deep inside him ... si-lence vast and frozen ... a message from Langston awaited ... Querido Xavier, deseas cenar conmigo esta noche? ... he called the number and a woman answered ... she would pass on his message, for this evening at 7:30 pm ... he set the clock and lay down ... at 7 he rose and washed up ... changed into fresh underwear, shirt, the socks he had hung to dry ... a pale lavender tie purchased in a store on College Street ... at 7:25 he headed downstairs ... expecting to see the American standing there ... he sat in a comfortable chair and waited ... he had brought a copy of Maeterlinck's poems ... he flipped through, barely reading, as his watch hand spun ... at 8:04 Langston walked in, palms extended in greeting ... his face gay and fuller, sporting a mustache ... he spoke in Spanish, almost formally at first ... Xavier replied in casual English ... apologies upon apologies, there were issues at the theater ... a dramatic piece beginning in a week ... too much to explain right now ... did the visitor want to dine near the hotel ... go downtown to the Village ... Xavier suggested Harlem ... Langston mentioned it was sixty blocks north, but they they could take the train ... there were restaurants still open ... he had one in mind in particular ... if Xavier was game ... the visitor urged that they take a taxicab ... he had a little stipend ... he would pick up the fare ... the doorman hailed one for them ... they climbed in and pitched right into conversation ... Langston asking about the various people he had met last spring ... the writers, painters, theater ... the social and political conditions in Mexico ... he offers some gossip about the celebrities ... he met in Los Angeles and during his stay in Carmel ... like the hearthrob Ramón Novarro ... Xavier describes the experience of Gershwin's musical ... he is one of the finest composers, Langston says ... not a colored man but he has something of us in his soul ... in no time they reach Harlem ... where the buildings shrink and the faces brown ...

At Robert Johnson's Dixie on 133rd St. they climb out ... Langston leads his guest into the mid-sized restaurant ... they cut up in here, he laughs, and I mean cut up ... Xavier doesn't understand the idiom but laughs too ... a fox-faced maître d' ushers them to a table ... the dining space is not especially full ... but all there are, Xavier notes, are black people ... no one gives him more than a glance, though several greet Langston ... I have to be on my best behavior, he whispers, grinning ... though you can get away with quite a bit in here ... Xavier again fails to grasp what he means but savors that smile ... the wall of reserve he observed in Mexico City has fallen ... a bandstand, empty but with some instruments, hunkers off to the side ... I was trying to think of all the people I want to meet you ... but I have been so busy with this play and all ... it is a budding disaster, not that that matters ... is it on Broadway, Xavier asks ... yes, at the Vanderbilt, it's called *Mulatto* ... like your poem: "Into my father's heart to plunge the knife / To gain the utmost freedom that is life" ... Yes, though there's a fuller story, actors, the whole deal ... I'm sure it is brilliant and I hope to see it ... If you only knew what they were doing to it ... but let's talk about something else, like your studies at Yale ... they chat about Xavier's classes ... his desire not just to write but understand the theory of theater ... to know drama's extensive history ... do they teach you about rich white Southern dictators, who fancy themselves producer-directors ... Xavier is not sure exactly what or whom Langston means ... is this the father he wrote the poem about ... he notices two fey men at a table, observing them ... Yale is one of the most elite schools, Langston continues ... they make sure not to let many, really any Negroes in ... Unsure what to say Xavier sips his water ... at another table he spots a woman's leg rising along the line of her table partner, another woman ... the waiter glides up to take their order ... a minute more to choose, please ... Xavier asks questions about Harlem ... when he'll be returning to Mexico ... Langston promises a tour of Harlem and the rest of the city when Xavier comes back ... the drinks, then the main dishes arrive ... the meal is passable, but there's the ambience ... all the restaurants, like the people up here, are suffering badly ... Xavier nods, affirming things are tough in Mexico City too ... we're still waiting, Langston adds, on President Roosevelt to help us, and I mean *us* ... we'll even take Presidente Cárdenas if he isn't too busy ... both laugh and launch into a discussion of poetry ... the poets of Mexico first, Langston lists all he knows, Cuesta, Gorostiza, Torres Bodet, Ortiz de Montellano ... then other poets leaving their mark in the Spanish language, Darío, Vallejo, Guillén ... the Chileans Mistral and Neruda ... especially the ones committed to the cause of political, economic and social liberation ... the Contemporáneos are not Communists, Xavier responds, but are quietly striving to transform Mexican literature ... what does he think of Borges, Langston asks ... the avant-garde without a political compass can easily become reactionary ... Xavier assures him there is no danger of this among his group ... you must read Alfonso Reyes, Gutiérrez Cruz ... what of the poets of Harlem, of America ... he has heard of some of the names but not many others ... Cullen, yes, a master stylist, Douglas Johnson, the powerful McKay ... Nugent, never heard of him, Bontemps, no, Grimke, Walrond, Brown ... he withdraws a little notebook and his fountain pen ... he has to ask Langston to repeat a number of them ... then the white ones, Crane, why of course, Crane came to Mexico a few years ago ... Eliot, certainly, so erudite and forbidding ... Pound, Williams, he is familiar with these, yes, and Bénet, Sandburg, Robinson, Millay ... Stevens? No. Moore? No. H.D.? No ... most are politically retrograde ... the whole passel including Hillyer, Coffin, as well as the Southern Agrarians (though Ransom is a good poet) and the rest not worth mentioning ... there are poets with far better politics, like Fearing, Rukeyser, Davidman, Beecher ... does he know any American poets who are of Mexican descent or write in Spanish ... he will send Xavier some issues of the newer periodicals he has appeared in ... they talk of Gide, Wilde, Proust ... through their ideas of poetry ... what makes it so necessary always ... especially now, even more than novels or essays ... like plays it is, Langston says, an immediate and economical way of reaching the masses ... promoting the ideas that will foster and allow revolution to flourish in society ... look at the bloody lesson of Mexico, Xavier says ... one should exercise caution when invoking that term ... he views poetry's role and power as more modest ... poetic language always carries the seed of something revolutionary ... merely by being a testimony to one's always complex and difficult interior journeys ... in language you need to lose yourself ... to recover yourself ... yes, Langston says, that too, so true ... still talking, they finish dinner, another round of drinks ... Xavier mentions an early train back to New Haven ... over Langston's gentle objections he pays the bill ... the male couple, now openly holding hands at their table, offer familial approval ... we are not afraid of night ... the next one will be my treat ... they walk down to 125th Street to hail a taxi ... shoulder to shoulder, fingers grazing ... Xavier offers to have the cab drop him off ... then abruptly says why don't you come back downtown with me ... have a final nightcap and relax ... Langston muses a second, then agrees ... there are places in Times Square where we can get a drink ... I have a bottle of whiskey in my room ...

The taxi knifes through the city's dark canyons ... the sky glowing blue as a gas flame ... Xavier presses his thigh into Langston's ... they are discussing the options in nightlife ... if this were a Saturday I would have many places to take you ... no bullfighters but we have some things almost as delectable ... Xavier laughs and says not everyone longs for a brute ... yes, Langston answers, a poet's touch can do the trick ... the taxi lets them off right in front of the hotel ... in the room Xavier takes Langston's hat, coat and scarf ... he glimpses himself in the mirror ... more cold, more fire ... pours each a little glassfull ... they sip in silence for a while ... Langston inspects the room ... the neatly folded clothes, small pile of books, the sheaf of poems ... Xavier asks Langston if he is keeping him from anyone ... no luck in that regard, he responds ... they pour through my fingers like water ... Ferdinand, A, C ... so beautiful, Xavier says to himself, it seems incomprehensible ... and you, I imagine you have someone back in Mexico City ... or someone new up in New Haven ... there is a novio at home, but things are complicated ... Always, Langston says, the toll you pay for your art ... he sits down at the desk ... please don't read those poems, they aren't ready ... ah, but this one is a gem ... "Somnambulant, asleep and awakened all at once / in silence I roam the submerged city." ... That one is titled "Nocturnal Estancias" ... Nocturnal ranches and stanzas, how intriguing ... I think my whole next book will be a volume of nocturnes ... I myself have written so many poems about the night ... That is where I truly live ... Xavier pours each another drink, takes off his tie and jacket ... Tás cansado ... Sí, un poco ... It is getting late, Langston says ... you have an early train and I a long trip back uptown ... Please, no hurry, finish your drink ... Langston knocks it back ... Thank you for a wonderful evening ... Thank you, and I will be your Virgil through the city next time ... Xavier passes him his hat and coat ... they embrace, peck each other's cheeks ... He departs ... Xavier slips out of his remaining clothes ... packs, sets the alarm clock ... he notices Langston's scarf is still on the chair ... he will mail it to the Emersons' when he reaches

New Haven ... he finishes off a cigarette, reads one of his poems ... not so bad, but not yet as good as he wants it ... climbs into bed, douses the light ... there is a knock on the door ... he listens, ignores it ... it persists ... he rises ... cracks it open ... I'm so sorry, Xavier ... but I left my scarf here I think ... please come in ... it's just over there ... Langston enters ... he does not light the lamp ... he wants to say something ... nothing to be said ... let hunger and instinct guide them ... in this confusion ... of bodies, he will show ... this one is mine ... slides Langston's coat from his shoulders ... the jacket, tie, underpants, shoes ... his lips on his lips ... their bodies bare ... together ... his chest on his ... armpits and thighs ... he guides his hand down there ... he kneels and tastes ... his hard sex ... of salt, silkenness ... he guides him to the bed ... they caress, and kiss ... this mouth is mine ... he climbs atop him ... dulce, tan dulce ... tastes his salt again ... takes his sex again ... in that blue darkness ... spit and sweat ... satin funk and musk ... sweetens his tongue ... opening ... he takes him in ... dulce, slowly ... again ... a double death ... ay morenito ... this mouth is his ... sweetly, mi ángel ... fills him ... the firm grip on his hips ... nipples, ankles ... fast now, angel ... moving together ... in sync ... this rhythm ... of men ... alone together ... a blues. ... fills them ... he feels him ... deep inside ... his soul ... ay negrito ... moans ... this man is his ... mi amor ... short breaths ... as one ... together ... sweet fire ... ay cariño ... they come ... to this ... yes, this ... this fire ... together ... cry sí, este fuego ... sí ... sí ... softly ... softly ... they lie ... beside each other ... in the crepuscular dark ... holding tight ... night pouring in ... to stir the blueblack shadows ... somewhere out there dawn ... on the horizon ... somewhere out there dawn ... and trains to New Haven, Harlem ... the open grave of life, this dying room ... its waning song ... will you write a poem ... about tonight ... I already have ... and you ... I have too ... who will you give it to ... you, my angel ... and you ... you, my very own ... our secret ... I loved my friend ... amid this solitude ... let us roam the night ... together ... loving ... living ... these blues ...

ANTHROPOPHAGY

The poet sleeps without the need to dream.

—Mário de Andrade

Every day the quickening passage of the years manifests itself around him, in him. The morning light burning its entry through the shutters, too bright to bear except in blinks, winks, the armor of fished-out-of-pocket spectacles. The endless clangor and perfume of the streets outside the windows, once a comfort, now a menace, requiring a miracle to survive another Carnaval. The heat, as if every oven, stove and kiln in Rio were firing, glazing him and all but the hardiest to half their size. The sheet music's notes, like the newsprint's accounts of the unfolding and distant world war, the dictator and Depression closer to home, all sliding inexorably away from his fingers and eyes. His knees, back, the ankles that rattle with each hike up a stairwell, each trek across the University of the Federal District's grounds. The liver's complaints after another glass of beer or cachaça, another snort of cocaine. All those words that gushed like water from a fountain, that now have to be hunted with an unsteady hand and head. The heart's berimbau quivering in irregular time, a rhythm only the reaper can and will discern if allowed. Except in those moments when the hours fall away, disappear, he lying on his side, in dreams or awake and a record cycles on the player, Debussy, Villa-Lobos, Pixinguinha, or a disc grooved from the recordings of catimbó from his journeys across the northeast, its sonorities drumming out a bridge between the present and the past; and behind him, beside him the one who—unlike the glittering young men in his circle of friends, the well-bred law students and witty budding writers who claim to celebrate him, the young, poor blond athlete from Porto Alegre he met in the stall on rua Conde de Lage seeking a sinecure, through his, the distinguished writer's, intervention, at the Ministry of Culture, the beautiful and not so beautiful sycophants who say they have read his *Macunaíma* and studies and poetry and the ones who have managed to mis-memorize a few lines—like this one, known only by his first name, gained in the passageway between the Budapesto's dining room and its kitchen, by his braided locks and his careful gait, trained through climbing the hillside shanties ringing the city, by his dark arms embracing, knotting around the writer's chest, their fingers interlacing, locking as he enters, moves, dances inside him, the beat mutual and infinite in its tenderness and knowingness; or later, the day after, crouching over his desk, having just finished breakfast downstairs once the cup of cafezinho and the bowl of half-eaten papaya, the glass of freshly squeezed orange juice have been cleared, the letters to Anita and Murilo and Henrique and Manuel written, the reviews for his column, and he begins the strophe,

> "Heroic anxiety of my feelings
> to awaken the secret of beings and things."

or

> "They are forms...Forms that burn, individual
> forms, jostling, a jingling of elusive forms
> that barely open, flower, that close, flower, flower, unformed
> inaccessible,
> In the night. Everything is night...."

and who need regard the message of the clock's hands, acknowledge the calendar's insistent story? Then, he rests the pen beside the typewriter and blotter and rises, puts on his straw hat to shield his rice-powered face and bald pate, bows the canary tie around his neck, and dives out into the afternoon, walking toward the competing planes of gold sand and the Atlantic's silvery waves, the lines blurring like a freshly painted watercolor. The Cariocas, beachcombers, bathers, the steady stream of vacationers from the nearby hotels pass him, on their way to the huts, umbrellas, the beckoning water. He is here, in Lapa, on the rua Russell, peering at the roofs of Niterói, and there, on the dais in the Municipal Theater in São Paulo, Oswald, Di Cavalcanti, the other radicals at either side of him at the podium, our Pierrot, our Miss São Paulo, our brown-skinned, bucktoothed hero with such character, beginning the excerpt from *The Hallucinated City*, to hoots and catcalls, while thinking to himself, then as now, we must never let the lies and the tears devour us, we must devour and savor the years.

III

COUNTERNARRATIVE

"If there is any genre in which it matters to be sublime,
it is evil, above all."
Denis Diderot

THE LIONS

"If a lion could talk, we would not understand him."
Ludwig Wittgenstein

G ood evening.

....

Or should I say, Good morning.

....

Of course it could be whatever we want it to be. I want—

....

Decree. Good morning, good evening, good night.

....

Under the circumstances you could lose sight—

....

—of such distinctions. Or forget them. Time of day, night time, time itself—

....

—slips through your grasp when you're....

....

Preoccupied. Aren't you?

....

I rib you but I can smell it. In my case, I have been, so much to do. Think about. You think about it, how common it is to say that, so busy. So easy to lose sight—

....

Of the mountain for a single peak, too. I, never. Too many do, though. You—

....

Want to speak. Your crying request. Here I am. There are some things you never forget, no matter how hard you try. They root, linger, you'd once have said. You can't forget them, I'd say.

....

You take time out of the equation, you can't take time out, forget.

....

So much does get lost in the transmission. But I came. On precious time.

....

I still am a man of few words. I had to learn how to use them from you. Once upon a time they could hardly understand me. You could. You, wielder of words. Language welder. Were.

....

There. That should be better. Now's the time to speak. Precious time. Yours.

M-.

Mmm. I doubt you'd believe it, but I hurried over. Even now, despite everything, still. You know I've always had an affinity for non-punctuality, all that messing with time, untimeliness as you used to describe it. Some things can't be rushed, and yet others can't be postponed. How do you un-time? Slip through its grasp? I learned from you.

Mmm....

I learned that it's best to keep time itself out of sync. Take its beat, remake it in your own. Be untimely. The drumbeat always sends a letter to the future. Say you happened to be the only one to arrive early for a meeting...and a bomb goes off. Wouldn't it have been better to be late then?

Mmm....

Or the chartered plane that you were to fly to that restive region went down mysteriously into the river, but if you arrived well in advance and boarded an earlier flight, you cheated fate, or the person attempting to shape it. All those other unfortunate people, though.

Mmm. . . .

The hands of fate, I suppose, or fate's handler. Hangman. Honcho. You know who I mean. All those car crashes, overdoses, bodies found at the bottoms of drained swimming pools, riverbeds, earthen dams, sudden bathroom electrocutions, sharp, heavy projectiles flying through windows while people were eating their morning meals, the staged robberies where the robber always manages to accurately hit the bull's eye of the heart, kidnappings without ransom notes, bones shattered into a thousand pieces so that they'll never heal again, disappearances, heads left in mailboxes, hands and ears and tongues stapled to doors before dawn, such a remarkable arsenal this particular fate possessed, wouldn't you admit? What I learned from you: how to glide out of fate's schedule. Un-time oneself.

Mmm.

Mmm. Though before we ever had need to speak of such things I can recall us sitting facing each other, just like now, what was it, twenty-five years ago? Just like this, our noses not touching but close enough that we filled each others' lungs. Do you recall that?

Mmmo. . . .

Sitting like this? Nostrils to nostrils, oily sweat and blood masking our faces in the sheer black silk of that night, we each could smell the other's throat exhaling the hours, the years, of endurance, our elation and fear, all flavored with tobacco and the cheapest palm wine, with every breath. The smell of death so near too, nearer than the tips of our noses, our lips brushing against each other, our chests and knees fusing as one, and the smell of life as well, potentiality, the horizon that we would seize.

Mmmo. . . .

Just like this, in darkness surrounding us like an empty arena, so dark that even after our eyes had adjusted and we could feel our pulses passing between us we still had to rely on our other senses to confirm we were still sitting there. The only sounds the intermittent gunfire, later the mines going off, the rockets, the ground a rattle beneath our soles, the dirt and grass and plastic we could not wash off our tongues. There you go.

Much better....

We even kept the radio off because we knew exactly what he would be saying: I appeal to you, vanguard of our nation's liberation, I appeal to you at this grave hour.

Grave hour, dire.

We could recite it by heart, with the flourishes and the drumbeats, the two of us, the emphases and the pauses, I because I had heard it so many times from his mouth and initially I believed it, as I did you, you because you had written it, such a way with words, like the griots, the oracles, you and I just like this, the night so enveloping we had only our senses to ensure we were still sitting there.

Sitting there, and here.

The monsters no longer have to send their mirage planes, vampire jets, canberra bombers and helicopters, purchased from their American and European master devils themselves, to rain down bombs upon us, to stamp out our freedom like a boot heel on a new and fragile bloom. They no longer have to ravenously slaughter our little children, the seeds of our future, in their schoolhouses or their mothers' wombs. They no longer have to destroy our factories, our banks and bourse, our villages and metropolises, all these the foundations of our freedom, they no longer have to salt our farms, uproot our trees, reduce our harrows and planters, our tractors and transport vehicles, to dust. They no longer have to poison our water engines and wells, these savage beasts who slaveringly covet the earth of our ancestors, these fossils who call us the missing link. They no longer have to take these steps, these demoniacal settler-colonialists, these aliens in our midst, with their cluster bombs and nuclear bombs, their handouts and NGOs and spies posing as missionaries bringing us the anti-salvation of their diabolical savior, their radioactive ideologies of capitalism and liberalism and individualism transmitted over TV sets and in records and books, through fashion and fads that wither our own indigenous culture and traditions like drought, in their pernicious pop culture which like a cancer devours the flesh and souls of our youth. No longer, my countrywomen and men, no longer, no longer. No.

No longer, those monsters.

No longer because they labor from the inside out now, through these Quislings in our midst, these walking tumors, these inhuman viruses, these beasts more depraved than any creature the gods ever bequeathed to us, these idolators among us who pray to the whiteman as their only deity and have pledged their being to sacrifice the black race to appease their abominable god, these psychopaths who have become impervious to reason and immune to the history and ethics and morality of our ancestors, the people, you, our people, more duplicitous and degenerate than the most unspeakable and unimaginable monsters ever placed or dreamt of on this earth, these traitors, these bootlickers, these parasites with their black skin and white hearts, cold empty hearts, lacking souls, these thieves who have conspired with the capitalist thieves in Washington and London, in Berlin and Zurich, in Toronto and Tel Aviv, to empty our pockets, strip our resources, rape our rich soil into a desert and turn our deserts into their tarmacs and derricks, this filth, this rot, this shit festering in our midst, circulating among us, like the air we breathe and the water we drink.

This filth, this rot, this shit, in our water and air.

But, my countrywomen and men, my fellow patriots, my fellow liberators, my fellow warriors, my sisters and brothers, my people, we have identified them and we must stamp them out. We will stamp them out, my people. We will cut them from the body politic, we will hack them out, we will dispatch the remains of their pestilence, ground to ashes and the memory of blood, and remit them and the foul scent that lingers after to those capitals that seek to destroy us, to Washington and London, to Berlin and Zurich, to Toronto and Tel Aviv and Johannesburg and Brussels and the Hague, and I shall be your tribune in returning us to the glories of our people, our past, our first days of freedom, of liberation and independence, but we must join together, hand in hand, arm in arm, armed in mind and body, we must, to wipe this pestilence out.

Hand in hand, arm in arm, this pestilence.

Victory is certain, once we extinguish this plague. Together. We. Will. Wipe. This. Pestilence. Out.

Out, in one draft. My ears had filled with versions of that speech since I was an infant.

Our leader did not believe a single word of it. I did, the rest of the country did, even the Quislings themselves knew what it meant. You did too, but in a different way. It was you speaking, as if with a microphone to your soul. The leader was ventriloquizing you, because you had placed not just him in your crosshairs, but everyone else. Including me.

Not everyone else, and at that moment....

At that moment—me. Brother Quisling. What perfume, my stomach wrenches at the thought, though I would be lying if I said I did not smell it then and suppressed it.

I heard it and like a stylus to wax, a nib to paper, a needle to a groove....

Sound. Your sense was sound, always sound, the most infinitesimal crackle or rustle, and you'd cock your head just so, as if the sound were right beside you, or behind you, or in front of you, just that quick, like a gazelle or a dik-dik, like you had invisible antennae instead of ears, a sonar, so exactingly tuned. The sound of words, of worlds. You could hear my mind's pulse back then, the beat of my dreams.

Yes, the pulse of everything, and beyond. Months.

Mine, now you can't have forgotten mine.

I can't have forgotten.

You have, gods help you.

I can't.

Mine was smell. Immaturity and ripeness, scents of all kinds, fragrances, stenches, nature's olfactory artistry and legerdemain, anything created by the hand or mind of a chemist, anything that could be marked by scent, even emotions, usually emotions, I mined them, except when the mephitic truth was right under my nose. Fear sends out a terrible perfume. The worst.

Yes, every scent, through glass or concrete. Months.

Because of all the engines, the gunfire, all those explosions, not to mention the music and noise in my childhood compound, I'll probably have to wear a hearing aid too when the time comes, glasses instead of these contact lenses for my eyes, and.... But I can still sniff a rose out of an open gravesite, or a shallow grave in an overgrown garden. A rose in a cemetery, a grave in a garden, there's a bit of poetry for you.

Blooms in graveyards in bloom, quite lyrical. Months.

I have no gift for poetry, like you, never did, but I sponsor a contest for our youngsters, ten categories, including rap and traditional epic. Some even recite that famous speech, or the revised variation I approved. They're very good. It's even televised and broadcast via satellite all over the continent, though the part about the Quislings I had to alter. Not so poetic that cut.

Our youth, Quislings. Months.

In our youth we were something, facing each like this in that ditch in the midnight clearing, your ears pricked and that invisible antenna, maybe it was other senses too, not just hearing but vibrations you picked up from the air and ground, and me, my nose like an elephant's or bloodhound's back then, us two boys from opposite ends of the country, you from the city and I from the bush, sitting and waiting, biding and plotting.

Months.

Months? Sitting and waiting? Planning, yes. Before that night— was it months?

Four. Waiting, requesting.

We weren't—you mean yourself, here. I admit to not having kept count. It could have been a month, or four, or four years. Not that I let problems fester that long. But as I said, I have been very busy.

I kept count. Four months since the last time.

So I wasn't so busy that a year passed. But I wasn't here the last time.

No. But I still kept count.

Still kept count, kept still, counting. How did you do that? A mental map? No access to a calendar, your schedule is staggered, and your placement in this room is regulated in an untimely fashion. No light or darkness, nothing to create a clock. I have gone to inestimable lengths to keep you out of time . . . and on this earth.

By sound.

Ah. Because I had to address of the problem of . . . toes or fingers.

You had to, no counting.

And sight, that light and dark. But I wanted you to talk to me, talk now, so I didn't order . . . everything.

To be able to talk, say everything, and nothing.

You see, you used to say I was inattentive, too lost in my own time. But I followed you like a scent every day for all those years, until you scrubbed me clean of you. I loved to hear you talk, do you remember? We would sit for hours, you talking, me all ears. I am a man of few words. You could spin vast webs of them, of numbers. Stories, plans, plots, systems. Nets, traps: I had to work my way out of all of them.

Nests of words and figures, which snared me.

First feet so that they will never run away. Then hands, so not even the simplest tools. Then eyes, so no recall of a single place you stash them. But keep the tongue and vocal cords until the end because they may have something else to surprise you with.

My later approach, almost to the letter. How I will surprise you.

You will.

Tell you something.

The baobab tree lives forever and offers shade, but not cassava fruit. Today smells like that evening in the clearing, you know.

I can't smell it.

It does. The stink of oblivion. Its anticipation. The smell that lies outside the smell. Fumes beyond and beneath it. Something worse, don't you agree, lurking there? You still have your nose.

Yes, no, nothing like that evening. I can't.

You can probably hear it in your voice, and mine. In the silence before I entered.

No, fumes, no sounds.

You probably cannot just hear it but taste it. That's how the oracle described it, no? A feeling so strong the ear tastes its contours? All that poetry like a radar. We survived but not the victims of that ambush. An open field, though, for you.

Yes, but no, it was an ordeal after that.

Every such situation presented itself as an ordeal, but you saw the window before you. You leapt right through. I followed you.

Windows, yes. Now, no.

It wasn't supposed to stay open for me. Yet every time when you tried with me you failed. After the first time, the failed assassination at the market, I realized I had to place my steps inside and then ahead of yours. Enter your frequency. The truth that I was next, your truth. That's how I knew. The acid in the tap. The radioactive isotopes those painters painted all throughout the house. Survival is a great motivator. Somehow you missed that.

I missed.

You did and didn't. You were watching but you couldn't see past your ken. The untimely horizon. I won't even use the metaphor of chess, which you banned, remember? Recall how you always beat me back then? Then you contrived to let me win, until I got the gist. You hated that you could imagine what the person next door or across the street was thinking but you couldn't figure out a winning strategy against your former protégé on that board. How many did you tear up or burn? It fascinated me that the king was so powerless, waiting to be taken. He should have been able to control his fate and the throne.

Powerless, and taken.

Terrified of knights—and pawns. A bishop, how ridiculous. The queen is the one who never gave a damn. I was the queen, then. But yoté, choko, checkers, backgammon, cribbage, senterej, go, poker, 21, roulette, I laugh at all those metaphors today because they point to chance and I don't take any.

No chance, no time.

Out of time. Except now.

No, I can't believe it.

That your clock is running out? That you will surprise me? Before it's too late. There was that class we took together while in exile, the philosophy of military strategy, or political philosophy, or philosophy of politics itself, something enthrallingly useless.

Yes. Plato, Machiavelli, Hegel, Marx, Heidegger, Schmitt—

All those damned Europeans, all that claptrap.

Emperor Frederick the Great, Teddy Roosevelt, Franco, Mussolini, Stalin, then a week for Mao, Trujillo, Amin, Pinochet, Bokassa...I imagined they've added Saddam, Cheney, Ghaddafi, the rest.

To what end? Our ancestors had more wisdom in their little toes.

My avatars, my favorite monsters.

At first I thought that was when you began formulating your schemes. But no, it was earlier. Before the philosophers, always political. You always had such ambition, foresight. Even in childhood, I envision, since I didn't know you then. Those stories about your youth, on the other side of the country, how you organized the local children, drawing maps in the sand, compelling them to strangle animals, memorize secret words. It took me a while to catch on, and up.

Then you were behind me.

Fully. Behind, until I passed you. Surpassed you.

Past me.

I want to say that I remember the exact moment but that would be too cinematic, too perfect. Like a still from a movie, or a literary scene. Is there a computer code for that? A simulation I can view on the nearest screen. I don't recall it. No need now to say I did. I was carrying out all of your plans, to the letter. Rewriting maps, strangling opponents, devising secret languages.

All my plans, opponents, letters.

I would say to myself, he foresees everything, moves men around like figurines. Without ever consulting the spirits, the oracle, those magical books from the Middle East and East and elsewhere. He has the insight of a seer and the might of a deity. That's why I called you, we all called you The Prophet.

The Prophet, men like figurines.

Because you knew how everything would unfold, how you would unfold it. No instructions needed. The Prophet foresaw the complex mathematics of circumstance and how his actions would affect them.

Prediction, or statistics, or complex systems analysis.

I never studied any of that in school. Perhaps military colleges should teach it.

Poetry, history, psychology, ban all of it.

You banned most of it. I thought you had a hologram of the world, of everyone else's head, in yours, a cybernetic game turning it every which way, the dates, the days, the figures, the complicated transactional interplay of everything materializing in its array, with the will to realize it. Even if that's not what it was like the metaphor works. You with your all your thinkers and dreamers, those bards, black, brown, yellow, white, whatever the color, that cannot save a single soul, including you.

Yes, my avatars, my monsters, I can hear their words right now.

You even wrote your thesis on Amilcar Cabral, another poet, one of ours.

No, Frantz Fanon. On the justification and cleansing power of violence, in the service of revolution.

Blood for the stanzas, odes to gore. That brain, so sharp, cutting even now like a well-honed trap, correcting me. I did say I want to be surprised, though the squeak, as you liked to say, cries out to be silenced.

Yes, that insistent noise. It became habit, the algorithms of reason, action, circumstance. I could place myself in the minds of others, their bodies, and view the world through their eyes, step where they stepped before they knew they would. What they would do I could always counter it. Equations for such things, code, scripts, texts, written or sung a thousand years ago, last decade, but something finer, more subtle too, that could not be written down, though I did.

Lyric poems, oral stories, short stories. You banned them all. I initially followed your lead, all of it except the most inane trash, though some of that can provoke enough sympathy to start people thinking. I realized that I would just have to tinker a bit.

That's dangerous too, I learned soon enough.

If you don't tinker, and control it. Yourself. I give them a steady diet of garbage, music videos from Rio, US reality shows, K-Pop, Mexican telenovelas, Bollywood gangster tales, Nollywood films about witches, fads, diet shows, hair shows, dubbed and scrubbed. Patriotic dramas, documentaries on the colonial wars. You can never go wrong denouncing the British and French. Louis XIV, King Leopold. Dead kings. You. Even a trickle of attenuated religion now and then, nothing to give them any hope or ideas. Thin as wartime broth.

One minute everyone is equal and the next minute they see that they're not, or they're appealing for help to a higher power. A god takes the shape of a man.

Mysticism, ritual, pageantry, emptied of content, Prophet. Rules to follow, without being told. The American evangelicals even endow some of it with a veneer of legitimacy.

Soon they start to see themselves as one in the same, all believing in that same figurehead.

None except that nation, and you know who that is now. We've always had more than enough minor engines of resentment among the ones who might do some damage, so I remove them, finding multiple other ways of pacifying the rest. Then it's South vs. North, East vs. West, this tribal yawping vs. that tribal yawping, the lighter ones vs.

the blacker ones, but with something to placate them all at the end. Nothing like a forgiving mirror.

A nation of narcissists, knowing nothing. You still have to be vigilant. I wasn't.

Is this what you screamed your lungs out for? Was that your story about reality? What do you hear right now?

Your voice.

With those ears? I should not have to waste a breath asking anything twice. What do you hear?

I hear your body ever so slightly shift in your chair, your thick buttocks cushioned by a very soft pillow, softer than a calf's sack. Though you love handmade suits from Italy and the UK in private, and your Nehru collars, African printed cloth and kufis in public, you have on a uniform, a plain one of ours of which you have many, a castle's worth, I can hear the faintest rustle of the duck, it's immaculately starched and pressed and hasn't lost its crispness because of this heat. You have on a black beret, fabricated and blocked in the Basque region of Spain, not the Chinese kind, though you have been to Shanghai alone several times within the last six months. That hat sits easily on your shaved head, smooth as an egg, though sometimes when you touch it the rougher, gray hairs that you didn't completely remove softly scratch against its inner lining. Instead of your usual patent leather driving loafers, you are wearing black steel-toe boots, thick soled, polished by peasants' tongues as I used to say, so shiny you could scorch the sun with them. You don't have on any medals, any jewelry, any makeup, any cologne, except a very mild deodorant manufactured in Cape Town whose combined fragrances my ears, let alone my nose, cannot make out.

I knew you had it in you.

You knew.

Can you hear how aroused your skill has made me?

Please.

Can you hear that?

Yes, I can hear your . . . pressing against the fabric of your. . . . Please don't.

Don't what?

You know. Please. I don't. . . .

Have these months not taught you anything? Have you completely lost the ability to see into the future? Put yourself inside my head like you used to. Your little hologram or code or poem or statistical algorithm or whatever it was.

Yes. No.

If I wanted I would have done that straightaway. If I wanted your wife, your mother, your father, your children, your grandchildren, the grandchild living in the penthouse condo in Abu Dhabi and the one working for the Royal Bank of Sweden in Stockholm and the ones cavorting like princes in their chateaus in Atlanta and Los Angeles, if I wanted your entire native ancestral village to lie prone before me as I entered them one by one, if I wanted to raze the entire village and rape all the crushed and dismembered and burnt bodies, if I wanted to destroy every vestige of every single soul that spoke the same language as you and rape their ghosts, rape your ancestors who were my ancestors, if I want to rape the vestigial mother and fathers of us all, if I wanted to rape the last embers of your existence and memory and then what wasn't even left after that, I would have done so. I can write the story of reality however I see fit. At any time.

No. Yes.

And if I instead wanted it to be as it was when we sat facing each other in the darkness in that clearing, when binding ourselves to each other not just to overthrow our supposed liberator, the tribune of the people, our leader with his bloodshot eyes and blood-drenched hands and blood-drained soul, if I wanted it as it was when we devoured each other that night, like lions, though we were both still cubs, when I shared everything of myself with you and you with me, or at least I thought you did, though you were even holding something back then. Admit a sick man into your home, but not your bed.

No. I was looking ahead. Yes.

You were looking ahead to the bead on my throat.

No, I was...looking back—

And as you entered me you were thinking instead of my bond, this will be a dagger, or a bayonet, or a Kaleshnikov butt.... You were thinking of terrors that would send the most extreme dystopian writers into paroxysms, that would make our ancestral spirits and the griots who have shared with us their stories shudder with envy and horror, and you would start as soon as you could.

No, not that night. I waited, until the time was right.

In time, then. With that burst of fear you feasted on your second chance. Try harder. I do want you to surprise me. How can you do that? If you don't do that...what else?

Do I hear?

Do you?

Yes. I hear your dyed black mustache curling upwards at the corners of your full lips as they bow into a grin, I hear those lips brushing against your teeth whiter than Kibo snow, I hear your pleasure at how this is going, how things have unfolded over these last few years. I also hear the sweat trickling down into the open placket of your uniform shirt because even though they have turned up the air and opened the vents this cell is still a dutch oven, I hear your flaring nostrils, flecked with the residue of an early morning snort of cocaine as you were listening to your favorite rap artist whom you flew in to perform at your daughter's 13th birthday party and who also put on a private show for you, your nose which is now smeared with some sort of paste made of Noxzema and miracle fruit, nevertheless periodically wrinkling at the stench, though they cleaned me up, several times this morning, they scrubbed me and this room up and down, every corner as well as the ceiling, before you would set foot in here.

The time had come.

I hear that you want to tell me what you are going to do to me but you want to draw it out on the one hand, but you are also ready to get back to all the things you had planned for today, beyond this. I hear that you are going to kill me, and take great pleasure in it.

I would never take pleasure in such things, certainly not with you, you know better than that, but you need to listen more closely. The man who listens to the wind hears nothing of life. Prophet, have you not been listening to me? To my words. To all these years? Or only to your own internal, empty silence?

Yes, this terrible silence.

Have you really forgotten me so fully? Purged the text of your memory? Prophet of Society you would recall that I took and still take little pleasure in the sorts of things you did, not in building airports or hospitals or reducing them to rubble. Not in appointing generals to march my armies or ministers to oversee the economy or human welfare or the mint. Not in bludgeoning them with my own fists when I have tired of the extent of their looting, even though I ordered it. Not in flushing towers of bureaucrats or rats, of democratic activists or patriotic neo-fascists. Not in standing beside yet another pale monarch or prime minister or even our browner ones, their many thousand-dollar suits or dresses or traditional garb smelling of the enslaved child workers and women who assembled them. Not lying with my wives in any of our hundred beds knowing that not even they would dare think of slitting my throat for fear of what would happen to them if such a thought entered their heads, nor with any of the whores in the most sumptuous hotels in foreign capitals, nor any of the others here or anywhere else in any of the countless beds I requisition for a night or a week or a month, depending upon my moods and whims, the circumstances. Not in giving speeches or proclamations or orders, not issuing decrees, ultimatums or threats. Neither in condemnation nor clemency. Not in rites or ceremonies, not before our gods or God, not before Christ or Allah or any other, not in our languages or in Arabic or English or Chinese or any other tongues. Not in the countryside or the savannahs, nor atop our highest peaks nor in the sea's mouth, not in the cities the colonizers left nor the ones you built nor the ones I willed into being. Not in pets or children or noise or silence. Not in telling the truth or in lying, both among your many arts, though I sometimes must. Not in a single one of these actions, or most others, including not taking pleasure in a single thing at all.

No. You used to enjoy our time together.

Yes, but those days are irretrievable, as you should have heard grasped by this point by my words, my tone, my weariness. It's an audience, really, not a conversation. You're not listening. I do take pleasure, however, in one thing.

Yes, something. Though wealth isn't it—

Once I thought, following your lead, O Prophet of Wealth, that I would take the greatest pleasure in riches. Vaults of treasure, buried deep in blast-proof bunkers, a mile into the ocean floor, vaults behind virtual walls of zeros and ones only the most brilliant of the geniuses I hired could penetrate. I thought I would feel pleasure bathing in money, sleeping in money, clothing myself in money, eating vomiting crapping fucking money. I followed your lead and had jewelry fashioned out of rhodium for every appendage, the entire interior of a tower in silver, a new arena for my birthday and it and everyone in it painted in gold leaf. Anyone there quickly grasped the appeal of the golden calf. To warn off anyone else it's now an abyss.

Yes. I once erected a massive obelisk wrought of platinum studded with red diamonds, jadeite, garnets, red beryl emeralds, black opals, all of them. It became a shrine.

Don't you think your dildo paid off our foreign debt? I give money away, some of it, why do you think the people love me so much? 100% of the vote, every election. It mints itself faster than we can spend it, look at how the vultures from every continent are circling our ports, such are the bounties the earth saw fit to bequeath us.

No. And it isn't power—

Power, that aphrodisiac as someone once said, I don't take pleasure in it either. Prophet of Power, that you were. Such a point of idiocy and a truism that money equals power, or some such thing, money buys power, power buys money, always the two shall meet and screw and someone ends up as the surplus in the equation. I can crap on the floor and order someone to lick it up. I can have an entire block of apartments leveled and raised anew in the span of a few days. I can throw every book in every library into a furnace and order that new ones be written to fill the shelves. I respect power, especially the power that hides in things, that resides in things over which we have no control, the power that surges up out of the pages of one of those books you torched, the ones some intrepid fool rescued, the power in one of those mountains looming over us that decides it is going to batter everything around it with its sublime volcanic breath. The power in atoms whirling about towards a bang that brought the earth into being and that will clear us all from this human plane. Would that a man should become a god, or what's literature, or politics, or physics, or the military for? Yes, but I don't take any great pleasure in it at all.

No. Though you wield it better than a prince. Or a king. Or queen, of the chessboard or the savannah. Better than I did. The king of the savannahs, the greatest lion of this nation that ever lived.

Yes that's how they refer to me. The Lion devoured the Prophet, though they're still hunting for you in Switzerland and Tehran.

Yes, voracious, eaten whole.

What gives me pleasure is... can you guess it?

No... I don't... I can't say. Not money, not power, not sex, not religion, not, not death. I... can't.

What do you hear?

I hear you leaning back, your face calming as you peer in my direction, your back arching as it settles into position, you briefly touching a crucifix, though you are not a Christian and haven't been one in a long while, that talisman that nevertheless rests uneasily in the valley of your chest as a kind of reassurance that you have stumped me and this is going to end horribly.

You've almost gone deaf, then. Listen.

No...please. Not laughter or weeping, not seeing me laugh or weep. Not even knowing that you have stumped me completely and there is nothing I can do. Not even screaming. No. I can't hear the answer. Please don't. I can't.

You can't? I don't want that smell to reach my nostrils. Try harder. Open one of those books in your head; turn on one of those screens. Listen, Prophet.

Yes. No. I can't. Not the fact that you even if I outwitted you now, as well as every single degenerate member of your cabinet, your military, your family, I would not leave here. I...can't. Don't, have mercy.

That smell is reaching my nose. Crossing the space between us. Listen, Prophet, listen. The roaring, isn't it fearsome? Pure poetry and science, beyond symbols or words.

No. You know how this will turn out, and are trying to will me to save myself, because you know I won't. I can't. Don't, though I give up.

I can smell the abyss your ears have become, your existence. Some prophet. That was your third chance, your time is up. Fearlessness. I take pleasure in that, tremendous pleasure. Unimaginable pleasure. Do you hear me growing hard at the very mention of the word? Do you hear my salivary glands filling, the sweat rushing into my pits, the adrenalin quickening my heartbeat? Fearlessness. Do you hear the dopamine surging through my brain as I think the word? A volcano surging through me. A terrible, sublime roar. I don't even have to say it, from it an entire world flows. That is what I thought we both had back then, chest to chest in that clearing. I remember how in our school that professor of ours called an extreme version of this mindset the greatest danger known to humankind, and I immediately looked at you, though at your core you were all fear. Fear, fear, fear. You were never fearless, though you had me fooled. The coups, the progressive changes, the preemptive attacks, the coronation, the wars. All fear's handiwork.

The reason I wanted to speak with you was just this. I am no longer afraid.

It was always fear. I can smell you trembling into the void. It's nauseating. What did you think was the true source of anyone's sovereignty? Did you take nothing from all the people you plastered on every wall? Yaa Asantewa and Anacaona, Toussaint L'Ouverture and Dessalines, the Bolshevik and the Long Marcher and the rest of them, Indira Gandhi and Golda Meir, the sage who defied Kennedy, Malcolm X and Martin Luther King Jr. and Patrice Lumumba and Thomas Sankara and Nelson Mandela? Those eyes staring back at you? Did you really not listen to the stories you told everyone else, Prophet, the stories they told you in response? Did you not take anything from our ancestors who survived the depredations of the gods, and later the encroachers from every corner of the continent? Of course they were frightened but were fearless nevertheless. Some more than others, all more than you.

No. Listen to me. I am no longer afraid.

Did you not learn anything from the brazen creatures who seized our mothers and fathers, who bought and sold them here and across the sea, who fought them here and over there and did not back down? The ones to whom you signed over so much of our matrimony and patrimony? Their puny bodies that melt in the sun, all their sicknesses of the flesh and mind and soul, yet they keep arriving. Their words, their ideas, their abstractions, the ones you love so much, gave them an armor of fearlessness. I, however, scare them out of their sleep, not infrequently. They never know what time it is with me. Did you not take anything from every single soul that dared to challenge you at penalty of things worse than mere death? What do you think allowed any of them, me, to survive you?

I screamed my throat onto the cement floor to tell you this, I'm not afraid.

The prison of hope, you used to say, which was easy for one who controlled the future. Did you not hear the clue? I gave you several. You with your statistics and plots, you who could place yourself inside the heads of others like the Trojans, or a medium. A walking antenna. You touched one of the keys aloud but could not open the door. Why else would I have worn that cross around my neck, invoke Christ of all people? What use is a prophet without his powers? Should I have roped it around your neck? Stuffed it your mouth? Rammed it in your....

Listen to me, I know what's coming. I accept it, I am not afraid.

You requested me for this? My time, for this? All that hollering for an entire season, for this? I must admit, you still have the power to make me even more cynical. The Prophet of Cynicism has created a Deliverer.

Why not parade me before my people, Deliverer, send me back to them, and let me die in shame at their feet? I won't fear them.

What people? You have no people anymore. Can't you smell it?

Bury me in the desert, Deliverer, cast me into the ocean near my home, you can broadcast it on your station, on the Internet. I won't fear it.

You have no home. No home, no state, no brothers, no sisters, no people, no lineage, not a thing. Truthfully, I could smell it all the way on the other side of the world, years ago.

Listen, you could force my allies out there to reveal themselves and to eat my beating heart, mount me on a steeple, but do it in the middle of the capital's main square. I fear nothing now.

Absurdities, who ever heard of such things? You have no allies, I was your last one. You are nothing and you have nothing. You are not even the ghost of a recollection any more. In the air, diving in the sea's depths, I could smell it, and can smell it now, it's almost unbearable.

Rendition me, send me to one of their special ops sites, let them lock me up in Guantánamo. Nail me in a coffin and mail it to the Hague. Have them fly in the drones. Wash your hands of me and cast me into theirs. I have nothing to fear.

I must be going. I'm a man of few words but I have a speech to give. I'm nauseated by the stench, and have been for too long.

Ransom me, you could buy whole blocks in Paris, London, Miami with my head. I'm not afraid. I—

A speech on a theme you spoke on many times. Everybody is a monster, but only the monsters know it. Cautionary tales for cautionary times. Absolutely nothing like it, this odor, not even death. It's enough by itself to kill.

I appeal to you, vanguard of our nation's resistance, I appeal to you at this grave hour. The monsters no longer have to send their superjet fighters, stealth bombers, hypersonic technology vehicles, and flocks of drones to rein down bombs upon us, to stamp out our freedom like a boot heel on a single bloom....

    ....

I hear you rising from your seat. Standing. Shaking your head as if under water, as if this alone could reset the clock. No longer smiling, your face muscles wiring into a grimace, your brow slashed with a frown. You are choking back the retch. Your eyes are boring in my direction, at what's left of me, propped up here.

    ....

Your eyes fixed on this still breathing lump in the darkness, I hear you pushing the chair back with your calves, you want space, I hear you pushing the chair back even further and you turn and move it to my left so that it is out of the way. I hear you unbuttoning your shirt with your intact hand, which you have learned to use as if it were the dominant one, the other, a prosthesis, dangles at your side, above the prosthetic foot, proving I should have cut off both sides when I could. I hear your shirttails falling over your belt, your pants.

    ....

I hear your removing the cross from your chest, so built up, sliding it up across the smooth skin with your long, thick fingers, your platinum pinky ring and your gold and ruby signet ring, your manicured nails, you are pulling it up out of the cleft of your chest, you have always been powerfully built, no less so today than when we were just boys, I always envied that of you, that body and the force that you carried in it, that force of feeling that was fearlessness, that was always the only ethics you clung to, fearless to do the worst things and the best, to commit unspeakable crimes and then not contemplate another horrific thing on this earth, I feared that in you, I knew, too late, that it would be my end.

....

I hear you lifting the tool from around your neck, you holding it in your left hand while with your prosthetic hand you are extracting a glove, two, latex, you hate it and are allergic to it but there's no other material that will ensure you keep me off your skin, my flesh and memory off you, you have doctors on call to give you a shot before you face the crowd once you leave here, you cradle the weapon as you wrestle the glove onto your right hand, your prosthetic hand which you use as if it had left the womb with you, your left one almost too large for the glove, the same hands that generations ago would have wielded spears, or clubs, or an axe or machete, the same hands generations ago that would have slapped a cow's or horse's flanks to move them into a pen, the same hands that would have wielded the spade to furrow the earth or hoisted the walls atop which the roof might sit, the same hands that would never have been found in a schoolhouse, or a college classroom, or a luxury hotel, or a castle in the middle of here or anywhere else, except cleaning such rooms, scrubbing them from corner to corner, scrubbing the pits the powerful crapped in, your hands, the one I did not cut off and the one I did, that could have torn off my own hands, my arms, my feet, my legs, my nose, my tongue, my ears, but didn't, that wasn't fear or cowardice but distress at having to dismember what you had come to completely, utterly love.

....

I hear you shifting the weapon to your false hand in preparation, now your real one, working by intuition, that was one of your gifts, unerring always, living by feeling, your feelings as light as wind and taut as a mainspring, all my planning and booklearning couldn't match it, and you so beautiful back then, so fearless, the greatest lion of our youth, always more so than I, you didn't know it because we didn't have a language for it, we had it but you didn't know it, we knew it but you couldn't speak it, that time would come, the leader feared that in you as much as your courage, or rather fearlessness, they are different, I was courageous but not fearless, I was daring, brave, impulsive, reckless, I put the bullet through his temple and so many others, I was not a prophet or saint but I was your apostle, apostle of what everyone loved and feared in you, most of all me, that beauty and the fearlesness.

....

I hear you leaning forward, your eyes having never left this lump of me, what's left of me, so beautiful, it was almost painful to look at you after my eyes adjusted to the blackness that night, you were too much to bear, it wasn't just the beauty or the fearlessness but that I knew it would come to this, I would have to get rid of you, I would have to destroy you, eliminate you, do what our leader couldn't do, one of us would remain in the end and it wouldn't be me if I didn't do it, I hear that, I hear you reaching forward . . . seizing hold of my chin with that prosthetic hand, the grip tight, firm as a vise, so tight I can barely speak, I hear you thinking that having to do this distresses you more than anything else, disgusts and dismays you, I hear you thinking this distress won't even kindle into rage, you will transform it somehow into indifference, I hear you thinking I could simply leave him here as he is to rot, no one would ever find him, you could pour in molten metal or concrete, just as I did to your parents, your siblings, your ancestral village and neighboring ones, unleash a torrent in minutes because no one would ever find me, none will, I hear you thinking that would be too easy, I hear you thinking I failed you completely when I had the opportunities to rid the world of you, I hear you thinking I did not do so out of pity or love but sheer ineptitude and greed and fear, not even the most stupid creature on earth would have let things come to this, I hear you thinking I slaughtered countless people but I could not manage to liquidate this earth of you, stamp out you, filthy degenerate lion Quisling, I was too afraid of doing so, not with my own might or that of my allies overseas, I hear you thinking you are going to flush this earth of me, but slowly, as you have been, reducing me to the nothing I've become, and that not even this will atone for all I've done, all the lies and betrayals, all the vast continent of discontent and destruction I wrought, and but you are wrong, I have now surprised you, I am hardly displeased with myself for having let it come to this, I am pleased beyond measure at everything I ever did and would do it again, and you hear now how I do not fear what's about to happen, how I am no longer begging but welcoming it, no more pleas, no more imprecations, I know what's due, how I would send my partisans into flight rather than rescue me, burn the gods, not a single one of them can save me and I would reject them if they tried, I hear you raising the bandanna gag from around my neck with that hideous freakish American hand, the sound of it makes me want to explode with laughter, your hideous freakish American foot, prosthetic, cyborgian, not human, I did that and not even all the money and the power in the world can make you whole again, your inhuman fingers on that same bandanna you pulled down earlier so that we could speak, as I requested for four straight months this time, every waking second of every day, screaming through that fabric so loud they could not not hear me, the same one I used to wear all those years ago, the one knotted around my neck that night and many days and nights thereafter, tonight, or today, I hear how in a few seconds you will stuff the ends of it into my toothless mouth, I should have pulled out all of yours, and your tongue, and your throat, I should have cut it out when I had the opportunity, I laugh fearlessly at my folly now, why should anyone fear a lion with only two paws instead of four, a lion unsure if it's a male or a female, a lion so unafraid of anything it is incapable of understanding the sheer terror of life and death, a lion who will itself be devoured by another waiting nearby, the lion's roar is anything but music, just animalistic howling, I hear how, in a few seconds or many, only you know the time, you will cock your arm back like a spring with the makeshift cross like a knife pointed out and swing it forward hard into my right ear over and over, and how you'll find my left until I am no longer crying out through this muzzle and you won't even have to let them know you're done, you'll scurry away knowing the same will eventually happen to you, one you've bred just like me who will come hunting, the bead's on your throat, I can hear that language clear as a bell, a whistle, can you hear it, you cannot, in fact, she's doing so right now, he's gliding right through to get you, in no time, the man who listens only to death hears nothing of life, your time will be up, out of time, and I'll lie here until—

    ....

    ....

    ....

    ....

    ....

Author's Acknowledgments

I would like to offer thanks to everyone, named below and unnamed, who offered support during the writing of these stories. I wish special thanks to the Mrs. Giles Whiting Foundation for the fellowship that aided me in completing them.

Many thanks to all my students, colleagues and the staff members, too numerous to name, at Brown University, Northwestern University and Rutgers University-Newark, to whom I offer deep gratitude.

Particular thanks to the New York Public Library's Stephen A. Schwarzman Research Branch, and in particular to Messrs. David Smith and Jay Barksdale, supervisors of its invaluable Wertheim Study and related programs, for all of their endless generosity and helpfulness.

Thanks also to the various editors who published versions of these stories, and to the institutions where I had the opportunity to read versions of them.

Thanks also to all of my teachers over the years, especially E. L. Doctorow, in whose workshop I wrote one of the first of these stories.

Many thanks to Dorothy Wang, who introduced me to the sheet music that led to "Cold," the story about Bob Cole.

Profound thanks to my fellow Dark Room Writers Collective members for their friendship, vision and superlative examples, and especially to Tisa Bryant, with whom I have shared these tales, and who suggested one, which she later published; and to the Cave Canem writers, for their friendship and stellar artmaking.

Many thanks to everyone at New Directions Publishing Corporation, especially Barbara Epler, and to my agent, Jonah Straus.

Also, an especial thanks to Jeffrey Renard Allen; Frances Bartkowski; Herman Beavers; Kevin Bell; Jennifer DeVere Brody; the late Rudolph P. Byrd; Alice Elliott Dark; Kwame Dawes; the late Gerard Fergerson; Reginald Gibbons; Thomas Glave; Rigoberto González; John Eric Hamel; Reginald Harris; Victor Hodge; Geoffrey Jacques;

Tayari Jones; Mary Kinzie; Serena Lin; Keguro Macharia; Dwight McBride; Francisco Mejia; Askold Melnyczuk; David Barclay Moore; Nathanaël; Jayne Anne Phillips; Robert F. Reid-Pharr; Sarah Schulman; Christopher Stackhouse; Christina Strasburger; Ella Turenne; Jerry Weinstein; Jay and Lois Wright.

And above all, a million thanks and love always to Curtis Allen.